ACKNOWLEDGEMENTS

Few books reach publication without valued contributions and assistance. I extend my sincerest appreciation to draft readers: Wayne Harvey, who exposed a potentially embarrassing timeline flaw; Ian 'Ezy' Loader; James 'Jock' Waiter, who appraised the manuscript as 'very feminine' (no compliment could please me more); and Freddy Dickson, whose grammatical conundrums would confound even the most esteemed English-language authorities.

Thanks to Steve, of West Mercia Search and Rescue, who assisted with search and rescue craft detail.

And to lawyer Regan, for advice about court venues under various circumstances.

Finally, a heartfelt thanks to my mother, Ann, who continues to offer unwavering support through this and other demanding projects.

BEYOND
ALL DOUBT

BEYOND
ALL DOUBT

PAIGE
ELIZABETH
TURNER

FARMERS
MARKET
THIS
SUNDAY

Matador
9 Priory Business Park,
Wistow Road, Kibworth Beauchamp,
Leicestershire. LE8 0RX
Tel: 0116 279 2299
Email: books@troubador.co.uk
Web: www.troubador.co.uk/matador
Twitter: @matadorbooks

ISBN 978 1785898 846

British Library Cataloguing in Publication Data.
A catalogue record for this book is available from the British Library.

Printed and bound by CPI Group (UK) Ltd, Croydon, CR0 4YY
Typeset in 11pt Adobe Garamond Pro by Troubador Publishing Ltd, Leicester, UK

Matador is an imprint of Troubador Publishing Ltd

MIX
Paper from
responsible sources
FSC® C013604

PART ONE

THE MURDERS

1

As THE EVENING'S dusk draws a translucent grey curtain across the sinking afternoon sun, twenty-two passengers board the late-afternoon river cruise. Patrons jostle for position to view shafts of orange sunlight bounce from the river like fiery sparks escaping a Guy Fawkes bonfire. Those who shun sunsets' romanticism retreat to the sub-deck where they struggle to digest the complimentary Devonshire Teas' crumbling scones. Others exchange the intense gaze of first-time lovers: eyes only for each other – oblivious to their surroundings.

A young couple exit the comfortably heated cabin, climb three steps to the deck and breathe in grey mist rolling across the River Avon in Evesham, Worcestershire.

Legend claims the town's name evolved from a herdsman, Eoves, a farmer for the Bishop of Worcester, who is said to have seen a vision of the Virgin Mary. In 701 AD, Evesham's abbey was built at that very location.

The small town holds its place in history. The Battle of Evesham, in 1265, saw Simon de Montfort, Earl of Leicester, slain with his small army in Greenhill on the northern perimeter of Evesham. Simon de Montfort was recognised as an outstanding English personality, an advocate of a limited monarchy, and an active and outspoken proponent of parliamentary and governance reforms.

Today, rural enterprise and clusters of satellite industries complement Evesham's bustling township. The River Avon flows through its heart and radiates a shimmering backdrop to the vast Crown Meadow. Summer nestles a string of permanently moored barges whose tubs of flowers, deck chairs and tables, television antennas, satellite dishes, and the wafting aroma of culinary delicacies afford domestic convenience to the weekend mariners.

Trevor and Juanita saunter arm in arm along the timber deck, beyond a white bulkhead propped like a lone kiosk on a derelict railway platform, and continue to the rear of the refurbished timber barge. Huddling like conjoined twins, they trail the arrowhead wake chasing across the river's surface. Trevor flops onto a timber-slatted seat whose identity succumbs to stacked layers of red, green and blue paint. The most recent décor – a yellow acrylic – is cracked and bubbled through neglect. He swipes flakes of the puckered paint to the deck, pulls Juanita to his lap and snuggles into her breast like a newborn baby pacified by the comfort and security of its mother.

Juanita embraces the warmth and happiness of newfound romance as she drinks the dew of Trevor's kiss. With limbs intertwined like convolvulus jacaranda, they absorb the tranquil evening of August fourteen.

'I love you babe,' Trevor whispers.

'Love you too.'

Trevor combs his fingers through her hair and rests them at the nape of her slender neck. With the flourish of an oriental masseur, he stimulates dense tissue beneath her lithe skin. As he kneads deep into Juanita's neck, he smothers her lips with breathless kisses and rises to the frisson of her electrified tongue.

Juanita closes her eyes and reclines into the emotion and anticipation pulsing through her body. She surrenders to sensuality's whisper, choosing to float above reality while selfishly enjoying the inner heat fuelled by twitches and spasms of hormonal yearnings.

Her stifled groans shrill down Trevor's throat.

Her arms clamp him in a chest-crushing embrace.

Her heart races and body shudders to orgasm's rhapsody.

Her eyes dilute and fix upon his: *Is this a new adventure in foreplay, or a gross act of rejection?*

She will never learn it is the latter. Her soft breath ceases like the exhausted wisp of an autumn breeze.

Trevor lifts Juanita from the seat. Cradles her. Kisses her cheek. Says goodbye. He glances over his shoulder to confirm his concealment from both passengers and occasional anglers chancing their luck from the riverbank. He flips her limp body over the side of the craft, the inboard motor muffling the faint splash. Her white cotton blouse inflates and bobbles atop the wash. Moments later, it collapses and descends, returning the glistening river to swans and ducks feeding on discarded scones.

Trevor dawdles to the cabin, awash with innocence – the look a child presents upon being admonished for teasing his sister: *What? Who, me?* No one sees that look, and no one pays him attention as he enters the foredeck where he will remain until the cruise terminates.

The captain manoeuvres the craft toward the recently restored Evesham pier, now protected by suspended tyres dangling like children's swings. Patrons preserve lasting memories of the cruise onto their digital cameras and smartphones: the soaring St Lawrence's church; Workman Bridge; the historic stone wall surrounding Evesham's famous abbey; and the meadow from where families pack away memories of the day's picnics and barbecues.

After shutting down the motor, the skipper casts two ropes onto the pier and lashes the boat securely to fore and aft mooring bollards. From the side of the craft he unfolds a rickety ramp and extends a trusting hand to the over-cautious as they disembark.

Trevor merges with the departing passengers. Barely five-feet-seven inches tall, he shuffles along like a child entombed within the surging exodus of a football match. His slate-black hair – greasy and unkempt – is contained by one of his many baseball caps, while his ears flare beyond, straining to capture patrons' chit-chat.

He mimics passengers exchanging cheerios, and waves to awaiting families as if to single out friends in the crowd. No one would know otherwise. He strolls to the riverbank, checks for telltale signs of his indiscretion and smiles as the increasing darkness falls upon his crime. He walks briskly along the footpath, whistling with the felicity of a child having plucked the toy from a McDonald's Happy Meal.

In three hours, he'll enter his front door. Alone.

Twelve months' earlier, at thirty-two years-of-age and twice divorced, Trevor John Taylor had proposed to Juanita Morales. He had detoured around the route to everlasting love, ejecting baggage, lack-lustre memories and promises of 'for better or for worse'. Like many in his position, he had accepted no responsibility for his situation.

His first wife, swept away by the freedom of a singles lifestyle, charged toward nightclubs, dancing and interchangeable relationships. His second marriage fell two weeks short of four years after his beloved Belinda, so deeply immersed in the Christian faith, found worshipping a fellow church member more soul intensifying than the joys of holy matrimony. Trevor floundered in emotional wilderness, desperately intent on sharing his life with someone. Equally at home with his own peace and solitude, he felt little inclination to re-enter the dating scene, where small talk, failed first dates and stand-ups intersected the journey to the prism of love.

His job as a self-employed electrical contractor afforded him a good income, although he spent little of it, choosing instead a reclusive lifestyle of watching television and playing computer games. One evening, during an internet search for a new computer game, a pop-up advert commanded his attention: *Filipina Joy. Find your life's love with a beautiful Asian woman.* Trevor clicked into the website. He'd heard stories, both good and bad, of internet dating sites, but never had he explored one. His introduction to the site was overwhelming, as was the beauty and eagerness of many women.

He clicked on an appealing portrait. The profile read like a professional's curriculum vitae; a two-page document supplying every conceivable piece of information required to successfully claim the vacancy. But Juanita Morales was not seeking a life-changing career – she was seeking a husband.

A photographic model of Philippine origin, her petite frame reflected God's idea of beauty. High cheekbones accentuated huge brown eyes peering from sculpted dark caves, giving her the appearance of a mystical cat. A snub nose and full lips complemented black satin hair, which meandered below her shoulders. She was twenty-two-years-old, five-feet-four and single.

Her profile was expansive: as a student, she had participated in many athletic pursuits. On leaving school, she obsessed over her trim figure, for it was her body that rewarded her with an envied lifestyle – a lifestyle she intended to renounce.

Juanita was not extravagant. She preferred a simple life to one crammed with the over-exuberance of her profession. She steadfastly refused invitations to parties and head-turning get-togethers, on those nights preferring to stay at home, sulking into her self-enforced isolation. The rigours of modelling, dealing with questionable agents whose sexual propositions would guarantee she'd 'make it to the top', convinced Juanita to withdraw from the artificial glamour. She longed to find a sincere, devoted person who would accept her for her own being – not as a pin-up object of satisfaction upon a men's room wall. Juanita craved a future where she could enjoy life with a home, husband and family.

For many years she had planned to leave the Philippines, a country from where young girls dream of meeting and marrying a foreigner, particularly an American. The Philippines is historically associated with the United States of America, originating from its attack on the Spanish Navy in the Philippines in May 1898. The country remains strongly influenced by the US as evidenced by its American English language education and the plethora of American television shows now enjoyed by most Filipinos. Many young women, and even younger girls, crave the luxury American lifestyle as a means of escaping their depressed life.

After brief consideration, reinforced by her friends' encouragement – *what have you got to lose?* – Juanita Morales joined the *Filipina Joy* website.

The marvels of technology, search engines and scrolling

photographs united Trevor and Juanita. They exchanged emails, quickly stretching to multi-page letters, texts, photos, and from Trevor, parcels of gifts. A strong friendship sprang from their exchanging each other's life and aspirations. Six months' later, Trevor visited Juanita. During intermission at a local cinema, he removed from his pocket a half-carat diamond ring, knelt between the close-knit rows of seats and said: 'Juanita. I love you. Will you marry me?' Two hours' later the pair returned to Juanita's home where Trevor, in keeping with both local and western custom, formalised his proposal as a request to Juanita's father. Within months, Juanita leapt into Trevor's arms at Heathrow Airport.

Initially, life presented many difficulties. Juanita missed her family. She knew no one in Bournemouth where she shared Trevor's home. They fought often, not physically, but with verbal venom enough to poison neighbours either side of Trevor's semi-detached home. Juanita eased slowly into new friendships but remained moody and despondent. It was not long before she confided in one of her new friends the torrid time she was suffering under Trevor. She considered acting on Trevor's taunts to return to the Philippines, but believed that doing so might deny her one of life's key opportunities. Worse still, she could not face the shame of being labelled a 'failure' by her family.

Over time, the emotional bindings of cohabitation frayed. The challenge of winning over Juanita Morales had enthused Trevor far greater than the prospect of living with her – a peculiarity generated by childhood eagerness of waiting for a Christmas or birthday present, only to quickly tire of the Lego bricks and marbles. There would always be more toys. And there would always be more women.

* * *

Two hundred metres upstream of Evesham's pier, Juanita Morales' distorted body lies partly submerged, clutched by riverbed reeds. A slick of matted black hair swirls around her opaque face, concealing the tremor of her final gasps. Resting on the surface an oversize fashion watch encircles her tiny wrist, reflecting a plea of 'help me' from the half-moon's chilling light. Its diffused glow captures the attention of a young couple enjoying the early excitement of courting. Arm in arm they creep to the water's edge, supporting each other's steps lest they slip into the Avon's gloom. They peer inquisitively through the assembled cavalry of reeds, expecting to score a valuable object ditched by a fisherman, or perhaps mislaid by another amorous couple. And then they see her.

Seventeen-year-old Graham Johnston reaches for her arm. Its chilled flesh sends him reeling. Too aghast to check for a pulse, he retreats to the riverbank, fumbles for his phone and with shaking hand calls 999. He stutters the gruesome find to an operator who directs him to remain at the scene until police arrive.

Graham soon tracks the blaze of flashing lights streaking along Abbey Road, their fluorescent haze tinting the stretch of mist compressing Crown Meadow. Two marked police cars enter the park and inch along the potholed access road before stopping at the Evesham Rowing Club. Uniformed officers alight and string crime-scene tape across the road to prevent admission of sightseers and other persons likely to contaminate the area.

Police and emergency service personnel share distaste for loitering 'rubber necks' eager to snatch glimpses of unfolding catastrophes, yet those same time-wasting sightseers are the first to complain when they're stuck at a supermarket checkout for more than thirty seconds.

Beyond the tape, a second pair of headlights bounce like erratic balls along the base of a karaoke screen. A silver Vauxhall Astra emerges from the grey-topped bitumen, its indignant driver waving his police identity to the tape-bearing sentry. Hauling himself from the driver's seat, the rotund Inspector Michael Marchant gazes toward the river. He shuffles beneath a park light, his ruddy face and red hair illuminating like a child's glow-in-the-dark figurine. Nothing else about Marchant glows. He is well into his fifteenth year with Worcester CID – on the outer. He'd commenced his career with youthful enthusiasm, but along the way had exhausted his stamina – akin to progressing beyond the reserves but failing selection into the major league. His abrupt manner and lack of finesse with junior members had prevented his promotional path extending beyond inspector. Marchant's career is now a seven-year flat line.

Conveying an air of authority at odds with his crumpled suit, he shouts to a nearby uniformed officer: 'Constable. Who's in charge here?'

'Er, no one, sir. PC Denning over there was first on the scene.'

'Denning!' Marchant roars. 'Here.'

Denning turns toward Marchant and glares. He curbs his intent to volley: *Who the fuck do you think you are?* before obeying the command.

'Good job containing the scene, Denning. Who found the stiff?'

'A young lad. Graham Johnston, sir. I got him to wait over there.' Denning nods to a moulded aluminium bench fronting the rowing club.

Marchant waddles toward Johnston. 'Detective Inspector Marchant, Worcester CID. You rang 999?'

'Yes. I can't believe this. We was just walking along the river when we noticed something shining. We looked down and saw her... the body.'

'You say "we" saw her. Who was with you?'

'My girlfriend, Mel.' Johnston raises his hand, fused to Melanie's, as an introduction.

'Did you see anyone else while you were walking?'

'No. We was talking and I wasn't paying attention to nothing but Mel.'

'We logged your call at 8.25 p.m. Is that when you found her?'

'I think so. I don't wear a watch, but I can check the time on my phone if you want.'

'No. Doesn't matter. All right, Graham, wait here for a moment. By the way, did you recognise her?'

'No. But I hardly looked. It was so awful.'

Detective Sergeant Olivia Watts signs off from a radio location call, springs from the passenger seat, and proceeds directly to the river's edge. She glances at the deceased as Marchant unceremoniously drags the body on to the bank. 'Probably done a few hours ago, sir.'

'Would've been daylight then,' barks Marchant.

'I realise that. People *are* killed during the day,' sneers Watts. 'I've called the Coroner's office. Groenweld's on his way.'

2

FROM THE AGE of twelve-years-old, Olivia Elaine Watts had longed to be a police officer. The initial attraction was no more than glinting buttons hanging from the uniform. Much later she was gripped by her father's devoted life-long service. Today, she relishes her position as an important contribution to community harmony and safety – a utopian, if not ill-conceived perception of the constable's role. Of analytical nature, she dives into covert investigations requiring tenacity and skill rather than seeking out straight-forward arrests where the offender, hoping to either hoodwink the arresting officer or broker a deal, confesses with haste. To complement her investigatory skills, she studies Forensic Applied Biology part-time at Worcester University. Her attendance is unpredictable because of shift work's toilsome demands.

Olivia's recent promotion to detective sergeant reared dissension among colleagues. Whilst excelling in the uniform division, she alienated herself from many officers because of her perceived 'tuppenny toff' poise. She inherited the label not from pretentiousness, but from the knowledge of her having been educated at the exclusive St Catherine's Girls' Grammar.

Frequent patronising and sarcastic comments, unappreciated by most, contrast her success. At twenty-four years-of-age, Olivia, despite having a lot to offer, also has a lot to learn. Packaged in an athletic five-feet-seven-inches, she is a woman possessed of striking features: short brown hair – recently streaked with ash blonde – deep blue eyes, the trademarked colour of Cadbury's chocolate wrappers, and magnetically-charged lips. Her ability to mix it with the boys during after-shift drinks and social evenings is welcomed, although some suggest she mixes *too* well.

It is no secret that Olivia often crosses the perilous boundary dividing work and leisure, a trait that has earned her another label: 'easy'. The tag is neither justified nor accurate.

It is also common knowledge within CID ranks that she loathes working with Marchant. No one has yet discovered why.

* * *

Doctor Erich Groenweld, a squat man with tonsured head and liquor reddened nose strolls out of the darkness, his mind focused not on the task before him, but on matters deeply embedded in his mind. He carries the look of a person who's drifted off into space: out of this world; daydreaming, walking straight ahead – robotic, some would say – eyes fixed on an imaginary whiteboard of computations.

Sixteen years' earlier, after completing further studies, he registered with the Home Office to continue his profession as a pathologist with the Worcestershire Coroner's Office. Forsaking his general practice at the Wolverhampton Medical Centre, he reasoned that working with the dearly departed would be akin to working in heaven. Groenweld had tired of treating common ailments, issuing certificates on Mondays to irresponsible employees hoping to extend their weekend, and he was fed up with children's whinges, gripes and tantrums, many of which were milder than those of his octogenarian patients.

He's lived alone for the past 10 years after losing his wife to London's Underground bombing of 2005. In silence, he focuses on early retirement, each morning compulsively obliterating the preceding day of his calendar with a huge felt tipped 'X'. He devotes the whole of his free time to a research project borne from fascination with geological and universal science. He shuns publicity, refusing to offer preliminary outlines of what he believes will revolutionise a long-standing theory, *and* provoke more debate than the God versus Darwinian theory of evolution.

In the current year he's taken more than six weeks' sick leave, comprising mostly of Monday morning hangovers. Whilst he is never truly ill, he spends whole days touring travel agents, dreaming, planning and collecting brochures of prospective retirement destinations. Spain heads the list. Many of his colleagues have joined Britain's retirement exodus to Spain's temperate climate. Groenweld's grey and pasty complexion might not benefit from relocating, but it does render him as fodder for office jokes: 'Erich. Are ye the walking dead or are you just empathising with your patients?'

Groenweld has worked alongside Marchant on many occasions; all instances of natural deaths, for there has not been a murder in Evesham since the Albert Road atrocity of 2003.

'Evening Michael. What have we got here?'

'Young woman found a short time ago by a passer-by. Not a gory one so I'll leave you to it.'

Groenweld snaps photographs of the deceased prior to conducting a preliminary examination. He dictates to a micro-recorder: 'Female. Approximate age mid-20s, Asian appearance, lacerations to the neck and thorax. Impressions to the front of neck, beneath left ear and left anterior deltoid. Clothes intact, no evidence of sexual assault. Rigor retarded due to immersion in water…'

'Watts!' yells Marchant. 'Have a scout around will you? Deceased has no bag or anything. Could've been snatched, but have a look all the same. And tread carefully.'

'Yes sir!'

Marchant returns to Groenweld: 'Can you give me an idea of how long she's been here?'

'Well, that would be nigh on impossible to establish without a witness. If, however, you are interested in knowing how long she has been deceased, my inclination is that it would be within the past five hours. I'll be more precise after the post mortem.'

DS Watts summonses a uniformed officer to assist.

They scan fifty metres north and south along the river bank – the limits of available light – probing dense reeds which waver in huge clumps alongside the water's edge. Spreading them apart with a small paddle, Olivia finds only scrunched-up potato crisp packets, chocolate wrappers and a couple of generic soft drink cans captured by the reeds. She suggests searching from a boat might be more successful, assuming the existence of a bag, and assuming it hadn't been stolen or had fallen to the murky river's floor.

'I'll arrange a craft for first light,' snaps Marchant. 'It's pointless continuing. We've got a reasonable description. Trot up to town will you, and check around. Maybe someone can put a name to her.'

'All right. Okay to take Denning with me?'

'Take anyone. Just go!'

Sunday night in Evesham is like walking through sideshows where only one stand remains open to extract stragglers' last few coins. Shops and cafés close simultaneously as if a huge switch shuts down trading activity. People scurry home, anxious to devour the traditional Sunday Roast (purchased as a pre-packaged microwave meal) or to snatch the final minutes of the delayed telecast 'Match of the Day', or maybe to preview the evening's proliferation of new-vogue reality shows dominating televisions worldwide.

Only two businesses survive the exodus. The Rainbow Café, an upmarket establishment struggling to attract the town's clique of trendy, cashed-up clientele, hosts a dozen diners. Another thirty, and the elaborate dine-in might reach break-even.

Watts and Denning wade through a smoky haze to the vacant bar. A flurry of activity sees cigarettes stubbed, stomped upon, and in one case, dropped into a coffee cup. Little regard is shown for the smoking ban introduced in 2007.

A trendy waist-coated attendant materialises from beneath the counter.

'Evening,' smiles Olivia, tilting her head and inhaling deeply, provocatively flaunting availability. 'Seen this girl today?' Olivia swipes her mobile phone to display a photo transferred from Groenweld's camera.

'Nup. Lucky to see anyone here. Real quiet.'

'Mind if we ask around?'

'Suit yourselves.'

The pair shuffle between patrons, leaving shortly after with no information and no free drink. They walk briskly to the Blue Haze nightclub where they fare no better.

Back at the riverfront, Marchant waves them off: 'We can't

achieve much more this evening. No one's reported missing. Yet. We'll call it quits and make a fresh start at 7.00 a.m.'

A support team erects a three-square-metre white marquee over the site to minimise the risk of early morning dew destroying undetected trace evidence. A diesel generator chuffs power into four halogen floodlights, transforming the riverbank to the luminance of Wembley Stadium. Marchant arranges static surveillance for the night, instructing two constables to roam the marquee's perimeter, whilst unofficially suggesting they rotate on the hour to the comfort of their patrol car. He need not have proffered the gesture. The constables would retreat to the vehicle immediately after his vacating the scene.

Watts returns to her small flat, a character-dripping one-bedroom unit carved from a large house into slices of rental accommodation. The late nineteenth-century stately home, built on the wealth of Britain's once flourishing economy, boasts 10 feet high ceilings, decorative cornices and ceiling roses, oak architraves restored to warm timber after being stripped of half a dozen once fashionable colours, sash windows that don't open because the same half-dozen coats of paint ensure they'll never again open, and a green porcelain bath and basin chipped by the misadventure of children's toys and errant mop buckets. In the bedroom, a huge light shade hangs by three brass chains between which spiders spin geometric autobahns.

Olivia steps into her bath – a customary treat after a long shift – lies back and absorbs the aroma of lavender perfumed salts. She broods over her lonely but tolerable life, legacy of prioritising her career at the expense of friendship and leisure.

She misses her mother and misses the days she'd helped dress her dolls. She'd applied Olivia's first make-up, plucked her eyebrows and chosen lipstick colours that did not make her

18

look ten years' older. Olivia recalled the day when she snuck back to Boots, and with her pocket money purchased the very colour that *did* make her look ten years older.

At nineteen years-of-age, after hearing the damning prognosis of her mother's breast cancer, she remained at her mother's side until the debilitating disease stole the mother Olivia had never truly known. Moving to Worcester was the first step in recovering from that loss.

Olivia fights the demons of permanent relationships, a fight that relegates her to casual flings with work colleagues. She'd once confided in a friend that reluctance to commit and loss of liberty were driving forces that prevent her from entering the contract of lifelong attachment. Her most recent steady relationship with Dave Stafford, a detective inspector with the National Crime Agency based in London's head office has fizzed to a surreptitious once-in-a-blue-moon dalliance. They'd maintained the low-key association for nearly eight months until a chance sighting by a fellow DI topped the locker rooms' gossip list. Olivia was not fazed by gossip mongers ridiculing her friendship with the inspector. Area command thought different, citing bad image and lack of professionalism as a poor example of standards expected to be portrayed by senior officers. Command persuaded DI Stafford to cease the relationship.

Not all commands are honoured.

Over the past fortnight Olivia has missed his company. During vulnerable moments of loneliness she craves his attention. Just a kiss. The touch of his hand on hers…

She drifts peacefully into the lavender mist, smoothing soft moisturising soap across her face, shoulders, neck and breasts. An electrifying tingle surges through her body, alerting carnal yearnings to the long-awaited attention. A coil of desire unwinds deep in her stomach. Ripples of fragrant water lap against aching thighs like small waves rolling onto the white sands of an isolated lagoon. She arches her back and traces a line of lather down her breastbone, over taut abdominal muscles, through wavering pubic hair –

A flash of inspiration suspends her intention: *If I were looking for a person of a different nationality, I'd ask one of their own. They always befriend each other. They're far more likely to know who's who in and around the area. I'll speak to Marchant about it in the morning.*

3

BOURNEMOUTH'S COASTAL COMMUNITY has been Trevor's home since birth. Like most who ponder holiday destinations, Trevor adopts the seaside sets' cross-migratory habits of trickling into rural areas, while the rural residents customarily invade beach resorts. He had no particular reason for choosing Evesham as the venue for a day out. It was simply a matter of fate. He unfolded a map, circled his index finger in the air and dropped it to the huge sheet like a person aimlessly selecting lotto numbers. But *he* had an ulterior motive. In a distant town like Evesham, he would be just another tourist. As would Juanita.

Within days of Juanita moving into his home, Trevor had regretted committing himself to another relationship. He blamed the power of the rebound. He relished independence and objected to anyone, including a doting fiancée, organising his daily activities. The heavy hand of discipline had moulded his childhood, bequeathing him an introverted personality unable to accept love and friendship as one of life's fulfilling joys. Trevor had long ago sworn that he, and only he, would control his future decisions and destiny. In moments of despondency, he admits that *that* creed *might* have contributed to the collapse of his previous marriages.

It didn't take long for Trevor to spout persuasive hints that Juanita return to her family in the Philippines. His attitude surprised her, but she reasoned that Trevor was thinking only of *her* best interests because of her unfamiliarity with the new country. He'd certainly grown fond of her, but the fondness was no more than a heavily diluted concoction of love and physical yearnings. His greater concern was the prospect of losing face in front of friends and family on telling them that Juanita had abandoned him. Instead, he would become an immigration scam victim.

Trevor arrives home at 11.00 p.m., slams over the kerb and straddles the footpath – Britain's accepted parking etiquette – and slumps down into the seat. He'd grappled his emotions for the entire journey, replaying the event over and over while trying to justify his actions – now concealed by a cloak of guilt. He walks trancelike to his front door, fumbles the lock, and then shuffles straight to his reception room. He stands transfixed before the chronicle of framed photos: hugging Juanita at Mactan Airport in Cebu where they'd shared their first kiss; posing in front of the huge Ayala Shopping Mall; sipping a drink at Juanita's home; and in an expensive platinum-framed montage, their engagement celebration at Jollibee's – a Philippine fast-food institution. The photos will soon join discarded papers, business paraphernalia and faded memories consigned to cardboard boxes in the garage.

He steps into the kitchen, swings his arm across the table and swipes three days' dirty breakfast bowls to the floor. Stepping over the shattered china, he drops two heaped teaspoons of instant coffee into a dirty mug and pours in water before it boils. He removes a carton of milk from the fridge, squeezes open the flap, takes a deep whiff, gags, and abruptly upends the contents straight down the sink. *Black will do.*

He assesses the situation: *Calm down. This is just another evening.*

But Trevor can't calm down and it isn't just another evening. He panics. *Shall I report her as missing, or just remove every trace of her presence? If anyone asks, shall I stick with my plan and say that she left me?*

Trevor knows that police will eventually appear on his doorstep: 'When did you last see her?'; 'Where were you on the night of August fourteen?'; 'What was she wearing?'; 'Can she swim?'; 'Does she carry a bag or purse?'; 'How long have you known her?'

Considering that scenario restores his confidence. Trevor believes he can outsmart anyone, although he saves deceptive practices primarily for work. Many times he's convinced customers that their switchboard is below standard and susceptible to flash ignition because of the demands of modern appliances such as televisions, DVDs, microwaves, fridges and freezers. He preys on pensioners, persuasively detailing how their old switchboard could fail while handling power fluctuations of modern conveniences. For one elderly woman who lived on her own, a new 'refrigerator' was her only electrical luxury. No television. No microwave. Not even an electric fan. Trevor's emphatic spiel persuaded her that today's fridges use power far greater than the old wiring is capable of handling. 'There's a great risk of the board catching fire,' was the crunch line he employed to educe fear. The customer, not wanting to risk life or property, readily agreed to the installation of a new switchboard – at an inflated cost of £247.00.

He compulsively adjusts charges when attending emergency callouts. Trevor never 'increases' charges – that communicates opportunism and greed. He applies the word 'adjusted' to all quotations and invoices, never letting on that the adjustments operate in one direction only. North. He lives by the rationale: *if they want me now they can pay through the nose. Who else will they get?* The unfortunate consequence for the consumer is that it is far too late when they discover they'd been overcharged.

Trevor changes into the role of deserted victim, phones Bournemouth police and adopts the voice of an emotionally broken man. 'Hello. I want to report my fiancée missing. I've looked everywhere for her.'

'How long has she been missing?'

'I got home from work and expected her to be here. It's nearly midnight now; she's always home. I can't get her on her mobile either. Gives that out-of-service message.'

The receiving officer stifles a snigger. No one reports an adult missing after only one hour. A young child, yes, but certainly not an adult. 'An hour's not long. She could be delayed, at a friend's or anything. Give her a while longer.'

'I've been home for an hour. She wasn't here when I arrived and she left no note. She could have been gone for hours.' He barrages the officer with multiple reasons of why it is out of character for Juanita to be absent. The officer, perhaps trying to placate his caller, suggests Trevor email a description and photograph to the Missing Persons office, 'just in case she panicked and got lost in an unfamiliar area.'

Trevor immediately fulfils the request, believing that acting with urgency will add credence to his concerns. He remains at the computer, clicks to his unpublished blog and two-finger types the day's entry:

August 14, 2015. Took Juanita to Evesham. Had a romantic late afternoon cruise on the Avon. Of course there are similar outings closer to home, but I wanted a distant place to deflect any suspicion that I would be involved in her disappearance. It was easy to get her on the craft. She didn't suspect a thing. Why would she? I knew, well, maybe I thought, that I did love her, but who can explain love in times of uncertainty?

We sat at the rear of the craft making small talk and cuddling like young lovers in a cinema. She gave her all to me. I know she had deep feelings. How could she not like a great guy like me?

I held her and cuddled her and when I traced my fingers through her hair and around her neck, her eyes gleamed as if she were expecting another romantic interlude. I sunk my fingers into the soft flesh of a neck that supported one of the most beautiful faces I ever had the pleasure of kissing. She grimaced and contorted as she struggled. Sure, it was cruel. Her face reddened, then flushed to a light pink, like the setting sun melting its imprint on Antarctica's icy glaciers. In the forefront of my mind, I saw my father disciplining me. He'd never choked me with force, but the strength of his fingers around my neck instilled the fear of life, or lack of it, into me.

Another thing I learnt from my father was the fear of water. One of his favourite disciplinary measures was to plunge me into a bath full of water and hold me under until I had expelled nearly every bubble of air from my tiny lungs. He did these things for only the slightest transgression, like accidentally breaking a toy, ripping a page from a colouring book, or, as occurred on more than one occasion, sharpening a pencil to the extent that it became too short to use.

I'm feeling a bit schizoid because I'm jumping all over the place. I don't have the patience to do that editing stuff so I'll just carry on.

Water is said to be the essence of life, of tranquillity, of love. We aspire to absorb the peace of water; to sway to its flowing cadence; to feel its energy cascading over the edge of a waterfall and the intensity of its power crashing and churning beneath the Niagara Falls; to gaze at the serenity of water-lilied lakes; and to experience the sensuality of water invigorating our deepest senses beneath a shower shared by two.

I won't brag about how I penned that flowery prose, but it is that piece of philosophic poetry, in which I capture the embodiment of life and all its living wonders, that inspired me to commit Juanita to perfect peace in the beauty and tranquillity of water.

Trevor returns to the kitchen, kicks aside errant fragments of crockery, and crunches six Weetabix into a plastic container. After an outburst of profanities resulting from his having thrown away the only milk, he pours the remaining luke-warm water from the kettle into the bowl. *Better than nothing.*

Thirty minutes after midnight he sits before the television and jabs the remote as if he were punching a text message into a mobile phone. CSI: Miami flashes onto the screen. He settles down to dinner.

At 6.45 a.m., a cacophonic rendition of 'Start me Up' by The Rolling Stones vibrates his mobile phone from a side table. He flays his arms trying to locate the noise, spilling the unfinished bowl of cereal in his lap. On picking up the phone, he sees that he'd slept for nearly six hours.

The house is silent. That is unusual. Every morning he'd woken to his darling Juanita's rustling and scratching as she prepared breakfast, packed morning snacks and lunchtime sandwiches, and draped a clean pair of overalls over the bedroom door. She had been a conscientious home-maker, constantly tidying, dusting, washing, putting things in their place – even when they were not out of place – all under the sufferance of missing her family and friends, expressly so she could build a happy and lasting life with the man of her dreams.

Trevor heads to work as if nothing has happened. In his mind nothing has happened – Juanita has simply gone missing.

4

WEST MERCIA SEARCH and Rescue volunteer Steven Jones launches the *Plastic Pig* from the Evesham Rowing Club at 0700 hours. The backup craft is so named because its moulded plastic construction makes it 'handle like a pig' compared to the modern inflatables preferred by most team members. The *PP*, just shy of four metres from bow to stern, regularly joins flat-water missions where rescues and evidence retrieval from difficult and inaccessible locations would pose risks to the lighter inflatibles.

Jones rips the five-horsepower outboard motor into life. Ducks flutter from cosy retreats, fleeing the riverbank like an Air Force squadron withdrawing from enemy threats. The motor splutters billows of grey, oily smoke, which, together with its 12,000 revs-per-minute shriek, rouse the calm early morning. Jones steadies the craft as DS Watts approaches.

'Morning. Shall I get in now?'

'"Get in?" I think you mean, "Shall I come aboard?"' counters Jones.

'"Come aboard?" You've got to be having a laugh. It's not a 35-foot pleasure cruiser. It's a bloody bath tub with two plastic seats, a few metres of rope and a couple of lifejackets. Get real,' says Watts as she steps gingerly into the wallowing boat.

Jones ignores Watts' admonishment, pushes the tiny craft from its mooring and angles across the flat water to the upstream location where Juanita's body had been found. With a lightweight fibreglass paddle borrowed from the rowing club, Watts probes through reeds and river vegetation, seeking the elusive handbag or purse.

'It's more than likely sunk by now,' Watts shouts above the spluttering motor.

'Depends what it's made of and what's in it,' replies Jones. 'Some things will float forever; others absorb water and drop within minutes.'

'Yeah – stop. I see something. Right in all that crap over there.'

Jones negotiates the craft through metre-high bamboo-like reeds. Razor sharp fronds claw the sides of the plastic hull, emitting the piercing screech of fingernails scraping an old school blackboard.

Olivia clasps both hands over her ears and clenches her teeth as the noise drills her head with the shrill of a thousand cicadas. She fixes on the bag – a brown leather clutch purse of the type often found in weekend craft markets – wedged within a clump of reeds. Using her expertise as a former star player in her school's lacrosse team, Olivia extends a long fishing net to salvage the purse.

After flinging the sodden leather bag into the boat, she dons the mandatory latex gloves – an obligation she considers futile given the item's condition – opens the clasp and gasps. No money. No identification. Nothing. She places it in a plastic evidence bag for signing over to the Forensic Unit. Robbery can now be considered a motive.

Jones and Watts return to the launch site where Inspector Marchant heaves on a cigarette. 'Found a bag. Nothing in it,' yells Olivia.

'Looks like we got us a Jane Doe then.'

Marchant flicks the half-smoked cigarette into the river and boards a Simmons' Scenic Cruises pleasure craft roped to the pier. He scans the timber deck, fittings and fixtures for signs of a struggle or evidence capable of furthering his enquiry. The door to the sub-deck buffet is securely locked. Marchant peers through its windows and notes the layout.

On disembarking, he questions officers returning from an expanded grid-search. One carries casts of footprints taken as potential identification evidence.

Marchant will later learn that they belong to Graham Johnston and his girlfriend.

For two years Barry Andrew Simmons has piloted Simmons' Scenic Cruises' tours along the River Avon. He'd earlier resigned his post as a Lieutenant Commander of the Royal Navy to accept a captain's role with a commercial shipping line. The new career's excitement dissolved as pressures and accountability of private industry surmounted the liberties he had enjoyed in the navy. Strolling away his frustrations on deck, lifeless towers of containers crushed the little remaining enthusiasm he held for the sea. Barry resigned after only one return commission from Southampton to Tokyo.

The resignation came too late to save his marriage, which had not attained even the lowly status of Paper Anniversary. The stresses of separation caused by repeated oceanic operations did not sit well with Felicity Simmons. Throughout the eighteen-month engagement, Felicity strived to conquer the recurring emotional voids. An extensive network of friends, a good job with her local council, and prolific contributions to magazine puzzle competitions ensured Felicity had little time to wallow in the ocean of sadness. She eventually anticipated the indulgence of doing as she pleased, when she pleased. After those opportunities presented themselves with increasing frequency, her dreams and aspirations floated away on the same waves as her cherished husband.

Barry Simmons had no notion that when he waved Felicity goodbye from Southampton dock one Sunday afternoon, he would never again see her.

He remained single, spending four months in solitude, moping about and feeling sorry for himself, before deciding to again offer his hand to female company. That presented a new problem: his perceived image of being an eligible, well-groomed ladies' man conflicted with opposing critiques which labelled him a middle-aged man trying to recapture the élans of youth. From a distance he was of striking appearance; the magazine-cover epitome of a serviceman: tall, broad shouldered with ponytailed sun-bleached hair fighting the transition to grey. But on approaching Barry Simmons, lines of wind-swept salt furrow his brow, and arched crow's feet radiate from his eyes – the harsh penalty of squinting into the sun and glistening oceans.

Social interaction rewards only the social. Barry shunned clubs and the embarrassment of approaching tables of single women; he rejected the growing trend of joining community bingo or quiz nights; and he was far too traditional to join the swelling population clicking their way to romance on social media and dating websites.

His spirits lifted at the thought of sunny afternoons in the garden and quiet evenings devouring Tom Clancy novels. In doing so, he would enjoy the freedom and clarity to plan his future: permanent retirement, reapply to the Navy, or consider a career tutoring seamanship and ocean charting.

A chance glimpse of an advertisement in *Boating Monthly* provided the opportunity for a life-changing experience. *'For Sale to Boating Enthusiast,'* read the caption above a quarter-page advertisement. *'River cruise business based in Evesham, Worcs. May be run part-or full-time. Two craft, mooring rights, full insurances, profitable operation. Excellent opportunity for person with river-craft expertise. Contact owner on 01386 451417.'*

Barry folded the paper and immediately phoned the number. He later inspected the craft and financial records, and paid a deposit, conditional upon the business's financial viability being substantiated by his accountant. Within a fortnight, he'd satisfied licensing requirements, paid insurance, and familiarised himself with the river's course and its many obstacles between Evesham Loch and Tewkesbury.

Today, Simmons knows every inch of the Avon in his operational area. He owns and operates two barges, both restored after the West Midlands canals ceased trade and transportation in the mid-1970s. He commands the bridge with the authority of a P&O cruise captain, broadcasting smiles from beneath the Two Pound Shop gold-braided cap, and he chats willingly to patrons keen to discuss weather, the course of the river or such other trivialities volunteered as conversation starters.

Booking a cruise from the Evesham pier is a low-key affair – pay by cash or card. No ID, no hassle. On boarding, passengers are required only to show their ticket stubs. There is no roll call or tallying names with bookings. Exit head-counts are an income-calculating exercise rather than a dedicated concern for the safety and responsibility of those under his watch – sufficient explanation of why an unaccounted-for passenger on yesterday's final disembarkment failed to arouse alarm. He casually glossed over the miscount. *No one could disappear from an evening cruise. I must have stuffed up my cast-off check.*

Fifteen minutes prior to the day's final departure, Trevor Taylor had purchased two tickets. With Juanita on his arm he approached Simmons and queried the price and duration of the cruise. He paid £20 for the tickets, which he handed to Juanita. They boarded the craft, accompanied by a group of tourists comprising bored locals, creepy birdwatchers, and guys who believe an outlay of £20 represents good value and adds valuable credits to their romance tally-board. Like sheep squabbling through a race to the dipping troughs, they stepped down to the below-deck heated cabin for their free Devonshire Tea.

5

SEVERE FUNDING CUTBACKS limit Worcester police station's efficiency. Five years overdue for a re-fit, Marchant's 'temporary' office is one of three segmented from the former typing pool. He likens it to the janitor's storeroom, minus the rows of detergents and disinfectants, musty mop buckets sitting beneath a rack of mops and brooms, and the crinkled copy of *People* magazine – left open at the centrefold – which would command more interest from the caretaker than would newsworthy columns.

Nicotine-yellow stains the ceilings. Walls resonate similar depredations of time. An assembly of certificates and awards shirk the drab décor. Centrepiece is a faded graduation photograph of fifteen years' earlier; a certificate of crime scene analysis; two Chief Constable's commendations – one of which humours Marchant's heroics in rescuing a young lad from an out of control dodgem car at a local carnival – and a few curled editorials sensationalising two arrests made eleven years' earlier.

His cluttered desk fronts the display. Most who attend Marchant's office pay no attention to his achievements; they repeatedly hear them in the incident room, they hear them in the staff canteen and they hear them on patrol. They are tired of listening to Marchant's self-aggrandising snippets of history.

They all know that during the past two years he has not solved one major crime.

Standing on the edge of his desk as a sick memento, a cactus rises eight inches out of a flesh-coloured ceramic pot, hand-formed in the shape of two oval roman urns. Cursive yellow handwriting etched into a small plaque screams: *To the biggest prick ever. Marilyn.* Only Marchant and two senior officers know that Marilyn was the former WPC who dramatically withdrew a sexual harassment complaint at the door of the Superintendent's office. The fact that Marchant has no conscience about preserving the tribute on his desk is a clear representation of his character – he doesn't give a damn.

He strolls into his office shortly before lunch and checks notes and updates passed on by night shift. Interrupted by a phone call from the forensic science laboratory, he learns of their recovering two ticket stubs from the river victim's purse. 'My off-sider told me it was empty,' Marchant roars into the phone.

'No one would have seen them in the wet bag. The paper'd become translucent and stuck to a divider. They're tickets for a river cruise in Evesham. Two people. No date, but the company is Simmons' Scenic Cruises.'

'Cheers for that. I know where they are.'

Marchant makes a mental note to reprimand Olivia for her oversight. Whether or not they were translucent is of no substance to him; her lackadaisical attitude had whisked by a vital piece of evidence. It would be only minutes before colleagues' jibes sing-song throughout the office that forensics is reaping accolades for the discovery.

Marchant frequently impresses upon his teams that evidence will rarely be located by cursory glances or inattentive fossicking. He expounds that the most complex cases are solved when the obvious is discounted and the investigating officer probes deeper into the crime's fabric. 'Double-checking is essential,' he hypocritically stresses. Never will Marchant admit to practising the beleaguered detectives' trait of complacency – accepting the obvious as fact.

He plucks Simmons' Scenic Cruises' phone number from an online directory and waits as it beeps through a maze of electronic diversions to a mobile.

'Morning. Simmons.'

'Good morning. Detective Inspector Marchant, Worcester CID. We're conducting enquiries into the disappearance of a young woman in Evesham. I'd like a few words with you at two o'clock if that's convenient.'

'Fine by me, but you'll have to make it 2.45. I'm on my way back from Tewekes' at two. Probably wasting your time if you don't mind my saying. I don't know anything about it.'

'That's okay. Just a few formalities.' Marchant preserves a snapshot of Simmons' demeanour, knowing that those with the least to tell have the most to hide.

On hanging up, his fax machine spurts out four pages. He snatches the top page and studies the pathologist's preliminary finding:

Female subject. Approximately 20 – 25 years old of Asian appearance, possibly Malay/Thai/Philippine extraction.

Superficial external bruising to frontal and both sides of neck (sternocleidomastoid, sternohyoid and omohyoid muscles) consistent with application of manual pressure pre-mortem.

Internal bruising to the epiglottis and lining of larynx.
Compression of jugular veins and carotid arteries. Rupture
of hyoid muscles. Hyoid bone fractured as is consistent with
strangulation.

White blood cell count determined that bruising occurred pre-
mortem. Bruising and blood lividity determined that cessation
of life occurred between 1900 and 2200 hours on the 14
August 2015. No sexual interference. Death by strangulation.
Asphyxiation evidenced by lack of water in lungs.

Marchant digests a mouthful of hamburger along with
confirmation that he has inherited a murder investigation. He
pushes the burger to the side – oblivious to the slick of oil
seeping into confidential files – and maps out the prospective
meeting with Simmons. He ambles to the Property Office,
signs out the cruise ticket stubs and commences the twenty-
minute drive to Evesham. Procedurally, he should request a
fellow officer to accompany him. Marchant, however, is so
appalled by Watts' recent negligence that he once again opts
to flout rules.

Mid-afternoon guarantees little traffic on the A44. He
slips in a CD of 70s hits and winds up the volume. The
Cranberries 'Zombie' booms from the Astra's six speakers.
Clipped hedgerows and razed yellow pastures flash by,
spinning Marchant's mind back six months to a casual end-
of-shift drinks session with Olivia. As the unwelcome images
materialise, he pulls into Crown Meadow and inches along the
pitted road to the pier where Simmons leans against the dock,
sipping from a stained thermos cup.

Marchant extricates himself from the vehicle like a

contortionist unfolding limbs from a suitcase. He pulls one knee into his body, twists free of the door, drops his head in a kow-tow, grabs the door with one arm, the roof with the other, and heaves himself from the seat with so much effort that he has to prop against the car to recover. He hoists up his trousers and approaches Simmons. 'Good afternoon. Marchant, Worcester CID. We spoke earlier. I'm investigating the death of a woman in Evesham last night. Found in the river. You know anything about it?'

'I heard talk of a body, it's all 'round town. I haven't paid much attention. It doesn't really concern me.'

'Were you on the river last night?'

'I'm on the river every day, but not at night. The last cruise leaves just before dusk – provided there's more than ten patrons.'

Marchant produces Groenweld's photo of the deceased. 'Do you recognise her as one of your passengers?'

'No. Don't think I'd recognise anyone, unless something really stood out. Pretty average people 'round here you know.'

'And how many of these "average people" did you carry last night?'

'About twenty.'

Marchant raises his brow. 'About?'

'Look, I'll check my log. I'm counting people on every trip; you can't just expect me to pluck the exact head-count out of the air. What's this about, anyway?'

'Any problems last night, or dusk as you call it?'

'Nah. Never have problems. Don't allow drink on board, and it's not the sort of place riff-raff gather.'

Marchant pulls the bagged receipts from his pocket. 'Are these yours?'

'Sure are.'

'So when were they issued?'

'Can't tell. We don't date them. Why?'

'They were found in the deceased's bag.' Marchant stops short. He won't give anyone a head start by arming them with too much information. He's confirmed the obvious – Simmons had issued the tickets – but he needs proof that the bag in which they were found definitely belongs to the deceased.

'Still don't see how I can help you. I'd issue sixty to eighty of those things a day. As I said, we had no trouble last night.'

Marchant departs with a queasy feeling.

Experience is a wise tutor. Marchant had long ago learnt that body language telegraphs guilt or innocence. Repetitive mannerisms, idiosyncrasies, hand movements and gestures all form part of a suspect's defence mechanism. Add to that, the fine beads of perspiration atop one's brow, the impromptu request for a cigarette or toilet break, or the 'Sorry-I'm-a-bit-tired-I'm-not-thinking-clearly,' excuse rushed into a sentence by a suspect clearly lying his ass off and you're half-way to cracking the case.

On his return to the office, Marchant fires a tirade at Olivia. He believes that smearing his team with frustration will spur them to greater productivity. 'Surely you can come up with a few leads on this? I've got the super on my back and I've nothin' to give him.'

'It's only been a day,' Olivia retorts, 'and the lab did find the boarding pass.'

'"It's only been a day",' mimics Marchant. 'Yeah. No thanks to you. We lost a good few hours because of your little blunder.'

Olivia had profusely apologised for her tardiness, yet she still wears the embarrassing stain. She loathes discipline and chastisement. It smacks of rejection, and rejection forms chapters of her childhood, long ripped from their leather-bound covers.

Marchant's offensive manner sears into her core: 'If you can't stand the heat get out of the kitchen.' No pussy-footing. He tells it straight. 'There's no place in this job for the weak-minded.'

Olivia snatches her bag: 'I'll be out for coffee.' She slams the door with such force that it reverberates through the office. Marchant stands aghast, lips bouncing like those of a ventriloquist's stuttering dummy.

Olivia merges with pedestrians braving the afternoon's chill: office workers on tea break, late shoppers, and a group of uniformed school students. She stops at a nearby café, drops her bag onto an outside table and joins the cosmopolitan latte set – pinkies extended – gracefully consuming coffees and croissants. Olivia has no inclination to join the ranks of pretentious sidewalk swankys, but does demonstrate her eligibility by ordering an egg and lettuce sandwich (stipulating reduced-salt butter in lieu of margarine), a vanilla slice and a mug of cappuccino – purely for the calcium content. Today is not one for calorie counting.

The full sun throws chaotic shadows across the footpath. Once a mall of generous proportions, it has now succumbed, like many, to the needs of vehicular traffic and their ever-expanding black thoroughfares. The remaining narrow strip provides a pleasant promenade of umbrellas sprouting from the brick pavement, shielding rickety tables from unwelcome summer showers. A young waitress slides a plastic tray onto the tiny table.

Olivia bites delicately into the sandwich and considers the investigation to date:

Fact: There were two ticket stubs.

Deduction: The deceased must have been with someone.

Fact: The small purse contained no money, credit or bank cards and no identification. And, there was no make-up.

Deduction: She could have been the victim of a mugging gone wrong, or, someone had purposely removed all means of identity –

The ringing phone in her bag interrupts her train of thought. She fumbles, and like most in that situation, answers it two seconds too late. Four seconds' later the phone beeps. She reads the text: Return to office ASAP.

Bugger him. I'm finishing this first. She places her phone on the table and ungraciously devours the sandwich before polishing off the vanilla slice. The phone gleams in the sun as if communicating a divine revelation. *Bloody hell. What an idiot I am. There was no phone. She must have had a phone. Everyone has a phone. We need another search.*

While Olivia ravages her afternoon snack, Marchant sifts through a stack of public appeal responses. His priority is to ascertain the deceased's identity ahead of all secondary information. Among the pages is a Missing Persons Report logged at 12.05 a.m., but not entered into the police database until 9.10 a.m. *Typical night shift,* he huffs. *Handballing to day shift the tasks they're too lazy to do.*

He scans the computer screen: *Juanita Morales. 22 years old, dob 2 September 1992. Petite build, Philippine national, missing from Bournemouth. Out of character to stay out. Not with known friends. No employment due to visa condition. Reported by fiancé, Trevor John Taylor, dob 6 May 1983.*

Marchant reels as Olivia bursts into his office. Disguising

41

his anger with a smile he announces: 'Our Jane Doe may have just been Christened. Juanita Morales. Looks like we're off to Bournemouth.'

'There was no phone,' pants Olivia. 'She must have had a mobile – everyone does.'

'Well, get onto it. Find out if she had one. We need the model and the service provider.'

'Maybe I can do that on the way to Bournemouth. What's there?'

'Guy named Taylor. Fiancé of a woman he reported missing some time last night. Bloody night shift didn't log it. Rang him just before. Seems pretty calm under the circumstances.'

6

MARCHANT AND WATTS settle into the Astra for the three-hour journey to Bournemouth. Olivia sulks in the passenger seat, despising her supervisor's incessant smoking and persistent replays of full-volumed Beethoven, Tchaikovsky and Rachmaninoff classics. She believes he abuses the foible solely to annoy her. Coarse rebukes keep her hand from the volume button.

'I'm driving. Helps keep me calm.' Marchant's favoured retort.

He always drives, having widely avowed that women shouldn't be permitted to drive police cars – they should be restricted to prams and shopping trolleys. He cites the lower threshold of panic displayed by women, and uses the analogy of a woman having never been crowned world champion in Formula One, Touring Cars or the World Rally Championship.

Only recently, *The Daily Telegraph* had headlined Marchant's true contempt for women over his lobbying Wychavon Council to proclaim stroller- and pram-free areas in the High Street between twelve noon and 2.00 p.m. 'This proposed by-law would avail pedestrians to unhindered movement during the peak lunch period,' he claimed. 'Women have plenty of time before and after lunch to wheel around their infants. I don't walk the sexist platform,' he continued in the editorial, 'I speak only in practical terms for the community's benefit.'

Marchant joins those who negate personal ideals to add credence to an argument, in much the same manner as a person claims: 'I'm not racist, but...' and then spits a bevy of abuse against Asians, Muslims and Europeans who 'steal' Brit's jobs (even though they're jobs Brits refuse) and against the British of West Indian and African heritage who toiled over furnaces, pushed shovels for fourteen hours a day, stacked supermarket shelves at night (invariably because employers didn't want to be seen employing 'blacks' during the day) and studied until their eyes wept blood so that they could provide a future for their family and in so doing make a worthy contribution to Britain's prosperity. *They* slogged the hard yards and succeeded while their Anglo-Saxon neighbours sat back, relishing their 'government sponsored' life.

The ensuing raft of public opinion against Marchant, mostly in the form of Letters to the Editor, crushed his aspirations to nominate for local council. The community's rage saw a flood of British National Party enrolment forms anonymously flutter to his letterbox, car windscreen and office locker.

Marchant turns down the music. 'How's your love-life, Olivia?'

The out-of-the-blue question strikes a nerve. 'I don't have one because I'm scared I'll end up with someone like you.'

'Aah, you could do a lot worse than be kept by a ravishing chap like me.'

'I don't want to be "kept" by anyone, thank you very much. Just drive and keep your eyes on the road.'

'Olivia, Olivia. You're much more pretty than the road ahead. Just as straight though.'

Olivia is not in the mood for personal attention, least of all from Marchant. She throws in a subject change as her favoured tack of wrong-footing those with dubious agendas: 'Michael. What do you think about someone reporting their wife missing and then doing her in? Or what about the other way around – killing her and then reporting her missing? It's not unusual, you know.'

'Yeah. Happens. They think we'd never believe a loving husband would kill his wife. But just remember, we have to approach this case with an open mind. In saying that, I reckon there's more to that Simmons guy than he's letting on.'

'I don't know about that. I haven't even met him since you chose to dart off yesterday without me.'

'Operational decision, my dear. Boss's prerogative.'

'Maybe, but it's difficult enough trying to catch crims without half the force doing their own thing and concealing information.'

'Okay, okay. Here it is. As you know, I saw Simmons yesterday afternoon. He runs two cruise craft on the Avon. Evasive bastard. Says he heard something about a body but didn't know anything. Didn't recognise the photo. Didn't even know how many he'd had on board that night. Confirmed the receipts were his – you know, the receipts you didn't find – but he can't say when they were issued. All in all I got nowhere. But, and this is a big but – not like yours my dear – the guy's hiding something. I may give you a crack at him later.'

'Why, thank you very much. I must be privileged.'

They turn into Alexander Road, a cul-de-sac of 20-year-old homes whose numbers are as chaotic as those of a Sudoku grid. A welcoming beacon: '*Taylor's Electrical Services* –

45

Specialising in all Current Problems' beams in yellow and black from the side of an erratically parked van.

'I think *he's* going to have a current problem,' smiles Olivia.

'Look. Gawking out the window. He's expecting us?'

Trevor Taylor appears in the doorway. 'Thanks for coming,' he smirks as Marchant and Watts stride along the footpath. Taylor's self-confidence reflects his belief that police have responded to the missing persons report. He has no idea that Marchant and Watts have pegged him as a potential suspect.

Taylor extends his arm. 'Come in. Have you found her?'

Both officers squeeze through the doorway and into a sparsely furnished reception room that yells 'bachelor pad', albeit blessed with a fragrant tinge of feminine influence. Best described as a work-in-progress, the tired and plain room boasts a gas log fire squeezed into the original fireplace. A huge television sprouts snaking strands of liquorice wires to a DVD player and Sony Play Station and then to a bank of five home-theatre speakers, clearly expressing the occupant's lifestyle. Scattered magazines, trade journals and boxes of financial records leave little space for furniture. A dusty mantelpiece accommodates tiny figurines of Asian emperors, Philippine jeepneys and an alabaster Virgin Mary. From a mock crystal vase, wilting flowers bow their heads in sympathy to the happy couple smiling from jumbled photographs.

Tatty worn carpet buckles across the floor as if a nocturnal creature hibernates within its warmth. A single couch with frayed arms hosts two pillows stained with age and coffee mishaps. The round light fitting, once pearl white but now a tarnished, sticky-bronze, harbours a twenty-year collection of insects, dust and grime.

'Nice home,' mutters Marchant.

'Thanks. I'm in the middle of doing it up,' replies Trevor, oblivious to Marchant's sarcasm.

If this is the "middle", I can hardly wait to see the finished product.

'You guys like tea or coffee?'

Given the state of the home, Marchant chooses to immunise himself against the risk of infection. 'No thanks. We'll just race through these few questions. Now tell me, when did you last see your fiancée? Juanita, isn't it?'

'Yeah. I got home from work late on Sunday after an emergency callout. I expected her to be here, but we'd had a bit of an argument earlier on so I thought she may have gone visiting someone – a friend or whatever. I rang a couple of times and left a message on her mobile.'

'Who'd you think she was visiting?'

'I don't know. She had her own friends. All Filipino; they just talk their own lingo and eat fish.'

'So what made you call the police if you thought she was at a friend's?'

''cause it was late, wasn't it. I couldn't find her so I wondered if maybe she'd been attacked in the street or something. It's just not safe for a girl to walk around sometimes, is it?'

Marchant chokes back a comment. 'Do you have a recent photo of Juanita?'

Trevor glances at the mantelpiece, walks over to his computer, clicks a few menus and displays a photo of the couple sitting in McDonald's. 'I emailed this to missing persons last night.'

'Yes, I know.' Marchant continues, 'Just wanted to be sure. There's been a girl found in Evesham. At this stage it would appear she matches the description of your fiancée.'

Trevor forces surprise. 'Evesham? That's ages away. What would she be doing there?'

'That's what we're hoping you can tell us.'

Taylor morphs into an animated character, gesticulating with every word: 'I can't imagine she'd know anyone that far away. As I said, I hardly know her friends. Did you bring her back? Where is she now?'

'I'm sorry to tell you Mr Taylor, but the person we found was in the River Avon.'

'Fuck me. She can't be dead. You mean she's dead?'

'All we can say at this stage is that a person matching your fiancée's description has been found. We need to confirm identity and notify family. I understand you're engaged, but you're not strictly family. I'm sorry to be harsh, but we can't comment any further.'

'That's all right. It can't be her. She wouldn't be that far away; she's never been out of Bournemouth.'

Olivia jumps in: 'Perhaps you could give us a list of her friends or contacts?'

Marchant shoots a scathing glare.

'Um, I don't think there's anything written down. She doesn't use a diary or nothing like that. Everything's in her phone. That's where they'd be 'cause she mainly texts to save asking me for money.'

Olivia continues: 'Is her phone here by any chance?'

'No, 'cause I was ringing her wasn't I.'

Marchant is clearly uninterested in his partner's line of questioning despite it being reasonable, and common, for a person to store all of their personal information in their phone. By Marchant's reckoning, today's generation should use a diary and log phone numbers in a Teledex. His gut instinct screams:

48

let's eliminate this guy and get back to Simmons, but instead, he says: 'All right. We'll head off now. Thanks for your time Mr Taylor. One of us will get back to you when we have further information about the identity of the woman found.'

Olivia isn't satisfied. She mouths to Marchant 'one moment' and shoots a barb to Taylor: 'Just before we go, where was your emergency call on Sunday night?'

'Emer –? Oh, uh, I can't think straight now. M-my brother's place. His power went down.'

'I realise this is a sensitive time, but I'll need your brother's address and contact details so we can note on file that we've exhausted all enquiries.'

Marchant stands aside, hands in pockets and with head bowed, scowls at Olivia.

Olivia ignores him. She's learnt to immunise herself from Marchant's 'what-the-hell-do-you-think-you're-up-to' look. She jots John Trevor Taylor's details into her notebook. 'That must be confusing, mustn't it, having nearly the same names?'

'Not for us, but some people get mixed up. We're nothing alike, anyway.'

Marchant reinforces his eagerness by grasping Olivia's elbow and leading her to the door like a child clutched by a remonstrating parent. He terminates the conversation, leaving Trevor standing gobsmacked in the centre of the room. 'Okay. That's all for now. We'll be in touch.'

Trevor peers through the window and tracks the silver Astra to the end of the street, unaware of Olivia pressing his brother's number into her phone. He triumphs over fobbing off the police despite his not expecting such probing questions. He has no real concern, believing that missing persons remain missing because, in the main, they vanish of their own accord.

Trevor has no contingency plan to defend himself in the event of Juanita being found; he believes that she'll rest on the bottom of the Avon. Waterway predators and micro-organisms will feed on her tissue until skeletal remains tumble away with the current. Only when Olivia asked about friends' details did he panic. He tried to re-assure himself: perhaps she's one of those investigators who leave no loose ends. Of course she'd check with friends to establish whether or not they knew of Juanita's whereabouts.

He brushes the curtain into place, picks up his phone and taps his brother's number.

* * *

'John here.'

'Hello John. Detective Sergeant Olivia Watts. You're Trevor Taylor's brother?'

'Yeah, why?'

'I suppose you already know this, but his fiancée's missing. I'm trying to locate people who've recently seen her. When did you last see her?'

'What d'ya mean, "missing"? I know nothin' about that. Last time I seen her was a couple of weeks ago when I dropped in on my way home from work to say hello.'

Olivia's glance to Marchant floats through the windscreen. 'And when did you last see your brother?'

'Then. The same time, a couple of weeks ago. Is there a problem?

'No. Should be all right. Just preliminary enquiries, but I may need to call you later. Thanks.'

Olivia ends the call and relays John's half of the conversation to Marchant. 'That Trevor's talking crap. His brother hasn't seen him for a fortnight.'

'We'll sort that out easy enough. Don't forget the guy's probably beside himself, wondering what's happened to his woman. He didn't show any of that nervousness I'd expect of a guilty person. Anyway, first off, I'm going to drill that Captain Simmons. It's been a long day and we've got a long drive ahead; I'll set him up for 8.00 a.m. tomorrow. Can you be in?'

Olivia rolls her eyes and reluctantly agrees to another early start, knowing it will not help reduce the swelling files of paperwork and pending interviews.

John Taylor wonders why a detective would phone him about his brother's fiancée when Trevor himself had not mentioned a word. He jumps to the phone. 'What the hell you got yourself into now, Trev?'

'It's better you don't know. Just a spot of bother I might need your help with.'

'I've told you before, I'm not helping you. It's about that Juanita bird, isn't it? The coppers already put the finger on me askin' when I seen her. I dunno what to say do I? They catch me on the hop like that; I dunno whether I'm sinkin' ya or helpin' ya. I just said I seen yas both a couple of weeks ago or somethin' like that.'

'So what did they ask about me?'

'Just wanna know if I knew about Juanita missing and when I seen yas both last. All I could think to say was I seen yas two weeks ago when I dropped in for a beer or whatever.'

'Shit. I told them I was around on Sunday to fix your power 'cause it went down. You remember that in case they ask you again.'

'I can't just change my story for you. How many times I gotta pull you out of the shit? This has been going on for too long now. I got my own life. Anyway, where is Juanita?'

'She's gone missing. I came home from work and she wasn't here. I reported it to the police and that's all I know so far.'

'So why d'ya want me to say I saw you on Sunday if you're on the level?'

'Look. I just need your help, okay?'

Trevor had manipulated his younger brother from early childhood. He stole John's toys. He took food from the fridge, and when later confronted by his mother, blamed John. As they grew older, Trevor had John do his homework. That progressed to bullying his brother into forging sick notes and handing them to his teacher while Trevor spent the day thieving from shopping malls or joyriding around the rail network.

Years later, after each began dating, Trevor found John chatting up *his* girlfriend. An intense physical fight erupted, during which John suffered a fractured jaw and broken nose. Trevor accepted that whilst the level of violence inflicted upon his brother was unforgivable, it did serve to scare him into never again trying to one-up Trevor in the brotherly power stakes.

Trevor continued the domination through to adulthood, at one stage discouraging John from moving to another county. John was ill-equipped to stand up to his brother, so he continued to be submissive. Until now.

'I can't change it Trev. You know I can't.'

'What are you, a weak bastard or something? It's easy. Just tell them you were mixed up.'

'I can't and I won't. I know you're my brother and we're s'posed to stick together and all that stuff, but I can't just change my story. I'll get myself in the shit. You work something out as if *you* were mixed up. Don't put it on me.'

'Yeah, right. Stuff you too. I got no reason to hang on here then, have I?' Trevor jams his thumb on the 'end call' button.

7

MARCHANT DRIVES THE return leg to Worcester while Olivia dozes in the passenger seat. To help stay awake, he figures a mathematical hypothesis of the cost to the community of police sleeping in vehicles whilst on duty. The calculation soars beyond six figures.

It is not unusual for partners, especially those rostered for night shift, to share brief naps. As the observer, the passenger's only official requirement is to maintain the duty sheet. Most police learn, during their first taste of operational duties, that the duty sheet is a fictional exercise completed at the end of each shift. Many officers choose to 'moonlight' during the day. Suffice to say that those who mow lawns, provide labour for cash, or serve summonses for private investigators, suffer varying degrees of sleep deprivation. Night shift affords patrol passengers the opportunity to partially recuperate for the forthcoming day. They'll slump into a fully reclined seat, monitor the local hot spots with half-open eyes, but see nothing until feeling a jab in the ribs two hours' later when it's time to swap roles.

Similarly, those tasked for office duties fall limply to their desktops at the dreaded hour of 4.00 a.m. Those commanding the rank of inspector and above simply lock the office door. No one will ever know they've catnapped for three hours.

Marchant diverts to Olivia's home, jabs her in the ribs – low enough to not be indecent – and instructs her to be on the doorstep at 7.45 in the morning.

At 10.00 p.m., Marchant walks into the station to see two officers scramble to a filing cabinet, a detective throwing darts in the meal room, and a sergeant indiscreetly playing solitaire on a computer. The duty board shows a uniform patrol tasked to known trouble spots including the popular licensed club trumpeting the incongruous name of White Elephant. A typical Monday night.

Marchant enters his office and gapes at a pile of papers dumped on his desk. He flings a half-eaten burger into a colleague's bin before glancing at the top sheet – a statement typed by PC Bailey – detailing information he'd taken from a Brett Davies.

Davies had reported finding a mobile phone under a seat of a river cruiser. The statement documents how, at approximately 5.54 p.m. on Sunday, August fourteen, he had handed the phone to the 'captain', but thought it suspicious when the recipient dropped the phone straight into his pocket rather than announce the find to disembarking passengers.

Marchant races to the uniform division and bellows abuse at the desk sergeant for not alerting him to the vital information.

'Just a moment, inspector. Bailey's on day shift. That's nothing to do with my boys. I'd respectfully ask you to check your facts before coming down here and blowing off steam.'

Many police stations foster rivalry between uniform and CID divisions. Worcester is no exception.

DS Watts creeps into her flat, aching for a call from Dave Stafford – a reunion that is long overdue. Rather than crawl straight into bed, she marks time, like a faulty CD striking a glitch on each rotation. The weight of the investigation, coupled with Marchant's attitude toward her, has taken its toll. She has avoided end-of-day drinks at the local, refused offers of social engagements from likeable colleagues, and offered false excuses to those with whom she would ordinarily share leisure time. Olivia prefers to not initiate contact with Stafford, but does wish to end the drawn-out run of lonely nights.

In truth, she is not totally alone. Theodore the goldfish, who also performs the same repetitious rotations as the aforementioned CD is amicable company; but there are limitations as to how long one can sanely interact with a Nemo caricature circling a glass bowl.

Theodore loses out when Olivia calls Dave. Voicemail: *Stafford here. Leave a message if you dare. If you don't, I won't care.*

'Hi Dave. It's me. Love to hear from you. Perhaps we can get together soon? Call me, bye-ee.'

The evening imparts dreary solitude. Boring. An evening unable to be rejuvenated by clubbing or a half-dozen cans of pre-mixed Gin and Tonic. She succumbs to her weakness. Olivia is an emotional eater whose will of steel occasionally falters under life's stresses. While some turn to drink and others to drugs, Olivia turns to the pleasure of Chocolate Bavarian desserts, cake, and Dave Stafford. She chomps, nibbles, and chews away an hour, waiting for his call. In vain. Driven by eagerness for companionship, she launches her computer, logs on to the internet and enters 'romance' in the Google search box. A page flashes onto the screen, featuring the top ten results – ten of 307 million. Another click, and she lands on a page of 'available' males. Daunted by seamy profiles of males seeking 'fun times', Olivia shudders at the thought of subjecting herself to the bevy of predators and online desperados. She closes the laptop and returns to the fridge.

Food. The great pacifier. But it won't choke Olivia's memory of an ill-fated evening with Marchant.

Shortly after arriving at Worcester CID, Marchant had promised to 'ease her into the new role' by treating her to after-shift drinks the local pub – tradition being that no one is 'properly' inducted into CID until they've downed a few pints with the team.

'They'll be here soon,' Marchant professed on catching Olivia's anxiety.

Olivia became suspicious after discovering that Marchant had 'conveniently' forgotten to convey the invitation to staff – thereby leaving her as his sole company. She downed a couple of Gin and Tonics – to do the right thing – and expressed disappointment at the botched arrangement. In consolation, Marchant draped his arm over Olivia's shoulder, dropped it to her lap and walked his fingers along her thigh. Goosebumps erupted. Nerves frazzled. As the new member of Worcester's team, she struggled with the prospect of jeopardising her position by fobbing off the very person likely to assure her future.

At any other time she would have slapped the offender's face, pitched a drink over him, and with head held high, stomped from the pub. End of story. Here, she chose to weather the storm and remain with Marchant as pint followed pint and his speech degenerated to a saliva-spattered slur. Olivia propagated the burden of guilt, conceived by woman's maternal instinct, after sensing the hurt (or frustration) she'd inadvertently wreaked on her supervisor. In normal circumstances, Olivia wouldn't have minded the attention. That night, however, all she wanted was to go home, shower and sleep. Solo. But she had not yet learnt that Marchant was of the 'no means maybe' brigade.

Marchant had interpreted Olivia's demeanour as a playful brush-off; he would not accept that Olivia was *serious* about not wanting to play along – he believed she was delaying the inevitable, solely to preserve her honour and propriety. He slid closer, grabbed her shoulders, pulled her into his chest and kissed her cheek. Olivia reacted instinctively. Waiving regard for her location and respect for her companion, she picked up his beer and upended the half-pint of lager over his head. The rebuke was instant and produced unexpected results. As if snapping out of a hypnotic trance with no concept of what had just occurred, Marchant adjusted his clothes, checked his watch, and said: 'Must be getting along now. Was a nice evening, Liv. See you in the morning then, eh?'

'Only if you don't call me "Liv" and only if you apologise for your conduct when you're sober. You obviously can't drive, so I'll drop you home if you give me directions. Let's go!'

'Yes ma'am,' slurred Marchant with a salute.

Ten minutes' later, Olivia swung in to Marchant's driveway. The porch light flashed on and illuminated the entrance beneath an angled portico reminiscent of an olde worlde church entry. Leaning against a pillar stood a woman with folded arms, glaring at the car as if a bank executive were about to jump out and serve a repossession order on the home. Her expression did not change as Marchant staggered like a wayward student reporting to his starched headmistress.

Obscene words shrilled from beyond the front gate. Olivia chuckled as she reversed from the drive. *So he's not the macho superman he pretends to be, and she probably thinks I'm his tart. I hope he suffers.*

Fifteen years' earlier, and only two weeks after graduating from the police college, Michael Marchant had married Geraldine Clements. They've endured the test of time, though not all fifteen years have been roses and chocolates. Whose has?

Michael knows friends who had married at a similar age, only to separate or divorce within five years. So much for the fabled 'seven year itch'; many didn't even reach the milestone to test whether or not the prophecy was true.

Geraldine too, has friends who'd married for love; forever after; till death do us part; all harnessing fantasies of Romeo and Juliet and the greatest modern variation portrayed on the silver screen: Richard Gere and Julia Roberts in *Pretty Woman*. On the screen, love is eternal; unconquerable by external influences. In reality though, love is malleable – but susceptible to having squeezed from it life's every pulse.

A harvest of wilted petals covers Michael and Geraldine's marital bed. Countless creamy chocolate centres have been rejected in moments of indifference and belligerence. Numerous words of love and anger have been spoken and retracted. And several nights have been spent apart – courtesy of the unresolved battle of wits, pride and stubbornness. On waking, there is no winner. Despite that extensive history, Michael and Geraldine celebrated their crystal wedding anniversary, proving that a turbulent marriage can achieve top billing for a matrimonial screenplay.

Geraldine, as a fifteen-year-old school sweetheart, had pledged her life to Michael. She had eyes for no one else and no interest in dating other boys. Her mother considered the friendship a passing fad. On turning eighteen, Geraldine announced her engagement. The Clements reluctantly accepted that Michael Marchant would inevitably be inducted into their family.

Michael and Geraldine's parents jointly lectured the benefits of meeting other people. 'You're so young, go enjoy yourself' (as if the couple weren't enjoying themselves – their parents just had no concept of the intensity of their enjoyment). Michael's father went on to profess the proverbial creed of maledom: 'Son, go sow your wild oats before even contemplating settling down.' Michael thought at the time: *I know all about the "wild oats" stuff, but what the hell does "contemplating" mean?*

Sadly, Michael has sown acres of extremely wild oats since marrying Geraldine, who, through the incalculable power of women's intuition and regular coffee mornings, discovered that Michael has flouted his vows and continues his youthful 'farming' in the car park of the Worcester police station, thereby justifying Geraldine's scornful look.

The Clash's 'London Calling' shrieks from Olivia's mobile, jolting her to the present. *About time. Now I'm right for the night.*

'Hi Olivia. It's Shannon.'

'Shannon?'

'Just passing by, as they say. Wondered if I could pop in and say hello?'

'Well… sure. Bit late, but I'm not doing anything. Come on up.'

Shannon Fowler had breezed through the police college with Olivia. They'd maintained sporadic contact after

Shannon's prompt exit from the constabulary. Flushed with embarrassment, she had never offered an explanation for her engaging in lascivious activity with a fellow police officer. Olivia filled in the blanks.

The police force has long been considered a 'brotherhood'. With women swelling the ranks, they now boast their own 'sisterhood'. All in all, both sexes combine to form a bond of members who support and stand beside each other under the most trying circumstances – save for sexual fraternisation whilst on duty, an activity that, through locker-room embellishment, paints personal reputations far darker than were the actual activities.

Shannon narrates a chronology of recent activities. Olivia responds similarly, but for ethical reasons chooses to gloss over the current investigation. Her conscientiousness is futile, given that most information is already in the public arena – few have not heard about the body in the river. Of those who have, many circulate cruel jokes: *Where's your local Avon representative?*

The morgue.

And, *Have you heard that Avon's new body-wash has been recalled?*

Consumer Affairs found that it failed to rejuvenate a customer.

Olivia sombrely explains her disenchantment with Marchant, and huffs at Stafford's continued avoidance. Tears stream from her eyes, the salty emotion dampening her shirtsleeve.

Shannon wraps Olivia in a consoling hug, offered and sought in moments of depression and emotional fragility. Shannon raises her head, and feels the pain in her friend's eyes. 'What is it?'

'I just can't win. I ring Dave and he ignores me; I won't see anyone from work because half of them start horrid rumours and the other half only want sex. There's nowhere else to find company. I'm tied up on this bloody investigation twelve hours a day and I've got… I've just got no release at all.'

'Come on Olivia. You know things work out in the end. Dave's probably on a job right now. He might be in a position where he can't call back.'

'And he may be in a tangled position with someone else and that's *why* he can't call. Stuff him anyway. He only calls when he wants something. What's so stupid is that I do exactly the same thing by calling him.'

Shannon fixes on Olivia's eyes, absorbing the hurt, the pain and the desire. She breathes a conciliatory kiss on Olivia's cheek.

Olivia winces, looks complacently at her friend and smiles. 'Thank you. That's just what I need, although I didn't expect it from you.'

'It's just what I need too, though I didn't expect to be giving it to you.'

They freeze with anticipation; the pose expressed by dizzy teens on a first date: *Shall I make a move or will it end in disaster?* Shannon drops to Olivia's lips but halts at the crucial moment. Instead, she brushes another kiss against Olivia's cheek.

Olivia returns the gesture, this time homing in to the hunger of each other's desire. 'Shannon. I can't do this.'

'Shh. You can, Olivia. Just let go.'

Never has Olivia ventured beyond male intimacy. Never even experimented, yet the idea knocks on an unlocked door in the penthouse of her mind. As emotional instability, workplace stress and aching desire meld, the door opens. A gust of thought blows away reservations: *what the heck. What's wrong with a little consoling?* She folds her arms around Shannon and slowly traces her tongue across Shannon's lips. A hint of strawberry lipstick heightens her anxiety. Shannon opens her mouth, allowing Olivia to offer sweetness unmatched by a male. Tongues flutter in the humid cage like captive butterflies engrossed in a frenzied fracas.

Guided by Aphrodite, Shannon unbuttons Olivia's blouse. Pauses at each opening. Expecting to be censored. She isn't. She nestles into Olivia's neck and paints soft kisses beneath her ear lobes, each kiss descending to the lace trim of Olivia's bra.

Olivia arches her back, inching higher to receive Shannon's pleasure. The point of no return advances. 'No Shannon. Not here.' She takes Shannon's hand and leads her to the bedroom. They drop into the quilted duvet like windswept seeds falling upon the vast acres of Louisiana's cotton fields.

Shannon leads an expedition through the plantation, gently brushing past silky stems as she captures the sensuality of nature's buds. 'Sshh, don't say a word. Close your eyes. Just lie there.' She places her knee between Olivia's thighs and then creeps over undulating hills, admiring, as she does so, sun-scorched peaks atop sandy white slopes. She slides through fertile valleys, pausing to savour droplets of moisture from the tips of delicate ferns. An intense subterranean contraction thrusts the gorge skyward. The earth groans like a latent volcano suddenly reactivated. Eruption imminent.

Olivia relishes the journey into foreign surroundings. She'd previously travelled only as a budget passenger with no trimmings and no Frequent Flyer points. She'd encountered harsh desert plains of rocky outcrops where prickly pear cacti dominate and cowboys ride roughshod, trampling all before them. And then they disappear, never to be seen again, leaving only a worn saddle and lecherous lacerations of the desert earth upon her back.

This time, as a content passenger, she relishes the exquisite adventure: the never-before-experienced sensations of dizziness transporting her to Hindenburg's heights until its explosion consumes all in its path.

Overwhelming satisfaction settles jittery nerves.

Shuddering spasms dwindle to serene tranquillity.

Stillness lingers until the new dawn.

8

At 8.00 a.m., a uniformed desk sergeant leads Barry Simmons to a vacant interview room.

Once carrying the esteem and respect of a commissioned Naval Officer, Simmons now presents as an aged, couldn't-care-less pariah. He's abused alcohol and cigarettes to compensate for the loss of his beloved navy, blaming, of course, the navy's cohesive camaraderie that inducted him into the drinking and smoking guild. The 'follow-the-leader' ritual recruited his idle hours, and encouraged the meek Marchant into the boys' club. As promotions elevated selected personnel, tobacco and alcohol dependence took its grip and was difficult, if not impossible, to reverse.

For Barry Simmons, alcohol stencils the navy's glory days to the forefront of his mind. The River Avon *is* the Pacific Ocean.

Simmons paid no regard to interview preparation. What could he contribute? After the previous day's discussion with Marchant he'd walked around the decks and cabin trying to recall who he *had* seen on the night of the fourteenth. He'd leant against the port-side railing, deep in thought: *There's that young part-timer who served the teas; she may have seen something, but she's a bit of a scatterbrain – don't think I could rely on her to help. Besides, Marchant hadn't asked about anyone else, so why volunteer* her *name? She was in the cabin all along and certainly wouldn't have noticed anyone fall overboard – if such a thing happened. That would answer the discrepancy of the miscount, but I can't admit that, can I? And what about that bloody phone? Nah, piece of piss. No one's going to call the cops and admit to finding a phone. They'd just keep the damn thing, wouldn't they? No one calls the cops for anything now, except maybe to complain about a neighbour's stereo or barking dog.*

Truth is, once all are aboard, Simmons sees little other than the river twisting and looping its way to Tewkesbury. He focuses on avoiding constant obstacles: storm-generated debris, floating branches, potential Olympic rowers sculling away at practice runs and the occasional group of mischievous children hurling rocks at the pitching target.

Marchant swaggers into the room and checks the DVD recorder and video camera. Watts follows like an obedient school prefect carrying her teacher's books. She nods 'hello' to Simmons and waits patiently whilst Marchant scans his notebook for the prepared questions.

Early in his career, Marchant found that suspects invariably present one of three distinct demeanours. There is the obliging public-spirited type who seeks gratification for his contribution, fully cognisant of his doing police a favour; there's the abrupt, belligerent model who typically conceals something, whether it be guilt, evidence, or a hatred of authority; and finally, there is the suspect who displays a common trait of the guilty – he has faith in his ability to outsmart both the police and the courts with smug 'no comment' responses. Marchant aligns Simmons with the second profile and continues to rely on his gut feeling that Simmons was complicit in Morales' murder.

Just as the 'no comment' is a favoured tool of the street-savvy suspect, the 'gut feeling' is a highly ranked resource of many investigators. The very nature of their vocation demands their prosecuting wrongdoers. The investigator is therefore predisposed to processing a suspect with the objective of prosecution, rather than holding back and impartially viewing the circumstances, evidence and suspect's account. They lose sight of the judicial objective: clear the innocent and find the guilty.

Omitting pleasantries, Marchant plucks a handkerchief from his pocket and wipes his brow. He nods to Olivia, and commences: 'Barry, I'm going to ask you some questions in relation to the murder of Juanita Morales. You do not have to say anything, but it may harm your defence if you do not mention, when questioned, something you may later rely on in court.'

'Yeah, yeah. Not a problem.'

'Were you conducting Avon cruises on the afternoon of Sunday August fourteenth?'

'Yeah, I am every day.'

'How many trips did you make?'

'Four. That's eleven, one, three and five o'clock – every two hours. Then I return on the even hours of twelve, two and four out of Tewkesbury.'

'I'm showing you a photo of Juanita Morales. Did you carry her on any of those excursions?'

'Might have. I'm not good with faces.'

'Come on, have a good look. She's a distinctive looker. The sort of woman you wouldn't forget quickly.'

'Listen, I got a boat to run and I carry about 20 people three or four times a day. I have no reason to remember anyone, whether they're a good looker or not. As I say, she may have been on and she may not.'

'Can you explain why she would have two tickets?'

'If she had two tickets, it seems pretty obvious that she did travel, doesn't it? – that's if they're definitely my tickets.'

'You've already identified them as yours when I showed them to you yesterday.'

'Okay then. They're mine. What are you suggesting?'

'I'm not suggesting anything. I'm asking questions. We just want information that will help identify who murdered this girl.'

'Who says she was murdered? She might have fallen overboard. She might have fallen from the riverbank before or after a cruise. I don't have information. I told you that yesterday.'

'So you concede she was on your boat?'

'No. I don't concede anything. I didn't see anything. Just piloted the boat to Tewkes' and back. And inspector, mine is not the only craft operating on the Avon.'

Marchant transmits a smug grin. 'Yes, but yours is the only craft operating as Simmons' Scenic Cruises. Now then, what's your lost property procedure for items recovered after your trips?'

'Most people realise they're missing something before they disembark. We have no need to keep records.'

'So no one's ever lost anything or left something behind?' Marchant creases a smile. 'I don't know how many times I've left an umbrella in a taxi or on a train.'

Simmons palms his chin. 'I didn't say nothing's ever been

left behind – it's just that I don't recall anything. I think it's natural for a person to check their possessions before leaving the craft, or a bus or a train for that matter. If you've lost umbrellas, that's a reflection on you, not the transport operator. Anyway, what the hell's that got to do with this woman? I've told you I didn't see her. What more do you want?'

Marchant's flush deepens. 'I'd like to inspect your property log.'

'There's no such thing. Listen. I just told you we never have lost property. I even make an announcement: "Collect all bags and personal effects before you disembark," near the completion of each journey.'

'Did you make that announcement on Sunday?'

'Sure. It's part of my docking routine.'

'So what can you tell us about a mobile phone found on the deck?'

'What mobile phone? News to me.'

'It's been reported that a phone was found and handed to you by a passenger.'

'Not true. No one handed me anything.'

'So you're denying any knowledge of a mobile phone handed to you on the fourteenth of August this year?'

'Of course I'm denying it. It isn't true.'

Marchant sifts through his file. 'I'm going to read a passage from a witness statement taken on the fifteenth of August: "I saw a phone on the deck near the rear of the boat. There was no one around so I didn't know who it might have belonged to. I just picked it up and gave it to the boat driver or captain or whatever you call him. It was a silver Nokia, one of those fairly new ones that do everything. This was very near the end of the return to Evesham because I wanted to shoot some photos from the rear of the boat. I dropped my camera case and when I bent down to pick it up I saw the phone under a bench seat." What do you say about that, Mr Simmons?'

'Yeah, sorry. That just reminded me. There was a lot on my mind that day, I completely overlooked it.'

'So where is the phone now?'

'I, er, um, sold it to that Cash Liquidators shop in town.' Simmons' deceptive veneer and initial denial of the mobile phone clearly enunciates his devious disposition.

Jotting details of the sale onto a Post-it note, Marchant scowls his thoughts across the table: *you friggin' shifty bastard.* He fires off a barrage of questions: 'Don't you think it would have been reasonable to hand it to the police or at least hold on to it in case someone came back for it? Did you think of phoning one of the numbers to find the owner? How much did you get for it?'

Simmons replies to only one: 'Ten quid.'

Marchant probes further, enquiring about en-route stops.

'We stop only at Tewkes.'

He asks about the availability of other witnesses.

'I had only a part-timer serving scones.'

And he asks if anyone had made enquiries about the phone.

'No.'

On that negative note, he winds up the interview: 'Thank you for your time, Mr Simmons. I'll refer this to my supervisor. In the meantime, we'll be making further enquiries. You may be required for re-interview at a later date. You're right to go.'

Marchant sees no merit in chasing a menial enquiry over a recovered phone. His obsession with Simmons' complicity clouds the link to the prospect of the phone dovetailing Olivia's proposition of Morales not having a phone in her bag or pocket. He throws Olivia a smile, slaps the Post-it note on her wrist and grunts: 'Handle that will you Liv.'

She glares, too nervous to return a barbed retort, and too thrilled to boast that her prophecy might materialise into a potential breakthrough.

DS Watts stands in awe of Evesham's Cash Liquidators shopfront. The left-side window glitters with jewellery: engagement rings sold in the aftermath of unresolved quarrels; family heirlooms sacrificed because money ranked higher than memories; and a snaking line of assorted jewellery, diamonds and cubic zirconia stolen from properties nationwide to support drug addicts' habits.

Many of Watts' burglary and theft enquiries steer her to pawnshops and boutique liquidation centres, which are, as every police officer knows, the first point of disposal for the amateur's haul of stolen goods. Undercover police posing as staff frequently snap photos of suspects unloading saleable items in the wake of their supposed garage tidy-up or spring clean. Some goods are clear pickings of burglaries; no legitimate owner would try to off-load three DVD players and two iPods for the price of a McDonald's meal for two. If thieves thought logically, they would realise they'd be better off selling their loot at a car boot sale where the margin of return far outweighs the element of risk.

Honest traders rely on a meagre profit margin to reward them for hours of sitting behind fold-up card tables, often in minus-zero temperatures. They might have sourced product through eBay or garage sales before adding a token margin, or they might have spent countless hours handcrafting timber models, woollen garments or gemstone pendants. On market morning, they rise as early as 4.00 a.m., load their car or van, and then drive up to fifty miles to the market location. The regulars score an asphalt apron upon which to set their stall while the newbies prepare ten square metres of sodden green pasture through which they, and the throng of bargain hunters, compress into a squelchy quagmire.

Thieves though, do not endure the practical and inconvenient methods of the honest. They have no expenses, other than fuel and tools of trade: gloves, balaclava, jemmy and screwdriver. They receive a one hundred percent return on their haul and accordingly are not interested in attending fairs, markets and car boot sales, preferring instead to dedicate their Saturday and Sunday mornings to burgling homes of the very people who do attend car boot sales and religious services.

Sitting on a low-level, burgundy velvet-covered shelf – the obligatory display material guaranteed to inflate prices by at least ten percent – shine ladies' and men's watches of every description, from the budget Argos chronograph to a questionably authentic gold Rolex.

The adjacent window displays a range of CDs and handbags, strangely complemented by a selection of power tools presumably stolen from an unsuspecting tradesman's van. The focal point of the window is a Chinese Dragon kite; its wings spread wide, iridescent colours of the rainbow chasing across its breadth and a tail of golden interlinked nuggets wagging a sign: *Ideal for celebrating Chinese New Year.*

The Chinese New Year is six months hence.

Olivia enters, examines an assortment of phones standing on a glass shelf, and selects a silver Nokia. A 'New Stock' price tag dangles from the screen. She discretely slides the back off the phone. No SIM card.

'We retrieve SIMs for privacy reasons,' calls out the observant manager. 'In most cases the seller transfers it to their new phone.'

Not so discrete after all. 'Or they trash it so you don't know it's stolen,' Olivia quips.

'Not us. We make sure that everything's legit' and has paperwork.'

Of course you do. 'What about this one?' she smiles, hoisting the reassembled phone into the air.

'Let's see. Mmm. Not here at the moment. Said he'd drop it in. A local guy.'

The battery is flat. Olivia plugs it into a power source above a nearby shelf, energising the phone with Nokia's signature tune. She flicks through the menus to 'phone memory'. Four numbers illuminate the screen: 'Babes' and 'JTT' which she recognises as UK numbers and two others: 'Mama' and 'Lola' with a '63' prefix which she assumes to be international. *This is the one.*

'You got a charger for this?'

The manager disguises a smile and ruffles under the counter. From a plastic tub he produces a small black Nokia charger complete with a car cigarette-lighter plug: 'Just happen to have one left.'

Yeah sure. What a coincidence.

Olivia makes the purchase, withholding her true identity should Simmons be informed, upon returning to the store, that police have possession of the phone. She hands over £35.50 for the phone and charger and heads back to Worcester while the store manager gloats over the deal's £23.00 profit.

Prior to logging the item in the Property Register, Olivia

copies the phone's stored files to her notebook computer. She follows with an online check of international prefixes and finds that '63' dials into the Philippines. Olivia has little geographic knowledge, as demonstrated by her reliance on a GPS to navigate her way around England, but she does recall from school geography that the Philippines is a close-knit group of 7,107 islands nestled in the South China Sea.

She plugs her new acquisition into the charger and presses 'mama'. Heeds a flurry of clicks and screeches. And then a ringing phone. *Good start.*

At 3.17 a.m., a mobile phone shrills in Edwina Morales' tiny home in the Philippine city of Cebu. With the slur of interrupted sleep, she mumbles: 'Hello.'

'Hello. Sorry to disturb you. Who's this?'

'Huh.'

'I'm a police officer in England. Whose phone is this?'

'*Unsa?* No English.'

A background shout, a rooster's crow that sounds as if it comes from *inside* the house, and muffled, indecipherable babble fill the phone before a clearly audible voice takes over: 'Hello?'

Thank goodness. 'Hello. My name's Olivia, a police officer in England. I need to identify the owner of this phone. Who am I speaking to? Do you recognise the number I'm calling from?'

'Is my sister's. Where is she? She's not call for one week already.'

Shit, Olivia murmurs under her breath. *How am I going to handle this?* 'All right. I have her phone. Your sister has been reported missing. We're trying to find her. I don't want to alarm you, but we need your help. What is your sister's name?'

'Juanita. Juanita Morales.'

'Where does she live?'

'In England. Near a beach. I don't have address. We only text, but I know it's called "bourne" something.

'Selbourne, Westbourne, Honeybourne?'

'No. Not like that, other way.'

'Other direction?'

'No. Something after "bourne".'

Olivia suppresses a joke about 'born again' Christians. The conversation is heading dangerously toward the conclusion she most fears. She timidly squeaks out the words: 'Bourneville, Bournemouth?'

'Yes, Bournemouth. Near the beach. With fiancé.'

Olivia falters. Takes a deep breath. Tries to not project her dismay through the phone. 'Do you know his name?'

'He is Trevor. I don't know family name. Where is my sister? Why have questions if you have her phone?'

'I'm sorry. Her phone was found on a boat and handed to the police. We're trying to establish if your sister was also on the boat. Can you send a photo of Juanita?'

'I send picture now.'

Olivia's phone bursts into The Police's 1979 hit, 'Message in a Bottle', signifying an incoming message. The picture clearly identifies Juanita Morales as the body retrieved from the River Avon. Olivia returns a 'thank you' text with office and personal contact numbers. She has little doubt that very soon she'll be assigned the task of conveying a death message to Juanita's parents. It is the one facet of policing that Marchant *always* delegates to female staff. 'It's the maternal, compassionate way you women handle such occasions,' Marchant disguises within the patronising instruction to junior officers.

Olivia takes a moment to evaluate the growing fragments of evidence:

The purse had been found in the vicinity of Juanita's body.
There were two tickets in the purse.
Morales must *have been on the craft.*

Trevor John Taylor is closely associated with Juanita.
He had reported her missing.
He had lied about his whereabouts on the night of the fourteenth.
He must *be considered a suspect.*

Simmons was evasive to Marchant's questions.
He was on the craft.
He denied knowledge of the mobile phone.
He discarded the SIM card, thereby adding to his complicity.
He must *be considered a suspect.*

9

TREVOR TAYLOR HAS difficulty applying himself to work. He rushes to complete his present job before lunch, at which time he will abandon the day's work and return home. His mind is an aerial photo of fertile farmlands – a patchwork of thoughts – germinating self-preservation. In one field, Marchant tends husks of information yet to unfurl. In another, the burden of guilt matures, wavering like ripened wheat in a stiff breeze. Taylor wanders into that field, seeking forgiveness. He prays – although there is not one religious grain in his body – to resume life as it was before he'd committed the unconscionable act. He drops into an earthy furrow and stares at the sky. An odd-shaped cloud appears. Nearly square. Vivid white. *God's message?* Trevor studies the cloud like a child viewing a pantomime from the front row. The opening scene shatters into a palette of greys before puffs of geometric black clouds announce the title: *Guilty*.

On arriving home, he ejects the sub-conscious, opens his diary, and pushes all work commitments into the following week. With a bundle of clothes jammed under his arm, he rushes out to his runabout car – an old Ford Orion – and commences the long journey back to Evesham. Drawn by curiosity and the need for information, he recalls a junior football coach's prized motivator: *Defence is the best form of attack*. He modifies the clause to suit his own agenda: *To be abreast of the news is the best defence.* The axiom accords with his late father's prophesy: "Forearmed is forewarned".

Taylor's defence will see him scavenge Evesham gossip for the status of the police investigation and use it to leap ahead of any future inquisition. And he has no doubt there will be one. Marchant's "We'll be in touch," vividly stamped that intent.

In the early evening, he ambles in to Evesham's One Stop convenience store, checks the array of newspapers and magazines featuring more flesh than the refrigerated window of the nearby butcher's and selects one of the local newspapers. He anticipates a substantial spread about Juanita, but finds nothing, not even a snippet in the Police Rounds column. The masthead tells why: he'd grabbed the previous week's copy. He buys it and discovers that the next edition will be available tomorrow.

The High Street hosts a selection of cafés and pubs. A 'specials' chalkboard on the footpath entices Taylor into the Rose and Thorn. He flicks his eyes left and right before sliding into a bench seat beside a tinted window. He studies the menu and the bustling High Street.

Pub banter clashes with a blaring television replay of Chelsea versus Liverpool. Shouts of 'ya too old' and 'kick the fucker' drown conversation attempted by the more sedate guests. Taylor zeroes in on the rowdy bunch's antics. They've already sussed him as an out-of-towner, just as he would pick the non-regulars in Bournemouth. He recognises the sideways glances, the inquisitive glares that question: 'What are you doing in our pub', and intimidating stares from the bar queue: '*I'm* a regular – you wait your turn'.

Behind his table, a group of women chat about marriage, husbands, boyfriends, cooking, and the body found in the river. Trevor tunes to the cocktail-fuelled conversation.

'I heard the proprietor of the cruise company has been interviewed.'

'Why? I thought it was an accident.'

'She fell overboard and drowned,' said another.

'If that was the case, someone would have seen it so it wouldn't be suspicious, would it?'

'Good point.'

'Marg, you know about this don't you? Didn't you interview the copper who's investigating?'

Trevor cranes his neck to identify Marg as she responds to the question.

'Yes. But you know I can't talk about any of that. It's highly confidential. There's a ban on releasing material until cleared by police.'

'But you can tell *us*,' one woman encourages.

Taylor clutches every word. *The police must be onto something. Of course they would be – they wouldn't just dismiss a drowning without a full probe into the death.*

He orders a Fisherman's Basket and continues eavesdropping, intent on learning more about Marg. He satisfies his own query after opening the local paper and chancing on a name credited to an unrelated story: reported by Marg Hegarty.

Marg Hegarty typifies the 44-year-old divorcee reconstructing life after the ill-effects of a calamitous marriage. She has re-invented herself with a persona stolen from her mid-20s. The twirled bun atop her crown has given way to a coiffured soft, blonde-tipped cascade that brushes the side of her prominent cheeks. Skin rejuvenation – Marg would never admit to Botox – has smoothed away worry lines of her 19-year marriage, and professionally applied make-up has transformed her features to those of a woman half her age. In short, she is a billboard for the increasingly successful makeover industry. Marg has learnt through experience that overt sexuality reaps rewards when trying to elicit information from unenthusiastic male interviewees. Through her revived youth, she intends to exploit that to her advantage.

Graduating in Journalism and English Literature, she has worked in the industry since her early twenties, preferring local papers to the national dailies. She desperately awaits the break that will see her rise above the specialists of local gossip, romance and sexual health advice and football reports. Her waning career provides little scope for her to realise that ambition. Reports and editorial posts constantly promote the names of today's young graduates, many of whom have already established themselves with prospective employers through work experience and freelance submissions. Marg also faces the disadvantage of gender. She suffers the wrath of political correctness and discrimination, and of companies preferring to employ males over women, and she experiences rejection from unscrupulous employers who continually contrive devious means to circumvent the system.

Marg has devoted five years to the *Evesham Record*, working from early morning until late evening. She is determined to prove her worth to her employer, and to the small local community that she dearly loves.

On the night of August fourteen, whilst enjoying her

customary mind-clearing stroll around a loop of the township, she was attracted to a flurry of flashing blue lights speeding through the Crown Meadow. Marg swung into duty mode and rushed to the local park where she milled with the growing group of similarly interested onlookers. One police officer struggled to contain the buzzing swarm. Another threw a beam of white torchlight onto the riverbank. On seeing a body laid out at the water's edge, Marg edged closer to capture discussions between police and public. She homed in on Marchant, introduced herself, and received the obligatory, 'No comment at this stage.'

Undeterred, she approached DS Watts with whom she'd had previous contact when seeking a contribution for a 'Homesafe' editorial feature. Olivia was more personable than her supervising officer but still checked her response: 'A body has been retrieved but not identified. The deceased is possibly female. I'm sure my DI will make a statement at the appropriate time, after relatives have been notified.'

And that was it. Just as expected. *Something's happened, but we won't tell you what.*

As Taylor studies Hegarty's editorial, a young woman approaches his table.

'Hi. I'm Amy.'

Trevor mutters 'hello' into his paper. No eye contact. No interest.

Amy, perhaps considering Taylor a better prospect than one of the locals, persists with her introduction.

Trevor hesitates. Looks up. Surprised. She is attractive, although overdressed in a Gothic theme. A huge black great coat drops beneath a black hoodie pulled loosely over her head.

Strands of black hair, tipped with purple, hang over his table. Black lipstick accentuates two lip piercings through which silver sleepers shine below a similar ring dangling from her nostrils. Two more and she could pitch herself as a chrome-plated Olympic Logo.

Her forest-green eyes gaze pleadingly into Trevor's.

He ponders. She is obviously available and ticks all the boxes in the male's '*Criteria for an Easy Date*' manual. Easy pickings. But he prioritises his objective over the temptation of a few minutes' fun in the car park or wherever they might shag their hearts out. Tonight, this clone of the Grim Reaper is just another thorn in his side. 'A man can't even enjoy his beer,' he mumbles.

Amy bends down, nose to nose, and shouts: 'Not good enough for you then, am I? Have your beer by yourself, you queer. See what I care.'

Trevor does not cope with rebukes. His inherited – or cultivated – personality disposition pierces his shell of confidence as had his brother done only two days' earlier. As a child, he broke into tantrums when told to tidy his room. Much later, he was extremely fortunate to finish his apprenticeship without reacting to fellow workers' jovial banter and taunts.

Trevor thinks no more of her – until the effect of three pints in quick succession trigger anxiety for vengeance. He downs the remainder of his fourth beer, slides the *Evesham Record* into his rear pocket and leaves the pub. *I'll fix her. I'll teach her for disrupting my evening.*

The more he dwells on her interference, (an interference that would have been welcomed by any other patron) the more he draws upon his euphoric adrenalin rush to exact retribution. And the formula for that retribution is clearly defined. A verbal barrage will be the starting point – words and gestures calculated to inflict emotional pain; an entrée to physical pain; the prologue to the main event.

He visualises the prospect of watching her retreat in fright, screaming, submitting herself, her whole self, as a gesture of apology. Trevor sees her pleading for life, offering anything: money, sex – yeah, probably sex, a girl's best negotiating tool: 'Please. I'll do anything.' He's heard that and seen it all before, but only on television. Taylor's constitution of resilience means that he won't be swayed by pleading or incentive. He'll just take out his knife; one hand gloved in preparedness – he isn't stupid enough to leave DNA or other evidence like finger prints – and he will plunge the knife into her flesh, reaping pleasure from the terror transmitted through her eyes.

It isn't his custom to carry a knife – he just left home with it. Like a scene replicated from an old American Express advertisement, 'Don't leave home without it,' he casually picked up the knife from the table and flung it into his pocket. As a twelve-year-old, he once took a small kitchen knife to school to settle a score. His parents had also witnessed his frequent anger management setbacks, *and* had been victims of them, but they discounted the outbursts with the disclaimer: 'Bloody puberty. He'll grow out of it.'

He hasn't.

The journey home becomes a three-hour DVD of strangulation and blood fused with love and desire. Grotesque images of Juanita and Amy hang like limp dolls from the rear-view mirror. Headlights of oncoming vehicles shimmer like the Avon, sharpening to the gilt edge of the knife that he sunk deep into Amy's back.

Trevor caresses remorse and satisfaction with no comprehension that such conflicting emotions could possibly be felt by a sane person.

On arriving home, he rushes to his computer:

August 16, 2015: Just returned from the Rose and Thorn. I don't know whether I should detail what I did. Maybe it's a bit self-serving; though I don't seek self-gratification. The scene was so gory. I don't know if I should alienate you, my dear companion, from the heart of my story. Certainly, you will judge me for what I did, and as I reveal more, you will pre-judge me for what I may later do because my quest for excitement is far from complete, so I'm reserved about confiding to you my deepest thoughts. I couldn't tell just anyone, that's why I can write what I like here, where no one will ever see, or learn of the motives that control me and the rewards granted me by satisfaction alone.

Wielding a knife carries the same euphoria experienced by one who carries the flag at the opening or closing ceremony of the Commonwealth or Olympic Games. The feeling of the firm grip in my hand is overly sensuous, the fluttering in the breeze replicates the hovering of razor-sharp steel so appeasing to my eye.

I had that feeling tonight when the voices commanded me to strike. I flexed my arm and thrust the knife into her soft flesh, watching it sink like an olive in a Martini. Blood surged in appreciation of its release. The sight aroused me. I wanted to see blood gush like torrents spurting from the oilfields of Iraq.

I watched her face grimace with life's last gasps. What'd she call herself? Emily or Amy? I hadn't been listening. I didn't care. I was too busy.

The experience haunted me as I returned home. Frames of images flashed by like watching an express train's windows race through Reading Station. Maybe I need help to stop the voices. I don't necessarily mind them; they're sometimes kind and encourage me to achieve things I have rarely been able to do in all my 32 years. But for some reason, my psychologist hasn't been successful.

I have complete confidence in the guy; I guess I should have after spending hundreds of hours in his office. I've never participated in the stereotyped lay-down-on-the-Chesterfield-couch type consultation. No. I simply sit at his desk and prat on for hour after hour – bit like I'm doing here, I guess. He's never let on what he thinks of me, even when I blame my conduct on my failed marriages. But he did help me through periodic episodes of despair after I once explained that years of marital bliss had dissolved like a mouthful of fairy floss and synthesised into a mush of masticated pink goo. That's what my marriages were like; they started huge, the two of us like pink fluffy foliage on the tree of life; soft, sweet, desired, and of course, full of sugar. No preservatives. No synthetic additives. Love a la natural. But the use-by date had been pre-stamped in a place unknown. Why? There should never have been one. By then, my delicacy was gone.

That was the turning point, I told the shrink. How could I have respect for women who pledge their love and life only to one day artlessly opt out? Yes, 'opt out'. A simple clause used to decline an extended warranty on a new television: 'I think I'll opt out of that'; or used to refuse all the hidden extras an insurance salesman puts to his client: 'I'll opt out of the nuclear damage insurance, and I'll opt out of the accident policy.' My wives simply opted to opt out of our marriage.

I must admit that I never set out with the objective of killing anyone. I just didn't want to be hurt again. I didn't want to get to the stage of being so strongly glued to romantic cohesion that my senses of compassion would again be destroyed. So I adopted the philosophy as endorsed by any Middle East national defence strategy: Get 'em before they get you.

10

PULLED FROM SLEEP, Olivia answers her phone.

'Where've you been? I've been ringing for hours,' yells Marchant.

'Huh? Sorry. Must have turned my phone down. What's the problem?'

'We got another one. Girl knifed in Evesham. Get here right away will you.'

Thirty minutes later Olivia crashes into Marchant's office where he lounges, feet on desk, sipping coffee. 'Well, well. Nice of you to make an appearance, Watts.'

'I'm sorry. I didn't expect to be called back in.'

Marchant leans over and takes a slurp of Jack Daniel's from a small decanter, which he'd retrieved from his filing cabinet. 'In this job, Watts, always expect the unexpected. And it is unexpected that we've got another body in Evesham. A bloody quiet town where nothing ever happens and now we got two stiffs within a week.'

'Two? So what's the connection?'

'No idea, but we'll find out soon enough. Let's go.'

There is no mistaking the Evesham crime scene, conspicuous by tanked patrons milling about the side of the Rose and Thorn. Police string tape between signposts, parking meters and plastic bollards. Two ambulance officers work frantically on a young woman lying on the pavement. A paramedic unit stops at the adjacent kerbside. Marchant pulls in behind, leaving barely enough room for the ambulance to exit. Watts corrals the curious crowd and calls for witnesses.

Few volunteer information in such circumstances. The community do-gooders shy away from dramatic situations, especially after dark. Well-to-do, responsible citizens become hesitant, reluctant even, to offer assistance. They fear reprisals from criminal connections monitoring proceedings from within the crowd, and they fear being identified as a worthy, community-minded citizen. Most of all, they fear paybacks: 'I don't want to get involved'.

Marchant examines the bloodstained body.

There is nothing rewarding about policing when tasked to the scene of a violent attack, especially in gruesome circumstances of blood-saturated clothing and blood-spattered walls and footpaths where crowds gather like vultures eager to ingest every last gasp of breath, every last shudder, all the time awaiting the final moment when the subject's head lulls to the side or the body suffers final involuntary spasms en-route to the cessation of life.

The girl is well – albeit radically – dressed and groomed; typical of a young woman out to enjoy a carefree evening. Her blood stains the footpath beside a disused doorway of the Rose and Thorn in Swan Lane, a tiny thoroughfare that stretches alongside the popular discount pub.

Marchant observes five cuts in the back and shoulder of her coat; two superficial and three that appear to have been inflicted by a blade of substantial size. A black bag lies nearby, its contents spilled along the footpath like overflowed winnings from a poker machine. Marchant rips his phone from his pocket, flicks on the camera, and photographs the deceased and immediate surrounds. To onlookers, the act might appear ghoulish, but even though Marchant knows that Scene of Crime Officers will shortly arrive, he is particularly interested in preserving time-stamped evidence of the bag and its strewn contents: coins, an expired rail ticket, Tesco dockets and a familiar looking business card: *Simmons' Scenic Cruises. Crown Meadow, Evesham.*

An ambulance officer steps aside and lowers his head. Erects a makeshift screen around the body. The young woman who enjoyed only 20 short years of life is shielded from the indignity of parading herself on the public thoroughfare, absorbing drunks' spittle and stale urine into her porcelain skin. Behind a window, patrons continue to revel: boozing, laughing and cheering; no one shedding a tear for this girl whose extroverted search for friendship resulted not in a happy union, but in pain and terror where her final struggle for survival constituted a feeble attempt at clutching soiled cobblestones as she tried to eke out a guttural plea for help. A life now extinguished, identified only by a gleaming gold necklace from which dangle three letters: *Amy*.

Despite police presence, or *because* of it, the group of bystanders swells, gawking for the self-gratification of witnessing the aftermath of one of the most heinous crimes of humanity. A second police car arrives. Its occupants disperse the clusters who finally accept that there is nothing left to sustain their interest.

Olivia, now thrust headfirst into investigating another murder, searches for a weapon. She stops at an industrial skip servicing a supermarket adjacent to the Rose and Thorn. Calling on her tomboy past, she clambers up its side, holding her breath to the fetid aroma of rotting and fermenting fruit. The torch's beam falls upon the prize — an eight-inch retractable pocket knife – cheap steel, plastic handle – of the type commonly seized from youths who claim they need protection, but protection from who or what, they never divulge. Such knives are readily available from craft and fishing stores and on the internet where free delivery encourages underage and unlawful purchases. Despite various weapon amnesties, the availability of knives and other offensive weapons is limitless.

She pulls on a latex glove, ungracefully balances on the edge of the huge bin, and like the beam of a see-saw, descends into the skip and picks up the weapon. A quick visual reveals blood smears sufficient to prove, or disprove, that she's located the murder weapon. As expected, the weapon bears no personal engravings or apparent identifying marks. She places it in an evidence bag and stands it beside the skip before resuming the search.

Inside the pub, Marchant furthers enquiries. A barman recounts a brief altercation with a non-local and a young woman. Because his attention was focused directly on that particular woman, he is unable to describe the male, other than his having dark hair, which 'fell below a cap'. He continues: 'It was no big deal, I thought. Just a lover's spat. Happens all the time.'

'But they don't all end up getting knifed in the back,' Marchant snaps. He ascertains that the deceased *is* the woman to whom the barman refers. She is known only as 'Amy', and is a regular patron.

Olivia scouts through a car park where she glimpses a couple cuddling in the rear seat of a small car. Not wishing to alarm the cavorting occupants, she approaches with louder than usual footsteps, taps on the window, and enquires about persons running through the car park in the previous ten to fifteen minutes.

'I was busy with my girlfriend, if you know what I mean. There was some sort of vehicle drove past. Might have been a Mondeo or similar. Right squealed out of here.'

Olivia continues surveying the car park and notices a CCTV camera, which she hopes has captured the departing vehicle. Deducing the pub, rather than council, would monitor the cameras, she returns to the pub and requests the manager run the camera's previous 30 minutes.

She begins to wonder if her witness *had* actually seen anything, because there is no footage of a Mondeo entering or exiting the car park. In the preceding 34 minutes only one vehicle, a blue BMW, had departed. At 10.33 p.m., Olivia phones control to obtain registered keeper details of index number P323 BAS. She scrawls the reply into her notebook: *Barry Simmons, 27 St. Peter's Road, Evesham.*

'Shit. Michael, look at this!' Olivia's excitement overrules her usual adherence to protocol.

'What you got?'

'Bloody Simmons raced out of the car park in a blue bee em.'

'Told you there was something about that guy. Just stick with me and you'll do all right. Find anything outside?'

'Oh shit!' Olivia drops her notebook and races outside, brushing past a local officer minding the door. Approaching the skip, she exhales relief on seeing the bag standing exactly where she had left it. She snatches it with a swift arm, hugs it to her chest like a long-lost favourite doll, and slinks back into the pub.

Marchant shoots her an inquisitive look. 'What was that? Emergency toilet break?'

'I left the bloody knife outside after I got side-tracked with the vehicle info.'

'You'll give me heart failure, Watts. You realise we've lost continuity of evidence now?'

'Of course we haven't. It was in a controlled environment. The locals were supervising.'

'Try explaining that under cross-examination, Watts, when you're asked if you preserved the exhibit's security from crime scene to lab. You bagged it, then secured it in the car safe. Okay?'

Olivia recognises the hidden message. She is not in favour of the frequently employed covering tactics, although when under a supervising officer's nose she knows it is better to toe the line than to uphold her strict moral code.

'Guv, we got a weapon and we got a lead.'

'No!' gruffs Marchant. 'You've got a weapon and *I've* got a lead. Simmons is mine.'

On the return trip to Worcester, Olivia again breaks the silence. 'Find out anything in the pub?'

'Not really. The girl's a regular. Seems she was making small talk around a few tables. Not a known troublemaker. Some suggestion she was trying to make it with a guy; no one recognised him as a regular. No substance in it far as I'm concerned. Just a few piss-heads who enjoy upping their social standing by giving coppers false leads.

'I'll tell you what we have got. We got Simmons at the river where that girl drowned, and now we got him right here implicating himself in this girl's death.' Marchant's head swells bigger than usual. He adds: 'By the way, you got the goods on that phone yet?'

'Working on it guv.' In police parlance that means Olivia has been too flat out to do anything. It also covers everything from checking a name in a phone book to a full-scale investigation.

Marchant continues: 'Very funny. We got no reason to question the statement taken by Bailey, so straight away we know that Simmons is pulling a shifty, because he lied about the phone until confronted with Bailey's statement. His whole credibility is shot.'

'So, do we have a link to Amy?'

'Of course we do. He just high-tailed it out of the bloody car park, didn't he. I've checked his background – no priors – this could be an instance of one of those mid-life brain-snaps. But the coup-de-grace is this – and not a word to anyone – there was a Simmons' Scenic Cruises business card on the ground, right next to the girl's handbag.'

'Fair scenario, guv, but what about this? Think about Taylor for a moment. He wants rid of his fiancée for a reason we are yet to uncover, and dumps her overboard. He phones his local and reports her missing, thinking that his concern will remove any possibility of his being considered a suspect. Don't forget the number one rule of domestic solution: the spouse in the house is invariably the louse. Sort of a true-crime version of Dr Seuss's *Cat in the Hat*.'

'Very true Watts. Still doing your homework? What you haven't considered is that on the streets things are different. Your house is small and there's nothing in it. You honestly think a guy wants rid of his wife or fiancée or whatever she bloody was, and he goes, "I think I'll drive her 100 miles away to a quaint little river and give her the permanent dunking treatment just like dropping a biscuit into a cup of tea." Then he drives all the way home, comes to his senses and rings his local coppers and sobs to them, "My fiancée's gone missing. I don't know where she is. Please help me; I love her so much."

'You're crazy, Olivia. Let's continue your little charade. Out of the blue he says, "That was fun. I think I'll go back to Evesham and find someone else to waste. I'm done with drowning, how about a nice stabbing." So he hops in his car, Olivia, drives all the way back to Evesham, stabs that girl Christ knows how many times – didn't even get a bit of action for his troubles – then drives back home and has another cup of tea – this time without the biscuit.'

'You're crass, inspector. You know that? At least we've sorted that out. I still say we have two suspects and that leaves us with a heap of work to do.'

'Maybe for you,' Liv. But I told you, I got Simmons and I'll have him on a plate before you even get a proper lead on your Taylor guy.'

'All right. How would you explain Taylor's evasiveness by trying to set up an alibi using his brother? That was definitely designed to remove him from the Sunday time-frame.'

'Olivia. How many partners have you spoken to who have been distraught over missing or losing someone? The guy was clearly out of it; probably hadn't slept all night, and then when push came to shove, he couldn't even put two and two together. No, Liv, that was what they call a crime of opportunity. Simmons clearly saw an opportunity to waste this woman – for what reason we don't know yet – and then, for some other reason we don't know, he does the Amy girl. Maybe he's one of those psychos set off by being served flat beer or given incorrect change. As I said, I'll have him on a plate as soon as I've established those unknown reasons.'

Olivia's forensic studies declare many serial murderers to be habitually driven by one common denominator: an incident or disturbance that caused affront during their childhood. Serial killers might target prostitutes, gays or religious fanatics as well as older women whose distorted image represents an authority figure or emotional loss of years past. Seeing that image superimposed upon an innocent person triggers within the perpetrator a need to exact vengeance and retribution, with the unfortunate consequence that the unknowing image-bearing woman becomes a victim, or, another victim.

Such killers employ various means to commit their crimes: poisons, guns, knives, arrows, spear guns, drownings, ropes, fire, explosives, drums of acid and bare hands. But victims of these acts are not ordinarily found in Evesham's unsullied rural hamlet.

Olivia considers her role in the investigation and ponders: Is there a connection between the two murders? Is it possible that Juanita and Amy knew each other?

Perhaps Juanita *had* fallen overboard. That isn't murder.

Perhaps Amy had argued with her boyfriend or a drunken crackpot who then stabbed her in self-defence. Huge call, so, okay, let's find the crackpot.

Life is full of crackpots; every village, town and county has one. Or many. Some undeservedly inherit the derogatory tag because during the journey along Conception Highway they fail to grab a chunk of specific genetic code. They alight at their destination with any one of hundreds of psychological or physical disorders.

Others though, earn the label because their bizarre beliefs or behaviour precipitates unconscionable conduct.

It is one of the latter who Olivia deems responsible for the Evesham murders.

By the end of her shift, Olivia has reached breaking point with Marchant. She's endured more than enough of his big-headed gloating of how he is on the verge of solving a double murder, at the same time ridiculing Olivia for her 'away with the fairies' theory about Taylor. She respectfully tolerates his sarcastic remarks. They cut deep, but determination to prove her theory overcomes everything that Marchant dishes out. Only after further ridicule during a meeting of task force detectives does she decide to ease the tension by constructing distance between them – both geographically and professionally.

On completion of her shift, she rushes home, showers, dresses in her 'special' lingerie, drops a few clothes in a shopping bag and heads for London. Tonight she will perform the lead role in her recurring dream of a secret rendezvous with Dave Stafford.

As late night traffic buzzes along the M42, Rihanna's 'Anti' CD blares from the rear shelf speakers of her outdated car. Articulated vehicles pull along plumes of muddy beads, smearing windscreens of following vehicles. Olivia dreads the conditions and twice considers turning back before accepting that Dave's open arms will offer far more pleasure than her apartment's solitude.

Dave's home address is officially designated as London, but physically sits beside busy Baker Street in Paddington – three miles from the city's heart. Olivia squeezes her car into a nearby street and walks to her beau's front door. Trepidation races through her mind: *Shall I do this? I feel so desperate.* Office whispers return: *She's easy. Screws her way to the top. Fun for the boys.* She throws the thoughts aside and knocks.

The door creaks open, Stafford wiping sleep from his eyes.

Olivia blurts, 'Hi Dave. I had to see you.'

'At two o'clock in the morning?'

'It's been ages. I need someone sensible to talk to.'

'So you've driven all the way down here? You couldn't speak to Marchant?'

'It's gone too far. I can't stand the guy. I'm thinking of transferring or leaving the force and that's why I want to speak to you. Now. I know I can do that confidentially. There's too many shortcuts; he's chauvinistic, abrupt, rude, it's… you know, some things just irk you and they're too hard to explain –'

'I don't confine conversations to doorsteps unless I'm entertaining Seventh Day Adventists or Mormons. Come on in. It's great to see you. Why didn't you ring? Oh, sorry, you did. Sit down and have a drink. Have you eaten?'

Olivia digests the multiple questions. 'No. I've had nothing since breakfast. I couldn't even eat in the office.'

'All right. I'll order in. Kebabs? There's an all-nighter down the road.'

'Yes. That'll be great. You know, my father, well actually my stepfather, once told me he lived in hope of me following his example. He would tease me with his favourite saying: "What's the best future for Watts? The police." That was ingrained in me from an early age. I felt pressured to join the force, but that's how we align with our family, isn't it? To do the things they want of us so we can make them happy.

'I sailed through the police college, becoming Dux of the class by a margin of three marks. Of course my parents were proud, especially my father, who later pranced around his office with my graduation photo. You know how I progressed through the various initial postings and served much of my time in uniform investigating petty thefts and minor assaults.

97

My tenacity of probing suspects rewarded me with many convictions, although it was not necessarily the conviction I craved – it was the thrill of the conquest.

'All the while I climbed the career ladder, but without clear direction. I did not want to commit my whole being to the force. I did not want to become – how should I say this? – a 'thin' person, defined only by my occupation. Some would call it 'married to the job'. I wanted, and am now sure *I do want*, to be more rounded, informed, and mindful of world and personal experiences. Not so one-track. Whilst I'm happy to pursue my father's dreams, I also want to pursue my own, and I believe I can do that in similarly related work. Working for myself would be the ultimate reward.

'After serving the CID for three years I experienced one of those moments where one reflects on their life and asks the question: "Where am I going? What am I doing with my life?" At 24 years old, I know I've got a lot to learn, but I also want to learn it for myself, not for someone else. I know of support staff who work as private investigators, performing mundane tasks of serving summonses and taking statements. Some work as consultants for insurance companies, trying to immunise them from fraudulent practices, while others work in the sleazy area of sleuthing behind the scenes to obtain evidence sufficient to satisfy clients that their beloveds are climbing into beds left, right and centre, behind their partner's backs. All too common now, so why engage an investigator when divorce is so simple? The reason is that many don't want the divorce. It's the old "I'll have my cake and ice it too", or whatever that saying is. There is popular opinion that it is not having the affair that is a problem, it is the humility of it being done to you behind your back and that is why many go to great lengths to obtain irrefutable proof that their spouse or partner is doing the dirty on them.

'I suppose I am not in the ideal position to be expressing that sort of opinion, but if I was at work and my husband was entertaining some young floozy in a hotel without my knowledge, I would be incensed. If it *was* with my knowledge, I would be equally incensed.

'Anyway, I've had the electric light bulb moment. I know I have to make the move, but I'm wise enough to ensure I cover my bases and plan my future with open eyes. I'm contemplating a month's holiday during which time I'll concentrate on completing a Private Investigator's Course. It shouldn't be lengthy or expensive, but it will suffice to equip me with a qualification that will afford me leverage should I wish to enrol in more formal studies as well as secure my application to the Association of Private Investigators.'

'Bombshell, Olivia. Have you finished? You're one wound up woman.'

'It's that Marchant who winds me up. I'll leave it to you to unwind me.'

'It'll be a pleasure.'

11

MARCHANT EXTRICATES HIMSELF from the grip of four hours' sleep. Pulls the phone to his ear: 'Marchant.'

'He's back.'

'Be right there.'

From a pyramid of soiled washing piled beside the bed, he snatches yesterday's clothes and fights darkness as he treads into trouser legs and claws into shirtsleeves. He drops a kiss on Geraldine's forehead before tiptoeing down the stairway and into the fresh morning where a giant sun struggles to end the night.

Marchant buckles into the Vauxhall's sunken seat and rolls out of the driveway.

The clear road – save for the few early morning delivery drivers and factory shift workers – allows him to tune to his dilemma. He won't budge from his position that both murders were committed by the same person, and, the likely prospect of the perpetrator committing further atrocities. The disturbing question is *when* the next victim will fall.

He detours through the local McDonald's where glossy, appetising facsimiles of fast food cram the acrylic signbox: large fries, Filet-O-Fish, the world famous Big Mac with its trademarked tongue-twister of two-all-beef-patties-special-sauce-lettuce-cheese-pickled-onions-on-a-sesame-seed-bun; the Quarter Pounder which should, given Britain's conversion to the metric system, be rebranded the One Hundred and Thirteen Grammer, and the heavenly caramel sundae, made all the more tempting with double syrup.

'Welcome to McDonald's. May I take your order please?'

Marchant, glued to the menu, struggles to muster willpower enough to maintain his cholesterol reducing, low fat diet. The challenge lost, he purchases three Bacon and Egg McMuffin meals with coffee and demolishes two burgers and two hash browns before completing the next mile. Too late, he finds no serviettes in the bag. *Fuck! Why me? I get eight of the damn things, or none.*

Four and a half hours' earlier, Marchant had dropped Olivia at the office before continuing to Simmons' home, where he arrived within an hour of Simmons' car leaving the Rose and Thorn. Neither Simmons nor his vehicle had returned by 2.00 a.m., at which time Marchant arranged for a night shift CID member to continue surveillance of the property.

DS Stanton drew the short straw.

Marchant pays no heed to the protocol of conducting interviews during reasonable hours. The ancient rule that stands for fairness is followed by few, least of all Marchant who is renowned for abiding by nothing at all. If challenged, he defends his right to the hilt; the right to protect the community and the right to provide the victims' family every possible resource to apprehend those responsible for horrifying crimes.

Three raps on the front window rouse the resident.

Simmons appears. From his bare, salt-ravaged upper torso hang two arms tattooed with distinctive seaman's insignia: anchors, snakes and hearts. On his left bicep, a garland of roses caresses the name 'Felicity'.

'Morning, Mr Simmons. Sorry about the early hour. I'm sure you remember me?'

'Of course I do. It's bloody 6.30. What now?'

'Just a couple of questions. Were you at the Rose and Thorn in Evesham last night?'

'I may have been. I get around. What if I was?'

Hampered by sleep deprivation, Marchant is not prepared to tolerate another session of ifs and maybes. He impulsively short-circuits the information gathering process and glares at Simmons: 'I'm arresting you on suspicion of murder.' Turning to his colleague in the time-honoured fashion of Hawaii Five-O's Steve McGarret, he grins: 'Read him his rights, Stanton.'

Stanton frowns surprise and embarrassment. He desperately wants to warn his supervisor about arresting Simmons solely on an admission of *possibly* attending a pub the previous evening. On that subject he remains mute, before parroting the legal caution with the sting: 'You're going to accompany us to Worcester where we'll conduct further enquiries. Anyone you want to notify?'

'Yeah, my lawyer. You guys don't know who you're messing with.'

Stanton whispers to Marchant: 'Guv, aren't we going to search the place? I thought that's what we came for?'

'Later. This guy gives me the willies with his maybes and what ifs. Just get him in the car and down to the station where I can work a bit of magic on him.'

Stanton leads Simmons upstairs and watches his charge pull on a black suit, striped tie and a white shirt whose emerald cufflinks wink beyond the jacket's sleeves. As a finishing touch, he applies a generous spray of sickly cologne. The bottle is clearly more expensive than its contents.

Simmons nods. 'Ready'.

Stanton clutches the suspect's trouser belt, steers him out to Marchant's vehicle and eases him in to the rear seat.

Marchant flounces into the front. The car groans. Stanton smirks.

'I bought you coffee,' grins Marchant. He hands Stanton and Simmons the lukewarm coffees – part of the two meals he'd already scoffed. He wolfs down the third before driving off. 'Sorry guys. Early breakfast.' Marchant continues: 'So, Barry, how's the cruise business?'

Refusing to be drawn into small talk, Simmons murmurs, 'Okay,' before resting his head against the door pillar and closing his eyes.

Marchant settles into his established interview routine pirated from the quiz show: *Who wants to be a Millionaire?* – ask a few easy questions to comfort the contestant, and then, when they're oozing confidence, as is Simmons, bang in the loaded challenge.

Simmons had decided against calling his lawyer, for two reasons. One: it is not a situation of such importance to warrant disturbing a professional at seven o'clock in the morning; and two: he questions the necessity for a lawyer when he's done nothing wrong. *What have I got to hide? If worst comes to worst, I've knocked off a phone – big deal; far cry from murder.*

Marchant is bewildered by Simmons' confidence. He had hoped the interview room's caustic setting would intimidate his suspect. However, the cheap faux-teak panelled walls, the plain table that cost double its worth because it had been sourced through the government's tender process, the tube-steel chairs securely fixed to the table's legs, and the imposing digital clock glowing above a two-way mirrored window, do not raise one eyebrow or bead of perspiration on Simmons' brow.

The austere room had not always been so drab. Marchant is one of few in Worcester who know the room's secrets. Beyond the teak panelling, deep cracks and gouges shriek the pain of suspects' heads, arms and shoulders bouncing from the walls. Three coats of gloss magnolia mask floor to ceiling blood-spatters resultant from detectives 'encouraging' offenders to cooperate. Smoke stains leech through successive years of fresh paint and cling to the ceiling – evidence of past offenders being primed with cigarettes to encourage quick confessions. Believers see in the ceiling a huge water stained apparition of St Jude, protecting and guiding the innocent as they fight to defend allegations.

Adopting an implausible character reversal, Marchant adopts the 'good cop' role, a technique he uses only on rare occasions where his grinning facade disarms suspects who know nothing about formal interviews and nothing about his ruthless, abrupt and abusive nature. With Stanton lolling in an adjacent chair, Marchant starts on Simmons: 'During the evening of August sixteen, your car was seen leaving the Rose and Thorn car park in Evesham. What do you say to that?'

'Well, if it was seen, it was seen. What do you expect me to say?'

'I put it to you that you were driving a blue BMW registered number P323 BAS.'

Simmons leans back and laces his fingers behind his head. 'Sounds like my car but I don't recall driving it.'

'Can you nominate a person who may have been driving it?'

'Not that I can think of at the moment.'

'Do you deny that you were driving a blue BMW last night?'

Simmons jolts forward, drops his elbows to the table and glares at Marchant. 'No, I don't deny it. You just roused me out of bed at bloody six-thirty. I can't instantly recover time-frames of where I might or might not have been at a particular time.'

Marchant flips a page of his notebook and continues: 'Tell me about the Rose and Thorn. Do you drink there often?'

Simmons eases back into the chair. 'I do, but I also drink at a few pubs around town, so let's dispense with the "often".'

'And who do you drink with?'

'What is this? I don't go through a roll call of drinkers hanging around the bar. I don't necessarily drink with anyone. I don't need to, because there's always someone wanting to spill their guts about something.'

'So did you talk to anyone last night?'

'Yep. Had a couple of short conversations.'

Marchant pulls from his folder a photo of Amy. 'Do you recognise this woman as one to whom you spoke last night?'

'Yep.'

Marchant stalls with surprise. 'So you don't deny seeing her at the Rose and Thorn last night?'

'Nup. Why would I? I just said I spoke to her, therefore I don't deny it at all.'

Marchant's heartbeat pounds to the impending triumph. He is breaking through the ice, or so he thinks, faster than an Arctic icebreaker. Experience has rewarded him with the ability to penetrate suspects' deceitful veneers. He understands the mannerisms liars embrace: how they search for words with sufficient weight to gloss over the truth, and how they paint pictures of integrity and honesty resembling a still life bowl of fruit. Marchant, however, will always pick out the rotten apple. He recognises the shifting and slumping in the seat after a particularly barbed question attacks the nervous system, and he sees the resulting muscle spasms protest against the stressful interrogation as the suspect tries to conceal his tension by giving nothing away. All the while, the suspect struggles to gather his ailing composure. He stammers an answer, deliberately stalling long enough to fabricate a plausible reply, but all he really does is inter himself deeper into the grave of criminal charges.

Marchant boasts that he can spot a guilty person a mile off. In truth, he spruiks the clichéd throwaway devoid of scientific data capable of reinforcing his assertion. Paradoxically, his conviction ratio does not support his claim. He demonstrates an uncanniness many investigators crave. His unorthodox interviewing techniques however, are spurned by most.

He proposes to gain confessions within the hour for both the Morales and Amy Doe murders. (As Amy awaits formal identification, she maintains the euphemism of the anonymous).

He continues: 'So what time did you leave the Rose and Thorn last night?'

'I don't know. What the fuck? I had a few beers, spoke to a few people and left alone. I had no need to monitor what time I ate, drank, pissed or left the pub. I left sometime before eleven so I could catch the weather forecast to be prepared for work today which is where I should be now, so if there's nothing else I think I'll leave.'

Marchant scratches his head as he tries to untangle the incomprehensible sentence. His brow furrows into a sheet of corrugated iron; his complexion flushes from pasty anaemic pink to deep crimson. He is not one to be dictated to by suspects or colleagues. Marchant rules his territory and no one leaves an interview until *he* decides when to dismiss them.

It had not always been like that. At school he'd been dubbed 'March Mallow' because of his softness. The taunts still echo from the assembly quadrangle: 'You're a girl, March Mallow'. He was an early victim of the teasing and bullying epidemic. It started with juvenile threats: 'Give us your lunch March Mallow,' and progressed to an occasion of his one day having to hand over his new bicycle to a fifteen-year-old fat kid two grades his senior. Michael had arrived home minus his bike and received a dressing down from his father. The castigation was not so much for having relinquished the bike; it was for having not stood up to the bullies. 'Listen son, what are you? Some sort of pansy or something? When I was a lad we'd not let anyone nick something of ours. We'd knock 'em out even if it meant getting into trouble from the headmaster – but we earned the respect of the spivs who tried to make our life hell. That's what ya gotta do son. Give 'em a hiding. A black eye or a blood nose is a good tutor. They'll never worry you again. Tomorrow morning we'll go get that bike of yours.'

The following morning a timid Michael accompanied his father to school. Marchant senior waited in his car while young Michael yelled out to Reginald Hoffman. 'Hey Reggie. Come here.'

'Come here yourself, March Mallow.'

Michael nervously complied. To divert Hoffman's attention, he scratched his head as he approached, then quickly launched his right elbow into the side of Hoffman's cheek.

Hoffman crumpled to the footpath, releasing the bike as he instinctively tried to brace his fall. Michael picked up his bike, glared at the stunned Hoffman, and said: 'There's more of that if you want it.' He rode off watching his father's car shrink in the distance, too late to witness the smile stretched across his dad's face. The euphoria of satisfaction inflated his chest. The pride of having stood up for himself overflowed with approval of having taken the first step toward developing the physical and mental toughness that would shape his future.

Marchant relies on it now: 'Well I haven't fuckin' finished and you're going nowhere until I'm ready.'

'I might remind you, inspector, that you have arrested me as a suspect. That does not give you the right to unleash your abrasive tongue after I have afforded you all due respect, despite being dragged here at this ungodly hour. Now, the way I see it, you can either substantiate the charges with evidence and invite me to refute same, or you can release me this very moment, which, by so doing, will obviate the need for my speaking to your governor and my lawyer.'

Whilst Simmons had long departed the Royal Navy, his presence of mind, while sober, remains as sharp as when he commanded 417 crew on HMS *Invincible* during the Falkland Islands tour of duty between April and June 1982.

Marchant has limited knowledge of Simmons' service record. The Ministry of Defence refused to release Simmons' classified information, offering service dates but withholding his majestic naval record. Marchant therefore, does not know that as a former commanding officer, Simmons was well versed in authoritative negotiation and legal protocol. But that is history. Today, he is suspected of two murders.

Marchant continues: 'Very well then. I'm charging you with the murder of Juanita Morales and Amy Doe, yet to be formally identified. You do not have to say anything, but it may harm your defence if you do not mention, when questioned, something you may later rely on in court. Do you wish to say anything in answer to the charges?'

'No comment in answer to the charges. As a separate comment I exercise my right to phone a legal representative.'

'Right? Smart-arse eh? A "legal representative". Right away Lord Simmons.'

Now who's the smart-arse? Simmons utters under his breath.

'Hey Stanton. Slip out and grab a phone for his Lordship, will you?'

Stanton rises from his role as corroborator, the purpose of which is to enable him to swear in court that the conversation between Marchant and Simmons is a true record of events. Stanton however, had dozed like a cat in front of a fireplace, raising an eyelid at the appropriate moment to convince Marchant or any passing officer that he was actually coherent, attentive and alive. Marchant is convinced he fails on all counts and regrets not summoning Watts.

Stanton returns with a cordless phone, plonks it in front of Simmons and fixes him a glaring scowl.

'I'm not using that,' protests Simmons, thumping his fist on the table. 'You probably got it wired to a recorder. I want to make a *private* call.'

'Who do you think we are, the CIA or something? This is as private as it gets. You got five minutes; make the most of it.'

Simmons arranges for his solicitor's urgent attendance.

12

RUPERT LLEWELLYN-JONES heads Worcester's renowned legal practice of Llewellyn-Jones and Jones, housed in a swanky glazed tower that rises like an oversize crystal vase from parkland abutting the River Severn. Its counterpart is immediately recognised as London's 'gherkin'. Solicitors joining the practice are said to be 'keeping up with the Joneses', an informal slur against those who choose to practice with the county's legal leaders.

Rupert had been grafted onto the tree of legal practitioners. His grandfather had started the practice in 1892. In 1924, his father joined as a partner and the legal office was renamed Jones and Jones. Rupert was encouraged to follow tradition and become a lawyer, but his predilection leaned towards the entrepreneurial pursuits of making money from business.

His youthful ignorance insulated him from the fact that law is the biggest moneymaking pursuit of all business ventures. However, with foresight beyond his years, he merged the two into his university curriculum, ultimately graduating from Cambridge with a double degree in law and commerce.

Rupert specialises in Commercial Law. Despite laws and regulations curtailing the manner by which legal practices can promote themselves, he exploits opportunities to elevate law in the same manner as do pro-active businesses, along the way fighting miles of government red tape designed to strangle aggressive marketing.

He seeks also to boast his legal expertise over his father's, as both Joneses compete for clients in a similar manner to Curry's sales staff fighting over prospective purchasers – commission driven rather than demonstrating a conscientious interest in customers' needs. So Rupert, striving for recognition in his own right, and against his father's strongest direction, added 'Llewellyn' to his name by deed poll.

The name was plucked from nowhere. Simply random. Never had Rupert known anyone by the name of Llewellyn. It is a name owned by people who have an affinity for hyphens, for all famous Llewellyns are hyphenated: Llewellyn-Smith, Llewellyn-Worthington and Llewellyn-Turner. One of the more celebrated was Baroness Annie Llewellyn-Davies of Hastoe (1915 – 1997) former British Labour Party Chief Whip in the House of Lords. So Llewellyn-Jones was born, adding a pretentious degree of class and pomposity, commensurate with the name, to the young lawyer.

He attends Worcester Police Station.

'Llewellyn-Jones. You're holding my client. I wish to converse with him please.'

The desk sergeant buzzes Marchant and whispers: 'I have a Mister friggin' hyphen someone or other to see that friggin' Popeye character. Hey, you wanna get a load of this guy. Straight from the manor. Got the Burberry coat happening, the Mr Sheen'd dome, and get this, he's got a friggin' cane topped with a friggin' silver skeleton's skull.'

Standing beside the reception counter, Llewellyn-Jones' acute hearing, perfected over many years catching testimony of timid witnesses, picks up every word.

He greets Marchant and receives his copy of the charges and a summary of events said to have occurred between the night of August fourteen and the present date. Rupert is straight to the point: 'Barry. I'm a commercial lawyer. I am well at ease with your purchase contracts and insurance indemnities, but I would sooner refer you to a colleague of mine. And I have to tell you, Barry, we have a problem with that phone. What happened there? What the hell were you thinking?'

Simmons shrinks. Tainted by naïveté, he'd anticipated Llewellyn-Jones walking into the station, arranging bail and walking out with him some five minutes later. Never had he considered re-acquaintance with his solicitor might be laced with negativity. He protests: 'A lawyer's a lawyer. All you do is represent my position, reword it into judicial jargon, quote a few statutes, cite a few references, and leave it to the judge. I'm totally innocent Rupert. Innocent. As for the phone, a passenger gave it to me when I was mooring. I thought nothing of it because no one had reported one missing. Later in the night I realised it was in my pocket. I know that technically, I should have handed it in to the locals, but I thought I'd just get rid of it, so the next morning I sold it to Cash Liquidators in Evesham. Only got ten quid for the bloody thing.'

'It's clearly incriminating. We'll work our way around it. It's a big stretch from unlawful possession of a phone to murder. Your alibis stack up?'

'Come on Rupe, you know me. I wouldn't even punch anyone, let alone kill them. There's something about this Marchant, I don't know what, but he seems to have a crick in his crawler about me, but I'm at a loss to explain why. He hauled me out of bed at bloody 6.30 this morning and dragged me here to interrogate me about two girls murdered in Evesham. I didn't even know there were two. You've probably heard of the woman found in the river –'

'Why the hell didn't you phone me earlier? This is a serious matter you know.'

'I realise that, but I wasn't going to call you at that time. All I had to do was give them my story. I had nothing to do with it. I thought they were just trying to trace her movements, but then the issue of the phone… well, it just slotted me in the frame.'

'No argument there.'

'Come on Rupert. Do you think a person interviewed for murder would, only hours later, commit the same crime? The scenario's preposterous!'

'Listen Barry. It's not me you have to convince. They have you on your boat when the Morales girl was killed and they have your car coming out of the Rose and Thorn when the other girl was killed. They have reasonable cause to suspect that you were involved. Were you driving your car on the night of August sixteenth?'

'Yeah, of course I was. Doesn't mean I killed anyone though.'

'I'm going to push for bail, but at the moment our chances are slim, unless you have something compelling to support an alibi.'

'Rupert. I don't know what to say. I don't have anything but my honesty.'

'All right. Let's see what we can do about getting you out of here.'

Llewellyn-Jones signals his request to leave the room. He walks briskly to Marchant's office. 'Inspector Marchant. It seems we have an absence of evidence linking my client to any crime. In the matter of Juanita Morales, we are in a position to negate any involvement of my client by virtue of his continued operation of the craft from the control podium, to which my client refers as 'the bridge'. Old habits die hard it seems. You've offered no evidence implicating my client with any contact or conversation with the deceased.

'In the matter of the girl known as Amy, you rely only on the flimsical proposition that my client's car, as one of at least 30, was seen leaving the location. To that, you connect the off-chance of a Simmons' business card found near the deceased's body, which is less than circumstantial if you're unable to prove its origin. It could have blown up from the river for all we know. You've offered no tangible evidence linking my client to that girl's unfortunate death. I'm prepared to put these matters, plus the excellent references my client enjoys, to the court if you insist on opposing bail. My client is no risk, no threat to the community and has strong community ties and support. If you are prepared to release my client, I assure you he will be both contactable and available at your reasonable request.'

Marchant is in a quandary; counter-bluffed. If he proceeds with a formal remand application to the Worcester Magistrates' Court he faces the embarrassing prospect of losing to Llewellyn-Jones, in part because the arrest was made only on suspicion – albeit in accord with the statutory requirement of 'belief on reasonable grounds' – and secondly because of the insufficient – non-existent, he reconsiders – evidential weight. His application based on 'gut feelings' would be promptly dismissed. Marchant buckles.

Throughout his career, Marchant has been pig-headed and pretentious – but always objective. Something encircling the current circumstances has infected his mind-set. He agonises over the brutality of Amy's murder, and the fact that she was taken in her youth. His long service as a detective has immunised him from the trauma of many horrors, but never will he, or any other police officer, accept death as part of the job. Nevertheless, he is compelled to acknowledge it in much the same way a child adapts to the cuts and scrapes of growing up: fall off a bike a few times and by the fifth time you don't cry any more.

Perhaps Marchant has reverted to a childhood trait of blaming the bike and not the rider in much the same way as he confines his enquiry to Simmons instead of looking at the bigger picture. Now, weighing up Llewellyn-Jones's articulate précis of his client's situation, Marchant does look at the big picture, and realises that he must piece together a watertight case bolstered by concrete evidence capable of sustaining the charges.

'Okay, Mr Llewellyn-Jones. I'm fine with that. We'll put it to the custody sergeant, but I warn you, he may not be quite so amenable. Consider my position though. It will take very little to solidify my case against your client, and when I do he will be right back here asking for you.'

'And so shall I be here, inspector. You can be assured of that.'

13

MARCHANT'S OBSESSIVE PURSUIT builds a stack of files from which he collates details of unsolved murders and violent attacks from the previous five years. He finds nothing to link Simmons to the current atrocities. He withholds information from colleagues – a habit that fetters the investigation, but he justifies his action by professing that silence prevents leaks and dissemination of information into the wrong hands.

He pitches Olivia no favours, despite her graciousness of not reporting his appalling behaviour during the *supposed* 'team' introduction at the pub. Whilst he continues to exercise caution over information he does give her, Olivia's mature conduct convinces him that she is the only person in the Worcester nick who will always stand by his decisions.

He should know better. A very thin line divides trust and betrayal.

* * *

DS Watts fights headlong into her own battle. Her conflict is not in Afghanistan or Iran – it is within the ranks, against Inspector Marchant. She abhors his penchant for releasing only snippets of the investigation, and she despises the system that forbids her formalising concerns that the investigation is hampered by Marchant's pig-headedness.

She sets her own agenda, and resolves to counter Marchant by proving that Trevor Taylor *is* responsible for the murders of Juanita and Amy. This, she must perform low-key, or 'under the radar'. She cannot risk the Chief Inspector learning that a member under his command is operating independently. The repercussions would see Watts sanctioned to other duties – 'other' defined as mundane clerical tasks. Whilst a detective's solo effort may not necessarily be counter-productive, the practice has been outlawed because of its propensity to impede progress, jeopardise investigations and put at risk not only the officer concerned, but also others who might be summoned to remedy an ensuing confrontation or similarly dangerous situation.

Olivia rushes to the Rose and Thorn where she harries Bob, an afternoon shift bartender, who promptly attaches a surname to Amy. Amy Anderson, Olivia learns, was a local; a regular attendee at nightspots, and rarely seen without male company. She enjoyed a wide circle of acquaintances, all cultivated by her convivial nature as frequently demonstrated in the Rose and Thorn. This is no revelation. Marchant had discovered as much.

Bob plays CCTV footage covering both inside and outside the premises. The basic system was originally installed to identify perpetrators of burglary and theft rather than to pinpoint minor infractions within the pub's walls. After a spate of drunken disagreements in the car park, the CCTV's capture area was extended to provide security, or perceived security, to patrons returning to their vehicles. The pub's proprietor acknowledges the cameras will not prevent crime – they provide only a placebo effect. It is the cameras' prominence, rather than their functionality, that deters misbehaviour.

One internal camera is not so prominent. Concealed by a small wall sconce, it records a wide-angle view of activities at the bar and cash register. Its practical application is useless, for management rarely check the security monitor wired into the administration office. Its backup DVDs lay beside, a clutter of silver discs.

Olivia asks for Sunday night's recording.

'You won't find anything there,' grunts Bob. 'Just shots of the bar. You'd get more joy concentrating on the outside.'

Eyes glued to the computer monitor, Olivia says nothing. Pans for gold.

A scene from one errant DVD changes the course of the day… slow, stop, rewind. Slow… Freeze. A face shielded by a cap. A distinctive cap. Four frames snap him walking between two cars. The blurred outline fuzzed and grained. A zoom-in refines the image to reveal a cap bearing the letters: TES. Olivia mulls over the letters. An acronym? A TESCO hat with two letters obliterated? Then it strikes her: Taylor's Electrical Services. And beneath the cap? Trevor John Taylor.

Olivia is ecstatic. She beams at Bob and plants a kiss on his cheek. 'Thank you. Thank you. This is amazing. Just what we need.'

Her ego deflates on finding nothing further. Dead end. No image of Taylor getting into a vehicle or leaving the car park. Nor is there an image of him with Amy.

She considers relaying the development to Marchant, but quickly shelves the idea, knowing that his preoccupation with Simmons will earn her another round of abuse. She's already told him, respectfully, that he is barking up the wrong tree, although at that time, she had no other tree to plant in Marchant's field of enquiry. She accepts the risk of contravening departmental standing orders by not reporting the new information to her supervising officer, knowing she would jeopardise, if it could possibly be further jeopardised, the working relationship between herself and Marchant. But only if discovered. She conceives a plan to monitor Trevor's movements, which in so doing would double as a practical insight into her prospective career change to Private Investigator.

Olivia's confidence over-shadows her ability to foresee potential risks, for she fully understands that undercover work without backup is fraught with danger. She pays heed to her reliable intuition, but discards all forms of rationality and adherence to police procedure to pursue her objective of apprehending Trevor Taylor for two murders. The first step is to devise a failsafe means of observing her target.

On shift's completion she races home, and from a drawer of character embellishments – she never calls them 'disguises' – she selects a swathe of long, dark hair extension, pins it in place and instantly assumes the role of seductive vixen.

Two years' earlier, Olivia hatched an alter ego. Applying 'Covert Operations' detective training principles, she sought to expose suspected deceit of her then boyfriend. She had become increasingly concerned and annoyed at the frequency of spurious phone calls: 'Sorry babe, something's come up,' or, 'I've got to work back tonight.' Olivia, immersed in the innocence of her first real relationship was yet to understand that she was another victim of the *I-need-a-quick-alibi-because-I've-got-a-hot-date-tonight* repertoire practised by many philanderers.

Steven was a fellow police officer who'd barely scraped

through the entrance exam. Best described as an example of Trafalgar Square's Nelson's Column – tall and erect with no defining features – Steven had neither the nous to conduct the most basic investigation nor to be cognisant of his girlfriend hatching a ploy to uncover his infidelity. He had not even conceived the excuses proffered to Olivia – he'd plagiarised them from a colleague.

Steven conducted his life as a creature of habit. The first anomaly Olivia faced was his penchant for lining up the different varieties of nuts from bulk packs of mixed nuts. Once laid out on the table, he'd package each type in separate resealable bags, and then consume only one variety at a time. He'd prepare the same breakfast of muesli each morning, save for Saturday, when he negated the benefit of the previous six days by indulging in a huge English Breakfast, doubling up on bacon and black pudding. He sorted his underwear by a ridiculous code: Maroon for Monday, Turquoise for Tuesday, White for Wednesday, and so on. The weekend caused confusion because he was continually frustrated with trying to remember whether Salmon or Sea-blue corresponded to Saturday or Sunday. He finally settled on Salmon for Saturday because both words began with 'sa'. He used two toothbrushes; one for morning, the other for night, reasoning that to be most effective, toothbrushes need a twenty-four hour withholding period to ensure that clinging bacteria will not survive.

By far the strangest trait, and perhaps evidence of a rare compulsive disorder (although tests revealed he was not afflicted with Asperger's Syndrome) was his devotion of exclusivity to an individual product or establishment. He frequented the same supermarket, same petrol station, bought the same shoes (often stockpiling if he found they were to be discontinued) and would attend only the one picture theatre. If a film he wanted to see was being screened at another theatre, he would simply miss the film or wait for the DVD. His predictability had both good and bad points.

Steven had romanced Olivia in the Black Lily seventeen times in three months. On the eighteenth invitation to talk and fondle in the rear booth, Olivia plucked the courage: 'Can't we go somewhere else, Steve?'

'Where would be better than the Black Lily?' he replied.

'We'll never know if we don't try.'

'I'm happy there. I feel it is our place.'

'And it was "our place" to your previous four girlfriends!'

So it was Steven's own undoing that prompted Olivia to head straight to the Black Lily after his call to apologise for yet another night of 'urgent' overtime. She walked demurely into the pub, slithered onto a bar stool and imitating Sharon Stone's renowned scene, seductively crossed her legs before an audience of nearby patrons.

Dark brown tresses fell like twirling treacle beneath her shoulder while a jagged fringe rested above precisely arched eyebrows. A black velvet jacket, adorned with chrome belts and buttons ensured she would attract testosterone-fuelled attention, although Olivia would not accept just anyone's attention – it had to be Steve's.

Her prey sat in the rear booth, drooling over a young rookie officer yet to learn that she would be no more than a conquest to many pseudo admirers. Steven sat mesmerised, mentally unwrapping his unexpected gift. Or maybe he was simply promising her his life as he had to Olivia.

Olivia, unable to discern whether he was in self-preservation or hunting mode, watched his eyes flicker around the room.

Steven looked directly at her. Olivia shifted her legs, diverting his attention from her face to the yoga-like fold of tangled limbs. His eyes dropped at the speed of a medieval guillotine. She turned to the bar and checked Steven's reflection in a smoke-stained mirror. Goose bumps erupted on her arms as he approached.

'Buy you a drink, love?' he whispered.

'Yes. I'll have my usual.'

'And what would that be?'

Olivia turned around, ripped off the hair extensions, and for the benefit of her audience, shouted: 'You know what I have, you cheatin' fuckin' bastard. I don't want your drink and I don't want you. Fuck off back to your urgent overtime.'

14

SHE SETS HER satellite navigation system for Alexander Road, Bournemouth. The rear-view mirror reflects wild hair, vibrant make-up and an artistic application of eyeliner that creates a fusion of eastern European and Asian appearance. Olivia's transformed characteristics echo both Juanita's and Amy's physiognomies.

Although only days since accompanying Marchant to Bournemouth, Olivia recognises little of the previous journey. On the verge of panic and about to launch the GPS through the window, she figures that landscapes viewed by drivers, as opposed to passengers, differ greatly – courtesy of differing focal points. As familiar landmarks spring from the horizon, nervous tension dissolves. She focuses on the motorway's rolling miles, finally appreciating the straight stretch that silences the GPS's robotic directives. The visual aspect of the unit is a boon; the vocal, infuriating: *Merge left; turn right fifty metres; turn around. You are headed in the wrong direction.*

She smiles at an irony only she can appreciate. The GPS unit is actually more valuable than her car, a 1973 Reliant Robin purchased through a local newspaper advertisement. At the time of her joining the police college, financial constraints limited her to dodgy dealers' MOT failures and private sales. The elderly widow who'd advertised the Reliant took a liking to Olivia, believing she would cherish the car like a well-loved pet.

A mechanical once-over, new brake linings and superficial rust removal ensured Olivia's happiness with the old but reliable transport. The three-wheeled aqua-blue bubble continues to turn heads at traffic lights and shopping centre car parks. Since moving to Worcester, she rarely uses the vehicle because of her home's close proximity to the police station. She is now reliant on her Reliant to complete the three-hour trip to Bournemouth.

On parking in Alexander Road, Olivia studies Trevor Taylor's work van which shadows a silver Ford Orion in front of his home. She rummages for a bottle of water from her oversized handbag, pushing aside snacks, camera, notebook and assorted items of make-up – all essentials to aid what she hopes will be a productive night's work. She keenly gambles on Taylor heading out for the traditional mid-week pint – and later into her web.

The down side of the plan is that she is unprepared for success. Her evening might parallel a 'normal' date: tolerate the frivolous small talk, be wary of spiked drinks; extol the ideal of only one goodnight kiss on the first meeting; and spell out ground rules of no one-night-stands or sexual merriment. She will not risk encouraging amorous behaviour for fear of him discovering the pepper spray canister concealed inside her bra. Recipe for a dull date.

She barely retracts her seat when Taylor bounds out of his front door, jumps into the Orion and edges from the drive. Olivia slinks below her window as Taylor innocuously drives past, and then she springs up like a jack-in-the-box barely in time to see him turn left out of the street. She starts her car, lurches to the end of the road and inches slowly around the corner. The silver Orion is 100 metres ahead.

Tailing a car is not the straightforward task as portrayed in movies. Olivia has participated in many undercover operations requiring invisible pursuits. In cities and on motorways the mission is simplified (but sometimes hampered) by the volume of surrounding traffic shielding the pursuer. In Bournemouth, the shield is transparent.

Bournemouth is a compact town split by a trickling stream, the Bourne, that never quite swelled to the status of river. Rising from steep ornamental banks, the town radiates to elevated heights where sweeping panoramas of both the township and the sea dominate the Dorset horizon. Renowned for its huge conference and convention centre, Bournemouth is a favoured destination for both holidaymakers and retirees.

Olivia props at the side of the road as Taylor spears into a car park. Déjà vu washes over her. *Was there a silver Orion in the Rose and Thorn car park? That would certainly confirm Taylor's presence and make it difficult for him to claim the person wearing the TES cap was someone other than himself.* She drives into the park and stops in line-of-sight of the Orion. Minutes later, she hitches up her skirt to an immodest length, and follows Taylor's footsteps through the side entrance of the King's Arms pub and into a small foyer walled with coats and jackets.

The pub has changed little from the era in which the King's Arms had thrived: when travelling kings arrived with their entourage of protectors and soldiers; when craftsmen plied trade from village to village, town to town, in search of employment from which they could hope to earn a few pennies to support their family; and when wayfarers, concealed in the woods beyond, emerged only during opportunistic moments to steal anything of value from vulnerable passers-by.

The lounge area has been fashioned by removing dividing walls between adjacent small rooms, thereby destroying the pub's historic configuration. Hefty oak beams support a daubed plaster ceiling which is stained by centuries of smoke from cigarettes, pipes, and the huge fireplace. The scuffed timber floor hosts threadbare rugs now reduced to a patchwork of hessian.

Covering a jumble of tables constructed from cheap pine and flimsy particleboard, embossed linen tablecloths soak up cheers and tears of beer, cider and the pub's speciality: Ploughman's Pie. A chalkboard menu welcomes all – in the proprietor's trendy words – to *an elite dining experience*.

A woman of fifty-hard-years stands behind the bar pulling a thick, black stout. She is of matronly disposition and one who comforts patrons seeking a shoulder upon which to shed their woes of domestic unhappiness, finance companies' continued demands for money which, if complied with, would reduce available funds for their next beer, or rejecting those who see her as a soft target for an evening dalliance after closing time. She is fine with the tales of woe, but the thought of making it with a drunk, slobbering local is far-fetched, for she has not made it with anyone for seventeen years, after her husband had up and left with a flirty, ten-years-younger, liquor company sales rep.

Under the cavernous bar's canopy, twinkling low-voltage lights illuminate inverted spirit bottles hanging below sparkling glasses. Four shelves of glossy cigarette packs conflict with the historic setting. But not out of place is swearing, dubious tales and exuberant behaviour of those who spend far too many hours, and pounds, in 'The Arms.'

Olivia saunters to the bar and orders orange juice. She adopts a false persona with which she can create tension and desire, while simultaneously conveying that she is not just another freeloader campaigning for a free drink or evening's company. Taylor glances over. Unable to detect whether it is she or a nearby unattached girl who commands his attention, Olivia walks to a small table and notices that Trevor, uncannily employing Steven's prowess of past years, is following.

He approaches from behind: 'May I join you?'

'I'm waiting for a friend. He should be here shortly.'

'That's all right. I'm Trevor. Quick drink before he arrives?'

'No, better not. He's the jealous type and would cause a scene. Thanks anyway.'

'Fine then,' Trevor blurts as he returns to the bar.

Olivia clenches her fists in frustration. *Shit. That was my moment and I blew it.* The make-up; the three-hour journey; the nerves. All wasted. Baffled by Taylor's abandoning his 'chat up' so abruptly, she composes herself and continues to observe him comb the room and approach only unaccompanied women as he glides methodically from table to table. It appears that Trevor is popular and well liked in his home town.

Or well rejected.

Propping her bag on the table, she rifles through the contents, pulls out her make-up, checks her appearance, and on replacing the compact flicks on her mobile phone's video recorder. She discretely films Trevor's antics until he leaves the lounge area. After ten minutes, he has not returned. Olivia ambles to the bar, hoping, with each step, to glimpse Trevor imposing his dubious charm on an unsuspecting female. She sees nothing.

Outside in the Beer Garden, Taylor consoles a sobbing

young woman, distraught after a heated spat with her boyfriend. Maree and Trevor had previously exchanged pleasantries but rarely progressed beyond informal gretings. That minor association invigorates Trevor to rescue her from the emotional doldrums.

Maree blurts her shattered feelings. Previously a pillar of support to friends in similar predicaments, she'd always given the advice: stay in control; don't let anyone take advantage of your situation; don't submit to false comfort. In her moment of greatest need, Maree disregards her own counsel.

Feeling at ease with Trevor and psychologically indebted to him, she discards her rigid constitution and throws aside natural level-headedness. Driven by the power of alcohol, an opportunity stands before her to avenge her boyfriend's tantrum. She drapes her arms around Trevor's neck and kisses him.

Taylor returns the kiss, slightly more passionately than Maree expects, and in so doing encourages Maree to shed her moral armour. She surrenders to his lewd advances and follows him to the ladies' rest rooms where they swiftly cling to each other in a squishy cubicle. With animalistic enthusiasm, they yield to the passionate entwinement of carnal desire. Maree releases an exhilarative sigh as Trevor slides his hand beneath her blouse and clumsily unhooks her bra. She kisses Trevor deeply, using him as the *ultimate* payback.

Trevor is accustomed to overcoming at least *some* resistance, but Maree erects no boundaries. She is well up for it, as 'the guys' would say. He caresses her shoulders, pulls the flouncy top over her head and nuzzles her neck –

Slam! Bang! The adjacent cubicle's door crashes open as if it has been kicked off its hinges. The interruption is sufficient to pull Maree from the clutch of delirious need and return her to commonsense. She looks at Trevor, who stands bemused at his prospective conquest's shifting attitude. Embarrassed about dropping her guard, Maree rearranges her clothing, rushes out of the cubicle, out of the rest room, and out of the pub.

Olivia drops onto the toilet seat in the next cubicle. She'd planned the diversion to avert the possibility of assault on the woman. Having confirmed that Trevor could not have left the establishment without her seeing him, she deduced he could only be in the men's or ladies' toilets. On entering the ladies' rest room, she saw a pair of men's shoes beneath a cubicle door. To the uninitiated, the sight of men's shoes in a ladies' toilet would seem out of place. It might even cause alarm. However, to the growing number of teens and young adults prepared to engage in instant hook-ups, it is not unusual for a girl to usher a guy, or in some cases a girl, into a cubicle for a romantic interlude or non-committal quickie.

Olivia lifts and drops the toilet seat like an alligator snapping its jaws. She knows someone rushed from the cubicle, but the strong sense of a person's presence remains with her. The sound of scuffling shoes prompts her to peer beneath the cubicle dividers. No feet. She intuitively looks up.

Trevor clings to the top of her cubicle, his fingertips turning a motley pinkish-white: 'You all right in there. Security. Sorry to be rude. I heard the commotion, rushed in, and wanted to make sure everything's okay.'

'I'm fine thanks. Just slipped on my way in.'

She looks under the door and watches the shoes exit the rest room. *Security? Why'd he say that? Quick thinker, I'll give him that.*

Now, she *does* need the toilet. She catches her breath,

thankful that Trevor didn't break in to *her* cubicle and commit unthinkable evil – with the high probability of getting away with it. Willing her heart to return to a safe beat, she studies the scrawlings of bored pub patrons: *'Annette loves Peter', 'John M is a cheating bastard', 'What do you get when you cross a man with a shopping basket? A basket case'.*

She sniggers at the thought processes of one going about their business in a toilet cubicle, concurrent with delving into their subconscious to transcribe newfound literary expertise onto the toilet wall in the hope of capturing an audience of prospective publishers, critics and Man Booker prize judges. Olivia has grown up with, and continues to follow, her mother's teachings – the '3W' process: wee, wipe and wun. Her father's crude variation was less succinct: shit, scrape and scarper.

Her thoughts churn and rattle like slurry in a concrete mixer. The evening has not developed as anticipated. On paper, the plan was flawless: sit at the bar, listen to Trevor's pick-up line, demonstrate interest and maybe accept one kiss. He would try to venture further at which time she would insist that he leave her alone. He would refuse and then she would formally introduce herself and arrest him. Great concept – poor execution.

Now she has nothing. She can do no more. She's lost her nerve and accepts that she will receive no further interest from Trevor.

A night wasted. This is not the event that will trump Marchant. *What is that saying about counting your losses and giving up?* She decides to head home, but abruptly succumbs to a bout of 'mental telepathy'. Compelled by curiosity and loose ends she stops at the bar, unsure of whether she's been alerted by a spontaneous reaction to the divine power of logic, or arrested by one of life's gems where one faces a premonition that everything will work out. She recalls a news item of an aged woman who impulsively walked into a lotto agency and purchased a Quick-Pick. The woman looked at the numbers: *what an absurd sequence. Why did I waste my money on that?* The following Monday morning, while reading the paper – and without even thinking about lotto – her eyes dart to a one column box sitting in the gutter of page two and see that she's won £1,277,612.

Olivia approaches the woman of fifty-hard-years: 'I left a jacket at my table and it's missing. Has anyone handed one in?'

'No miss. Nothing tonight. Not yet anyway. Wait 'til later when they're off their head. Then we'll have jackets, bags, mobile phones and anything else that hasn't been stolen.'

'Are you sure? It was only half an hour ago?'

'Hey love, if anything was handed in, I'd know about it.'

'Okay, I'm sorry. Could I see someone from security please?'

'Security? You some kind of comedian? I am security. And I'm the manager, bouncer, chief cook and bottle washer. Security? Bloody hell, love, whaddya think this is, the Hilton?'

'If it was the Hilton a guy wouldn't have been standing on the john peering over me in the ladies' toilets. He clearly identified himself as security. Guy about 30ish, dark hair and maybe five-seven, five-eight. So either you're crapping me or you have a freak running loose perving in the women's toilets.'

Olivia walks off, satisfied that Trevor had adopted the security officer ruse as a means of gaining her trust. Unfortunately, she is disadvantaged by having not seen whether

Taylor had been wearing a uniform. The prospect is remote given that he'd worn casual clothing in the bar.

Assessing the evening, Olivia considers her overall investment productive. Every piece of information contributes to the huge mural profiling a suspect and his antecedents. She's witnessed Taylor's leisure-time modus operandi which closely reinforces Marchant's description of events as had occurred at the Rose and Thorn, and she's witnessed his ingenuity and quick-wittedness – the hallmark of a person determined to get what they want at all costs. Satisfied with her evening's activity, she waltzes out to her car and heads for home, via Alexander Road.

The silver Orion has not returned.

15

MARG HEGARTY BOUNDS into her office at 8.30 a.m., determined to unearth new information.

Whilst dining at the Rose and Thorn, she'd observed Barry Simmons cranking poker machine handles and venting frustration each time the machine failed to jingle coins to its tray. She'd been concerned about his low-level tantrums and his manner of bashing the machine in sync with audible obscenities. She had witnessed his animated conversation with Amy – a scenario later communicated to Marchant during the course of his interviewing pub patrons. She was unable, however, to detail Simmons' movements during the moments immediately before and after Amy's death.

That recollection of Simmons antics prompts Marg to grab her notebook and micro-recorder and return to Evesham's Pier. She parks in Waterside Drive as the first wave of shoppers head towards Bridge Street. A rainbow of decorated barges bob alongside the dock. Simmons' craft, moored at the pier on the opposite side of the river's seventy-metre span, dwarfs them. She chastises herself: *Great start. And I'm supposed to be an investigative journalist?*

She rushes along the riverbank, over the Workman bridge, past the shopping mall entrance, across the edge of Crown

Meadow, and arrives at the pier to see Simmons transferring rubbish from his craft to a council bin.

Marg had long ago learnt about interview scheduling and the importance of making appointments by telephone or sending a letter of request. Today, she'd just bang off an email. Experience has taught her, however, to abandon professional protocol in favour of the 'ambush' method – arrive unannounced. The questionable strategy favours the female gender because a male will happily encourage a woman's attention, even if she's selling a multi-level marketing 'business opportunity'. Accordingly, Marg harnesses the approach when requiring information from high profile subjects. Perhaps it is that form of borderline harassment that sees official surveys rate reporters and media personnel beneath car salesmen.

'Morning. Mr Simmons? Marg Hegarty, *Evesham Record*.'

'I got nothin' to say, though the amount I spend on advertising should guarantee me a fair go. I've been plastered over your paper for two murders; I don't want further exposure, good or bad.'

'I'm here to give you an opportunity to respond. We're running this as a front page lead whether you comment or not. The police media release paints a bleak picture; we wouldn't be responsible to not offer you the right of reply.'

Simmons gruffs: 'Thanks. I appreciate your interest. All I can say is that I'm innocent of this stuff. My lawyer's handling it and he's told me to speak to no-one.'

'Would you care to comment on your being seen at the Rose and Thorn on the evening of August sixteenth?'

'I care to comment that there were about 80 people there at the same time.'

'And what time was that?'

'That's all you get. I've got to get this going now.' Simmons replaces the engine cover and starts the inboard diesel.

Sensitive to his temperament and wishing to avoid aggravation, Marg accepts the blatant hint and returns to her car. She uses the five-minute walk to replay the voice-activated recorder secreted in her pocket. The only detail Simmons offered was that there were 80 people in the pub. That is no clue in itself – the pub could hold 80 patrons on any given night – but it does inspire Hegarty to further her enquiry at the Rose and Thorn.

As she unlocks the driver's side door, Simmons' craft rumbles alongside the nearby landing. 'Stop. Wait a moment,' he yells, gesturing wildly with one arm.

Marg drops her bag into the car and looks up to see Simmons scurrying towards her.

She recoils in fear.

'It's alright. I'm sorry. It's been a hard couple of days,' Simmons puffs as he approaches. He's hustled only 20 metres from the dock but looks as if he's just completed the London marathon. He lunges forward, buckles, and falls against the rear of her car. 'Perhaps we could do this another time. I understand you've got a job to do and I don't particularly want to be offside with your paper. How about I give you your interview at the pub tonight?'

Alarm bells clatter. 'No. I think we should keep this on a professional level Mr Simmons. My office will be fine. Now, how about you. Are you all right?'

'Fine. Just a bit of a turn. Back to business, it wasn't really the professional level I was thinking of, if you don't mind my saying.'

'I'm flattered, but no thanks. Long-standing policy – I don't mix work with pleasure.'

Marg hadn't mixed work with anything since her previous beau left without notice eight months' earlier. Injured by the insult, she'd rejected the few ensuing invitations and focused solely on her career, as do many suffering failed relationships.

Her waking hours are predictable. Work, sleep, work. The pattern continues into the weekend when Marg drafts forthcoming editorials. A Sunday shopping expedition rewards the six days' work, highlighted by a midday all-you-can-eat pig-out at Chinese Dream. On returning to the High Street, she purchases armfuls of kitchen gadgets and cookery books that will never defray the emotional and physical interaction she so desperately craves.

On rare occasions she'll phone Samantha, her twenty-year-old daughter, who lives and works in London. They force snippets of conversation about work, television programs, and Samantha's egging on her mother to 'get on with life'. The advice carries no merit as the coveted mother / daughter relationship had collapsed six months' earlier, after their equally fractious behaviour fostered intense arguments – generally over Samantha's continued urging her mother to 'find a good man'. Marg repeatedly countered: 'There aren't any.' The passing of time has not diluted her resistance.

Simmons pleads: 'Just in case you change your mind, here's my card. I'm always available on the mobile and the other number has an answering machine. I assure you I'm above board. It's just so much easier to speak casually.' Simmons returns to his boat, wondering what Marg had expected to wrench from the proposed interview.

Marg flicks the card into her car, notes the encounter, and heads for the Rose and Thorn.

She pushes through heavy, swing-doors and walks directly to the bar. A Dewar's Whiskey clock flashes 10.05 a.m. Marg is surprised to be the only customer.

'Late breakfast or early lunch?' asks the bartender.

'Second breakfast. On the move. Working early. I'll have coffee and a ham and cheese toastie.'

'Good job if you can sit in a pub eating breakfast while you're working,' he grins.

'Yes, it is. Maybe you can help me,' enthuses Marg. 'I'm investigating the drowning of that young girl the other night.'

'Your lot have been here often enough. I've told them everything I know.'

Marg studies him. 'Ah, I remember you. You were working on Tuesday night. I was sitting over there with a group of friends on the night of that terrible attack. Therefore, I'm not just a drop-in trying to siphon info from you. I'm a regular, so I do have some first-hand knowledge. Was the girl a regular too?'

The barman switches personas. 'Yeah. Amy's in here all the time. She knows, sorry; she knew all the regulars.'

'You know Barry Simmons from the river?'

'Yeah, I know Simmo. Everyone does. He's an all right guy.'

'Was he here on Thursday night?'

'Hey. I told yous everything. I'm not going through all this again. I'm a busy man. I've got lunch trade to prep for.'

'Sorry. You must think I'm the police. I'm from the *Evesham Record*, so you haven't told us anything. As I said, I was here on the night so it's understandable that I pursue this in the interest of that poor girl. And don't forget the other girl dragged out of the Avon. If you can help, I'd appreciate it. I'll keep you anonymous if that's a concern.'

'All right then. There were a few guys Amy was talking to. Don't really know who they were 'cause I was hardly paying attention. I think she left shortly after talking to them; 'bout ten o'clock maybe.'

'Was she with Simmons?'

'Yeah, she had been, for some of the time, but as far as I'm aware, she ended up leaving on her own.'

'You tell the police this?'

'Yeah lady, and I showed them CCTV of the car park they were interested in.'

'Could I have a look at that?'

'Could if I had it. They took it. Seemed pretty interested in a car leaving the car park.'

'D'you know whose it was?'

'Yeah, bloody obvious. The female copper yelled out something to her colleague about Simmo leaving the car park in a blue Bee Em.'

Marg accepts that as putting Simmons clearly in the frame for Amy's murder, despite his being only one of 80 people drinking, chatting and partying at the Rose and Thorn. She smiles at the thought of tactfully editing the independent confirmation into a lead story. Sipping a second coffee, she continues: 'Can you think of anyone who could give me an idea of who was last with Amy?'

'If I could do that, the police would have already sorted it. As I said, Amy always plays the crowd. There's not one person I saw her with exclusively, and even if I had, I doubt I'd be spilling those beans to anyone.'

Suitably rebuked, Hegarty resolves to ascertain if the police, or Marchant in particular, are pursuing other leads. Setting aside her ambush philosophy, she contacts the Coroner's office and makes an appointment to see the presiding physician, Doctor Groenweld.

16

DR ERICH GROENWELD extends his report writing assignments into the lucrative arena of overtime. He regularly stretches a thirty-minute draft to two hours, raising constant guffaws from colleagues who compare him to a housewife flitting about her business at 100 miles per hour in an illusion of efficiency. The simile describes perfectly Groenweld's productivity: an illusion.

He has no time for reporters who, from his experience, distort and embellish facts to create editorial sensationalism. He has adopted a constitution to treat all reporters with equal disdain. Today, he makes a rare exception.

Marg Hegarty has trekked through the many hazards of journalism: insults, erratic hours and secondment to the coalface of some of the nation's most heinous crimes. But delays cap the list. For reasons she cannot fathom, journalists are denied the same courtesy and professionalism as extended to doctors and dentists, business managers and school principals. Time management is important to everyone, but journalists are expected to wait. Join the queue. We'll see you when we're ready. Then, when the interviewee *is* ready, he will erect hurdles and barriers to circumvent even the simplest conversation. He evades speaking 'on the record' with the claim of his not being authorised.

Fortunately, Doctor Groenweld is of the 'old school' who refuses to give visitors the run around. He is interested only in retirement and publishing further articles about his flat earth theory.

He invites Hegarty into his sterile office. 'Well, young lady. I believe you're interested in the medical analysis of the drowning victim? Perhaps I'll give you a little of my background before we get started.'

'Fine,' smiles Hegarty, believing that allowing him freedom to gloat about selected career highlights will encourage him to provide detailed answers to her questions. There is also the prospect of stumbling upon a good story, but she is mindful of licensing him to waste her time with old war stories – another workplace hazard – and untold variations of medical breakthroughs often proffered by eccentric doctors and academics. Marg stands by another creed: the journalist's charter to listen. She is not one to cut short anyone's will to talk.

She studies Groenweld's anaemic bulk. Stifling a chuckle, she sees a 60-year-old clone of The Fat Controller from the Thomas the Tank Engine series.

'Make yourself comfortable Miss Hegarty.'

Marg accepts the cheering words as if Groenweld is priming her for a lengthy tutorial. She remains stiff-necked with notebook on lap.

'You're obviously aware of my duties as Coroner – to investigate and report on the manner of death of other than natural passing. What you probably do not know is that I also provide geological expertise to police who require forensic analysis of soil samples, vehicular and pedestrian footprints and geographic locative identification. That evolved from my long held passion for all things geological.

'Some eight years ago I commenced a research project. Only recently I have concluded, with proof, that the Earth is flat –'

Marg pulls her brows together as if trying to replay the revelation. *The earth is flat?*

'– Oh, I'm sorry. By your startled reaction, I'd say my research has evaded you. I must say that I've received a somewhat disappointing backlash from most sectors of the media, although I'm consoled by the fact that many of the world's greatest scientific discoveries did, eventually, silence the sceptics.

'My conclusions are based upon the dominant role of the number 'three' as a factor in astrological and biological life. The starting point is incontrovertible. The earth is the *third* planet from the Sun. Its circumference is indisputably 24,900 miles, while the equatorial diameter is 7,900 miles. What is immediately obvious is that the circumference is *three* times that of the diameter – assuming we accept that the world really *is* round, or close enough to it for argument's sake.

'To dispel that, we must consider earth's gravitational forces. As a simple exercise, imagine the world as a basketball. Now, if one were to sail across the seas to the extremities of the Southern Hemisphere – the underside of the basketball – would the boat float upside down or fall out of the water into infinity? Would a plane barrel roll beyond the equatorial juncture to ensure all passengers remain seated upright as opposed to being suspended upside down? The answer, of course, is an emphatic no. There is but one conclusion – the Earth is flat.

'Let us examine the North and South Poles. I don't refute their being 24,900 miles apart, but – and here's the key difference – they are 24,900 miles apart on a flat surface.

141

Imagine an A4 sheet of paper, laid flat. We have north at the top and at the bottom, south. Yes, I know. You're about to ask: "What happens at the Earth's limit? – at the edge of that sheet of paper." To answer that, Miss Hegarty, I must recite meticulously sensitive detail and formula.

'It involves the phenomenon of astro-transportation from the limit of the North Pole to the commencement of the South Pole. This marvel necessitates computing the difference in light years between the two points, and the relative time in physicality of travelling 24,900 miles across a flat surface. The significance of the equation is the factor of the speed of light, which travels at 299,792,458 metres per second – nearly *three* hundred million. That figure may seem insignificant – until you recognise the formula used in all speed of light computations exalts the number *three*: 3×10^8 ms-1.

'Fellows of the National Science Laboratory have credited me with the terms, 'window to the sky' and 'window of opportunity'. It was from the first reading of my 'astro-transport' theory that these now clichéd references were stolen. I can reveal with certainty that the reason lost explorers in the Arctic regions were never found was because they had already astro-ported to Antarctica.

'Do you have any idea of how many people send me satellite snapshots and videos of the Earth by day and the Earth by night; all trying to convince me that I'm a raving crackpot?'

Marg realises Groenweld is not speaking rhetorically, but actually addressing her. 'Absolutely not. I couldn't imagine. No. I have no idea.'

'Of course. You wouldn't. It's all illusion. Accepting a vision of the earth as round is akin to one observing a mirage in the middle of the Sahara. Both are merely figments of one's imagination, promulgated by scientific factors. You know that above the Earth lies a moisture-laden stratosphere comprising 78% nitrogen and 21% oxygen suspended in millions upon millions of liquid droplets. Those droplets distort refractions of light captured by huge stellar cameras. It is those cameras that *falsely* reproduce the earth as round. Watch this –'

Groenweld collects a droplet of water on the end of his pen and photographs a book through the droplet. He displays the image on a computer screen. The book appears round. 'See? As is generally accepted, a flat object observed through a droplet of water will appear distorted and round. Just as the book was flat before being photographed, so is the earth. This is my proof.'

The Doctor enlarges the photo and enthusiastically performs a calculation that verifies the book's data as the same factor as Earth: 3 to 1 circumference to diameter. 'See? The prophecies of the number *three* and its relationship to earth are unique. The earth is the *third* planet from the Sun. All things on earth are *three*-dimensional. There are *three* stages of matter: solid, liquid and gas; *three* primary colours: red, blue, yellow; and *three* components of food: protein, carbohydrate and fat.

'It was on the *third* day The Holy father created the earth. The birth of Christ was signified by the *Three* Wise Men. The Lord rose after *three* days! Jonah returned unharmed from the whale after *three* days and *three* nights. Christianity had placed its own reliance on the number *three* and furthered that with the *Holy Trinity*: the Father, the Son and the Holy Spirit.

'But not only has Christianity adopted the number three as a figure of worship. So too has Hindi. Its deity Ganesh, is blessed with *three* right and left arms and *three* right and left legs. Hindi also recognises 'Trimurti'; a *triad* of the gods Brahma, Vishnu and Shiva.

'These divine instances of the number *three's* relationship to earth and life are too important to dismiss as coincidental.

'Life itself is dependent on the number 'three'. A woman will enjoy – or endure – *three* trimesters of pregnancy. Three trimesters – *three* times *three*. Now, let's study conception itself, or more particularly, the sperm. The protagonist of life is a *three*-part cell: the head, containing a nucleus; a middle portion containing mitochondria and a long tail known as the flagellum. The fertilised egg will be identified by one of only *three* available human chromosomes: XX, XY and the rarer XXY.

'The Third World is often used as a derogatory term for underdeveloped countries or communities. Whoever coined the term 'Third World' did so because of the significance of the number *three*.

'Consider also the Third Reich. That is a fact of history in its own right. Whilst said to be conceived from the existence of previous empires of The Holy Roman Empire of 800 to 1806 (the First Reich) and the German empire of 1871 to 1918 (the Second Reich) it remains ponderous why the Nazi regime of January 1933 to May 1945 – which professed to be above all – would anoint itself as 'Third'.

'What about today's world? Look at the literary and entertainment appearances of the number *three*: Three Blind Mice; Three Little Pigs; Three Stooges; Three Musketeers; Three Amigos; Three Men and a Baby; Three Times a Lady and The Three Tenors.

'Society has been hoodwinked with information from eminent professors down to pop groups. Take the Bee Gees for example – and note, in the main, they were a group of *three* brothers – Barry, Robin and Maurice Gibb, who sang, in the opening line of their composition, "World": "*Now I found that the world is round.*" Did they have scientific foundation for the lyric? No. Of course not.

'What about sport? Olympic events of *Triple* Jump and *Tri*athlon. Cricket – *three* stumps and the hat trick of *three* consecutive wickets. Adidas clothing – *three* stripes.

'It is with accolades to persons like myself who have sacrificed countless hours to enhance the educative process with twenty-first century conclusions that there is now a definitive answer. What about your own profession, Miss Hegarty? What do you write to indicate a thought provoking moment?… yes, an ellipsis. *Three* dots!

'Look around your office and home. Both survive on power generated by earth's resources. How is that power delivered? The power point. Power points have a *three*-pin plug. What's the safe terminal of the plug? Earth! That's damn compelling evidence that *three* and the earth are as one.

'Sorry. I may have gone off the track a bit,' wheezes Groenweld. 'Perhaps you feel you're getting the *third* degree. Sorry about that. Now remind me why you're here?'

'Doctor Groenweld. I am impressed by your credentials and your theories, and I'd love to feature you in a future edition, but for the moment I am here because two women have been murdered. I hope you share my concern that anything we can do to help resolve this will hopefully prevent any further casualties in the community.'

'First of all, Miss Hegarty, we cannot be sure the two murders are related – two different MOs, of which I'm sure you're aware. Second, there's little a journalist or reporter from a country throw-away can do to "resolve" this as you call it.'

Marg withholds her wrath. She has long defended country

145

papers or 'throwaways' as Groenweld so callously belittled her employer's product. She tries valiantly to recover the lost opportunity. 'Doctor. I did not come here to debate you. My sole interest is advising and protecting the community from any further violence. If you care to contribute to that cause, I will take a few notes. If not, I'll continue to pursue my own line of enquiry and wish you good day.'

'Don't get me wrong Miss Hegarty. There's nothing I can give you. One girl was found at the water's edge, strangled, and the other was stabbed and died at the scene. Preliminary evidence, which I cannot disclose at this stage, may help identify the person responsible. It will, in due course, be passed on to Inspector Marchant of Worcester CID.'

Hegarty feels like a bride jilted at the altar. *So I sat through all that flat earth garbage for what? I'll give him a feature all right!*

17

'WHERE THE HELL is she?' Marchant grumbles to no one in particular. 'Anyone heard from Watts?'

'No, guv,' chorus three detectives struggling with newspaper quiz questions secreted beneath crime reports.

Marchant picks through a confetti-like smattering of Post-it notes for obscure messages and checks his diary, just in case he's forgotten an earlier absence notification. He calls her mobile and tells the 'out of area or phone switched off' message to fuck off. Marchant allows his team members liberal flexibility, but insists they report absence or illness at least one hour prior to shift commencement. He also expects to be advised of early morning enquiries necessitating an officer's absence for more than two hours. He readily acknowledges the unpredictable nature of police work: a new lead requiring immediate action; an interview that runs to excess; or dealing with a minor crime that a detective could not hand-pass to uniform. He extends only one concession to the forthright officer who bashfully confesses: '*Sorry guv. I'm a bit embarrassed about this. I slept in.*' But Marchant accepts *no* excuse for a member not phoning in.

'I'll have her arse for this. And –'

'Bet you'd love that guv, or maybe you already have,' interjects Stanton to the smirks of his colleagues.

'Nah. She'd never let the likes of the guv near her. Too much class for 'im,' shouts another.

'I dunno,' bellows Stanton. 'She might cop him in a moment of desperation.'

'You'll never know. And anyone else in this unit who thinks they can do as they please, you'd better think again. Stanton. Since you're so chirpy, you can get 'round to Watts' place and roust her up. If she's not there, find her. And take one of these clowns with you.'

During Stanton's first week at Worcester CID, he'd earned the dubious distinction of master of odds and ends. As the new guy, he was the natural choice to follow up the odd file, take home the odd witness and collect the odd lunch order. He would end up making coffee and end up answering calls of duty like a playful puppy who'd graduated with honours from the Canine University of Obedience.

He is openly gay. Out of the closet. Proud of finding himself. Expressing his sexuality. For the record, he wears every other similar cliché attributed to those who proclaim to be no different than anyone else – they just prefer to fall in love with their own gender. He objects to Marchant calling him a 'raving poofter,' but never does he have the gumption to take the matter further, knowing full-well that Marchant pays no heed to Human Rights and anti-discrimination legislation.

He wears the gaudiest suits, designer discards from Elton John's and Boy George's elaborate collections, and he speaks the distinctive dialect of gay culture – the lisping, semi-droned, over-animated speech pattern poached from select sectors of window dressers and graphic designers.

Stanton's forte is his proficiency in locating people. A wizard with missing persons files, he ascribes his success to an inherent ability to educe information from the depressed and forlorn. He empathises with their situation, and consequently obtains details rarely acquired by officers far above his seniority. It is not for those qualities that Marchant dispatches him to find Olivia – it is because he wants him out of his hair.

Stanton lopes along the footpath as if unaffected by gravity, each step suspending him in mid-air before gently setting him down again. His embarrassed colleague dawdles ten metres behind in a poor attempt to disassociate himself from the rubbery sergeant.

Stanton hurdles over a three-foot-high wrought iron front gate as he approaches the huge home. Affixed next to the front door an aluminium plate shines with eight apartment numbers and their corresponding tenant's names. Beneath number four: O.E. Watts. No mister, miss or misses. Just plain initials and surname. Generic identity. Stanton presses the buzzer and waits. And waits. A folded magazine wedges open the polished-brass letter flap. He peers through the slot and hollers. No answer.

He tracks a right-of-way to a side gate which leads him to the building's rear yard. Surprised to find the gate unlatched, he enters and scans the yard before knocking on the rear door. No answer. He peers inside and satisfies himself that nothing appears out of place. Stanton is not unduly concerned, but won't risk returning to the office without assuring himself of Olivia's well-being.

He door-knocks adjacent neighbours' homes but receives no response, perhaps due to the area's fashionable embracement by young working couples. Directly across the road his theory collapses. It is Stanton's luck, or misfortune, to knock on the door of Esmé Watford. Every neighbourhood boasts its own Esmé. The local gossip and know-it-all. The unofficial Neighbourhood Watch, Crimestoppers representative and parcel receiver for all nearby residents. If anyone is able to elicit every smidgen of information from such a valuable resource, it is the flamboyant Stanton.

Mrs Watford opens the door before Stanton's knuckles rap the glossy green paint.

'Good morning ma'am. You look divine today. I'm looking for a colleague of mine from across the road. Olivia – you might know her.'

'Oh yes, love. I know Olivia. Nice young lady, too. You know, I saw her leave yesterday afternoon, carrying a bag of some sort. Looked like she was taking a few days off, you know that job of hers, so demanding sometimes, all those different shifts she does, on call and all, especially with everything that's been going on the last couple of weeks with those poor girls in the paper; I bet she was working on that, you know; I wasn't particularly watching what she was doing, just dusting me window ledge and I just chanced upon seeing her—'

'Was it a large suitcase or an overnight bag?'

'Oh, they're everywhere. One of those carry-alls they lug 'round on their back. Can't do 'em any good, you know. Curvature of the spine, that's what they'll get. The kids in the shopping mall carry them, goodness knows what for; those young lads have probably got cans of spray paint in there ready to graffiti another bridge or sign; they certainly wouldn't be carrying school books; most of them are running around the streets all day—'

A voice booms down the hallway: ''oo is it, Es?'

Esmé reaches up to Stanton's ear and whispers, 'Don't worry about 'im. It's me other 'alf, Doug.'

Stanton freezes – an erect modern-day version of The Thinker. He splutters: 'Excuse me? Have I missed something? You're living with half a duck?'

Esmé breaks into raucous laughter and yells down the hallway: ''ey Doug. Get a load of this. Are you me man or 'alf-a-duck?' She turns to the red-faced Stanton, 'Sorry love, it's me other half; you know, me 'usband, Doug. Wants to know who's at the door.'

'Oh, all right Mrs Watford. You best get back to him. At least I now know that Olivia's safe. Thank you. Have a nice afternoon.'

'You wouldn't like a nice cuppa' with us would you?'

'Another time maybe. I really must be getting back now – it's the impatient boss.'

Stanton leaves, head bowed like a fool, but none the wiser about his colleague. *Carrying a bag indeed. She could have been going to the local gym.*

Olivia frowns a what-are-you-looking-at-me-for? look when, at midday, she strides into the CID office. Marchant assumes his preferred position: feet on desk, *Daily Telegraph* in hand. 'Afternoon Watts. Nice of you to grace us with your appearance.'

'Thanks, guv. Nice to be here.'

'Over here. Now!'

Olivia awaits the dressing down. Her intention had been to drive straight from Bournemouth to the office, but tiredness fell upon her so quickly that she retired to the Taunton Services Centre for a quick nap. The aftershock of Taylor's presence in the toilet cubicle had stretched the nap to a deep sleep.

'Sorry guv. I planned to be here early this morning but

slept in. I don't know what else to say, other than I went down to Bournemouth to work on Taylor, but got nowhere.'

'I could have told you that, Watts. We've got Simmons and he's going down. While you've been frigging around down the beach, I've been working my arse off completing the prosecution brief.'

'Guv, you did say I could pursue Taylor if I believed in it.'

'Yes. Rhetorically speaking. I didn't expect you to take me literally.'

'To be honest inspector, and with respect, I sometimes don't know how to take you at all. But can't we move on to the job at hand for the moment?'

'You're on a losing streak, Watts. I got Simmons nailed. Won't be long and we'll have his prints off the weapon.'

'Not likely. We'll need a lot more. Have you got a hand match from Morales' neck?'

'Bloody hell, Watts. You reckon he left bloody fingerprints on her neck?'

'Please don't treat me like an imbecile, inspector. There will be forensic evidence of the finger span from tissue trauma. We know that Simmons' is a big man with workers hands, whereas Taylor's are much smaller. I still say we've got to haul him in.'

'On what grounds?'

'Reasonable grounds for suspecting him to be guilty. Phone records. Remember when we first spoke to him, he said he thought Juanita was late because they'd had an argument and she might have been at friend's or whatever? He's already admitted phoning her before ringing the police.'

'Bloody hell Olivia. I've had my arse chewed off for acting on suspicion, and I've got the biggest arse in the job.'

Biggest head too, thinks Olivia before saying: 'There's

something else guv. Last night he was at a pub and had a girl in the ladies' loos. I think she was willing, but that's not the point. After she left, I saw Taylor peering at me from the top of the cubicle. He announced himself as security, but the proprietor later confirmed that she employed no security personnel.'

'Good bit of info, Liv, but it don't mean shit. It don't mean he killed two women. I told you. *Simmons* is the man. Anyway Liv, we're off to forensics.'

Olivia flinches at Marchant's abrupt manner, grateful to still be assigned to the case.

* * *

Dr Richard Thomas sprints into the forensic laboratory's administration foyer. 'You're here for the knife report, I take it,' he asks Marchant.

'Yeah. Treat me.'

'Assailant wore a latex glove. We've recovered a fine blue thread from the hilt of the knife. Being analysed at this very moment. What will interest you is that the thread is not consistent with the colours of the clothes the deceased was wearing.'

'Right. She had a black coat and, er, not much underneath, as I recall. We need that analysis yesterday. We have a suspect and this could be the thread we need to sew him up.'

'I don't share your humour, inspector. Give me twenty-four hours.'

'Eight.'

Olivia remains dutifully silent, restraining herself from venturing her prognosis that there should be two suspects. She defers to Thomas after hearing him dictate *his* terms to

Marchant. She feels redundant; a file carrier; a highly paid paradigm of successful Women's Liberation thrusts that elevated women in the work force.

Women's employment conditions have improved ten-fold since Olivia's childhood. The days of suppression and subservience have since been legislated out of society. Women's organisations, together with cell groups of carers and support staff, sprout in community centres and council offices. Rallies pronounce women's equality; wages escalate to near-parity with male remuneration; specific advertising for males is denounced – save for legal exemptions; and greater career opportunity for women is paved, or enforced as some proclaim, via the route of Affirmative Action legislation.

Today, there *is* more equality and opportunity for women. But lumbering in the constabulary's Jurassic Park survive chauvinistic dinosaurs like Marchant.

* * *

Marchant shouts: 'Hey Watts. Be a good lass and trot down to forensics for that thread report.'

Olivia bites her tongue and obediently strolls from the office while Marchant licks the top off a cappuccino. On a bad day she would stand her ground and aggressively defend her position. Today, she considers the strange anomaly that sees her to go 'toe to toe' with aggressive male suspects, yet when it comes to Marchant she simply folds and accepts his unwelcome comments. *Put it down to respect for the job, not the person.*

One hour later, she flings an envelope onto his desk. He ignores the contemptuous gesture and turns his attention to the report:

"Pure wool, five-ply twisted yarn, dyed Indigo Blue. Fibre samples match product manufactured by Northern Woollen Mills of Yorkshire, batch number 188901. Retailed through selected department and handicraft stores across UK. Used predominantly in the manufacture of cardigans, jumpers, scarves, gloves and woolly hats."

'Time to slam a search warrant on Simmons' place,' Marchant barks.

'You're taking a punt that he's got a blue jumper made of this thread?'

'He'll have one. Nothing surer. Fits his profile – plain and ordinary.'

'You've only just let him go. He'll claim harassment, *and* he'll have a good chance of proving it.'

'Not if we nail him first.'

18

TREVOR TAYLOR WAKES from an unbroken sleep. No nightmares, no hot sweats and no regrets. The absence of Juanita's cuddles rekindle memories of joyful nights where seductive whispers of 'I love you' were a solemn pledge for life.

He has shed the fear of further police enquiries – believing that interest in him has waned. One facet haunts him, and that is his hastily discarding the knife while fleeing Swan Lane. He hopes it will now be a rusting speck in the stinking acres of refuse feeding flocks of ibises at the Pinvin landfill site. Taylor is ill-equipped to recognise that supreme confidence is the bane of many now languishing behind prisons' walls.

He has not contacted police since reporting Juanita missing five days' earlier. Thinking logically, or as logical as a concerned future husband might think, he phones Marchant to enquire whether a positive ID has been established. Marchant responds curtly that the woman *has* been identified and that DS Watts is notifying relatives. When pushed for further information, Marchant offers a terse, 'I'm sorry to tell you, Mr Taylor, your fiancée died under suspicious circumstances. Our investigation is on-going.'

Taylor leaves for work, intending to complete the two jobs he's rescheduled. The sight of a police car parked at the end of the street elevates his heartbeat. It descends after he observes an officer in heated conversation with an adjacent resident. The scene reignites the shame of his recently chastising his brother.

He bears guilt of that indiscretion. It is not the first time an incident has resulted in one brother exercising silence over the other. Throughout their teens, there had been disputes over shared friendships, with Trevor claiming most were *his* friends because he was the eldest, and John claiming they were *his* friends because they liked him better.

Many of those childish traits stalked them into adulthood, culminating in the incident where John tried to seduce Trevor's girlfriend. That episode resulted in a six-week hiatus from both sides.

On another occasion, Trevor 'borrowed' his brother's credit card from his wallet and withdrew five hundred pounds from the local ATM. John spotted the deficiency on his monthly statement. After double-checking transactions, he reported the discrepancy to his bank, which immediately commenced an investigation. The full story emerged after the bank released transaction logs linked to a CCTV monitor's capture of Trevor pocketing money from the machine.

John insisted that Trevor be charged. Only at the last minute did conscience and the family bond compel him to withdraw the complaint. They did not speak for four weeks.

It had always been a test – an exercise in resilience – as it is now, of who will break. Each brother is equally determined. In this instance though, Trevor accepts responsibility. Choosing to insulate himself against further rejection, he sends John a text:

Hello, hope all's well ☺ ☺.

* * *

Marchant summonses Olivia to his office. 'We've got to look at this again, Liv.'

'I'll not be looking at anything while you call me that bloody name. It's Olivia. Please?'

'All right *Olivia*. We gotta look at this situation. How'd you go with that phone found on Simmons' craft?'

'I think it's a leap trying to connect the phone I bought in Cash Liquidators to the one found on the craft. Brett Davies identified the phone as a silver Nokia that does everything – but he can't identify who dropped it. Anyway, how many hundreds of thousands of silver Nokias are there in this bloody country? We know there's a connection between Davies handing the phone to Simmons, and we know Simmons sold the phone to the store. Later, out of the five dozen phones in Cash Liquidators, I happen to find a silver Nokia. The defence would make a meal of it. Don't forget that it was *you* who reminded me about continuity of evidence.

'However, on the credit side, even though there was no SIM, I'm sure we're saved by the fact that the numbers stored in the phone's memory were all kin or contacts of Morales. We've certainly got balance of probabilities, and I guess we'd have to rely on strong circumstantial. Oh yeah, and I eventually got onto Juanita's sister in the Philippines. Perhaps I should go and interview her.'

Marchant glares at the ceiling. 'If anyone's going anywhere, it'll be me. But there's one place you can go and that's back to Bournemouth. It struck me earlier after that Taylor guy rang. I did your job for you and told him his fiancée had been positively ID'd. We need more info from him about Morales' movements. We need to know how and why she came to be in Evesham. Was she messin' 'round with someone else? The good captain maybe? A bit of online adventurism that turned into playtime while hubby's at work?'

'But she—'

'No need to butt in. Figure of speech. I know she wasn't married.'

'Have we checked if she was seen in Evesham prior to her cruise? Shopping? Lunch?'

'You do the footwork, Watts. Speak to people, check debit and credit card details, check lunch-hour CCTVs.' Marchant rattles on like an industrial compressor in front of a building site – all puff, noise and a lot of hot air.

'Guv, we've missed the boat, so to speak, on half of that stuff. How are we going to find out if she was shopping or lunching or having an affair with someone one hundred miles away from where she lives?'

'You're a fuckin' detective aren't you, Watts? Remember? That's what we do. We walk the streets. We talk to people. We turn over every leaf and leave no stone unturned in our quest for truth, justice and the British way.'

Bloody hell, this guy's lost the plot. Too much superman or late night American TV.

'Yes, guv. I'll get onto it right away.'

Having canvassed Evesham businesses only days earlier, Olivia had mined nothing. This time she pumps local Filipinos for information. Three nurses, a shop assistant and a business owner's wife contribute nothing. That does not mean that they don't know Juanita; it means only that they won't admit to it. They subscribe to the unwritten law: silence is the best defence to everything. No Filipino would betray a fellow immigrant who might be overstaying their tourist or student visa.

Day by day, the likelihood fades of locating anyone who

had seen Juanita. Undaunted, Olivia enlarges copies of the photo received from Juanita's sister, considering that a better option than using the coronial photo of the deceased with its pale face and bloated cheeks, the matted hair of a Rastafarian reggae artist and smudged make-up of a young girl returning from a late night Halloween party.

With the flourish of a Royal Mail postie, she criss-crosses Evesham, calling on cafés, newsagents and supermarkets. She queries staff of clothing shops touting year-old fashions, proving that the invisible date line between London and Evesham leaves Evesham lagging a full season behind fashion trends. Staff at the public library where visitors and tourists book computers to email family and friends both in United Kingdom and overseas cannot help; nor can staff of three doctors' surgeries and the hospital.

Juanita is unknown in Evesham.

Olivia strolls to the pier where she composes a mental analysis: *Why was Juanita here if she knew no-one? Could she have been dumped somewhere upstream? If Barry Simmons is the favoured suspect, why, in such a busy setting as his boat, had no one seen them together?*

That is the perplexing question. *I'll bet Marchant's obsession with Simmons' guilt means that he hasn't thoroughly checked alibis.* Olivia remembers from the ticket stub fiasco that Simmons had no passenger inventory. That doesn't erase the possibility of his recognising local passengers. She would need only one to verify that Simmons had piloted his craft all evening and had not been seen with Juanita. *Eliminate the innocent to find the guilty.*

Olivia returns to the office and unravels her unproductive morning.

'Surely someone's seen her,' Marchant rants.

'Have you checked with Simmons about a passenger list?'

'Sergeant Watts. What I've checked and what I haven't is not for you to question. What do *you* propose to do next?'

'Inspector. I'm finding it increasingly difficult to work with you. We are supposed to be working together on this case. Pooling resources. I ask a simple question about the information to date and you treat me as if I'm questioning your integrity. I'm working hard on this too, and my interest in passengers who were on the cruise on the night of the fourteenth is relevant to the suggestion I was about to make. I—'

'Have you finished, Watts?'

'No I haven't. You claim Simmons is the prime suspect, yet we cannot conclusively tie him to the murder of Morales, let alone both girls. The sooner we either link him or clear him, the sooner we can widen our horizons and broaden our search parameters. I am sure that Trevor Taylor knows more than he is letting on, but you seem to be limiting my enquiries to your own agenda. I'm just about jack of this, and just about up for a transfer. Now, do you wish to share any information about Simmons' passengers?'

'Let us acknowledge, Sergeant Watts, that I am the supervising officer here, and I will not be challenged on the direction I choose to lead an enquiry. If you think you can do better, go right ahead.'

'Fine.' Again, Olivia rushes from the office with welling tears. She reaches the sanctuary of her car, drives out of the station car park and five hundred metres along the road props in a 'No Standing' zone. She explodes like an over-inflated balloon. Her vocal roar and outpouring obscenities, amplified by the cluster of commercial buildings, resonates through her mind like a street busker's thumping beat box: *That fucking bastard. The work I do for him and he treats me like shit. All I did was ask a simple question. I could have interviewed Simmons and found out if there was anyone he knew on the craft. I know what Marchant's all about. He just doesn't want to be outdone by anyone. But that's not my style; I'm just looking at the wider picture and trying to nail the bastard who killed two women.*

He's the same as my father was when he got lost going to my Auntie's place. Dad would never open a street directory. Come to think of it, a couple of my boyfriends had the same affliction. Do they think they're above looking in a street directory? Thank goodness for GPS. It's remodelled a whole generation.

Anyway, dad's parked at the side of the road, scratching his head and swivelling his neck at street signs and signposts. I piped up, "Dad, I know the way. If you turn right at the next traffic lights, that'll take us to a petrol station where we turn right again then it's only one street away."

Dad didn't believe that an eight-year-old kid could come up with the right directions, but I knew, because all a kid does when they're out in a car is look out the window. An adult is looking at roads, traffic, the speedo, and crapping on to the passenger. Dad was always talking to mum about the last case he'd solved; how he was going to get a promotion and all the time he was talking he had one hand on the steering wheel and the other under her skirt.

Gee, I was so naïve; there I was in the back seat with gloves on in the cold of winter. I thought dad didn't have gloves so he kept his hand warm in mum's dress. And those little groans mum stifled. Uh, yuk.

But dad yelled at me when I was only trying to help. "Olivia, you don't know what you're talking about. I'm driving the car; you don't need to say anything. Haven't I ever told you that children are meant to be silent and not seen?" Bloody hell, he didn't even know *how to recite a simple proverb.*

Now *what am I on about? I've just been crapped off at work; I'm sitting in a car on the side of the road, bawling my eyes out and talking to myself about my dad and his peculiar antics. Marchant's no different. Wants to rule the roost. Well that's okay by me because I have my own roost. I'm going home, packing a bag and then heading off to nail Taylor. This time I'll have him on a plate and I'll make Marchant squirm. Then he'll squirm even more when he reads my resignation.*

Four mascara-blackened tissues later, Olivia drives home, makes a proper pot of tea – teabags will not suffice – and packs a bag of personal necessities. Focused on locking the building's front door, she does not notice a red Peugeot parked across the road, and does not see its driver crouching inconspicuously in the front passenger seat.

Olivia is a cauldron of boiling emotion as she merges into M5 traffic at Worcester. Law-abiding citizens dutifully obeying a ten miles-per-hour roadwork limit do not help soothe her demeanour. Marchant has penetrated her thin veneer of resistance, prompting her to adopt the 'I'll show him' revenge, rather than step back and calmly resolve their professional indifference. Now, fuelled with keen desire, nothing will inhibit Olivia's resolve to acquire the necessary proof to incriminate Taylor.

Heading the plan is the need to accept that marching out of the office in a huff will, in all likelihood, result in serious disciplinary action. She cannot rely on the feeble excuse of 'personal difficulties' as a reason for deliberately abandoning her shift. That is essentially what she has done. AWOL. She acted irrationally, and withdrew into herself thinking only of proving her point against Marchant. But she hasn't finished with him. She intends to see this through to its conclusion – no matter what.

She phones Marchant: 'Inspector, it's Olivia. I've just come down with a severe stomach cramp. Women's problems. I've got to get home, so I won't be in for the rest of the day. I'll phone you in the morning.'

Marchant's response stuns her: 'Okay Liv, take it easy. Bye.'

That was it. He either doesn't care, or places little value on Olivia's contribution.

With the horizon razed of commitment, Olivia maps out the afternoon. To aid passage through dangerous territory, she plans to resurrect her flirtatious honey pot persona with the proviso that she'll stop short of blatant submission. Olivia's ability to control a male simply by sexual innuendo is masterful. Ironically, the attribute has not been consciously developed – it is merely a consequence of her continually being 'hit on' by fellow colleagues. She finds it easier to pacify them with subliminal hypnosis: to have them believe that one day they will join her in the spider's lair. What she does not know is that Amy Anderson had embodied those very same characteristics in her approach to Taylor.

The Gloucester exit siphons off crawling traffic, leaving Olivia's Reliant – built in opposition to motorways – struggling to maintain even sixty of the 70 miles-per-hour limit. No Reliant driver has ever been ushered to the roadside by an over-zealous traffic officer surreptitiously working motorways by hiding behind bridges and overpasses from where he targets vehicles with his laser speed recorder, and then moments later destroys the poor motorist's evening or weekend by slipping through their window a £100 fine. For Olivia those days are far behind. The red Peugeot is not.

Under the mid-afternoon sun, Olivia parks in front of

Trevor Taylor's home, hoping to save valuable hours waiting for him to return from work. Her wish is granted, for most tradies honour POETS day – their acronym for Piss Off Early, Tomorrow's Saturday.

Contrasting her previous visit, she proposes to hide nothing. This is official. She flicks on her mobile phone voice recorder and walks confidently to the front door. Knocks twice. Checks her bra to ensure the pepper spray canister is concealed. It is a losing battle, for there is little in her bra to compete with the can.

From the red Peugeot parked nearby, Marg Hegarty regards the scene.

Trevor opens the front door with a welcoming, 'Hello.'

'Olivia Watts, Detective Sergeant. I suppose you remember me?'

''course I do. You found my fiancée. What can I do for you?'

'A few more words, Mr Taylor. If you don't mind.'

'I don't mind. Always happy to help those who've helped me, though finding my fiancée dead wasn't really that much help. Have you found her murderer yet?' Taylor beams the amicable look of having been touched by God. The sinless smile that confirms God lives within – *I can do no wrong; I'm here to help you with whatever you want.*

Olivia could not know that Taylor had not spoken with God or held His book since attending compulsory religious instruction lessons some twenty-five years' earlier. 'Perhaps I could come in for a moment.' She follows Trevor into the reception room, eyes drifting around the walls. No change since her previous visit. *At least he could have cleaned up.*

'We need to contact Miss Morales' next of kin. Do you have her parents' contact details?'

'They'd be in Juanita's phone. I've never needed the numbers, but I know the family address in Cebu in the Philippines. Hell, I'm still so shook up about it.'

'I'm sure you are. Is her mobile phone here?'

'You asked me that last time. Like I told you, I haven't seen it, not that I've been looking for it you know. She used to leave it on the table, so I suppose she would have taken it with her when she went out.'

'Perhaps you could ring it for me now so we can listen for it.' Olivia suggests this as a subtle means of obtaining Juanita's number. She has no doubt the number is stored in Trevor's phone, and has no doubt that that number will correspond exactly with that of the silver Nokia stored in the Property Office.

'Yeah, sure.' Trevor grabs his phone and selects a pre-programmed number. 'Turned off or out of area.'

'Just let me jot down the number. We can try to trace it later on.'

Trevor volunteers the Virgin Mobile number.

'Trevor. Outside on the front step, you asked if we had found your fiancée's murderer.'

'Yeah, right. I think I should be able to be told what's going on. I mean, we were going to be married. It's been nearly a week and still I'm no better off with knowing what happened to her and why. I even rang your guv and all he told me was that the investigation's ongoing, whatever that's supposed to mean. I am a taxpayer, you know.'

Olivia sighs. *Here we go again. The age-old justification for lambasting public servants, politicians, police and anyone else whose salary is drawn from the public purse. We pay your wages so why haven't you got a result? Why aren't you out there chasing murderers and sex offenders instead of raising revenue with speed cameras and on-the-spot fines for this, that and the other?*

Olivia ignores his underlying gripe. 'Yes. There is information we can give the next of kin, but unfortunately, as you were not married, there's very little we can pass on – I seem to recall my inspector saying as much. We do have a strict protocol of first informing family or relatives. And my inspector's correct in saying the investigation continues. You have told us that to your knowledge, Juanita knew no one in Evesham or even beyond Bournemouth. That's mainly why I'm here, so we can gather as much information as possible about Juanita's movements and about her friends. That aside, what makes you think she was murdered?'

'Well… I just thought… I mean, being in Evesham and all… in the river, she didn't go there by herself. She wouldn't drown herself.'

'I can't understand why you would think such a thing. We've never said she *drowned*; only that she was found in the river.'

'If she wasn't swimming when you found her, she must have drowned. Do you think I'm stupid? Anyway, if we're going to talk like this, I think I'll get my solicitor.'

Olivia steps back. *Solicitor? Who calls a solicitor unless they're worried about something?* 'No need Mr Taylor. It's just a casual enquiry for identification. I didn't come here to stress you at this sad time. I offer you my condolences and thank you for your time.'

'I'm sorry too. I just miss her so much. I put two and two together I suppose. Someone turns up dead just like that and you think the worst. I guess it's just natural.'

The word 'natural' ricochets in Olivia's mind. Taylor's demeanour is an antonym of natural. A bunch of helium-filled balloons masquerading as unasked questions follow Olivia from the property.

19

Doodling hieroglyphics on a notepad, Marg Hegarty watches Olivia stroll, glum faced, to her car. She'd lagged behind the clipped-wing Reliant Robin for three hours, playing a hunch that sooner or later, DS Watts would lead her to a gold mine of information. She ruminates: *Why are we here? What for? Is she on a day off, visiting family? Is she attending a seminar of some sort under her own steam? Is the constabulary so short of vehicles that they'd actually expect her to fulfil duties using her own private vehicle? Or is it a 'pool' car? Surely, no one would still own one of those things unless they were a collector of strange and peculiar advances in British industry? – assuming, of course, that the Reliant Robin was considered an advance.*

Marg has already breached the Editor's Code of Practice, and will, given the right circumstances, breach it even further. She is ill-equipped to handle anything other than cordial interviews, but then again, no one foresees their interview turning sour. In rare cases of the public turning to aggression, it is usually a camera operator who takes the brunt of abuse.

Marg knows nothing of Taylor, but surmises from the case Olivia is working, that he is either a suspect or witness. There can be no other justification for a detective to invest over six hours travel, thereby suggesting to Marg that someone other than Simmons is of interest. And now, her reward awaits – a guaranteed front page lead.

She retraces Olivia's steps to Taylor's door. Knocks. Fans her face. Tries to settle her nerves.

Trevor answers, expecting Olivia's encore. On seeing the middle-aged woman, his smile creases into an inquiring frown.

'Yes?'

'Oh hi. I didn't want to disturb you while you had company. I'm Marg Hegarty from the *Evesham Record* and I'm hoping you can help me with some information about the woman found at Evesham.'

Trevor stands mute after coupling her name with the reporter who had sat behind him at the Rose and Thorn. With no enquiry as to how she had located him, he responds only with: 'I got nothin' to say to the papers.'

'Does that mean you do know something, but maybe you're just a bit reluctant or untrusting to say anything?'

'*The woman* you so callously refer to was my fiancée.'

'Oh, I am sorry.'

Taylor reconsiders. Perhaps she does have information about Juanita. Perhaps she's discovered that he'd been present in the pub on the night of Amy's death. Those scenarios change his perspective. 'Okay, come in, but only for a while. I have to go out soon.'

'Thank you. I won't trouble you for too long.'

Marg replicates the same reaction – the craning neck and scanning eyes – as had Marchant and Watts on their first visit. She follows Taylor to the reception room and sinks into the uncluttered end of the worn settee.

Marg poses a question to pinpoint his position: 'You've

been questioned by the police in relation to the missing woman, sorry, your fiancée, in Evesham?'

'Huh? You mean you don't know what's going on? No one's missing. My fiancée was found dead in the river.'

'The police are reluctant to confirm any details until positive identification. However, our information is that they have attended here and spoken to you. It therefore follows that you are either able to confirm the deceased's identity, which you've just done, or, they consider you a suspect. That compounds their problem, because there is already a suspect: the proprietor of a boat charter service in Evesham.'

Taylor receives this as good news because, despite his unproductive research trip to Evesham, he's been unable to scrounge any case developments. He calms, knowing that attention focused on another person must dilute interest in him. Without telegraphing his elation, he coolly replies: 'I don't know anything about any boat or charter service. But obviously, if someone's under investigation, then I am interested.'

Marg exhausts information gathered from the Rose and Thorn and from Simmons himself. She continues with her friendly, non-business approach: 'But if you're also a suspect it seems that the police will leave no stone unturned to break your story. They'll interview you in a calm and shrewd manner because they'll expect you to hide facts. They'll gain your confidence and side with your explanation or version of events, all the while steering you to a position of doom, to the trapdoor where you fall into a room of loaded questions that no amount of defending, back-pedalling or diversion will save you. If you give the wrong answer, you're gone. What we need to do is give them something that proves conclusively that you have no knowledge of your fiancée's disappearance and that you have never been to Evesham. Can we do that?'

Taylor recognises deceit beneath her empathetic attitude. He's used it many times. *She knows something. Bitch is carrying an ace up her sleeve. That's why she's here: get the story and take it straight to the cops. We'll see about that.*

Just as winter's snap melts to spring, Trevor's iciness thaws from tension to fervour. 'Well, I think we can. There must be something I can contribute. Like a drink?'

'No thanks. I'll be driving back soon.' But she quickly changes her mind, choosing to accept the offer to prolong her visit. 'Oh, okay. I'll be right if I stick to a small one.'

Taylor retreats to the kitchen and returns with two large glasses of Bailey's Irish Cream. 'Small enough?' he asks as he passes Marg the silky alcoholic liqueur.

Apprehensive of his guest's motives, Taylor plans to extract from her every detail of the police investigation. He believes she possesses a swag of information, and fears the consequences of her knowledge.

Marg gulps the drink as if she were downing a milkshake. She looks to Taylor: 'What sort of work do you do? How long have you lived here? How did you meet your fiancée?'

Taylor replies slowly and deliberately as Marg's eyelids waver and flutter like a threatened butterfly. She slumps low into the settee. Taylor utters a few more words, satisfying himself that Marg has entered the realm of unconsciousness.

She closes her eyes to Trevor John Taylor, Barry Simmons, the *Evesham Record* and the investigative world of journalism. She enters the deep sleep of anaesthesia. A world of no gravity and no movement. A world of unawareness, screened by a black curtain drawn across the faint flickering of what once was. A world that whether round or flat would surely impress Doctor Groenweld.

The no-prescription sedative he dropped into her drink had been easily sourced through three clicks on the internet. Taylor sits, engrossed in her catatonic gaze of helplessness and vulnerability. He thrives on the elation of holding supreme power over a person. Control. The ability to fulfil his desires under the artificial aphrodisiac of domination fuelled by suppressed anger.

A pang of sexual desire zips through him. He strokes Marg's face as he had Juanita's only one week earlier. Yearnings swell within him. He wonders why arousal burns deep. Marg isn't physically appealing, although her complexion does belie her forty-four years. But she is there. For the taking. *She'd never know if I gave her a bit of a quickie as a send-off.* He looks at her shirt, gaping across her breasts; a hint of white bra gleaming like powdered snow resting upon a wheel of potter's clay. He leans down and undoes a button. Then he ejaculates. Involuntarily. Embarrassingly. The sexual stimulus was not precipitated by thoughts of the act itself; it was the power. The heightened moment of fulfilment attained by exercising the ultimate dominance – the act of killing.

Taylor has no doubt that he can kill a person in his own home. There will be bodily discharges and the body itself to dispose of, but that won't present an insurmountable problem. A crime of opportunity. Silently. Professionally. Permanently. His brain transmits only single words. Do. It. Now. Who would ever know?

At many pubs he'd dropped tablets into drinks and invited himself to the girl's home, but never stayed long enough to see her wake. If she did. He'd have his fun: inhaling her unconscious moans and whispers and moulding her lifeless limbs into shapes of submission. The poor girl would not have a clue what was going on, what indignities she was suffering, or in fact if she was suffering at all.

This time he dropped ten tablets into Marg's drink. The effect of 10 milligrams of Hypnodorm was instant. And like any medication, symptoms are affected, and often magnified, by the presence of alcohol and other medications. Taylor has no knowledge of what, if any, other medications Hegarty might have ingested that morning. He can't imagine her taking The Pill or similar contraception; she may have taken tablets for blood pressure, headaches or even chilblains. Taylor does not care. He is on a high and has to act.

He bounces into the kitchen and removes a carton from his sparse pantry. Leaning over Marg, he unrolls the cling wrap and winds it around her head like a Sikh winding on a turban. He winds lower than a turban, straight across Marg's peaceful face. An air bubble forms beneath her nose, rising and falling like an artificial lung resuscitating an ailing patient. Her body twists in manic contortions. Limbs jerk in slow motion as if she were Judy taking a hiding from Punch in a carnival sideshow.

Taylor reaches over the coffee table, grabs his phone and presses 'video'. He props it against a stained coffee mug and records Marg's plight: arms waving, legs thrusting back and forth, the air pocket in the cling wrap slowly flattening. Agony slides from her face, contorting features like a stocking mask distorting the identity of a bank robber. He winds the wrap, tighter and tighter until blood vessels burst through unreleased pressure. His mind snaps back 20 years to the time he circled the village maypole, winding streamers around a terrified six-year-old girl as he lashed her to the pole.

The wrap muffles her plea for life. Marg departs the world as an Egyptian Mummy with a crystal head.

20

JOHN TAYLOR HAD contemptuously ignored his brother's morning text. Wiped it from his phone. Jettisoned it into cyberspace.

Like most people trapped in anger's clutch, John's spirit mellows with the passing hours. Silence's sentence is a consequence of the brothers' frequent discords – but a handshake and beer apology epitomise the national antidote to animosity. On the way home from work John visits his brother.

He taps on Trevor's front door and waits an inordinate amount of time before noticing the reception room's curtain swish to one side. A silhouette shrinks beside the rustle.

He pounds again, opens the letter flap and shouts, 'Come on Trev, I know you're in there.'

Trevor opens the door. Feigns surprise: 'Shit John, what're you doing here?'

'Sorry mate. Wanted to patch things up.' John edges past his brother and into the hallway. 'What the... who's she? What ya done here? Fuckin' hell Trev', what ya done this time?'

'It's not what you think, John. Was just a small disagreement. I tried to quieten her and she became, er, permanently quietened.'

'Fuck me Trev'. I'm outa here.'

'Come on little brother. I need your help with this.'

'I can't do nothin' for ya. Don't even know why I came 'round. Who is she? How'd she get here?'

'I don't know. Car I suppose.'

From Hegarty's bag Trevor plucks a set of car keys. A dangling Siamese cat lucky charm flashes a digital time check: 15:37. He spins around to the front window, points the key outside and presses remote unlock. A red Peugeot winks from the kerbside.

John looks at the handbag and then to Trevor. 'Okay. Let me think about this. Who the fuck is she an' where the fuck's she from?'

Trevor stalls. 'Marg something or other from a newspaper. She was talking to me about those murders in Evesham.'

'And of course you don't know anything about them, do you?' John grabs her bag and pulls out a clip of business cards. '*Evesham Record*, Industry Estate, Evesham. Where the fuck's that?'

'It's in the Midlands, sort of West Midlands, in Worcestershire, you know that Worcestershire Sauce stuff…'

'Fuck Worcestershire Sauce, you idiot. I thought you didn't know nothin' about those murders, but now you know where fuckin' Evesham is?'

'The coppers told me, didn't they, when they found Juanita. I looked it up. You don't think I don't care enough about where my poor fiancée was dragged out of some Godforsaken river?'

'Forget it. We gotta get rid of this bitch. I tell ya what we're gonna do. Get that shit off her face, wash that fuckin' glass properly, wipe this bag all over with that Spray 'n' Wipe shit, an' then we gonna carry her out to her car together as if we're walking her 'cause she's pissed. Got it?'

'Yeah. What do I do first? Just kidding, just kidding.'

'Then you're gonna drive her car to Evesham and park the car in the back of her fuckin' office and I'll put my neck on the line and drive you back in my car. Okay?'

'Yeah, sure. Sounds fair to me.'

John rifles through the handbag, pockets £60.00 and throws the bag to Trevor.

Darkness envelopes the street before Trevor and John walk Marg's limp body to her car. Anyone watching would think she is a football player with a broken ankle being assisted from the pitch. Trevor jumps into the driver's seat, slams it back until it clunks against the stop, and drives off.

His shirtsleeve drips with perspiration wiped from his brow. He shifts irritably in the seat, trying to free himself from the grip of clothes saturated with nervous sweat. Fifty metres along the road, he cranes his neck from side to side, continually checking the rear-vision mirrors for police. Trevor has not rehearsed a plan to absolve himself should such a confrontation occur, but he sure as hell knows that John, who is following, will turn up the radio and keep driving. He fishes his phone from his jeans pocket and taps John's number.

His brother's voice is indecipherable above the traffic noise and whining differential of Marg's high-mileage Peugeot.

'John, it's Trev. Can you hear me?'

'Just. What now?'

'This is shitting me. What if we get pulled over?'

'We won't if you just act normal.' John adds: 'If that's possible.'

Trevor drops the phone as he swerves to avoid a car in front of him – one of many piloted by drivers who indiscriminately change lanes without indicating and without regard for those whose lives they endanger. Straining to keep Marg's wallowing car steady, Trevor clamps both hands on the steering wheel, slows, and promptly regains control. John pulls alongside, mouths 'keep it cool' and then falls back into the line of traffic.

To calm his jittery nerves, Trevor lifts one hand from the steering wheel and delves into Marg's CD collection. He slips Black Eyed Peas' *The E.N.D* album into the player. He fails to recognise the analogy of the title being synonymous with his passenger's demise. For the next fifty minutes, he head-bangs along the motorway, in strict adherence of the speed limit.

As Gloucestershire's Ashchurch exit approaches, he activates the car's GPS. The stored menu glows: 'work'. Whilst Trevor remembers the way to Evesham, one touch of the Tom Tom screen plots a direct route to the *Evesham Record* car park. Twenty minutes' later, he eases into the empty parking lot, thankful to have arrived without incident. Anxious to decamp the scene, he does not waste time by transferring Marg to the driver's seat.

John, thinking more rationally, grabs a travel blanket from the back seat, makes a neat fold, and lays it over the woman.

'There ya are, Trev. If anyone comes past, they'll just think she's sleepin'. No suspicion at all. We'll be enjoying burgers at home before anyone suss's somethin's wrong.'

'Thanks for that. I don't know what I would have done without you.'

'Thanks nothin'. The best thing you can do is forget all about this and those other bitches you done. If I was you I'd be moving somewhere else 'cause somehow, sometime, the Bill's gonna catch up with ya.'

* * *

Marchant lingers in the office, sipping Jack Daniel's and glancing at the Rose and Thorn CCTV footage. Congestion smothers the identity of many patrons standing at the bar. Multi-directional views show people milling around tables and poker machines, and others appearing at toilet doors. Scenes of the car park pan through a wide-angle camera.

He flicks the remote with the ferocity of a twelve-year-old brandishing a Game Boy: shoot, bash, jump, fast, slow; hoping to spot a clear image of Simmons – the key to substantiating the blue thread connection. Half a bottle of JD later, Simmons jumps onto the screen. Simmons, standing with a group of people beside a table. Simmons, wearing the jumper or cardigan similar to the one seized from his home. Despite the constraint of black and white footage, Marchant swears the cardigan is blue. His smile nearly splits his lips after viewing the next frame: Simmons holding Amy. Could be a cuddle; could be a remonstration; could be nothing. He takes a giant gulp from his glass. *Got ya, you bastard.*

In the background Marg Hegarty holds an umbrella-covered cocktail. The Jack Daniel's primes him: *What's that all about? Who the fuck ever thought of putting a bloody umbrella in a fucking drink. You can't eat it. It does fuck all. At least with a slice of lemon, a cherry, an olive, or even a fucking worm, you can munch on the fucker. But an umbrella? Maybe some wise-guy disguised one as an IUD to give women a subliminal message that "it's on". The old hidden message trick. A sharp conscience picks up on those sort of things.*

The scene jogs his memory of Marg describing to him the brief interaction between Simmons and Amy on the night. The few notes he'd jotted on the sixteenth hide amongst indecipherable scratchings. Only now acknowledging her significance to the investigation, he vows to obtain her statement. Through experience he knows that Hegarty will insist on trading, rather than giving, information. *No rush. I'll see her first up in the morning.*

Whilst it is too late to contact Hegarty, Marchant does not consider 10.00 p.m. too late to phone Olivia. As far as he is aware, she has no nightlife or interest outside work. He imagines her baking muffins or painting her nails; reading Mills and Boon 'Sexy' series, or pampering a pet Chihuahua on a soft settee in front of a *Jeremy Kyle* episode recorded earlier in the day.

What he doesn't know is that Olivia devotes most of her social time to completing her forensic studies at Worcester University and rolling through the private investigator course. For relaxation, she completes, or half completes, newspaper crosswords. Stacks of unfinished puzzles bend a bookshelf, awaiting the day the remaining clues rush into her head. That day is far from arriving.

He also does not know that Olivia has never turned the page of a Mills and Boon, although she has followed a similar genre as evidenced by Danielle Steele, E.L. James and Jackie Collins paperbacks filling another shelf.

Olivia rolls over, stretches to her bedside table and answers the phone.

'Hi Liv, what you doing?' Marchant's perverse enjoyment of abbreviating Olivia's name hums through the phone.

'I was enjoying a nice sleep, thanks very much.'

'Good. You were dreaming about me then.'

'I said it was a nice sleep. If I was dreaming about you, I would be waking up in a psychiatric hospital. What's so important to phone me at this time?'

'Got a couple of stills of Simmons at the weed and

prickle. I know you're blind to this, but we've got him with Anderson. I've also got a witness from the local rag who may have seen her with him. We're off to interview her first up in the morn. Need you here at eight, Liv. And by the way. I think we should have an unofficial chat about your abrupt disappearance yesterday.'

'Um, yeah, okay. I'm sorry. I'll be there, but don't count your chickens and all that stuff. It's not him.'

'You're not still on that Taylor kick of yours, surely. This is it. I've got him. Told you so all along.'

'Look guv. Even though you've just woken me and I'm not thinking too straight, there's definitely something going on with Taylor. He asked me if we'd found Morales' murderer. Kind of strange isn't it, when all we've let on is that her body was found in the river? I didn't pursue that, other than to ask why he thought that way. He just said it was a natural thought. He had Morales' number in his mobile, and of course that is to be expected. But I bet if we get onto Virgin we will find that he'd made no calls to her phone on the evening she went missing. Surely, if your loved one is missing, the first thing you'd do is try to get them on the phone? And that's exactly what he said he did. Remember?'

Marchant was above sending up Olivia's comment. The 'Virgin' jokes had swept across Britain, and the world, since Richard Branson [now Sir Richard] formed Virgin Records in 1973.

'You're absolutely right, Watts. That is exactly the first thing they'd do, and it's exactly what I did yesterday when you didn't front nor answer your phone. I rang the pub and kept up my objective investigation and that's why I've now got a result. Go back to sleep and continue your dream in Fantasyland. See you in the morning.' Marchant slams down the phone before Olivia can reply.

She is unable to resume the sanctity of sleep. Like most people disturbed from the depths of dreams, Olivia cannot simply sink her head into the pillow and drop off like commuters on a train. As a young girl, she would sneak into her mother's side of her parents' bed, and snuggle into the warmth where sleep would descend upon her within minutes. Waking to her mother's soft morning kisses, Olivia remained in the warm cocoon until it was time to dress for school. The weekends were better. Her step parents would take turns tickling her until she bounded out of the bed and raced to the toilet. She'd then run back and jump in for the next round.

Such was her favourite recollection of childhood. Full of joy and surprises. No complex situations; no responsibility; no rules other than putting away toys and brushing teeth; no adults criticising, admonishing, abusing or teasing. And no Marchant.

Cherishing those memories Olivia returns to sleep.

21

Two decades earlier, Edison Edwards had joined the *Evesham Record* as a junior reporter. The wiry youth who once sported a frizz of black, unmanageable hair is now the paper's editor. And bald. He is rarely seen without his tartan trilby.

Habitually first to arrive and last to leave, he drives into the *Evesham Record's* car park at 6.20 a.m. on Saturday morning, surprised to see another vehicle isolated in the centre of the black expanse.

Saturday mornings are a three-hour think tank, commencing with Edwards chairing a round table discussion between journalists and advertising staff, and finishing with his authorising proof composites and page layouts. Edwards' Saturday morning generosity permits staff one hour's grace to their starting time – no one is required before 9.00 a.m. Most staff see the shift not as grace but as an imposition.

As one who keeps tabs on staff activities, monitoring comings and goings from his office window, Edwards struggles to recall who drives the red Peugeot. Impulse leads him to the French car where he observes Hegarty reclined in the front passenger seat: *Ah, that Marg's had a late one and decided to sleep it off.* Recalling his own youthful experiences, he believes it more productive to allow Hegarty a couple of hours kip to sleep off her intoxication. A conceited and selfish employer, the decision is not for her benefit, but for his own. Edwards leaves her be, preferring to enjoy early morning solitude as a prelude to the hectic morning. Having never developed the British custom of tea drinking, he brews a percolated coffee to share with the morning dailies.

Edison Edwards insists that every minute of his employee's working week be productive. So intent is he of quantifying his staff's output, he calculates the word content of reporters' editorials and features against their weekly salary. Their productivity must return a word rate of less than ten pence per word, meaning that each reporter must deliver a minimum of four thousand words per week. Hardly a tall order on newsworthy weeks, but during non-eventful periods the overuse of 'padding' springs from many columns.

At 9.05 a.m., Edwards stands at his mezzanine-level floor-to-ceiling windows, sipping his fourth coffee and watching words and photographs dart across computer screens. Except one. He walks to the opposite window and fumes at the sight of Hegarty still slumped in her car.

Compassion does not occupy a spot on Edwards' employer responsibilities' list. *She can sleep in her own time. We've got a deadline to meet.* He approaches her car and gasps at her pallid appearance. He raps on the window. No response. He lifts the door handles. No result. He rips out his phone and jabs 999.

A précis of the call is transmitted to a local patrol. *'Suspicious situation in* Evesham Record *car park. Possible drunk or overdose. Reported by a Mr Edwards, the company's proprietor. He'll meet you on site.'*

Two uniformed officers dispatched to the scene exchange banter about having to provide a heart-starting coffee elixir to another victim of Friday night pub-crawls. Slotting into the car park alongside Hegarty's car, the smiles dissolve from their faces. They flush as white as the cadaver, suddenly realising they have driven into a crisis and a crime scene.

PC Green takes charge while his colleague gapes at his first fatality. Green peers into Hegarty's car. All doors are locked. The keys dangle from the ignition. He thrusts his baton through the rear passenger window with skill enough to avoid showering the occupant with glass. A check of Hegarty's wrist convinces him that life is ended. He pulls the blanket over the woman taken far too early.

His training governs the next steps: call in a situation report; tape off and contain the area; and detain all witnesses. He finds no witnesses in the immediate area, save for Edison Edwards standing at the building's entrance jotting everything onto a notepad – no tablets and smart phones for the outmoded Edwards. Six cars and two motorcycles – all staff vehicles – sit on the bitumen. Green's colleague, PC Drummond, stands frozen behind the patrol car. 'Come on Drum, I need your help here. Grab the crime tape and posts will you. Give it a wide berth. I'll have a quick scout around.'

Green scans the *Record*'s two-storey offices, observing heads in windows more interested in police activities than the paper's next edition. He approaches Edwards and directs him to ensure all staff remain in the building until further notice.

Marchant sits in his office flicking through *The Sun*.

Olivia rinses the morning's coffee mugs.

Marchant snatches the phone. 'Bloody hell. I was just about to head over there to see a reporter. Be there in fifteen.'

'Olivia. Let's go. We got another one.'

This time, total silence joins the journey from Worcester

to Evesham. Marchant admonishes himself for not rejecting Llewellyn-Jones 'you've got no evidence' spiel and churns over the prospect of Simmons having committed another murder after being released without charge.

Watts churns over the prospect of Taylor having committed another murder after she'd failed to convince Marchant that Taylor should be the prime suspect. She bears guilt of having done all she could, apart from pierce Marchant's belligerent carapace.

On arrival at the scene, they acknowledge uniformed officers, limbo under the crime tape, and approach the Peugeot. At first glance, Marchant is certain that Hegarty has been dead for more than twelve hours. 'Christ, Liv. It's that reporter. Why? Where does this end? She wouldn't have been my first choice to twirl around the dance floor.'

Olivia is dumbfounded. Speechless. But only for a moment. 'Don't you ever stop? We've got a dead woman here, possibly a victim of crime, and all you want to do is turn it into a prop for your pathetic stand-up comedy routine. Have you no respect at all?'

'Come on Liv. A bit of jesting. Not going to harm anyone – least of all her.'

'You're right, it's not. I should remember to make generous allowances for your insensitivity.'

Marchant turns his back on Olivia's outburst and refolds the wrap over the deceased. A mobile phone falls from beneath the ruffled blanket. Marchant sweeps it up, slides it into his pocket and removes his own. He calls Doctor Groenweld to request his urgent attendance and then orders PC Green to extend the perimeter tapes. He looks up to see Edwards surveying the scene and scribbling notes like an enthusiastic reporter on his first assignment.

For a publisher who has worked with words for more than twenty years, he has few to offer Marchant. He cannot say when Hegarty arrived; confirming only that the car was there at 6.20 a.m., and he is unable to offer any detail of Marg's lifestyle or evening activities, other than to suggest that she lived 'in isolation'. That means little to Marchant. Isolation from whom or what?

She had not been assigned to any particular event, having during the week submitted only one item: an interview with Barry Simmons. Her desk is clear, as always, yielding no clue of current projects. Edwards produces Hegarty's personnel record and contact details. The 'Next of Kin' section notes Samantha Hegarty of Earl's Court, London. The next line reads: Spouse / partner: 'Not Applicable'.

'Take care of this will you, Liv,' says Marchant as he hands over the file.

Olivia accepts the task of delivering to Samantha the devastating news of Marg's demise. She does not mind searching electoral rolls, checking local libraries, gyms and other clubs for information of a deceased who may have exchanged fragments of their past with another member. Maybe they'd fled a partner after an abusive relationship; perhaps they'd changed a career path or moved to another county, or in Marg's case, to another newspaper. The challenge of the investigatory process means that Olivia will have to knock on a door in Earl's Court and sombrely utter the words: 'May I come inside please?'

Never has she been able to discern which is more difficult; uttering those five words, or suffering the expectant stare from the doorstep as if the relation were experiencing a delayed reaction of confirmation of news they had already gleaned from *the other side*. It is always the same. Olivia walks inside, each slow step replicating the trance-like motion of the person she follows. She takes command: 'Sit down please, Mrs Smith. Would you like a cup of tea?'

Mrs Smith couldn't give a damn about a cup of tea – she wants to know what a police officer is doing in her house. She refuses the beverage and within moments accepts a photo. It elicits no reaction.

'Mrs Smith. Is this your daughter?'

'Yes. What's happened to my baby?' Many times Olivia has faced that very question. Every woman's child is a 'baby,' no matter their age. In moments of grief and moments of joy, one's offspring is viewed only in a state of infancy.

'I have some bad news. I'm sorry to inform you that your daughter met with an accident and she's no longer with us.'

That's the soft version. In the police training academy no one ever believes that they will one day have to deliver the death message. The jokers in the academy devise their own message: *I've got some bad news for you. Your son carked it last night. Stabbed to smithereens. Twenty-eight times, not too deep though. Don't be alarmed – you won't notice when he's dressed up in the morgue.*

Olivia wishes *that* person were able to witness the avalanche of emotion, the cascading tears and fault lines etched into the face of a parent or spouse who's lost their loved one.

Within hours, Olivia will face that very situation.

22

GROENWELD DIVERTS FROM his journey between home and office, arriving at the scene forty minutes after receiving the call. He pronounces Hegarty dead at 10.17 a.m. and notes that she has been so for 15 to 20 hours. No initial evidence points to cause of death, but he marks minor trauma to the nasal passages for further examination.

Scene of Crime Officers mill around Hegarty's car, dusting for prints and lifting a number of impressions for identification. An officer kneels on the asphalt, scanning the ground beneath the car. He will not risk the career-damning prospect of evidence being located after the car's removal.

'While you're down there,' Marchant shouts.

Here we go, mumbles the SOCO officer. *The usual lewd suggestion offered to anyone found on his or her knees. Heard it all before.*

'Just run your torch under the seats. Might find something to show how the stiff offed herself.'

'You one of those psychics or something, guv?'

'No. Just naturally intelligent. Why?'

'Empty diet Coke can, business card and a couple of tissues.' The officer reaches under the seat and removes the items with a gloved hand.

'Well, come on, come on. Give it here,' Marchant grunts.

The officer passes up the Coke can.

'Not that shit. Bag the can and tissues for DNA. Give us the card.'

Marchant snatches the card. A familiar name bounces off the glossy red print: *Simmons' Scenic Cruises. Crown Meadow, Evesham.* Now he's smiling. 'Bag this as well and get prints ASAP.'

* * *

At the West Mercia Police Forensic Centre, Dr Erich Groenweld scrubs up to prepare for Marg Hegarty's autopsy. His assistant wheels the deceased alongside the operating table, grabs two corners of the plastic underlay and in a motion bordering on disrespect, hauls her from the gurney. Two medical students stand nearby, anxious to note procedures which, on every excursion, see one or more of their number faint or run from the auditorium.

The sterile theatre, stainless steel gleaming like a five star commercial kitchen, hosts an unintelligible calmness – the peaceful serenity of death. The body rests, the soul of believers having already risen to heaven or God's home of everlasting peace. There can be no transgression against the dead – until the surgeon's knife traces the first incision. Peace is violated and never again, with or without religious conviction, will the person be whole.

For Groenweld, who recently reached the century of autopsies and celebrated in the time-honoured manner of a Test Cricket batsman by waving his scalpel high in the air, Hegarty was just another job on the daily list.

He scans from head to toe, a sequential order practised

over many years that ensures no sign of foul play or natural cause escape his scrutiny. He picks off minute traces of plastic film from her left eyebrow, and detects bruised and burst nasal capillaries which he details as consistent with smothering. With the aid of a small penlight, he removes from the nasal passage two miniscule specks of plastic film of the type used in food packaging. Their location within the nose suggests that his subject had inhaled the foreign matter with short, sharp breaths immediately prior to the occlusion of the air passages. The only obvious external injury warranting investigation is post-death trauma to the underarms.

He observes similar adhesion of plastic film to hair follicles at the base of the subject's neck and instructs an assistant to take close-up photographs of the afflicted areas. They will be tendered to the foreseeable coronial enquiry and court proceedings.

From his instrument tray he removes a scalpel and slices a huge 'V' across the deceased's chest and then proceeds to harvest blood and organs for examination – minus one student, who predictably capitulated to the shock of human dissection.

Blood analysis reveals no disease or infection, but does show a blood alcohol volume of 114 mg alcohol per 100 ml of blood. Of greater concern is a strong concentrate of the drug 'Hypnodorm', a medication prescribed to those with sleep difficulties, but also prevalent among the many concoctions ingested by nightclub troopers.

Tangible evidence of a non-natural death.

As Groenweld dissects Hegarty's body, police investigators comb her car for fingerprints and bodily fluid residue. Dusted door handles return negative results. Hampering the examiner's mission is the 'proliferation of prints overlaid and smudged into one giant pattern of loops, whorls, ridges, cores and deltas,' writes Dr Richard Thomas, concluding that Edison Edwards' clammy fingers had compromised the doors.

Thomas inspects the vehicle's interior. The steering wheel has been wiped clean, as have the gear knob and indicator stalks – the common car thief's cursory effort to insulate himself from identification. Thomas's seven years in forensic service tell him that few vehicles present evidential traces on the steering wheel or doors. He philosophises that many criminals learn their craft from watching television shows such as: *The Bill*; *Midsomer Murders*; *Broadchurch* and the plethora of CSIs produced across America, testament to USA's soaring crime: *CSI: New York, CSI: Miami* and *CSI: Los Angeles*.

But Dr Thomas did not learn *his* craft from televised fiction. He could easily conclude that Hegarty had transferred to the passenger seat to ensure a comfortable sleeping position. In so doing, she would have had no reason to slide back the driver's seat to its limit. Therefore, he deduces, someone with legs longer than the deceased's had driven the car to its resting location. In moving the seat, the driver had left a clear thumbprint on the seat adjustment lever.

Thomas collects further evidence. He lifts fingerprints, most of which are perfect specimens, from CDs scattered on the front seat, and from one in the player. As a final coup, he extracts a perfect thumbprint from the GPS touch screen.

In his laboratory, he examines four independent sets of prints. After excluding Hegarty's, he analyses the remaining sets to hopefully identify the car's most recent driver. That objective is not straightforward. To match prints with those recorded on file assumes the suspect's prints have previously been entered into the police database, either as an offender or a person logged for purposes of security and identification.

Dr Thomas runs an elimination program. Two sets are not recorded. The computer flags an alarm on matching the third set – Simmons, Barry Andrew. Whilst Simmons has never been in trouble with police, his prints, along with those of all service personnel, have been loaded on the police database for identification purposes in case of casualty during armed conflict.

Marchant's phone vibrates across his desk.

'I said no calls,' he remonstrates to a young constable. 'Can't you see I'm snowed under with these fuckin' stiffs turning up all over the place!'

'I think you'll want this call, sir. It's a Dr Thomas from forensic.'

Marchant raises his brows in hope that the good doctor will be sharing a result. He grabs the phone and beams relief upon hearing that a set of fingerprints has been identified.

'We're in the money,' breaks Marchant into a discordant jingle. He gives up when six of his colleague's hands simultaneously clasp against their ears. 'Let's see if he gets out of this one.' He punches a victory fist into the air and beckons his team to his office.

'Listen up guys. I've just had confirmation that a set of fingerprints belonging to one Barry Andrew Simmons has been lifted from Marg Hegarty's car. As you all know, she was found dead in her vehicle. Of further interest is that she died by asphyxiation, not in the same manner as the Morales woman but by plastic film either held to her nose or across her face. We now have five independent scores of evidence against Simmons.

For those of you who were enjoying a Saturday sleep-in, I'd like you to know that I found one of Simmons's business cards on the floor of the deceased's vehicle. (Marchant shamelessly withholds the SOCO officer's contribution.) Of course, there may be a perfectly good reason for that, but unless and until we can establish that, it joins the steaming pile of shit we've got against him.

'The other points are photographs from the Rose and Thorn and the contents of Hegarty's note book, which I later confirmed with the pub barman, who, incidentally, will identify Simmons as having been in the pub at the relevant time.'

'I don't think he ever denied being there,' chips in Olivia.

'Give it up, Watts. Now, if I may continue, we'll do this by the book and arrest our illustrious captain first up in the morning. Before you lot clear off for the day, I want to run a quick briefing. Where's Stanton? Off with the fairies?'

'Yep,' calls a voice from the back of the room. 'He's taken his wand and gone for a leak.'

'One of you guys, get him here *now*! And Watts, you in on this, or are you still up in the clouds about Simmons being innocent?'

'I'd like to keep an open mind, guv.'

'Can't be much more open than it is now. Whatever was in there's evaporated. So let's get on with this. We'll bring Stanton up to speed when he glides into the office.

'What we've got is three murders within a bloody week. All different MOs. First, we got the Morales woman, who was found on the riverbank at Evesham. Cause of death asphyxiation. We've got Barry Simmons in the vicinity, both in time and location; we can be reasonably sure that Morales was on the craft on Sunday the fourteenth. DS Watts will bear with me that his attitude was, to say the least, cagey. But we got the best line on him due to a public-spirited Brett Davies stating that he saw Simmons pocket a phone that he, Davies, gave him after finding it on the deck of Simmons' cruise ship or barge or whatever the fuck it is.' Marchant's recitation of Brett Davies' statement reminds him of his own actions at the *Evesham Record* car park. He drops his hand against his pocket and feels the distinctive shape of a mobile phone. Someone else's.

'Inspector, don't forget I wasn't privy to your initial meeting with Simmons.'

'Not a problem, Watts, because anything you missed there, well, we covered it in the Record of Interview, didn't we.'

'With respect, sir, if I didn't hear the first interview, how the heck would I know if I missed anything?'

'Watts. You know the drill. You will only be corroborating the ROI, and only then if necessary. We've got so much on Simmons; he'll probably plea to the lot or try to swing a deal with that friggin' Rupert the friggin' bear. Now if I can continue –'

'So you've totally ruled out Taylor?'

'What is it with this Taylor infatuation? The guy's lost his fiancée and you want to slot him for it?'

Olivia douses temper's flames before protesting: 'I'm not eager to "slot him" but I believe we're premature with Simmons. Nothing adds up. There's no motive and there's no common thread.'

'Well there is a common thread, and that's what we got on Simmons for the Anderson girl knifed in Swan Lane. A thread from his bloody gay cardigan for goodness' sake. Talking about gay, where is that bloody Stanton?'

'Probably waxing his legs, sir,' a young DC weighs in.

'Inspector. I'm really trying to be respectful here, but I wonder if we're really being objective enough? There were no prints on the knife—'

'Come on Watts, the guy's wise. Wore a glove.'

'—we've got no motive, nor have we for Morales for that matter, but we do have Taylor, who lives one hundred bloody miles away, identified at the scene.'

'Just blown your own theory, Watts, because Taylor was not identified at the river, or implicated at all in his fiancée's demise.'

'Doesn't mean he wasn't there, though,' Olivia snaps.

'What now?' Marchant yells into his phone. 'Well you tell me doctor, what the fuck's Hypnodorm? They play football in those things don't they?'

'Think you'll find that's hyperdome.'

'So the stuff's a sedative? For insomnia? Right doc, thanks for that.'

Marchant replaces the phone and leans against the edge of his desk. Pensive. 'Now where were we? Look, that was Groenweld. Seems our intrepid reporter took an overdose of sleeping pills. The doc's not finished yet; just wanted to get that info to us ASAP. That doesn't affect tomorrow's operation. Remember, Simmons' prints are on her car and that, in the circumstances, makes her death suspicious. So, this is what we're going to do. The four of us, including you DC –, er, who are you again, sorry DC Lane, yes, the four of us – shit, afternoon Stanton – I was just saying, four of us are going to Evesham to arrest Simmons for three murders. Be here at six sharp; we'll wake him while he's dreaming about some bloody sea shanty. Watts. You up to this?'

197

'I've said what I believe and I'll say it again; I don't think we've got enough on him.'

'Well, I'll say this again DS Watts. We've now got plenty, and we'll have even more after I've interviewed him. If you don't agree, maybe you can get a job with Llewellyn-fucking-Jones.'

In the silence and privacy of his office, Marchant retrieves the mobile phone from his pocket. A yellow filament inside a light bulb glows as a screen saver. He scans the menu. Could be anyone's. But of the twenty-five numbers, none remotely identify with newspapers or media services. He presses last number redial.

'Hello. John here.'

Marchant jumps at the instant answer. 'Uh, sorry. Think I got the wrong number. Who's that?'

'John. John Taylor. Who's that?'

Marchant jams his thumb on 'end call'. *Holy fuck. What the hell's going on here?*

He turns off the phone and throws it to the back of his drawer.

John Taylor hates being hung up on. He's had his fill of telemarketers phoning at meal times – landline or mobile, they get him either way – trying to sell electricity plans, phone and internet deals, holiday plans, insurance, wills and health care – the list goes on. And then there are the donation seekers for this charity and that. 'Sorry, not interested,' he politely replies.

But no way does the insistent caller accept that. No. They've been groomed – brainwashed with auto-responses – to object to everything but an order. 'Wait 'til you hear what we've got for you. You could be missing out.'

'I'm happy with the service I'm getting, thanks. Gotta go.'

'Sure you can't—'

At that juncture John slams down the phone, or presses end call (but not before adding a barrage of expletives) checks his phone menu to see if the incoming caller listed their number and if so, calls back the company to complain to a supervisor. All well and good in theory, until the supervisor unwinds the very same spiel as parroted by the original caller. Dead loss. Another hang up.

This time John checks the caller's identity and recognises the number. Double checks it. Trevor's. *What the fuck. He's got a nerve hanging up on me after all I've done for him over the past few days.*

He calls Trevor's number: *The number you are calling is in use or out of area.*

Fearing another catastrophe, he scoots around to Trevor's home and screeches to a halt across his drive.

Trevor bounds from the front door: 'Hi John. What's the rush?'

'What's the go, phoning me and hanging up?'

'Couldn't be me. Lost me bloody phone, didn't I?'

'Well someone's found it and they just rang me and hung up. I thought you was in trouble. Again! So where the fuck did you lose the phone?'

'If I knew that I would have gotten it back by now, don't ya reckon? I think it's in that newspaper bitch's car. I dropped it when some ass-wipe crossed into my lane. Tried to pick it up, but couldn't reach it, then in all the commotion when we got to Evesham, well, I just plain forgot it.'

'Fuck me. You know what that means, don't you?'

''course I do. Gotta buy a new one, don't I? Had some good stuff on it too. Reckon I could have anonymously uploaded the glad-wrapped head onto You Tube.'

'Shit Trevor. Don't you ever think? How come you can wire a 50-room mansion, but when it comes to your own wiring, you're just fucked in the head? You know who's got your phone? The bloody coppers, that's who. They found it when removing the stiff, then later on they check to see if it belongs to her. Of course it doesn't. So what do they do? The old last number redial trick, and bingo – *my* fucking phone rings.

'Pretty soon the Bill will be on to me, but maybe even before that, they'll be onto you after getting your details from Vodafone or BT or Virgin or whatever you're on.'

Trevor looks nonplussed. 'Guess I'd better start working out some answers for 'em.'

23

At 6.55 on the late summer morning, Marchant, Watts, Stanton and Lane park fifty metres into the narrow dead-end street. Crisp leaves, fallen during a period of confused seasons, litter the bitumen while sunbeams slither over chimney pots, weaving their way between twisted television antennas and satellite dishes. A jogger shuffles by, dragging a plume of condensation. A postman-allergic kelpie heels at the gateway of his master's home, snapping loud and fierce, forcing the jogger to cross to the other side of the road.

Marchant and his team, dressed in fluorescent orange vests, clamber out of their vehicles and scamper to Simmons' front fence. A neighbour wrapped in a pink dressing gown cowers as she picks up the morning paper from her front yard.

On this day, Marchant follows implicitly the letter of the law, not wanting to subject himself to Rupert Llewellyn-Jones bellowing about illegally executing a warrant. At precisely one minute after seven Marchant heaves three swift kicks into Simmons' front door.

'What the hell? a voice hollers from inside.

'Search Warrant, Captain Simmons.' Marchant passes the document through the now open door.

Stanton and Olivia rush inside as DC Lane, a qualified computer technician, zeroes in on Simmons' computer which sits in a study alcove compressed beneath the stairs. He powers on the desktop case and runs a program through the hard drive, checking all file formats, particularly those deleted in recent weeks.

Forensic technicians have the programs, and ability, to recover files users think have been obliterated by Microsoft's Recycle Bin and permanent deletion programs. The gurus know that deleting programs from a computer is like swishing away remnants of evening meals down the sink. There will always be telltale evidence clinging to the grease trap, just as remainders of bad friendships and attempts at manipulating family photographs for humorous birthday cards remain deep in the core of every hard drive. The computer's owners defend sensitive deletions: 'I was just looking,' or 'I was trying to monitor my kids' searches,' or the honest John: 'my pornography interests change weekly.'

But there is nothing of interest on Simmons' computer.

Stanton mopes around the kitchen like John Inman in a scene from *Are you being Served?* He looks in the freezer, under the kitchen table and behind picture frames. Marchant takes him to task: 'What the fuck are you looking for, Stanton?'

'Anything that's not obvious, guv. Many a clue has been found in a freezer.'

'So have you found a body in there?'

'No guv. That would be *too* obvious.'

Marchant shakes his head and walks upstairs.

Kitchen completed, Stanton opens the bathroom door and steps back as a musty odour assails his nostrils. *Talk about rising damp.* A dripping shower rose paints a brown, rusty stem down the head of the bath; four or five towels reek foetid dampness, and the toilet bowl inspires Stanton to hum the Christie hit 'Yellow River'. Sitting askew on the wall next to a grimy window, a shaving cabinet hides behind its crazed mirror. Stanton prises open the mirror door and inspects the damp contents: shaving brush and lather, nail clippers, comb, Dr Scholl Corn Pads, a faded blue pack bearing the smudged words 'Hypnodorm' and a four pack of Tesco medicated soap.

As he picks up the Hypnodorm packet with his lace-trimmed handkerchief, Olivia pushes aside clothing in Simmons' wardrobe to reveal a stack of cardboard boxes.

The wardrobe doubles as a document storage centre. Olivia checks two boxes of suspension files labelled 'SSC Current Year', carelessly rummaging through folders as if they mean nothing to the investigation. She learns another valuable lesson – never take *anything* for granted, *especially* in a criminal investigation. As she flips a folder marked 'Sundry Expenses' one receipt stands out like a Geisha walking through Jerusalem's main street. A lump of disappointment clogs her throat as she acknowledges the significance of the small slip: *Cash Purchase. 1 only 8-inch Universal Handee Knife.*

'Anything of interest?' Marchant gruffs.

'Nothing out of the ordinary. Few jeans, tracksuits, jumpers from a Salvo's shop or favourite granny and a collection old admiral's uniforms. I reckon the guy was in the Village People's YMCA video.'

'Perhaps you could be a bit more serious and focus on the knitwear, Watts. Anything blue?'

'Only this cardigan I've put aside. It's about the same colour as that thread.'

'Shit. That's the prize we're looking for. Hundred to one it'll check out. Bag it, Watts. On second thoughts, first make sure it doesn't belong to Stanton. It's about his right whack.'

Olivia would love to say, *bag it yourself*, but knows she'll regret it. Sheepishly producing the receipt, now secured in a clear evidence bag she says: 'Guv, there's also this.'

'Holy shit, Liv. We got the daily double. That's a wrap. *Now* tell me you've got sympathy for Simmons.' Marchant thrusts his palm against his forehead. 'Speaking of "wrap" we need to see if there's any of that food wrap stuff here, you know, that clingy, plastic shit. Get down to the kitchen and have a scout around. You'll have to head back to the friggin' boat too, because I'm sure there'll be some in the friggin' galley or whatever the fuck it's called.'

They bound downstairs where Simmons lounges in a plush floral settee. Stanton accompanies him on a pouffe. 'Quite at home there, sergeant?' Marchant sniggers. *Man on a pouffe with a sailor.* He continues: 'Barry Simmons, I'm advising you that we have seized this cardigan from your wardrobe.' He holds up the item: 'When did you last wear this?'

'Buggered if I know. Sometime last week maybe. Why? Do you fancy it?'

'I wouldn't be such a wise guy if I were you,' Marchant counters. 'This jumper, which you probably think transforms you into a weekend fashion icon will be analysed by our forensic team for evidence believed to be consistent with crime scene exhibits retrieved from the Rose and Thorn in Evesham.'

'Fat chance.'

'We're also taking this receipt and packet of pills. We'll speak to you about them at the station.' Marchant beams a rare smile, knowing the seized items will meet the necessary standard of proof required to convict Simmons. He has no doubt that the cardigan matches exactly the colour and type of thread that Thomas had retrieved from the knife that killed Amy Anderson.

'Barry Simmons. I'm arresting you for the murder of Amy Anderson. Other charges may follow.' He recites the legal caution and continues: 'You can get dressed and lock everything because it could be a while before you return.'

'You lot never let up do you. Back to that? Amy? I told you I don't know anything about that.'

'Just like you didn't know anything about that phone handed to you. Save it for the judge. You right now?'

'Yeah, but I want my phone call.'

'You can make it from the station. Cuff him, Stanton. Be gentle with his wrists.'

They return to Worcester where Simmons is interviewed and charged with the murders of Juanita Morales, Amy Anderson and Marg Hegarty. He offers little more than denials and vague alibi evidence. Llewellyn-Jones repeatedly interjects, recommending a one-hour delay for legal briefing. Simmons refuses, standing by his view that telling the truth politely and courteously will afford him the best chance of satisfying the police enquiry.

Llewellyn-Jones scoffs. 'Telling the truth is no guarantee to establishing innocence.'

Despite the seriousness of the charges, the interview concludes within two hours.

Simmons subsequently appears before the Worcester Crown Court and is remanded in custody until 9 November. Rupert Llewellyn-Jones's lengthy bail application fails to gain his client temporary relief. Most barristers would not even attempt to convince a judge to release into the community a person charged with three murders.

Leaving the dock, Simmons looks to the gallery, unable to discern the attitude of the few supporters – mainly business and service acquaintances – who gaze catatonically at the floor. He offers a less than confident wave. A court officer steadies his other arm and steers him from the rear of the court through a series of hallways to the holding cells. The provisional lockup evidences spoils of the day's long wait: empty polystyrene coffee cups, the contents of some which have been spilled – accidentally or in contempt of authority – over benches and walls; a screwed up newspaper; lunch wrappings; and an abandoned binder of charge documents.

Simmons directs little thought to his future – he is more concerned about his next meal. He demolished the shrink-wrapped lunch-time sandwich pack in short time, although it was hardly sufficient to sustain the nutritional and energy requirements of a teenage school student. He presumes there'll be nothing else until he is returned to prison. And he is right.

News of Simmons' court appearance and remand draw a gathering of boisterous and abusive protesters to the Worcester police station. A superintendant addresses the growing crowd but retreats as the group surges forward, chanting: *We want Simmons, we want Simmons.* With concern for their own as well as the public's safety, police command act immediately and arrange for Simmons' transfer out of the county to an undisclosed location.

He arrives at Wandsworth Prison where the cell door slams finality on his life. Perhaps all new prisoners experience the same feeling of helplessness on taking in the lifeless horizon, where concrete walls and razor wire become the new vista; coming to terms with the realisation that all things past are now lost or irretrievable; and dwelling on thoughts that question motives of legal practitioners. Simmons flops on to the bed but immediately rises to pace the floor and wade through a marsh of silence and reflection. He has no interest in the television, not even to glimpse reports of his court appearance.

Hunger escapes him. He drops his head between his knees. Turns his thoughts to bail: *Will Llewellyn-Jones find someone to support my alibi? Will legal discovery unearth facts capable of clearing my name? Will police look deeper into evidential matters?* He answers his own questions: *not bloody likely.* But he will remain optimistic. He knows he has done nothing to warrant imprisonment. He has tried all avenues to plead his innocence to police and to his own solicitor, each time crashing against barriers of non-interest.

He considers his personal losses and the family he will miss, not that he sees them often, but he now regrets having not done so. That guilt drives him to revisit the past where he hopes to repair damage inflicted on loved ones because of selfish devotion to his own pursuits. And he thinks of Felicity standing on the Southampton dock and the huge void that swallowed him shortly after.

He wonders what will happen to his business. Stalls on the thought. He owes HSBC £20,000 in repayments on a loan he'd taken out for improvements and overhauls of his craft. The bank might cut its losses and abandon the craft, leaving the council to deal with their removal, or it could try to sell the business 'as is' at a 'fire sale' price. *They'll serve notices on me for a few months, but what the hell can I do?* He succumbs to the thought of his enviable credit rating triggering warning lights on computer screens and weekly demands constantly spitting out from printers across the nation.

There is no one he can enlist to manage the operation in his absence. In all probability, it will fall to the mercy of souvenir hunters. He cringes at the thought of scavengers climbing all over his boats, unscrewing bits and ripping off pieces: *I got a piece of that Simmons boat; you know, the murderer guy. Reckon I could get a few quid for it on eBay.* He sees his life's investment as a floating carcass of marine-ply ribbing and a skeleton of iron framing left to rot and rust. *Bloody hell, I could be here for thirty years or more. I can't even plan for what I might do on release. I'll have croaked it by then, surely. Friggin' Rupert.*

The muddle of conflicting images coaxes Simmons to sleep.

Hours later, the harsh reality of incarceration fills his awakening eyes. No hopping out of bed and trotting to the kitchen to make a coffee or hot chocolate. No eggs and bacon on toast. Now, he will stand to attention at the cell door on a siren's command. He will wait until unlock before grieving in front of a bowl of soggy cereal in warm milk and, if lucky, a couple of slices of warm toast.

Prison. The hours wind into a huge lingering question mark: *How did this happen? Why didn't police look at all the evidence? Why did Llewellyn-Jones brush me off as if nothing I said was true?* For Barry Simmons, declarations of innocence mean nothing apart from added stress. Although the prospect of appeal hovers, the process could stretch beyond twelve months.

A four metre by three-metre concrete enclave replaces his former stately home. No conveniences other than a small basin, stainless steel toilet and a magazine-sized television. His three small meals, claimed nutritionally sound by Health Department academics, have presumably never been taste-tasted by their assessors. The spattering of pleasant meals comprise generic ingredients sourced from supermarket 'end of line' shelves and clearance bins.

Requests for paper and stationery to pursue legal matters are ignored, or at best, satisfied after an unreasonable delay. Magazines and books left by supporters are not received – the excuse offered that staff must have lost them. Contemptuous treatment becomes the accepted manner of officer to prisoner interaction. He fights ridicule after uttering the fatal words: 'I'm not guilty. The coppers set me up.'

'Too right. You'll have something in common with the other 1400 prisoners who are not guilty. Dream on, idiot.'

He forces adjustment to prison culture. As one who has spent the majority of his working career giving orders to subordinates, he finds himself at the prison officers' behest. Where he had once directed the address of 'sir' to decorated and commissioned officers, as he too had been addressed, he now bestows the very same title upon twenty-year-old prison officer graduates.

He adapts to 6.45 a.m. 'wake up' announcements, sirens and bells summoning all to lunch and dinner; assembling five times daily for prisoner counts; wearing prison greys, or whatever fashion colour is in vogue at the time; he adapts to working menial tasks of factory work akin to the simplicity of a sheltered workshop; and he adapts to prison officers pledging to do all they can to help him – but when push comes to shove they have not one minute, nor one ounce of compassion, to spare him.

All this time Barry Simmons knows that someone in the community committed the crimes. He considers Marchant as guilty as the actual offender, because Marchant's negligence and narrow-mindedness cost him his freedom, his business, and all that goes with it: credibility in the community; weekly income and provision for the future.

He had worked tirelessly to arm his lawyer with information and material sufficient to lodge a successful bail application. He wrote to local members, government ministers and the Home Secretary requesting a review of the police evidence. Most did not offer the courtesy of a reply while others simply advised him to await legal process. 'We must maintain government and judicial separation.' All well and good, Simmons replied, but who takes overall responsibility for judicial process? Put under pressure, ministers and their staff responded with only cursory pro-forma generic responses: *'This government leads with judicial initiatives that galvanise the community and identify and penalise those who see fit to transgress against society. We proudly boast that our departments are staffed by qualified, experienced personnel capable of administering the law and also proficient in identifying flaws either within our policies, or attached to laws which have passed through generations of revision and fine-tuning. We thank you for bringing your concerns to our notice.'*

In the lead-up to the hearing, Simmons receives regular video conferences from his solicitor. Llewellyn-Jones shows no confidence in his client receiving a not guilty verdict. 'You're up against it,' Rupert proffers. 'We can't just hang our hat on your credibility and long-standing service record. That may have worked in the navy, but here, in the real world, it stands for jack shit.'

Simmons is tired of hearing clichéd references to 'the real world' as if there are two different worlds; a real one and one behind bars. From the 'inside' however, there are two distinct worlds – one ruled by freedom and democracy, the other by containment and autocracy.

'Listen Rupert. This *is* the real world whether you like it or not. You're not sitting in this hole rotting away. I'm not talking about relying on service records and credibility. I'm talking about relying on honesty and justice and your expertise to put forward the case of my concrete alibis proving I had nothing to do with those deaths. I thought you had more faith in me than that. How many years have you known me? How many years have you handled my affairs?'

'It matters not how long I have acted for you or whether I trust you or not—'

Simmons interjects, 'Well I may as well start afresh with someone else, because if you don't trust me for my honesty, how the hell will a jury?'

'Calm down, Barry. The crux of this relies on what is *put* to the jury. That's what will convict or discharge you, not our relationship. At this stage, the prosecution has a solid case. We've covered this many times; we've discussed the phone, the photos of you at the pub, the damming bloody thread of your jumper and the fingerprints. You're tied to each of those women.'

'I may as well just plead guilty then. You're full of telling me what they've got, but I've heard nothin' about what we've got.'

'Honestly, Barry. We've got nothing.'

'You're bloody kidding me. It's not as if they've got a photo of me killing anyone. What about Hegarty? How can you believe I killed her when I was home on Friday from 8.00 p.m. and before that I was on the river?'

'No one's come forward to confirm that.'

'All right. So where was she killed? Who saw me? Am I on CCTV? Of course not. This is one giant shamble. Can't you see through it?'

'Doesn't matter what I can see. It matters what the prosecution put to the jury to support their case. Reasonable

211

doubt doesn't cut it anymore. Of course I plan to attack their evidence. We might make progress examining the police, but remember, they're regarded as experts; they're in the box every week and they'll back each other to the hilt. I see them every day, reviewing and rehearsing notes and statements, geeing each other up. Put yourself in the jury's position. Who are you going to believe: a person charged with three murders or a reliable police inspector with fifteen years' experience?'

'So what am I looking at then? Thirty? Thirty-five? Forty?'

* * *

The committal hearing proceeds as scheduled.

Simmons repeatedly nudges his solicitor, pleading with him to submit a more powerful defence. Months of preparation have armed Llewellyn-Jones with nothing concrete to support his client. Instead, he concentrates on testing the evidence of potential witnesses.

From Barry Simmons' perspective, the committal proceeding does nothing to consolidate his not guilty plea. He hoped his legal team would uncover crucial evidence sufficient to clear him. He'd visualised the court announcing on this day: 'Case dismissed'.

'We won't win it in the committal,' Rupert consoles. 'We don't want to arm the prosecution with our strategy.'

'What?' Simmons protests. 'We haven't even discussed strategy.'

PART TWO

THE TRIAL

24

Marchant strides ahead of Watts as they rush from City Thameslink station to the Central Criminal Court, better known as the Old Bailey, so named by the street on which it stands. The multi-court complex has administered London justice since the early 1500s. The confused architectural features evidence rebuilds and repairs over its 500-year history. The massive semi-Gothic construction was destroyed by the Great Fire of London in 1666, was rebuilt in 1774, and then 170 years later, severely damaged in World War II. It has since been extended and has suffered services upgradings, enforced by legislation rather than by necessity. Today, it stands as a plain brick structure accentuated by neatly corbelled windows. A row of towering Roman columns decorates its entrance, upon which rests a miniature replica of the St Paul's cathedral dome.

The detectives hustle beneath a small archway, pass through high-tech x-ray pedestals and wands, and walk into a huge open space. Shards of sunlight pierce the eighty-foot dome and bounce off tessellated floor tiles to the accompaniment of Olivia's heels. Marble statues complement intricate carvings which compete for attention with the baroque-style painted ceiling.

'The day of reckoning,' Marchant grins.

Olivia walks on in silence. Only days after Simmons' arrest, she and DS Stanton had been transferred to the Community Policing Squad. Marchant had recommended Olivia because of her 'personnel skills' and conscientiousness. The fact that the move coincided with Simmons being charged was not lost on Olivia. Her contribution to the investigation had been overlooked, convincing her that she was well out of favour. She continued to remonstrate against the prosecution, but finally accepted that after Simmons had been charged and remanded in custody, nothing could be gained by pursuing Taylor.

Olivia firmly believes she's been transferred to Siberia to share tea and biscuits with juvenile offenders' parents, shop proprietors and school truancy officers, and to fulfil the local constabulary's political agenda of 'creating a uniformed police presence to demonstrate our connection with the community'.

On entering the courtroom, she assumes a seat directly behind the bar table. Marchant approaches the prosecutor who confers accolades and back slaps for the arrest and inevitable conviction. The camaraderie is interrupted by two court officers who lead Barry Simmons into the court and secure him in the dock.

The tipstaff calls the court to order.

Two loud raps echo from the judge's door.

The judge enters.

His associate monotones: 'All rise. All those having business before this court please remain standing and you shall be heard.'

His Honour, Justice Ainsley, resplendent in legal regalia of white collar and black flowing robe, looks down upon the court. He is encased in an acre of Mahogany which has been cut, chiselled, shaped, and sanded into a huge table adorned with carved facia. Bordering the huge bench's perimeter, corbelled gussets brace generous risers on which rests a wide document ledge.

The judge dispenses with trial pre-requisites, counsel submissions and jury selection in short time, enabling him to commence proceedings before lunch. He nods to his associate, similarly wrapped in a smaller but equally prestigious desk from where she will relay documents and exhibits to His Honour.

She stands and recites the Crown's Presentment: 'Barry Andrew Simmons. You are charged that on the fourteenth day of August 2015, at Evesham, you did, contrary to the common law of England, unlawfully kill Juanita Morales, being in the Queen's peace, with malice aforethought. How do you plead?'

'Not guilty.'

'You are further charged that on the sixteenth day of August 2015, at Evesham, you did, contrary to the common law of England, unlawfully kill Amelia Roslyn Anderson, being in the Queen's peace, with malice aforethought. How do you plead?'

'Not guilty.'

'You are further charged that on the twentieth day of August 2015, at a place unknown, you did, contrary to the common law of England, unlawfully kill Margaret Jane Hegarty, being in the Queen's peace, with malice aforethought. How do you plead?'

'Not guilty.'

Olivia studies Simmons' gaunt structure. He has shed at least seven kilograms since appearing at the committal hearing four months' earlier. Despite the dramatic transformation, his posture exudes confidence – but the six words aired fear.

The prosecutor rises. Black robed, the size of a two-man

tepee. White skinned, evidence of his waking hours spent in courtroom combat and legal library swotting. If he is lucky, he'll absorb a little Vitamin D during the short walk between chambers and the court complex. An unmanageable comb-over squirms beneath a yellowing horsehair wig, while a few straggling tufts relax on his collar. 'Godfrey Postlewaite, Your Honour. I appear for the Crown in this matter.'

'Yes, Mr Postlewaite. Go ahead.'

Postlewaite pauses and looks around the courtroom. Satisfied that he's commanding the attention of every pair of eyes, he looks directly to the jury and repeats the charges. 'The Crown presents that on the dates aforementioned,' he pauses and points menacingly to the dock, 'that man, Barry Andrew Simmons, did wilfully murder three women: Juanita Morales, Amelia Anderson and Margaret Hegarty.

'The Crown will show that Barry Simmons, while conducting a river cruise in Evesham, did, at an unknown location on the River Avon in Evesham, Worcestershire, murder Juanita Morales by strangulation before coldheartedly disposing of her body overboard. Miss Morales' body was later recovered from the river alongside Evesham's Crown Meadow.

'Ms Morales' purse, which contained two Simmons' Scenic Cruises tickets, was later salvaged in the vicinity. You will hear Mr Brett Davies testify of finding Miss Morales' phone and handing it to Mr Simmons. When questioned, Mr Simmons initially denied knowledge of that phone, but later directed police to a Cash Liquidators store in Evesham from where the phone was retrieved. Evidence supporting that will be placed before you.

'In the matter of Amy Anderson, you will view evidence

showing the defendant in the company of Miss Anderson at the Rose and Thorn hotel in Evesham. Shortly after leaving the hotel Miss Anderson was brutally stabbed outside the premises. A fibre matching an article of clothing owned and worn by the defendant on the night was removed from congealed blood on the knife. You will hear evidence of ownership of that particular weapon.

'The third victim, journalist Margaret Hegarty – you'll hear her referred to as 'Marg' – had unintentionally relayed to the defendant prejudicial information she had collated in the course of an assignment. We will show that Mr Simmons, fearing exposure by Miss Hegarty, brutally killed her. Within that evidence, you will hear of Mr Simmons' fingerprints being lifted from the deceased's Peugeot sedan.

'When you have heard and weighed all of the evidence, the Crown will ask that you find Mr Barry Andrew Simmons guilty of the murders of these three innocent women who were ruthlessly and heartlessly deprived of their life, their hopes and their aspirations.'

Rupert Llewellyn-Jones, against the wishes of his client, had instructed a barrister newly appointed to the bar, and one rapidly earning senior counsels' respect for tenacious cross-examination.

'Belinda Pace for the defendant, Your Honour.'

Her black robe veils a physically fit and mentally alert go-getter whose striking image is shattered by the absurd horsehair wig perched atop blazing-red hair.

'Members of the jury. Mr Barry Simmons stands before you an innocent man. I offer this not as an introduction to a fancy legal speech, but as the rule of law. Mr Simmons is innocent until proven guilty of these charges. Each of you must find, beyond reasonable doubt, that Mr Simmons did commit the acts as charged.

'My role is to present to you matters and evidence capable of proving that Mr Simmons is not the person responsible for these crimes. We will show that at best, the case against Mr Simmons is no more than vivid speculation founded upon circumstantial and superficial evidence. We will show that Mr Simmons had no relationship with any of the deceased and that there is no evidence linking him *directly* to any crime. I emphasise 'directly', because the Crown will present evidence of threads, fingerprints, the sale of a mobile phone and a welcoming hug in a pub, all of which will be used to connect Mr Simmons to these despicable crimes.

'You will hear the term "reasonable doubt" throughout this trial. His Honour will explain that later in the proceedings. At this early juncture, I ask you to consider very carefully all of the evidence you are called upon to consider. Your careful scrutiny of evidence and testimony will compel you to return a verdict of not guilty.'

Postlewaite opens proceedings with Graham Johnston's evidence of finding Juanita's body. He continues with Dr Erich Groenweld and Robert Sebastian – otherwise known as Bob the barman from the Rose and Thorn – and four of the pub's patrons, who contribute nothing positive to the prosecution's case. Dr Richard Thomas and Edison Edwards follow. Employing the tradition of Hollywood scriptwriters, he saves the climax for the last possible moment: the police statements. They fasten together the events like pieces of a jigsaw.

The court calls Inspector Michael Marchant.

Marchant swaggers confidently to the dock, swears the

oath and begins his testimony: 'I've been a police officer for 15 years, the past six as Detective Inspector with West Mercia Police, based at Worcester CID.'

Postlewaite guides Marchant through his statement, a lengthy 32 pages of detailed investigation into the three deaths.

'Inspector Marchant. Let me just clarify some matters in your statement. You say that on the evening of August fourteen you attended Crown Meadow in Evesham where you observed the deceased at the water's edge of the River Avon?'

'That's correct.'

'You arranged for the attendance of the Coroner, and you subsequently had a conversation with Dr Erich Groenweld?'

'I did.'

'Did you form any conclusions from that conversation?'

'I did, and that was that the deceased had suffered possible asphyxiation by strangulation. That was later confirmed in the pathologist's report.'

Postlewaite looks to the jury. 'Subsequent enquiries led you to interview certain persons and from those interviews you had reason to conduct a formal interview with one suspect?'

'That's correct.'

'Would you please tell the court, inspector, who that person was?'

With practised courtroom expertise, Marchant looks directly at Simmons, scans past the jury and returns his answer to the judge: 'Mr Barry Andrew Simmons.'

'Mr Simmons. The defendant.'

'Yes. That's correct.'

'Two days later, inspector, on the sixteenth of August, you were called to a second incident in Evesham?'

'Yes, I was. Sorry, *we* were. I was accompanied by Detective Sergeant Watts. It was a general call; a stabbing at the Rose and Thorn pub.'

'And again your enquiries and interviews led you to formally interview a suspect?'

'Yes.'

'And that suspect was again Mr Simmons?'

'Yes, it was.'

'Some days later you were called, general or not is of no consequence, you were called to an incident in the car park of a business, the *Evesham Record*, if I have that right, on the morning of August twenty?'

'Yes, but that was not so much an incident that occurred there, but the result of an incident.'

'All right. All right. But as a result of that investigation you had cause to formally interview and charge a suspect?

'I did. My investigation culminated in retrieving evidence from Mr Simmons' home, and subsequently charging the defendant, er, Mr Simmons. That evidence is one XL-sized pale blue knitted woollen cardigan, a receipt for an eight inch knife, and a packet of tablets prescribed to Mr Simmons.'

Postlewaite takes three evidence bags from the bar table and displays the contents to Marchant. 'Are these the items you seized from Mr Simmons' home, inspector?'

'Yes. They are.'

Postlewaite hands the bags to the clerk. 'I tender these as exhibits One, Two and Three, respectively, Your Honour.' Then to Marchant: 'And you tender the Record of Interview between yourself and Barry Simmons as a true and complete account of your conversation?'

'Yes. I do.'

Postlewaite shuffles a few pages from his manila folder, looks to the jury and back to the judge. 'No further questions, Your Honour.'

'Thank you Mr Postlewaite. I see this as an appropriate time to adjourn for lunch. Miss Pace, do you have matters to put to Inspector Marchant?'

'I do, Your Honour.'

'Very well then. We shall resume at 2.15.'

The jury files out. Marchant creases a wry smile, relieved to have completed his evidence-in-chief.

Whilst pigging into a free lunch, courtesy of the Crown Prosecution Service, Marchant prepares for the next session by reviewing his statement in concert with Postlewaite's pointers to potential questions.

25

THE LUNCHEON ADJOURNMENT over, legal personnel and public file into the court. A chattering hum fills the gallery as families discuss previously heard evidence, forecast outcomes, and pass back snatches of jovial banter between opposing counsel.

At 2.18, the court resumes.

Belinda Pace had eaten nothing, her appetite giving way to nerves, and impatience to attack Marchant. She rises with an air of royalty and then confounds the moment with feigned carelessness – a deliberate ploy to unsettle the witness. 'Mister Marchant. Oh, I apologise, it's inspector, isn't it? Inspector Marchant. Please bear with me for a moment. I may skip around a little before chronologising the events you have presented. You have no uncertainties about Mr Simmons' involvement in these matters before the court?'

'No I don't. We conducted an investigation and from that obtained more than ample evidence to refer the case to the Crown Prosecution Service.'

'Right. In the matter of Miss Morales, did Mr Simmons admit to any acquaintanceship or knowledge of her presence in Evesham?'

'No. He didn't.'

'So is it your case that because Miss Morales' body was found *in the vicinity* of my client's boat, a boat you cannot *prove* she was on, Mr Simmons has become the sole suspect?'

Marchant defiantly hoists his eyebrows. 'The deceased's bag was found nearby and the accused had taken possession of a phone later found to belong to Miss Morales. Enquiries excluded the possibility of any other suspect.'

Olivia shrinks into her seat. *What enquiries? The enquiries you prevented me from pursuing?*

'We've heard no evidence of proof of ownership of the bag you claim to have belonged to Miss Morales. Did the bag actually belong to her? Had you considered the possibility of it having been snatched, valuables taken and then thrown in the river?'

Postlewaite rises from the bench, hands in the air in animated exasperation. 'Objection, Your Honour. My learned friend should confine her examination to one question at a time.'

Pace interjects before His Honour responds. 'I withdraw that, Your Honour.'

Judge Ainsley musters the slightest amount of energy required to simply wave his hand as a direction for Pace to proceed.

She resumes: 'Inspector. Do you have proof that the bag found near the deceased's body actually belonged to her?'

'Not of ownership, but—'

'Thank you inspector. Have you considered the possibility of it having been snatched? Perhaps valuables were removed and the bag thrown from anywhere along the course of the Avon in to the river?'

'Yes. We have considered such a possibility and we concluded that as the bag had two of Simmons' tickets inside and had not been reported as lost or stolen it was fair to reason that it belonged to Miss Morales.'

'Yes. "Fair to reason". And those tickets were unnamed and undated?'

'That's correct.'

'So, it remains that there's no actual *proof* that the tickets or bag belonged to Miss Morales. Let me ask you this: Is it not possible that the bag *had* belonged to another person and it had been snatched by an unknown offender who, whether he took the cruise or not, dropped or disposed of the phone and the bag?'

Simmons grins. 'That's purely speculative.'

'But no more speculative than what you've proposed. You present no proof or witness to state Miss Morales was on the craft.'

'That's correct.'

'Did you examine the craft, inspector.'

'Yes. I inspected the upper deck and familiarised myself with the craft's layout and the location of the bench where the phone was found.'

'Inspector Marchant. Did you, for instance, examine the control area or helm?'

'I had no need to.'

'Really? Did you not check the speed capacity of the craft, or if, for instance, it was fitted with autopilot?'

Marchant reddens, clearly embarrassed. 'I conducted the investigation to solve the manner by which Ms Morales met her death, not to acquire an interest in the electronic functioning of river craft.'

Pace contains her delight. She glares at Marchant and glances to the judge. 'I'll repeat my question: Did you not check the speed capacity of the craft, and whether or not it was fitted with autopilot?'

'No. I had no need to.'

'Thank you, inspector. Returning to the phone you just mentioned, the phone you claim Mr Simmons sold; how did you establish that Miss Morales owned the phone?'

'As I gave in my evidence, we have a statement from Miss Morales' sister confirming the phone number.'

'Right. Let me digest that. She confirmed the number… now that doesn't actually confirm ownership of the phone, does it inspector?'

'Of course it does. It couldn't be any clearer.'

Pace mimics Postlewaite's earlier ploy of stalling before the jury. She takes it a step further and removes a mobile phone, of the same model tendered in evidence, from her pocket. 'Your Honour, I beg the court's indulgence for one moment.' In front of the jury, she removes the back of the phone, slides out the SIM card and then turns to the witness: 'How can you say that, inspector? You purchased a phone from Cash Liquidators with no SIM card. With no SIM card, the phone has no number. Does that not surprise you, inspector?'

'Why would it? It had her sister's, her mother's and her fiancé's phone numbers stored in the memory.'

'But with an open mind, inspector, is it not possible that the phone *could* have belonged to a brother, a sister, a relation or *any* other person who made regular contact with the deceased or her family?'

'I suppose it could have.' Marchant edges in a proviso: 'If any of those people were in Evesham.'

'Very well. Can you then exclude the possibility of a relative or friend having been in Evesham at the relevant time?'

'That wasn't part of the investigation.'

'So, are you telling the court, inspector, that you cannot

rule out the possibility of a friend, or associate of Ms Morales, having accompanied her or simply been present in the Evesham area at or near the time the phone was recovered?'

'Put that way, I can't rule it out.'

'So, I therefore put it to you, inspector, that you can't be absolutely certain that the phone in evidence is the phone sold by Mr Simmons? What I mean to say is, you can't exclude the possibility that, say, a member of the public also sold a similar phone to Cash Convertors and *that* was the actual phone found on the deck?'

'I can't exclude it, but it's too far-fetched to be a reality.'

'Finally, Inspector Marchant, are you presenting a witness who will give evidence to this court that they saw Miss Morales with Mr Simmons, or that they saw Mr Simmons strangle Miss Morales?'

'No, but—'

'Thank you inspector. Moving on to Miss Anderson; you established that she was a regular patron of the Rose and Thorn hotel in Evesham?'

'Yes.'

'As was Mr Simmons?'

'Yes.'

'And you've produced a witness statement and CCTV stills of Mr Simmons in conversation and embrace with Miss Anderson?'

'That's correct.'

'Would it be fair to say, Inspector, that Mr Simmons was not the only person to have spoken to, or to have embraced Miss Anderson on that evening?'

'Yes, that's fair. Footage shows that she seemed to know a few people there.'

Pace maintains the neutral demeanour of a seasoned voter walking to a polling booth: 'And you subsequently identified and interviewed those people?'

'Not all of them. They were not linked to the crime as was the defendant. None of them left the premises.'

'But you can't know that, Inspector Marchant. You cannot know who walked out during the commotion, just as you cannot know who left immediately before or at the time of Miss Anderson's leaving the establishment. I suggest that all you rely on is the footage of Mr Simmons coincidentally ending his evening at around the same time of this unfortunate incident. In fact, inspector, isn't it true that you arrived at Evesham some seventeen minutes after receiving the job allocation from the 999 operator?'

Marchant pauses, takes a sip of water and a deep breath. 'I weighed particular acts and responses with circumstances as they presented at the time.'

'Yes, but I've put it to you that there was a seventeen minute delay before your arrival. Isn't that so, inspector?'

'It is so, but that had no bearing on who we did or didn't interview. The locals had taken initial control of the scene. I had no reason to question their professionalism.'

'So, do you have a witness statement or CCTV footage implicating Mr Simmons in any violent activity with the deceased?'

'No.'

Pace spreads her arms wide in an exaggerated expression of dismay: 'You don't? May I then suggest that that is because Mr Simmons had absolutely nothing to do with Amy Anderson's murder?'

'You can suggest that, but it's not true. We have forensic evidence.'

'Ah, yes, the forensic evidence,' Pace repeats with a smug grin. 'And what might that be, inspector?'

'A thread retrieved from the knife which was found at the scene and identified by residual blood as the murder weapon.'

'Ah, yes, the blue thread. Is that *all* you have Inspector Marchant?'

'That's conclusive enough.'

'Yes inspector. Conclusive proof that the thread belongs to a cardigan of the type Mr Simmons was wearing, but not conclusive that he murdered Miss Anderson.'

Marchant shuffles in the witness box, agitated by Pace's repetitive questions. He enunciates the depth of his case. 'There's plenty of proof when you take into account that Mr Simmons' car was recorded on CCTV leaving the Rose and Thorn car park at 10.33 p.m., and the fact that we found his business card on the ground with the contents of Ms Anderson's belongings.'

'Very well, inspector. Did Mr Simmons offer a reason for leaving the car park at that hour?'

'Yes. At first he wasn't sure if he was driving the car on that night. In a second interview he gave a flimsy excuse about needing an early night.'

Pace seizes another opportunity to heckle the prosecution's witness: 'Inspector Marchant. What do you consider made Mr Simmons' reason 'flimsy'? Did you enquire as to his state of health or his working hours?'

'Sorry. It was just an expression. He told me he needed an early night.'

'So it's fair to say that at the time, you had no knowledge one way or the other of whether Mr Simmons *genuinely* had to retire early?'

Marchant flinches. 'Yes. That's fair to say.'

'In any event, inspector, Mr Simmons did not deny his being at the Rose and Thorn?'

'No, he didn't.'

'Let me move on to the business card you've just told the court was – let me read back your evidence – yes, "found on the ground with the contents of Ms Anderson's belongings". That is your case, is it not?'

'It is.'

'Isn't it true that Mr Simmons admitted to knowing Miss Anderson?'

'Yes, but statistics show that many cases of violence are inflicted upon those known to their assailant.'

'Thank you inspector. Perhaps you could confine your response to answers without added comment. One final question with regard to Miss Anderson, and I just want to clarify this: is it your case that the blue thread is crucial, the hinge-pin if you like, of Mr Simmons' complicity in the killing of Miss Anderson?'

'Most definitely.'

'Would you then tell the court, how much blood-spatter or residue was found on Mr Simmons' blue cardigan, and by that I refer to the cardigan seized during the execution of a search warrant on Friday the nineteenth of August and tendered to this court as Exhibit One?'

'There was none. He was fortunate—'

'None? There was *none*?' Pace reels in exasperation in another over-animated spectacle to the jury. 'Would you care to explain that? A frenzied knife attack on a woman… stabbed at least five times… and the assailant walks away with not one drop of the victim's blood on his clothes?'

'I can't explain it, other than to say that he must have discarded a jacket or cloak.'

'But you're not leading evidence on that are you? I mean, you've located a knife at the scene, but with all your searching, and your "more than ample evidence" as you've testified, you have not produced this jacket or cloak that has not been mentioned by any witness in their evidence?'

'Em, no.'

'No,' Pace adds for effect. 'Thank you inspector.'

She performs another paper shuffle, giving the jury time to digest the final fact. 'Now Inspector Marchant, I'll turn to the matter of Miss Hegarty. You rely on a fingerprint found on her car, and the proposition is, or motive as you claim, is that Mr Simmons felt threatened by information possessed by Miss Hegarty.' Pace pauses before slowly spelling out Marchant's impression of Simmons' feelings. 'F-e-l-t threatened. Exactly what threats did Mr Simmons reveal to you that he felt from Miss Hegarty?'

'Em, nothing concrete, but Miss Hegarty interviewed him a few days earlier. I believe that she'd unearthed further information about him.'

'That's closer to the truth, isn't it, inspector. *You* believed Mr Simmons felt threatened. You don't have notes or a record to support this hypothetical conversation between Miss Hegarty and Mr Simmons?'

'No. But there is a diary note of her meeting Mr Simmons at Evesham's pier on the eighteenth. August that is.'

'Well let me summarise this for the jury. Your case against Mr Simmons is based upon a bag, whose ownership is unknown, and the fact Mr Simmons sold a phone – the owner of which is not known. A single thread found on the murder weapon is declared key evidence, but there was no blood on the cardigan from which you claim the thread originated, and despite the existence of a ten-month-old receipt that bears no *direct* reference to the actual murder weapon, you cannot prove the knife was owned or used by Mr Simmons. And from a solitary fingerprint on Miss Hegarty's car, you conclude that Mr Simmons killed her? Do I have that right, inspector?'

'In very simplistic terms, that is correct.'

'Good. We'll keep it simple for the jury – with respect to the members.'

After a brief adjournment, Postlewaite calls DS Watts.

Olivia walks confidently to the witness box, gives evidence of attending each scene with Marchant, being present during the search of Simmons' home and present as corroborator during the subsequent interviews.

'That concludes my examination of this witness Your Honour.' Postlewaite resumes his seat.

Belinda Pace strides to the witness box. 'Detective Sergeant Watts. You've been partnered with Inspector Marchant for the whole of this investigation?'

'For most of it, yes. Some enquiries we conducted separately.'

'So it's fair to say that there may be some of the inspector's conversations and enquires that you were not privy to?'

Bitch. Olivia freezes. She knows Marchant would have said that she had been present during the whole enquiry. It's one of those unwritten rules; the informal convention that police corroborate each other's evidence. Never before has Olivia been challenged on this. She now faces either lying or exposing Marchant as a liar.

'My inspector had an initial chat with Mr Simmons while I conducted other lines of enquiry. To my knowledge, it was not formal; it was in the early information-gathering stage. I was present during the first official enquiry at the Worcester police station and for the subsequent Record of Interview.'

'And what was your view of Mr Simmons' involvement in these crimes?'

'I didn't form a view. I keep an open mind and collect evidence and information to arrive at conclusions based on fact.'

'How very admirable of you Sergeant Watts.' Pace withholds a smirk. A smirk of confidence in the battle of woman versus woman. 'Let us examine some of that evidence. Perhaps we'll start with the phone. You've sworn in your statement that you purchased a phone at the Evesham branch of Cash Liquidators?'

'Yes. That's right.'

'And that is the phone marked as an exhibit; the silver Nokia as I recall? Could you please tell the court how you established a link from that phone to Mr Simmons?'

Olivia grabs a breath. 'Information received revealed that a member of the public had handed a phone to Mr Simmons. I subsequently purchased that phone after Mr Simmons advised its whereabouts.'

Pace carefully plants a question to evade the issue of her client having sold the phone, despite that point already having been heard by the court: 'Was that phone owned by Miss Morales?'

'It had her numbers stored in the memory.'

'I'll repeat the question. Was that phone owned by Miss Morales?'

'To the best of my knowledge, yes.'

'The best of your knowledge. So did any of those numbers link Mr Simmons to Miss Morales?'

'No. They didn't.'

'*None* of Mr Simmons' business or personal contact numbers was in what you're claiming to be Ms Morales' phone?'

'No.'

'Perhaps you could tell the court who those numbers did connect to?'

Olivia again gasps for breath and blushes. Sips water from a plastic cup. 'Her relations in the Philippines and her fiancé.'

'And did you conduct enquiries with any of those people?'

'Yes. I spoke to Miss Morales' sister in the Philippines and her fiancé in Bournemouth. Inspector Marchant and I later travelled to Bournemouth where we interviewed the fiancé, Mr Trevor Taylor.'

'Was Mr Taylor ever, shall we say, a 'person of interest' in the disappearance and murder of his fiancée?'

Olivia pauses, desperately wanting to answer 'yes', backed by the foundation for her belief. But she'd had only a hunch, the famed women's intuition. 'No. We eliminated him in the early stages of the investigation.'

Pace shuffles more pages. 'Now, Sergeant Watts. You also attended the Rose and Thorn on the evening of the sixteenth of August?'

'Yes I did.'

'You located a knife, and that is the knife you've tendered to the court?'

'Yes.'

'And you were present during the search of Mr Simmons' home when various items described by Inspector Marchant were seized?'

'I was.'

'And you attended the car park of the *Evesham Record* on the morning of the twentieth August?'

'I did.'

'So your attendances at these scenes, these scenes of violent crimes, would have endowed you with a wealth of pertinent information capable of aiding the investigation?'

'Most definitely. Yes.'

Pace gazes to the jury with a get-ready-for-this expression and then fires the question: 'Could you then tell the court, Detective Sergeant Watts, why you have not detailed all that knowledge and evidence as a written statement attached to the brief?'

Olivia blushes, barely perceptible to the jury. 'Inspector Marchant wanted only direct evidence. That's why I detailed in my statement direct conversations with witnesses, searching for and finding a knife in the precincts of the Rose and Thorn and noting times of receipt and transfer of forensic evidence. My inspector was satisfied his statement comprised detail sufficient to sustain a conviction. It is accepted practice that a subordinate officer only corroborates.' Olivia cringes upon demeaning herself as "subordinate".

'Thank you. No further questions, Your Honour.'

Postlewaite rises. 'That closes the case for the prosecution Your Honour.'

Justice Ainsley replaces his disinterested look. 'You are leading evidence Miss Pace?'

'Yes, Your Honour. '

'Very well. We'll adjourn until 10.00 a.m. tomorrow morning.'

As the court clears, Olivia rushes to the ladies' toilets, charges into a cubicle and sits, head throbbing with guilt from having compromised her own ethics and morals. Never has she treated the law with such disdain to be so embarrassed over her actions. She tries to suppress anger and anxiety generated by her knowingly having lied on oath, solely to match Marchant's evidence. And then she'd walked straight into Pace's trap. Pace will now be certain something stinks.

Certainly, Marchant had eliminated Taylor, but never had Olivia.

The road upon which the Old Bailey sits, similarly named, bustles with people rushing home from work. Buses generating more revenue as mobile billboards than through passenger fares, clutter the road. Thick, black diesel billows from their exhausts and hangs as a carcinogenic fog before seeping into the lungs of those accustomed to ingesting the oxygen-depleted concoction.

Taxis dive into kerbs like black crows plucking prey from the footpath. They depart with similar urgency, intent on delivering their fare and returning with another income-producing chattel. Seasoned drivers know that a spinning meter returns a reasonable wage.

Marchant and Watts step out of court, squint into the remaining daylight, and say nothing of the trial lest they be overheard by an errant jury member enroute to the railway station or bus stop.

Under most circumstances, there is little to discuss during a trial's early days. Witnesses experience the competing emotions of confidence and anxiety, and they fear cross-examination –

but only if they intend to lie or distort the truth. Competent barristers understand the necessity to 'read' those witnesses, and the jurors, to anticipate and assess reactions to evidence, testimony and points of law, the sum total of which will help them determine the direction of their case. The prosecution might think it is ahead. The defence thinks likewise. In reality, no one is ahead because a trial can turn on the testimony of the final witness – often the defendant himself.

Marchant relies on his witnesses, Groenweld, Thomas and Watts, as seasoned courtroom campaigners to add fact and credibility to his case.

'How'd you go Liv?'

Olivia shudders. She feared the question. 'Okay, I think. Pace tried to bring me undone by claiming I was not present at all your enquiries. I had to be frank, but smoothed it over by saying I was present at all the official interviews. And she asked me if I had formed a view of Simmons' involvement. I flustered a little and said that I don't form views. Then she gives me this patronising, "How very admirable of you Sergeant Watts," la de da bullshit. Guess we'll see what she's made of tomorrow.'

'Yeah, tomorrow. Want a drink?'

'No thanks. I'm heading for an early night,' Olivia replies as she heads off to a rendezvous with Stafford.

26

THE COURT RESUMES at 10.00 a.m.

Belinda Pace has encouraged her client to give evidence, despite the Crown owning the burden to prove its case. 'Show the jury the person you are,' Belinda coaxed. 'Evidence-in-chief is straight forward; I'll guide you where I can.'

Simmons narrates a broad outline of his naval career and cruise business, in a speech designed to negate the prosecution's anticipated battering. Anaesthetised by the jury's overwhelming presence, he articulates a credible account of his activities on the relevant days. He denies involvement in the murders, and claims the whole episode had been 'a huge error of judgement by the police'.

Pace had worried him with the premise that upon completion of his evidence he would be barraged by Postlewaite, whose job it is to confuse him, make him nervous, rile him and do anything within – and beyond, some would say – court etiquette to break his story.

Postlewaite's moment arrives. Time to shine. Time to engage in a battle where words become the ammunition fired at his foe. He glares at Simmons. Shows the court that posture without communication is an essential component of courtroom procedure. He flicks through notes, glances at the judge and looks toward the jury to ensure each member is captivated by his attention-seeking act.

A regular offender before the courts is immune to such intimidatory treatment; they've seen it and felt it all before. They simply ignore the barrister, look around to friends and supporters or gaze at the courtroom ceiling. Simmons though, sits transfixed in the witness box, knees clamped together and feet shaking – the latter fortunately shielded by a facia panel.

'Mr Simmons. You run regular charter cruises on the River Avon. Correct?'

'Yes, that's right.'

'On the night of August fourteen, how would you describe the weather conditions?'

'It wasn't night. I departed the final cruise late afternoon, around 5.15. As best as I recall there was no breeze and what we call normal tidal flow.'

'Do you recall Miss Morales on your craft.'

'No. I don't.'

'It's not your claim is it, Mr Simmons, that Miss Morales was not on your cruise?'

'I don't know whether she was on it or not; I just know that I didn't see her.'

'Are you saying that the police have not shown you photos of the deceased?'

'No. I'm not saying that. I said that I haven't seen her. You asked me about August the fourteenth and I responded to that. Yes, I have seen a photo, but I'm not to know whether that is actually the deceased.'

'Mr Simmons. I'll ask you to confine your answers to a yes or a no.'

'That is fine so long as the question is clear and unambiguous.'

Postlewaite spots Justice Ainsley's ruffling robes and

frowning face. He pauses, hoping His Honour might warn Simmons about his attitude. He doesn't.

'Mr Simmons. I am showing you a ticket found in Miss Morales' purse. Do you recognise it?'

'Of course I do. It's a passenger ticket for my cruises.'

'So it's fair to say that Ms Morales was a passenger on your cruise?'

'She may well have been, if that was her ticket, and if she had actually boarded.'

Postlewaite splutters the next question: 'Is it your evidence that you *forgot* to seek the owner of a phone handed to you at the conclusion of the cruise?'

'Yes. That's correct.'

'And you subsequently sold that phone?'

'Yes.'

'How many other items of lost property have you sold?'

'Er, none.'

'You mean you've never had other items handed to you? You've never found bags, umbrellas, magazines, purses or hats on your boat?'

Pace rises to return an earlier compliment: 'I wonder if my learned friend could contain his cross-examination to one question at a time.'

Simmons doesn't wait: 'I've found some, but I've never sold them.'

'Is that so, Mr Simmons? You've *never* sold them. So, tell the court, Mr Simmons, what did happen to those items?'

'I may have kept a cap, but most I'd just give to the Salvos or other charity.'

'So that's hardly fair to those who have paid you for entertainment when you turn around and rob them blind.'

241

Pace jumps to her feet. 'Objection, Your Honour. Relevance.'

Postelwaite responds: 'Your Honour. Mr Simmons, by his own admission did not seek to return a mobile phone. He has also admitted not returning other items. It goes to credibility of the witness, Your Honour.'

'Overruled. You may answer the question Mr Simmons.'

'I did not rob my passengers. I chose to let others benefit so that's why I gave the things to charity.'

'But you didn't give the phone to charity.' Postlewaite skips to his next question before Pace can rise. 'Mr Simmons. I refer you to your Record of Interview taken by Inspector Marchant and signed by you on the sixteenth of August. Do you remember that interview?'

'Yes.'

'At page three, question forty-seven, you answer: "Who says she was murdered, she probably fell overboard." Do you remember saying that?'

'No, but if it's there I probably said it.'

'Is that your proposition, Mr Simmons, that Miss Morales *was* on your cruise and she fell overboard?'

'It's neither a proposition nor a stab in the dark.' Simmons immediately regrets the use of his clichéd response, but continues so as to not draw further attention to himself. 'I was simply offering the detective an alternative to his suggestion that the girl was murdered.'

'Very well, Mr Simmons. If we accept that reasoning in conjunction with your statement that the weather was fine, with normal tidal flow I think you called it, could you tell the court how many other people on your *pleasure* cruises have taken to simply falling overboard?'

242

Simmons glares at Postlewaite. The question is impertinent. 'No one has ever fallen overboard on one of my cruises. I run a safe ship with an enviable record of no losses either in my own business or during thirty years with the Royal Navy.'

'So, according to you, Miss Morales simply leapt from your boat, strangled herself, and gurgled to death in eight feet of water only metres from your mooring–'

Pace throws her hands in the air as Postlewaite injects his next question. 'Would you tell the court about your relationship with Ms Morales?'

'I can't. There was no relationship.'

'Perhaps you could then tell the court about your relationship with Ms Anderson?'

'She was an acquaintance.'

'An ac-quain-tance.' Postelwaite snaps the word into three pieces. 'And just how ac-quain-ted were you?'

'Miss Anderson used to work for me part-time, serving teas and cleaning. We always said hello and exchanged a few words whenever we crossed paths. We often ran into each other, as I did with many acquaintances.'

'I'd like you to look at this photograph, Mr Simmons.' Postelwaite hands over a still taken from the Rose and Thorn's CCTV footage. It depicts Simmons with his arm around Amy Anderson in a half embrace. 'Is that you being "acquainted" with Miss Anderson?'

'Yes, it is.'

'I tender that Your Honour.' Postlewaite hands the photograph to the judge's clerk.

'I would also like you to look at this blue cardigan which police removed from your home pursuant to a Search Warrant executed on August nineteenth. Do you recognise that?'

'Of course I do.'

'Were you wearing that on the night of August sixteenth at the Rose and Thorn?'

'I don't remember.'

'Let me help your memory, Mr Simmons. I can recall the photo if that will help.'

'It's all right. I may have worn it.'

'Yes, Mr Simmons. I suggest to you that you *did* wear it. I would like you to take a close look at a blue thread inside this bag.' Postlewaite passes over Exhibit Five.

'Yes, I see it.'

'Do you recognise that?'

'Not specifically. It could be from anywhere.'

'Yes, it could be. But I put it to you, Mr Simmons, it's not from anywhere. This thread was found on the murder weapon.'

Postlewaite spreads his papers, stalling for effect once again, knowing that the jury will draw conclusions from his linking the blue thread to the murder weapon.

'Your Honour. I tender a report from West Mercia Forensic Laboratory marked Exhibit Four, that identifies this thread as originating from the same manufacturer and batch number of wool used in the production of Mr Simmons' blue cardigan. Your Honour may wish to refer to Inspector Marchant's evidence – page 28, line 14, Your Honour. The thread was removed from the blade of the knife used in the attack on Miss Anderson. That is the knife tendered during Detective Sergeant Watts' evidence, Your Honour.'

Simmons feels reality and freedom slip away. His earlier confidence that Rupert and Belinda would breeze through the case like a quick trip through the local supermarket dissipates. He is stuck in the checkout queue. *Am I going to get through here or is someone going to plant something in my pocket and charge me with shoplifting?*

He understands the damning significance of the blue cardigan. Jury members will logically conclude that because he was wearing the cardigan he must have killed Amy Anderson.

During a Naval hearing some years earlier, an incident occurred where one of his seamen was found with stolen food in his locker. The accused did not put it there; it was inadvertently placed in the wrong locker by a culprit who became disorientated in the dark after stealing food from the kitchen.

In the overall running of a naval vessel, the incident was not of seafaring significance, but what now haunts Simmons is the fact that it is so easy to be implicated in a crime, and no matter how much or how hard one tries to clear themselves, they end up being crucified by a justice system that purports to stand for equality and fairness to all.

Postlewaite takes advantage of Simmons' despondency: 'I put it to you, Mr Simmons, that you did kill Miss Anderson after she rejected you. You were enraged; you followed her out of that pub and viciously stabbed her until she collapsed to the ground. You then left her for dead and decamped in your car, which we know was captured by CCTV at 10.33 p.m.'

'That's ridiculous.'

'Perhaps then, you could tell the court, Mr Simmons, how the thread came to be on the murder weapon?'

'I can't offer any reason because I did not have the weapon and I did not see Amy after I left the pub.'

Simmons shakes short, sharp tremors of nervous tension. He wants to pull on the blue cardigan to insulate him from the shiver enveloping his body. And he wishes that Postlewaite would stop addressing him as Mr Simmons every few minutes – Mr Simmons this and Mr Simmons that.

'And that brings us to the knife, Mr Simmons.' Postlewaite produces a clear evidence bag: 'Could you please tell the court if you recognise the content of this bag?'

'It looks like a receipt that was taken from my business files.'

'And you buy knives for business; for conducting customer-friendly cruises on the Avon?'

'I can't remember why I purchased it. I've tried, but I can't remember.'

'Perhaps then, you could tell the court where the knife is at this present time?'

'I've tried to think of that too, but I can't recall.'

Postlewaite cannot tally the number of times he has challenged the elective memory-loss of an accused person. He can provide no explanation as to whether the phenomena is a trait of the guilty or a genuine lack of recall. If pressed, he would back the former. Either way, the prosecution will strive to twist the response to its advantage.

Postlewaite takes the bag from Simmons and shows him another. 'Could this be the knife that you purchased; the knife that is the subject of that receipt; the knife that killed Miss Amy Anderson?'

'Well, er, it could be. I can't say that it's not; all I can say is that I didn't use it, I haven't seen it, and I did not kill Amy.'

'You did not accidentally drop a business card at the scene, or, heaven forbid, leave it as a calling card or warning because you hadn't expected she would die?'

'That's ridiculous.'

'But isn't it true, Mr Simmons, that you were observed,

and photographed, leaving the Rose and Thorn in your BMW shortly after the murder?'

'I never denied being there. It's just an unfortunate coincidence that I left at about the same time as the incident.'

'So what you're telling the court Mr Simmons, is that it is an unfortunate coincidence that Ms Morales died with two of your tickets in her bag, and that it is an unfortunate coincidence that you were at the same pub where Miss Anderson was stabbed to death, and that it is also an unfortunate coincidence that your fingerprint was found on Ms Hegarty's car after her murder?'

'I didn't kill her and I couldn't imagine how my print got on her car. Maybe it got there a few weeks before when I was talking to her at the river. I may have leant against her car when we were talking.'

'Very convenient, Mr Simmons. Your life is full of amazing coincidences. And I suppose you're going to produce a witness to support this revelation?'

'We were on our own.'

'Of course you were Mr Simmons, of course. Just like you were on your own when you killed her.'

'Objection, Your Honour.' Belinda Pace rises, faced flushed the colour of her hair. 'My learned friend is clearly patronising the witness. He is commenting and grandstanding within his loosely-framed questions.'

'I withdraw my last, Your Honour.'

'Yes, Mr Postlewaite. Proceed.'

'Do you have trouble sleeping, Mr Simmons?'

'Well prison's not the easiest place to sleep; we've got a feeble excuse for a mattress—'

'That's not exactly what I meant. Isn't it true that you're

dependent on sleeping tablets? Hypnodorm, if my notes serve me right?'

'I'm not dependent on them. I used them some years ago when I had difficulties in new employment after leaving the navy. My doctor prescribed them.'

'So you have no use for them now? You haven't used them for two years?

'That's correct.'

'I wonder if you could tell the court then, Mr Simmons, why a packet was stored in your bathroom cabinet at the time detectives conducted their search?' Postlewaite passes over another evidence bag. 'This is the packet, is it not, that was in your possession?'

'Yes, it looks like it, but I haven't used them. They're probably expired anyway.'

'Yes, like your friend Miss Hegarty—'

'Your Honour!' Belinda Pace shouts from the bar.

'Withdraw that, Your Honour.'

'Judge Ainsley peers over his glasses. 'Mr Postlewaite. You strike me as a man of experience enough to know the limits of cross-examination. Let there be no more of that.'

'Yes, Your Honour. I apologise.'

But the damage is done. The jury will link Simmons' Hypnodorm packet to the autopsy evidence given by Groenweld.

Postlewaite simulates a subdued manner as he continues examining Simmons: 'You've heard Inspector Marchant's evidence of Miss Hegarty's notation of an interview with you at Evesham on Thursday, August the eighteenth. Do you dispute that?'

'No. She saw me and offered to report my side of the

story. I told her my lawyer's handling it. I remember now; I was a bit abrupt and felt guilty about it, so I motored over the river to catch her before she left. I ran up to her car and nearly collapsed – I think I grabbed hold of the boot-lid or rear door pillar. That'll be where my fingerprint came from.'

'Convenient. One final question, Mr Simmons, or perhaps it's more of a conundrum: is it your position that you've mistakenly been accused of not one, not two, but three murders – all of which bear connection to you?'

'Yes. That's the situation and if it had been investigated properly I wouldn't be sitting here – you would be addressing the guilty party and not me.'

Postlewaite looks directly to the jury and extends an arm towards Simmons: 'The guilty party. Thank you Mr Simmons.' He throws a smug look to the jury, then to the judge: 'No further questions, Your Honour.'

Judge Ainsley glances at the clock. 'Any re-examination Miss Pace?'

'Only one question Your Honour; requires only a brief answer – shouldn't delay the afternoon adjournment.'

Counsel had been warned to not infringe upon His Honour's 2.00 p.m. pot of tea. Pace leans against the jury box and casually puts her question: 'Mr Simmons. Could you tell the court your habits, relating to business promotion, when you meet people for business or pleasure?'

Simmons projects a cheesy, salesman-like smile as if he expects the answer to instantly exonerate him. 'I always hand them one of my cards. If it's a business person the number and details are always a source of reference; if it's a personal contact, it becomes a small advertisement – I have received bookings simply from handing out business cards.'

'And had you given cards to Ms Anderson and Ms Hegarty?'

'Most definitely. Amy had had one for ages – she often rang to see if there were any spare shifts available. I couldn't oblige because I'd put another girl on. I gave one to Miss Hegarty on the day she approached me at the Evesham pier, just in case she wanted to contact me again.'

'Thank you. No further questions, Your Honour.'

Belinda is now anxious to present a solid closing address that will leave the jury with the most powerful reason to find her client not guilty.

And closing addresses are all that remain.

'We shall adjourn until two-twenty.'

27

TIME IS IMMEASURABLE in a court of law. Hours evaporate into minutes, the marvel likened to watching an enthralling two-hour movie: you're captured by the opening scenes and swept away with the plot; you unravel the twists and turns and hook the red-herrings; you solve the dilemma, peg the blossoming romance or determine how evil will conquer good, and then whoosh – the credits scroll up the screen and you're left hanging in desperation as you might be after being turned down between the sheets on your wedding anniversary.

The courtroom provides similar drama – without the popcorn.

Christian Abernathy leads the jury into the court. Hilary Chevalier's beady eyes scan the courtroom as she tails the twelve jurors.

Marchant and Olivia sit pensive, briefcases squeezed between their feet.

Instructing solicitors remove files from attachés and clerks page-mark reference material with pieces of torn envelope and Post-it notes.

Postlewaite and Pace look like Batman and Batwoman topped with coiffured horses' tails. They chat amicably while awaiting the court's resumption, at which time they will continue their battle of wits, knowledge and perceived superiority.

Simmons shuffles to the dock in a suit crumpled by transportation, constant dressing and undressing for security strip searches, and sleeping away nervous tension in the court's holding cells.

The public gallery swells with 60 people; friends and relatives of the deceased on one side, supporters of Simmons, including a delegation of naval officers, on the other, and a spattering of press and freelance journalists in their reserved pews.

The court resumes as scheduled. Postlewaite enthusiastically launches his closing address. With practised effect, he stands and reels in the jury with a spellbinding oratory: 'Members of the jury. You have heard the testimony of eight witnesses, and of qualified academics who specialise in forensic and photographic evidence. You have seen fragments of evidence and learnt of its origin. These pieces of the puzzle may count for very little on their own – we must look at them as forming a nucleus. Each piece of evidence completes a link in a chain; a chain of characteristics of the defendant's behaviour if you might. Let us start with Juanita Morales. It is ludicrous for the defence to contend that a bag snatcher would simply discard a mobile phone. They present no evidence of this hypothesis, and that, members of the jury is all the defence relies on – presenting you with a hypothesis in the hope you will conclude that a reasonable doubt exists as to Mr Simmons' complicity. I tell you, members of the jury, that there is no doubt.

'You must discount this supposition by examining the fictitious offender's motive for snatching a bag. There is only one reason: he steals to obtain something of value. Presumably, the bag would contain money or items worth selling. The snatcher has a vested interest to profit from the theft. It is not, therefore, a plausible scenario that a thief would simply discard an item as saleable as a mobile phone.

'You can take Mr Simmons at his word when he boasts of his thirty-year history of not losing anyone under his command. You must therefore reject the theory, floated, if you will, by Mr Simmons himself, that Miss Morales fell overboard.

'What we do have is opportunity. We can take as fact that Simmons' Scenic Cruises tickets were found in Miss Morales' bag and therefore accept she *was* on the cruise. It is a matter of considering inferences. Direct evidence is something that you see or you hear, but that is not the only way you determine facts. You may also draw conclusions or inferences from facts that have been established by direct evidence. That is, if a witness's evidence convinces you that a certain thing happened, you may be able to conclude or to infer from that fact that something else also happened. The process of drawing inferences is something we do every day. When we wake up in the morning and see a blanket of white outside, we would conclude that it snowed overnight, although we did not personally see it snow. That would be drawing an inference. In a criminal trial you are only allowed to base your decisions upon reasonable inferences. You must not base your decisions on guesses or speculation.

'Mr Simmons might have taken the opportunity to slip to the rear of the craft to dispose of Miss Morales. Next we know, a member of the public has picked up Miss Morales' phone and responsibly, though unwittingly, hands it to Mr Simmons. Mr Simmons doesn't want to hold on to incriminating evidence, so at the very next opportunity he sells it to Cash Liquidators. He doesn't care about the money. He just wants rid of the phone. Why didn't he throw it into the Avon or a bin? Fear of it being found, because he, Mr Simmons, the defendant, knew that there would be an intensive search for any evidence of Miss Morales' murder. Unfortunately for Mr Simmons, the police were one step ahead.

'Now, let us examine the defence's proposition that a thread from Simmons' jumper simply clung to Amy Anderson by "cross-contamination" as they eloquently put it. Members of the jury… you have seen the CCTV stills. You can accept Mr Simmons' evidence that he was acquainted with Miss Anderson. In your deliberations, study the photo. They embraced face to face. Mr Simmons' arms are wrapped around Miss Anderson's waist. Are we expected to accept from the defence that this one minuscule thread innocently and mysteriously jumped from Mr Simmons' cardigan, onto Miss Anderson's waist and then miraculously wriggled its way to the knife punctures in the young lady's shoulder? What is the likelihood of that? It would be like dropping a Roman coin from a plane 20,000 feet above the Midlands and later learning that an 8-year-old boy picked it up on his way home from school while walking through a 50-acre paddock of mature barley. However, this 8-year-old boy would not have rushed from the paddock like Simmons raced from the scene of Amy Anderson's murder.

'You've seen the footage of Mr Simmons leaving the Rose and Thorn car park, only minutes after Miss Anderson suffered the frenzied stabbing in the adjacent street. You cannot accept that as one of Mr Simmons ill-fated coincidences. But if, amongst your number, you do give credence to that proposition, think reasonably, members of the jury. If Mr Simmons did not himself attack Miss Anderson, he has not offered any evidence or description of another person who must have, given the time frames, been in the immediate vicinity. I think you will reason that all the evidence points to Mr Simmons having, on the evening of sixteen August, savagely and brutally taken Miss Anderson's life.

'Shortly after, panic deepens when he fears that journalist Miss Hegarty holds incriminating evidence. To save himself, he resolves to also eliminate her. I apologise for the expression, but the man was desperate. He leaves *his* fingerprints on her car – that can't be disputed. He admits to speaking with Miss Hegarty and Miss Anderson only because overwhelming evidence supports his interactions with both women. He has no alternative. The evidence is irrefutable. We call it confess and avoid; confess to the minor facts like the meeting, but avoid responsibility for the eventual crime. You can rely on the evidence seen and heard in this court that led to the killing of three women in six days. You do not need a motive. All you are required to do, by law, is form a view that stands the test of "beyond reasonable doubt".

'Ladies and gentlemen. Don't be fooled by Mr Simmons' long-standing service record. He has been trained to disregard human life – in a battle setting I might add – but nevertheless, he is conditioned for killing. He compulsively took the lives of three young women, covering his tracks as he did so. Whether it was personal rejection or a lust for power, it matters not the catalyst behind his behaviour. You must penalise that behaviour and protect the community by finding Barry Andrew Simmons guilty of all charges.'

Postlewaite's final instruction hangs in the air.

Belinda Pace rises. Smiles. Mentally tweaks her summary, now made all the more difficult by Postlewaite's thought-provoking closing. Pace however, has earned her reputation from 'winging it'; from her ability to devise and revise on the spot.

'"Protect the community",' she repeats. 'Members of the jury. Let us for a moment think about that. For thirty years Barry Simmons protected the community. He is a distinguished naval officer with an unblemished command record. For the past two years, he has promoted his charter service within the Evesham community. He employs local staff. You do not need protection from Barry Simmons. You need to understand how the police have been remiss in fully investigating these crimes. They have circumvented established procedures, jumped to conclusions and settled for whimsical snippets they choose to dress up as evidence.

'Let us for a minute examine the logistics. We have heard that Simmons' craft is not fitted with autopilot, although even if it were, the meandering nature of the Avon would provide difficulties too complex for its operation. We have also heard that Inspector Marchant was not vaguely interested in the craft's operation. Had he approached the investigation objectively, why would he not enquire about the craft's operating procedures? Was there a co-pilot or navigator? If that were the case, the defence concedes that there might have been an opportunity for Mr Simmons to vacate the bridge. But the very essence of Mr Simmons' defence is that *he was* operating the craft for the duration of the journey. You must question how it could be possible for Barry Simmons to take time out to murder Juanita Morales – at the rear of the craft, remember – and then walk the length of the craft back to his post as if nothing had happened. All in view of twenty passengers, mind you, and on a river that meanders like a slithering Anaconda.

'Not satisfied with that, two days later he is said to have

stabbed Amy Anderson to death. What links him to the crime? A solitary fibre. Remember, there is no proof of ownership or possession of the knife, and more importantly, no fingerprints or DNA attributed to anyone, let alone Mr Simmons. Certainly, you have seen a receipt for the knife, but remember, we are talking about evidence – hard conclusive fact. There is no evidence to prove that the murder weapon was the subject of that receipt. You cannot 'infer' that it was and you cannot assume.

'A complete and methodical search of Barry Simmons' home failed to locate blood on *any* clothes *or* shoes. You must carefully consider why there is no blood on the blue cardigan of which the prosecution relies so heavily. Further, and this is crucial, the police failed to locate any blood in his car, traces of which we would expect to find if Mr Simmons had stabbed Miss Anderson five times and then immediately jumped in his car and driven off, as the prosecution would have you believe. You must consider the probability that had Mr Simmons committed this crime, his clothing would have been stained with blood. If that were the case, members of the jury, I suggest you'd expect to find this blue cardigan had been discarded in the skip along with the knife and not found in his wardrobe. And remember, forensic analysis showed no evidence of recent chemical residue from dry cleaning or domestic washing. But what was not in the skip was the mysterious cloak or jacket the prosecutor would have you believe Simmons wore.

'Balance this with Mr Simmons' own evidence: he openly admits to seeing and talking to Ms Anderson at the hotel. You must consider why he would do that if he had something to hide.

'You've heard the prosecution stretch this fantasy even further by suggesting that Mr Simmons murdered Miss

Hegarty because of information she had. Let me repeat Mr Marchant's account of Miss Hegarty's conversation: "I saw Barry Simmons at the Rose and Thorn talk to Amy Anderson and hug and kiss her." That's it. No date to confine it to these allegations, mind you; it could have been any night, but let us just accept that it was the sixteenth of August. There may well have been another twenty patrons who hugged and kissed Amy that night – she did enjoy, as you have heard, a reputation of having many acquaintances. There is no harm in that, and you must not draw any conclusions therefrom. She enjoyed socialising and she enjoyed a reunion with her previous employer. In the thousands of pubs across England, patrons might have left at 10.33 p.m. We cannot suspect them all of committing a crime that happened only moments earlier. The prosecution relies on CCTV. But what does it show? A couple hugging and a vehicle exiting a car park. Hardly compelling evidence against Mr Simmons. To set that point even firmer, my learned friend offered you a lengthy explanation of the use of 'inferences' in an attempt to tie the Crown's evidence together. So let me talk about inferences. Can you, members of the jury, infer that because Mr Simmons drove his car out of the car park at a certain time of the evening, he must have killed Miss Anderson? Of course not. Neither can you conclude that because Barry Simmons' business card was found near Miss Anderson's body it must have been dropped or left there by Mr Simmons himself. It is not unreasonable that as a former employee, Miss Anderson would have his card for any number of reasons.

'Finally, just bear with me for a moment longer, police find a solitary fingerprint on Miss Hegarty's car, on the rear door mind you, not the driver's or front passenger door –

the rear. That is the only link to Mr Simmons. We have heard of Mr Edison Edwards' fingerprints being excluded. How many others were excluded that we do not know of? And let me put this to you: the learned prosecutor says you do not need to find a motive – and that is true. However, *he* chooses to cite as a motive Miss Hegarty's apparent knowledge of incriminating evidence against Mr Simmons. Pay no heed to that because you have heard that Barry Simmons had already told Miss Hegarty that he'd referred the matter to his lawyer. Remember his words: "All I can say is that I'm innocent of this stuff. My lawyer's handling this and he's told me to speak to no-one." There was no threat to Mr Simmons, but even if there were, it could not have been resolved by disposing of Miss Hegarty.

'I ask you to consider the testimony of Inspector Marchant. His admission of being firmly focused on conviction and safeguarding the community opens the door to non-objectivity. Has he presented a strong case against Mr Barry Simmons? I say to you that he has not. There is doubt as to whether Juanita Morales was on the river craft. If you accept that Miss Morales *was* on the craft, you must reject the notion that Mr Simmons had the opportunity to kill her or throw her overboard. There is doubt that Mr Simmons saw Amy Anderson for more than a fleeting "hello hug" and there is doubt that Mr Simmons had the opportunity to kill Miss Hegarty. Certainly, the police lead no evidence of her having been at Simmons' home or on his boat. They also lead no evidence of Mr Simmons having attended Miss Hegarty's home. All you have heard is that she was murdered at a place unknown and found in her car in Evesham. That is where you must rigidly apply the benefit of "reasonable doubt".'

Pace had struggled to explain the term "reasonable doubt" in the few court contests of her short career. She'd heard trial judges go to great lengths, often in convoluted terms, to convince the jury panel that beyond reasonable doubt is the highest standard of proof available. She'd seen juries tussle with the concept and apply the standard in reverse – in a matter where a defendant's testimony was so far beyond believability, the jury did doubt it and determined it to be a lie. Some of her former clients had presented testimony so remote from reality that the jury automatically discounted its authenticity.

She reinforces Simmons' position to the jury: 'Mr Simmons did not know Miss Morales and there is no evidence linking him to her death. The fact that he had her phone was a minor slip of character; the foolish act of a man who sought the thrill of opportunism at the expense of honesty and responsibility. His deceitful answers to the police paint him as evasive – but not guilty of murder. His friendship with Amy Anderson was neither illicit nor clandestine. Simmons had no more than greeted her hello. The evidence given by Marchant referring to the blue thread found on the murder weapon must be considered no more than peripheral coincidence.

'I ask you to accept that the thread was simply a cross-transference when Simmons hugged Amy. You cannot exclude the possibility that the thread from the cardigan adhered to the blood-saturated knife after slicing through Amy's coat. Simmons' leaving the pub had no impact on the evidence, because, once again, no one had seen him commit the crime. I say that you cannot conclude that it was Mr Simmons who killed her. And why not? There are far too many variables to be able to conjoin them as one act reliant upon the other.

'The prosecution has shown nothing concrete that you can seize to prove beyond reasonable doubt that Mr Simmons committed these crimes. On that basis you must return a verdict of not guilty.'

28

THE FOLLOWING DAY's proceedings begin with Judge Ainsley delivering to the jury a summary of evidence, legal directions and deliberation guidelines. On completion, the twelve jurors enter a cold wooden room whose walls will later resonate human intolerance. Twelve jurors who know each other only by first name and occupation – and some do not remember even that – begin the task of determining the future of Barry Simmons.

Fortunately for some, and unfortunately for others, Hilary Chevalier has been elected jury foreperson. A retired private college teacher, her demeanour and carriage suggest she's retired *very* recently. Her hair coils into a beehive above a round, puffy face. Like a 1950s headmistress she screeches at her 11 charges as if they are delinquent students. *Who voted for her?* whispers a reckless voice from the class.

Miss Chevalier, as she prefers to be addressed, calls the room to order. 'Where do we stand at this minute? I think we should have a show of hands. All those who say "guilty"?'

Five hands, including hers, shoot into the air. Two slowly follow.

'Of the remaining five, are you decided or undecided?'

'No way known he's guilty,' shouts Christian Abernathy, who has announced his occupation as student. He is in his third year of law at Reading University, and a member of a radical fraternity that endorses stringent carbon reducing measures. Christian passionately champions his causes and strongly opposes denigration of conservative policy.

'Not guilty,' vote another two males.

'Undecided,' reply in unison the remaining two.

'Then we have some work to do,' says Hilary.

She lays out the prosecution exhibits. The labelled plastic bags look like a selection of bargain oddments from a car boot sale: Knife, jumper, fibre, box of pills, forensic data sheets, Juanita Morales' handbag and mobile phone, Amy Anderson's coat, Marg Hegarty's notebook, copies of testimony, stills from the CCTV footage and excerpts from Simmons' Record of Interview.

Fixed in her tutorial carriage, Hilary continues: 'Our task is comparatively simple. He is either guilty or not guilty; we have only to decide one of two results.'

'How prophetic,' interjects Christian. 'I'm sure none of us has to be told what we're here for. We're all adults, you know.'

'Yes, young man. I'm sorry – I didn't catch your name. You are quite right. We are all adults. And as adults we should be acting responsibly and respecting the views and authority bestowed in me as the elected foreperson.'

Christian frowns. Discerning that he and Hilary are attracting the scrutiny of ten pairs of eyes, he does not want to appear confrontational. To the contrary, he states his view to gauge support. Rather than launch a full-scale attack on the woman he's labelled 'the old biddy' he replies: 'I apologise. I just felt you were overstating the obvious.'

'Now that we've cleared that up,' continues Hilary, 'we can proceed with the task at hand. We can assume that the police would not have charged Simmons with three counts of murder had they not had sufficient reason.'

A hand shoots up from the end of the table. 'Yes, Mr Abernathy.'

'Madam forelady. We cannot assume anything. That is not our role. If we assume police had good reason to charge Simmons, then we might as well assume that he is guilty and hand over our verdict this minute. Our deliberations and decisions must derive solely from fact. If we accept that police preferred charges by "good reason", which you have not defined, we can only arrive at a definitive conclusion by accepting the evidence or lack of evidence they had before them. We cannot *assume* that any such evidence is conclusive proof of guilt.'

Around the table jaws drop. Three or four murmurs of 'I agree' peel from the assembly and fall heavily on Hilary's ears. 'We're not getting off to a very good start here. Perhaps Mr Abernathy would care to *assume* the position of foreman?'

'I'm not sure I interpret your reference to 'assume' as respectful or contemptuous. However, I am happy to make my contribution to deciding the guilt or otherwise of Mr Simmons as an equal member of the jury panel.'

'Here, here. We must all be equal,' says Tom Dickinson, a casually dressed gentleman of middle age. Tom is indescribable. He is one of those depicted on television as 'just normal' – just another person in the street. The man next door. Perhaps it is his short, brown hair, average height of five foot nine inches and green eyes that set him as one of the general male population. Or, possibly the way he dresses from a Primark budget catalogue: average jeans, average windcheater and average runners. His children would all be of average looks, average abilities and average intelligence – thereby continuing the theory of evolution into the next generation.

He addresses his fellow jurors: 'I sat on a jury in this very court four years ago. I'll tell you that it wasn't the crime of the century, but it was one where each jury member respected one another and gave a little rope to the idiosyncrasies and mannerisms of each other. Look, we have seven guilty, three not guilty and two undecided. If we take into account the two undecided, we have the potential for a nine to three or a seven to five vote – nowhere near unanimous. As our forelady suggests, let us first consider the exhibits. Do they amount to evidence that will allow us to find that Simmons is guilty beyond reasonable doubt?'

After an hour of cross-table power broking and testosterone charged suggestions, amicable discussions ensue. As with any group discussion, there will always be non-contributors. Their colleagues will wonder if they're interested and they'll wonder if they're even paying attention. In most cases, the silent ones absorb every pearl of information, classifying and sorting it into cerebral compartments at the ready for future retrieval.

At the end of the table sits one such juror who would prefer a simple shoplifting case over a triple murder. At eighteen-years-old, she'd barely scraped onto the jury eligibility list. She's said nothing all morning, her introduction the only contribution: 'I'm Julieanne Newton. I'm unemployed, but I only left school three weeks ago.'

A couple of jurors picked up on that. An unemployed person with pride will always qualify why they're unemployed. 'I just got retrenched'; 'the company went broke'; 'we moved address and I couldn't get to work.'

No one with self-esteem wants to be labelled as the

stereotyped unemployed: the unemployed by election, avoiding work, flipping over advertised vacancies in local papers, walking past Job Centres and failing to be pro-active by canvassing prospective employers and distributing Curriculum Vitaes throughout their business district.

Yes, there are genuine unemployed, but those with a strong work ethic invariably accept a job of any vocation, enabling them to maintain respectability in the community, and responsibility enough to provide for their family.

Julieanne is embarrassed about her status, but not afraid to meekly reveal her thoughts. 'I came into this room undecided. So far, I've thought about these things (pointing to the exhibits) and I think if someone murdered three people, the police would have tons more evidence.'

Christian, realising he has an ally in Julieanne, looks across the table and smiles.

'Well said,' says Hilary. 'We have a good cross-section of opinion. How are we all going to decide as one?'

'If a few of us have doubts, we won't,' replies Christian.

A court assistant steers a rickety trolley into the room. The selection of tea, coffee and sandwiches is a calculated tension-breaker. It encourages jurors to informally gravitate toward those with similar leanings, and it allows for their points of interest to be shared and discussed in a congenial manner rather than one of stiff-necked formality.

Groups form. Some discuss the case; others continue introductions, talking about work, home, babies and the tremors swaying between their forelady and Christian Abernathy.

Deliberations continue through the short afternoon. In courts of law, mornings and afternoons generally span two-to three-hour blocks. Beyond that, the attention span of jurors, counsel and the judge wanes.

Near the end of the day, Hilary calls the table to order. 'How do we say now?'

Christian glances at Julieanne and mimics, "How do we say now?" accentuating the movement of his lips like an African woman in an elocution class.

'All those who say "guilty"?'

Eleven hands shoot above the table. The earlier mature and responsible Tom Dickinson holds both arms aloft.

'Mr Dickinson. We need show only one hand for our vote, thank you.'

Tom smiles and retracts one arm.

'So, we are ten to two. Miss Newton and Mr Abernathy are undecided.'

'I'm not undecided, Hilary. I *am* decided that Mr Simmons is not guilty.'

'Me too,' adds Julieanne.

The judge's tipstaff raps twice on the door and enters. 'Madam forelady. We are nearing 5.00 p.m. Have you reached a verdict?'

'No sir. I think we are a little way off yet.'

'We shall reconvene in court where his Honour will discharge you for the evening. He will warn you that after leaving this room you are not to discuss these matters with anyone, not even amongst yourselves. We shall resume at 10.30 in the morning.'

The jury files into the courtroom where Judge Ainsley repeats, word for word, the directive given moments earlier by his tipstaff.

Simmons is remanded in custody and returned to Wandsworth.

Jurors escape the court's precincts and head for home where they hope to relax in domesticity. They won't. For seventeen hours, their minds will churn with testimony, evidence, submissions, and jury room squabbles before they again convene to fulfil their obligation to the community.

Hoping for an early result, Marchant and Watts had braved the day within the court precincts. The lack of verdict means another day of ultra-marathon travel half way across England. They head to City Thameslink station where they shuffle like coal miners down the shafts of the Underground to commence the two and a half hour return trip to Worcester. They clamber aboard the 5.22 p.m. with seconds to spare.

'This is not going to be cut and dried,' Olivia says for the umpteenth time. She has continually tackled Marchant over his charging Simmons. She has also taken the painful step of furnishing a report to inspector Marchant, noting the grounds for her belief of Simmons' innocence, but had stopped short of going over his head to take the matter to the Chief Inspector or Superintendent of crime.

Olivia is mindful of the repercussions of transgressing against fellow officers, having seen, first hand, a WPC ostracised for her indiscretion against a senior colleague. That situation arose during a physical arrest where an offender had to be restrained. Admittedly, her accompanying officer did employ more force than was necessary to accomplish the task, prompting the offender to subsequently file a complaint against the arresting officer. When the WPC was called to detail her version to the enquiry, she told the truth: 'I witnessed the offender being restrained with sharp punches to the stomach.' She may as well have resigned on the spot for not following the unwritten practice of: 'I'm sorry sir, I did not actually see what my partner was doing. I had my head down, compiling notes at the time. I regret that I'm unable to help.' Others in similar situations simply offer watered-down accounts of the events under enquiry.

The following week the whole shift ignored her. Power in numbers. Some refused to work with her, relenting only after being threatened with disciplinary action for misconduct. Her locker had been broken into; honey poured over her uniform and boot polish wiped around the brim of her hat; one officer purposely forgot to buy her lunch when he ran the lunch errand, and another graffitied her name in captions over animal photos. One ingenious computer literate member went too far by creating promiscuous invitations on her Facebook page.

She resigned within a fortnight.

While Olivia enjoys a respectable standing within the force, she does not want to jeopardise her position, despite her intention of resigning in the foreseeable future. She maintains only professional respect for Marchant.

'Home and hosed,' Marchant responds to Olivia's prophecy. 'Juries are wise to people like him.'

'And I hope they're wise to people like you, too!' Olivia tries to pull the words back into her mouth. Too late. Marchant raises his arm and swings to strike her, but stops half an inch from her nose. 'You fuckin' bitch. You haven't got a clue, Watts.'

Papers rustle, earplugs from iPods fly around the carriage like glow-worms, and heads turn towards Marchant's coarse words. 'The sooner we rid the world of scum like Simmons, the better off we'll all be. Sometimes they just need some added help in exiting society and I'm not one to refuse that. You and your self-righteous cause of doing everything by the book helps no one and the sooner your type realise that you're best suited to an administration desk somewhere in the boondocks of personnel the better off we'll all be. Now let me sleep.'

Olivia has no problem letting him sleep. She even considers leaving him be beyond their station. She gazes at his reflection in the window and sees a man so incomplete that his only way of gaining acceptance from anyone other than his wife is to manipulate and contrive his way to the pinnacle of success. His sleepy smile suggests his subconscious is riding high on a wave of accomplishment. *Heaven help us all if he secures convictions.*

As the train pulls in to Oxford, Olivia accepts that she'd forced Marchant's limit of tolerance. She decides to not chance her luck any further. She wakes him.

29

ELEVEN MOTTLED JURORS dressed like animated liquorice allsorts, each carrying a cup of tea or coffee with tell-tale froth seeping through the lid's breather, extend their morning greetings, exchange chit-chat of the previous evening's television shows, and bid 'nice day coming up' and 'hope we're home for the weekend' superficial exchanges. Christian and Julieanne chat like newlyweds on a honeymoon. They speak nothing of deliberations, choosing to relive the delights of the previous evening.

Hilary, dressed in black skirt and black jacket, is the black liquorice. The dull, flavourless blob of molasses frequently orphaned in the bottom of the packet.

The second day of deliberations begins in earnest. Hilary resumes her position at the head of the table, drinking tea from the cardboard cup as if it were fine bone china, the obligatory pinky raised high above the lipstick-smudged rim. 'I think we should get started. An early day is a productive day.'

Half a dozen heads turn toward Hilary in silent protest. Disobeying her command could earn a dunce's cap and ten minutes in the corner.

'Are we any further advanced? Should we vote again?'

A fresh vote remains deadlocked at ten to two with the same two steadfast in their vote of not guilty.

The judge's tipstaff enters and queries the status of deliberations.

'Same as yesterday,' replies Hilary. 'We may have a problem.'

'The court will convene in ten minutes. You can direct any concerns in a note to His Honour.'

'Madam forelady. Have you reached your verdict?'

'No, Your honour. Nor are we likely to.'

'Madam forelady. There is a long way to go until we reach that stage. I suggest you return to your deliberations and perhaps offer more consideration to what each of you say. Think wider and broaden your discussions. We shall convene again before lunch, unless you advise my tipstaff earlier that you have reached a verdict.'

The court adjourns. The jurors return to their deliberations, skirmishing through an atmosphere of despondency and uncertainty. For ten days they've sat as one, listening to hours of testimony, witness examinations and cross-examinations, and forensic scientists speaking in lingo and jargon that few outside their sphere of expertise could understand. For ten jurors, facing yet another day of trying to convert Christian and Julieanne to return a guilty verdict, the task seems insurmountable. The couple's stance infuriates Hilary; her nine followers condemning the two dissenters' fierce resistance.

Christian will not compromise his integrity at any cost. Justice is justice, he'd professed on more than one occasion. Now, to the other jurors he asks: 'How could you send this man to prison for the rest of his life if he's innocent?'

'And how could you turn him loose if he's guilty?' a Chevalier supporter shoots back.

'We won't get anywhere by arguing,' Hilary snaps. 'Perhaps

we should restate the weight of evidence against the accused to assist Mr Abernathy and Miss Newton. Firstly, we must believe that Miss Morales was on the river cruise. Just because no one saw Simmons kill her doesn't mean he didn't. He demonstrated the necessary guilty mind by concealing her phone, and I, for one, do accept it was the deceased's phone. *And* he claims he didn't see Miss Morales. I challenge anyone to go to any function of predominantly white people and not be aware of a person of different race. This would be especially so for Mr Simmons, because as a male he would surely have noticed Miss Morales, who was, judging by her appearance in the photographs, a stunning woman.'

Christian interjects: 'Pure speculation. Ever heard of beauty being in the eye of the beholder? Are you aware of racism statistics and the widespread opposition to Britain's migration policy?'

'Just blown your own theory, Mr Abernathy. On that basis, Mr Simmons might just have been one of those racism statistics who actually abhorred having an Asian on his white-skinned, Anglo Saxon cruise. You can keep throwing in curly suppositions, but there's far too much weight against him. There is no doubt he killed Amy Anderson. You cannot accept the one-in-a-billion chance of cross-contamination. One thread of his jumper was found on the knife. Of course it came off his hand. We would be remiss in our duty if we found otherwise. We are aided by the photographs of his association with the deceased and of his driving out of the car park. There can be no clearer definition of beyond reasonable doubt. And then there's the fingerprints found on Hegarty's car. That wasn't a case of a mugging gone wrong. Simmons had to be rid of her to remove any suggestion of his involvement. Even if he was not privy to whatever Miss Hegarty might have known, *he* might have thought the worst. Perhaps she had eyewitness details? Yes, there I do speculate, Mr Abernathy, but the facts speak for themselves. Simmons is guilty.'

Jurors discuss and evaluate Hilary's elongated précis. Two knocks at the door interrupt the verbal void as the lunch trolley squeaks into the room. 'Tools down,' Tom calls out. 'I can't eat and think at the same time.'

'It's not you who needs to think,' Hilary retorts.

'Yeah, there's only two who need miss their meal so they can concentrate on the verdict.'

'I've thought about mine, and I'm sure Julieanne's thought about hers too,' shouts Christian.

'Better think again,' a heckler named Max shouts.

'Order in here please,' hushes the tipstaff. 'We know you face a huge burden; there is bound to be some friction between those of you from opposing camps. Enjoy your lunch and think of something other than the case for an hour.'

With difficulty, general discussion surfaces and then fragments into emotion, humour, joviality and sarcasm like flakes in a kaleidoscope shuffling into a different shape with each speaker. Christian and Julieanne remain on the outer, speaking only to each other for the whole hour. And they talk beyond the hour and into the next.

'Would you two care to join us?'

'We're deliberating,' says Christian, who is now more obsessed with passion for Julieanne rather than fulfilling his duty to reach a verdict.

Hilary continues: 'The court reconvenes at four o'clock. It would be nice to go home for the weekend with a clear mind. Can you imagine how we'll suffer if we're worrying about whether you two will have a change of heart or not? If you don't, Simmons will probably be fed back into the community on bail until a retrial.'

'We're still talking.'

And so they do for the following hour. One juror compares their whispering like lovers in an afternoon television soap opera: *Like the sands of an hourglass…*

The jury room's mood thickens with tension, perspiration, and hopes to deliver a verdict, any verdict, so long as it is unanimous. Jurors clash over the relevance of exhibits and argue over legal definitions – What is *beyond reasonable doubt?* Is one to be 'positive' of certain facts; nearly positive?; or most probable? Justice Ainsley had devoted ten minutes to that very conundrum. The jurors left the court none the wiser. What might be 'reasonable' to one person may not be reasonable to another. 'So why doesn't the system convict on beyond *all* doubt?' one of the jurors ventures.

Perhaps the jury system should be reviewed. Are all jurors 'reasonable' people? They are selected under a presumption of wisdom: they sit in the court as a cauldron of collective knowledge and experience. But what sort of experience? Can a bus driver or council gardener, for instance, determine ownership of DNA helixes, foetal haemoglobin from spattered blood deposits and entry angles of knife wounds? Generally not. They must rely on testimony of learned doctors, scientists and professionals in their respective fields. But those professionals are examined from opposing sides of the judiciary – the defence and the prosecution – knowing that their testimony will be attacked. The prosecution witness will have his expert testimony discredited by the defence in the same manner as the defence witness will have her testimony discredited by the prosecution. Accordingly, the expert evidence of a professional witness is *predetermined to be flawed*. Most 'reasonable' jurors are not equipped with knowledge sufficient to determine what aspect, if any, of that particular evidence is *flawed*.

Delivering justice is akin to delivering mail: it goes astray, it is delayed, or it is simply not delivered. Frequent headlines tell of DNA evidence having freed prisoners *after* they've spent up to 40 years in prison. [Ricky Jackman and Riley Bridgeman were freed after serving 39 years for the 1975 murder of a Cleveland, Ohio, businessman.]

Innocence Projects boast similar triumphs in the United Kingdom. These judicial back flips stem from conclusive proof that accuseds could not possibly have committed crimes for which they had been convicted. In at least one case the accused was not even in the county during the crime's commission. Police, however, aided by the Crown Prosecutor, still managed to *convince* a jury otherwise. Thank goodness for the House of Commons vote of 9 November, 1964 [which became law in 1965] to end capital punishment. By that time, 11,305 men and 633 women had been executed since statistics began in 1735. No one will ever know how many of those were innocent.

At 3.45 p.m. Hilary calls the collective to order. The sombre and jovial air abates like the prelude to a storm. The last joke has been told; resultant laughter escapes through dusty air conditioning vents. Some members struggle to crystallise their final decision, trying desperately to reinforce or justify their stance. Others had made their decision in the first minutes of deliberations – or earlier. Hilary prays for unanimity; she hoped to have been discharged the previous night, for she is none too pleased about missing today's bingo afternoon at the Chelsea Ladies' Auxiliary.

'We have not long left in the day so we shall now vote.'

Hilary double-checks the hand count. 'Are we all agreed?' Nods, murmurs and bowed heads acquiesce.

Seconds later the familiar double knock on the door drums through the twelve jurors. 'Have you reached a verdict?'

'We have sir.'

The tipstaff lead the jury members into the courtroom. Some fix their eyes on Simmons; others look to the floor in embarrassment as they give nothing away, not even the slightest hint of the decision that will impact upon the next 30 or more years of Simmons' life. If he lives that long.

Judge Ainsley utters his most important request: 'Madam forelady. Have you reached a verdict?'

'We have Your Honour.'

'And what say you in the matter of Juanita Morales?'

'Guilty, Your Honour.'

'And you are all of that mind?'

'We are Your Honour.'

Judge Ainsley recites the same words with the same intonation, for verdicts in the matters of Amy Anderson and Marg Hegarty.

Hilary Chevalier replies with equal drollness, 'Guilty, Your Honour.'

'Thank you. Members of the jury, I'm sure you've faced a difficult task deciding the fate, or otherwise, of a fellow human being. It's obviously an extraordinarily difficult job to sit in judgment of a fellow member of the community, so I now thank you on behalf of the community. I have no doubt you've encountered an onerous task but it's a system that works and it relies on people like yourselves taking time to do this generally thankless task.

'Remember that you are not permitted to discuss matters of the court or jury room. Thank you again, Madam Forelady and members of the jury. My associate will escort you back to your room from where you will be discharged.'

Simmons stands motionless in the dock, unsure whether to shout out in protest or maintain composure and respectability. He accepts that proceedings could have swung either way, but never had he truly accepted that he would be found guilty.

His Honour continues: 'Mr Simmons. You have been found guilty of three counts of murder. You are remanded in custody until March twenty-one, at which time you will stand before me to be sentenced for your crimes.

'Remove the prisoner.'

Jurors file out of the court, led by an emotionless Hilary. Others jostle for position, anxious to return to their daily business; some chat as if leaving a school reunion; but all are pleased to have finished for the week. They paid little attention to Judge Ainsley's appreciation speech, preferring instead to celebrate being shot of the burden. It has been an imposition on their lives; a disruption to work and domestic responsibilities of taking children to and from school, washing, ironing, lawn mowing, preparing midday and evening meals; sacrificing pre-arranged commitments such as attending health clubs; and foregoing long-established routines that have thrown their life so far out of synchronisation that they will need two or three days to resume normality. If the community is so grateful, why does it reward jurors with such a pittance when the legal fraternity receives salaries that tower far above the average wage?

Christian and Julieanne dawdle dizzily behind the group as if they've stepped out of a fun park's Rotor ride. They reach for each other's hand and try to squeeze the guilt from their veins. Christian is in awe of Julieanne. It was her inviting him to share her weekend that totally dissolved his personal ideals.

None of the jurors understood why the pair suddenly dumped their "not guilty" stance. Some had witnessed the developing bond, but that had no effect on Christian and Julieanne, who, by virtue of their early determination, had been on the incommunicable outer. The pair relented not to the pressure of those advocating "guilty", but to their own weakness of desire, of wanting to explore their newfound love in the sanctity of weekend peace without the prospect of a weekend recall hovering over their head. Many important decisions have been consummated by the endorphins of love and lust. Try to justify the decision-making processes (and their consequences) of King Henry VIII.

Christian and Julieanne mutually excuse abandoning Simmons with the rationale: *the others may have been right. We couldn't change their mind so we only delayed the inevitable. There would have been more pressure placed on us to change our vote. Perhaps we could have stood stronger had there been three of us sharing the same view.*

They depart the Old Bailey; the one place where the layperson believes that all wrongs shall be righted and the perpetrators of such wrongs shall be punished as prescribed by laws enacted by their peers; the place where the judiciary is charged to oversee the mechanics of justice so that no person will suffer legal indiscretion; and the place where the finely balanced scales of justice should never tilt in favour of the more plausible at the expense of absolute truth.

Christian turns to Julieanne. 'What have I done? I compromised my ideals. My love for you outweighed my love for justice.'

'You're so sweet.'

279

30

Olivia bolts to the station, drawing in traffic noise, sirens, horns, and the thunder of Qantas QF 9 on its approach to Heathrow, all in an effort to block out Marchant's boisterous gloating.

'Slow down will you. I told you so, Liv. Told you all along. You going to apologise? Shall we kiss and make up?'

Olivia stops and turns to Marchant with such fury that pedestrians watch in expectation of a violent domestic dispute. Abandoning self-control, she shouts: 'You revel in your glory of sending an innocent man to prison. Aren't you ashamed of what you've done?'

'Olivia. Look at yourself all wound up. What did you say to me months ago about being one-track fixated on Simmons?'

'I said you weren't considering other factors, or something like that.'

'Aren't you the same with this Taylor character? It's over Olivia, time to move on. New cases, new glory to seek. New horizons of crime waiting to be explored.'

'Maybe. But the sun hasn't yet set on the old horizon.'

'It will, Liv. Then you'll be as blind to the night as you've been to the day.'

'Maybe *I'm* blind, but his lawyer's not. You see her dart straight for the registrar's office? Old Ainsley hadn't even ripped off his wig before Pace lodged intent to appeal docs.'

The conversation tames after they board the train for their final trip to Oxford. Marchant magically produces a whisky flask from his briefcase while Olivia sips bottled water. She stares through the window, trying to reconcile how she'd so badly let down Barry Simmons by failing to unearth evidence sufficient to charge Trevor Taylor. Certainly, she'd been constrained by Marchant restricting her activities, but even had she discovered vital information and evidence, Marchant would have dismissed her findings – as evidenced by prior conduct – simply to preserve his own reputation.

Olivia needs help, but no one within her own office would dare tread behind Marchant's back to support a cavalier's quest to contest a closed-file crime. But there is one person outside her office upon whom Olivia can rely. Inspector Dave Stafford.

Olivia steps into her musty home. Sleep and coffee hang in the air. Five hours' daily travel to and from London had constrained her home life to only sleep, showers and snacks. Windows remain closed, dishes unwashed, clothes lie on the kitchen floor in front of the washing machine and snake a trail along the hallway to the bathroom and bedroom. She sheds her court attire and throws on a cheap tracksuit – a weekend market special that looks the real deal, but was probably knocked up by an illegal immigrant in a backyard outhouse for two pounds and sold for fifteen.

Pushing aside thoughts of dinner, she phones Stafford's mobile: *Stafford here. Leave a message if you dare. If you don't, I won't care.*

'Hi. It's me. Please call, I need your help.'

She phones his office, hoping to find him pressured into another fifteen-hour day.

'Hi. Could I speak to Inspector Stafford please?'

'Inspector? Who's calling? He's been a DCI for three months now.'

'Sorry. It's DS Watts from Worcester.'

The line crackles as Olivia's call clicks through. 'What's this DCI stuff?'

'Hi Olivia. Long story. Been following your case though. Another one off the plate eh?'

'Dave. That's what I need to speak to you about. Can we meet? Sort of officially; I don't know how to explain this. Simmons shouldn't even have been charged.'

'Bloody hell, Olivia. You've left it a bit late for that, haven't you? What's going on up there, if you'll excuse the pun?'

'Just help me please. I'll come to your place if need be.'

'No. If you've got concerns, we'd best keep this under wraps. I'm off this weekend. How about I come to yours – home, not office. I can be there in the morn.'

'Fine. But not before 6.00 a.m.'

'Very funny. You'll be lucky to see me before nine.'

Olivia plucks case notes from her bag, having had the complete file intact should it have been required in court. She is sufficiently organised to never be caught out. She lives by the words of a sign hanging in Worcester police station's firearms registry: *It's better to have it and not need it than to need it and not have it.* She memorised the words and adopted the phrase as a personal creed. She now applies it to everything: carrying make-up; a spare battery for her mobile phone; her canister of capsicum spray; and, she is embarrassed to reveal, an emergency condom.

She clears the table of the morning's unfinished breakfast cereal and half-cup of coffee, and throws over a fresh, dark blue tablecloth. The police insignia on the corners remind her that she'd 'borrowed' it to protect her hair from the rain when leaving a staff function six months' earlier. She contemplates changing it, but hopes Stafford will see the funny side of it being legitimised for police work.

She divides the paperwork into three piles: Juanita Morales. Amy Anderson. Marg Hegarty.

Stafford taps on her door at ten minutes after nine and walks straight inside. Less time in the hallway means less time for neighbours to second-guess the comings and goings of another *Coronation Street* or *Neighbours* visitor. A reunion kiss stifles Stafford's: 'What's this mess I have to sort out? This could blow up into something major if it's what I think it is.'

'Much worse.'

Olivia details selected pages of the prepared piles to Stafford, slapping Post-it notes to various sections for later discussion. She feeds Stafford the chronology of events culminating in Simmons' conviction, and apologises for not speaking out earlier – the reason being that she believed Simmons' defence team would present sufficient evidence to bring an acquittal.

After four hours of scrutiny and discussion, Stafford announces: 'Olivia, we've got to get all this in the open. We can't save Marchant's arse; he's taken too many short cuts. The guy won't stop at anything to fuel his bloody ego. Bloody CPS shouldn't have approved it. I'd almost bet he's slipped them a sweet underhanded deal.'

Olivia heaves a sigh of exasperation. 'I've got no real allegiance to Marchant, and it's not as if I want to sink him, but on the other side, Simmons is languishing in a bloody hell-hole for something he's had absolutely nothing to do with. I don't want to sound bigheaded, but I told Marchant all along that there was more to this case and I told him I felt that Taylor was the one we should be pursuing. Marchant was just so consumed with Simmons – almost as a personal vendetta – and his only acceptable result would be conquest. Stuffed if I know, but he pissed me off something bad every time I mentioned Taylor's name. In one of his rages, he told me to go it alone so I went all the way to Bournemouth to get more goods on Taylor. Could have got myself in the shit too, after I found him peering over a toilet cubicle at me.'

'So you would have been in the shit in more ways than one! Poor little Olivia,' Stafford consoles as he lays an arm across her shoulder.

Olivia moulds into the crease of his body. He kisses her forehead. She steals the gaze from his eyes and returns the flaming expectation. Heat welds them together. Hands probe for zips, buttons and belts, trespassing every fence and barrier until they simultaneously breach perimeter security.

Stafford sweeps Olivia into his arms, stumbles to her bedroom, sets her on the bed, and draws the thick curtains. The room exhales light and fills with darkness like a solar eclipse. 'So, DS Watts. I think I might start another investigation.'

'Proceed Chief Inspector. Inspect your crime scene, but please, no tape.'

There is a future, Olivia believes, for both herself and Dave. She is absorbed by his compassion and she relishes the prospect of a long-term relationship. Dave would continue with the MET while she promotes her agency for a few years before settling down with their first child.

Pangs of guilt rush through Stafford's head, and just as suddenly dissipate. He cannot tell Olivia about his newfound love. There is no way he can brooch the subject without jeopardising both their personal and working relationship: *Once this is over, we'll probably never see each other.* He justifies his deceitful encounters with the belief that if no one knows, then no one's hurt – the mainstay of cheaters across the world. He shuns the truth: when practising infidelity, *someone* will be hurt.

By late afternoon Stafford is fully apprised of the triple murder enquiry. 'Okay Olivia. Here's the plan. This may be the wrong way of going about it, but I'll make an appointment to see the Chief Constable. You must realise that I can't keep you out of this; I'll be asked how I got involved. It's no problem that you rang me because we worked together way back. You had serious reservations about the course of justice and I was the only one you could turn to.'

'Fine with me, but I feel bad about Marchant.'

'Keep your feelings for Simmons. If he is innocent, Marchant's got a lot to answer for. Now that I've done half your work, I've got to take a nap. I need to be alive for tonight.'

'You'll be lucky.'

Olivia acts on Stafford's suggestion to probe deeper into the evidence. 'Something'll be there. You've just missed it. Glossed over it like an advertisement in a magazine. It's there if you really look for it. Evidence presents itself in many ways. Sometimes it stares us in the face; catches us unaware.'

Olivia is nonplussed. *I've been through every inch of this bloody file. If anyone was going to find anything, I would have found it long before the trial.* Nonetheless, she keeps looking – scanning documents, photos of evidence and of the deceased, witness statements and CCTV stills from the Rose and Thorn. Nothing has changed. Nothing is new.

Ninety minutes into her third review, she loses all objectivity. *Throw in the towel and slip into bed. Someone's waiting for me. For a change.*

She studies the downloaded phone menu glaring from her laptop. It strikes her in the face like the gloved fist of Rocky Balboa. *Why the hell didn't I see this before?* She scans the menu earlier copied from Juanita's recovered mobile phone. Five photos in a picture file parade Juanita and Trevor in front of Evesham landmarks: two in front of The Round House in Market Square, one beside the massive Abbey church and another two alongside the River Avon near the Simmons' Scenic Cruises mooring. *Bloody hell,* she scolds again, eventually consoling herself with the fact that she'd passed the phone over to Marchant, who himself had inspected the contents of the phone's memory. *I wonder if the bastard knows about these?*

Olivia shudders with guilt for having not checked the phone thoroughly. Had she have been more technically-minded, or perhaps passed the phone to a colleague conversant with its operating software, she might have found this crucial evidence in ample time to present as incriminating evidence against Taylor. The photos are not in the default photo folder, but in a rarely accessed screen-saver file. They are clearly date stamped: '14/08/2015'. She enlarges the photos and overlays a grid sheet, in the form of a crime-scene search pattern, which enables her to inspect every square inch of picture with the objective of gleaning anything that might confirm the imprinted date. She wants more than just the save date on the phone, because a wise barrister would argue that the calendar facility was malfunctioning or that someone had created a false date imprint.

The Abbey church parishioners' noticeboard leaps from the grid, its shiny black lettering advising mass times of 6.00 a.m., 9.00 a.m. and 6.00 p.m. Unfortunately for Olivia, the general notice does not specify particular dates.

The snaps taken alongside the river yield nothing.

The historically significant Round House in Market Square, as the pride of Evesham, is portrayed on a variety of local postcards. Because of its recurring presence, Olivia would ordinarily pay no attention to yet another representation of the fifteenth-century building – *nothing's changed, same old Round House*. But now, when the examination of every minute detail is significant, the Round House, or more precisely its foreground, promise more. An 'A' board, sitting on the brick courtyard, stands like a beacon protecting a roadworks site: 'Farmers' Market this Sunday', it shouts in fluorescent orange letters. Again, it is a general notification with no specific date. Olivia pounces on a Worcestershire Business Directory and finds that Evesham's Farmers' Market trades on the second Sunday of each month. The relative Sunday in August is the fourteenth. 'Certainly not conclusive, but difficult to refute,' shouts Olivia. 'Right in front of me.' *And he said he'd never been to Evesham.*

Taylor and Juanita stand about 30 metres in front of the market sign. Viewed two-dimensionally, Juanita's arm rests beside the sign. A pinhead of brilliance draws Olivia's attention to Juanita's right hand. A blazing engagement ring. *That's nice,* Olivia thinks. *No expense spared. So why the hell wasn't it on her hand when we recovered her?*

Olivia swells with excitement as she once did after winning a pink teddy bear in a shooting gallery sideshow. *I've got him. I've got him. Better still, I've beat Marchant. How the hell am I going to tell him about this?*

With unabandoned excitement, she screams: 'I've got him.'

'Huh? Got who? What are you on about?'

'Dave. I've got Taylor. He's in photos with Morales at Evesham. Five of them. They're date stamped fourteenth August. He's fucked now.'

'Olivia! That's not you. Such language doesn't become you.'

'Sorry Dave. I just knew this for months. Knew there had to be something we were missing.'

'Not so quick. They may not be admissible. You will have to show why they were not presented in the original evidence, especially as it will be contested that the phone was extensively checked. Remember that it was you who discovered the Morales family names and numbers in the phone. Because these photos hadn't surfaced earlier, in all probability it will be suggested that the phone has been manipulated and your new 'evidence' planted.'

Olivia flashes a smug look. 'You know they can't do that. I copied the files, remember? The phone's still locked away as evidence because of the potential appeal. Anyway, you can't just put a picture on a phone and date it. And look at this! She's wearing the exact same clothes as she was wearing when we pulled her onto the riverbank. Look, that's the bag – clutched under her arm. No one can say that's fabricated.'

'Olivia. I don't doubt that you're right, but I've seen what ten-year-old kids can do with these things. Nothing is beyond them. I know one who could have you arm in arm with Neil Armstrong on the moon and you would have a difficult time denying it.'

'I *was* there. I had a gravity-free affair with him. You'd have no concept of how much fun I had banging on the steps of Apollo 11.'

'Very funny. Explains why you're so spaced out about sex.'

'Dave. Enough of the devil's advocate stuff. We've got to push forward. Seriously. What can I do with this? If authenticity is our first priority, shouldn't I get it over to the lab?'

'That may not be the best move at this time. Whip up a statement of your findings and note a phone call to me. There's no doubt we'll have a problem with Marchant over this. If he knows you've been sniffing around behind his back he could make things extremely difficult for you, irrespective of whether you're right or wrong.'

'Not that it *hasn't* been difficult losing my place in CID to Community Policing you mean? I've got a horrid feeling that he may have seen these. He may have examined the phone with greater scrutiny than I did, although I'm not really doing myself any favours by suggesting that. No wonder he wanted me out of the way.'

Together they contemplate Marchant's reaction to their combined intervention in *his* case. He would erupt violently, throw books across his desk and abuse anyone within earshot. He would demand answers: *Who the fuck do you think you are, snivelling around checking on my work. Haven't even got the bollocks to ask me about whatever you're looking for.* He would consider Olivia's deceit worse than being investigated by the Independent Police Complaints Commission, because he considers her to be one of his own. In addition, he would shout endorsement of the jury's verdict, insisting, in the crudest possible terms, that both Stafford and Watts butt out of his business. But it would be too late.

Another problem for DCI Stafford is his immersion in an exterior constabulary's caseload. NCAs are generally shunned by officers like Marchant who believe that they are being overridden and treated as incompetent imbeciles.

He phones a colleague in Professional Standards and seeks guidance about how to officially present the new evidence – delicately avoiding Watts' costly omission. He subsequently meets with the Chief Constable with a request to interview Taylor.

Stafford takes from the meeting the predictable farewell: 'We'll get back to you.'

31

SINCE THE COMMENCEMENT of Simmons' trial, Trevor Taylor has browsed the morning dailies in his local newsagent. Saturday's edition of *The Sun* headlines: '*CRUISE CRAFT CAPTAIN CONVICTED*', with the text continuing: '*Evesham business owner, Barry Simmons, was yesterday convicted of three counts of murder. Despite continued protestations of innocence, the Worcestershire identity was found guilty after only two days' of fierce jury-room deliberation. He will reappear for sentencing next year on March twenty-first.*'

With the name 'Simmons' glowing in the forefront of his mind, Taylor sees him as his saviour. He thinks nothing of that innocent person facing the remainder of his life in prison. He pulls out his work diary and slashes a red line through March twenty-one.

After returning from Evesham with his brother on the unforgettable night of August nineteen, Trevor had fully immersed himself in work and computer games. Only twice had he visited his brother, who repeatedly encouraged him to leave England. 'Set up in Spain,' he enthused. 'Everyone's doing it.'

'Why would I leave and draw attention to myself?'

'Oh yeah. That's the smartest thing you've said for a while,' John replied.

Today, after four months of worrying when the next police officer or reporter would knock at his door, Trevor exhales relief. He'd panicked over his brother's prediction that he'd be arrested because of the information on his phone; he'd rarely left home or socialised; and he'd ventured into town only for essential shopping. Now, he can restore life to normality (by his definition) to plain sailing across a calm sea – as Simmons would say. Time to celebrate.

He grabs his new phone, calls his client's number and offers the unconscionable excuse of a sudden death in the family as a means to absent himself from the morning's installation. He drives home, drops his work clothes to the floor and walks to the local pub. It is not yet open. Trevor doesn't care. He strolls to a nearby café where he devours a celebratory English Breakfast.

* * *

DCI Stafford completes his submission to the Chief Constable and prepares responses for the inevitable difficult questions he will face arising from his association with DS Watts.

He attends the office of Chief Constable Janine Nash, and presents the folder of evidence against Trevor John Taylor. His request for the investigation to be re-opened gains momentum when Nash learns that it is Inspector Michael Marchant who headed the original enquiry. Some six years' earlier, after being promoted above him, she'd crossed swords with Marchant who had challenged the promotion, citing abuse of the *Sex Discrimination Act 1975*, re-framed by Harold Wilson's Labour Government. Only on finding little support from colleagues did Marchant withdraw his objection.

Nash has charged up the promotional ladder through recognition of her working firmly, but fairly, within the framework of operational guidelines. She does not tolerate discrimination or abuse of power within the workplace, and she stringently objects to supervising officers denying members input. It is her view that the best teams are those able to feed off the thoughts and experiences of each other. A firm believer in the 'open door' policy, she is a leader in mediation and conflict resolution.

Stafford treads gently: 'I hope ma'am, that you would be kind enough to advise Inspector Marchant of this development. I'm sure you appreciate the difficulty of me doing so. I also have reservations about the welfare of DS Watts, who has constantly protested about the conduct of this case directly to her inspector. Sergeant Watts felt she had no one within her office who would afford her a fair hearing, hence her 'off the record' approach to me as a former supervising officer.'

'I'll have no officer under my charge intimidating anyone,' Nash interjects. 'I shall direct the case files to be couriered and entrusted to your office, DCI Stafford. I shall also recommend that DS Watts be seconded to your office until resolution of this file. I hope, for both our sakes, you are right about this. Whatever the result, we can expect huge media interest. I'm not sure we can keep a lid on this because it won't take long for word to leak of disturbing rumblings over Simmons' conviction. Fortunately, this might not be totally unexpected. I hope, however, that we're applauded for opening our minds to remedying a possible injustice, but one never can tell with what slant the media will choose to decorate this. I'll prepare a response to the foreseeable "do you think you'll get it right this time?" barbs from the Sunday tabloids.'

Stafford glows with relief. 'No problem ma'am. I'm of the belief this will be quite straightforward, given the material we've uncovered. We'll be through in no time.'

'Famous last words,' chief inspector. 'Over confidence is traditionally the curse of our adversaries.'

Having agreed to make her third trip to the seaside town by train, Olivia walks into the Bournemouth police station canteen at two o'clock in the afternoon. Stafford shares a corner table with a clutter of files, photos and reports. Also standing on the table is a battered anodised aluminium milkshake container – probably misappropriated from a nearby café – that wears three decades of dents, crumples, scratches, and a couple of lovers' names scratched around the base.

'Hi, guv. Let's go and get this guy.'

'You want coffee first?'

'Nah, leave it 'till we've got Taylor.'

Olivia excuses herself to tuck her overnight bag in a corner of the police station's locker room. She nervously rechecks the contents of her brief case, not wanting to be caught short of anything during the interview. There'll be only one opportunity to spring the element of surprise. And it *will* be one heck of a surprise.

Thirty minutes' later, they turn into Alexander Road and share a smile on seeing Taylor's work van. With no need to hide their presence, Stafford pulls up directly in front of the drive.

He taps a soft unofficial knock on the door, like the faint tap of a nervous trainee satellite TV salesperson on their first day of 'prospecting' in their 'exclusive territory' where the door swings open and Mr Resident sees the shiny black satchel at the feet of one of Britain's recently naturalised citizens; he is shown a catalogue of glossy satellite dishes, televisions, and banners of new release movies that he can enjoy for only two pounds per week (on the 'easy-plan' 48-month contract) and he listens to the stuttering, pre-programmed twenty-something-year-old enthuse how nice a day it is, even if it's blustery, pouring with rain and four degrees below zero.

Taylor opens the door. Colour drains from his face. The stale stench of male BO escapes the doorway. Olivia utters the words: 'Trevor John Taylor?'

'Yep.' Beer-breath assails the detectives.

'I'd like you to accompany us to the local station to help our enquiries in relation to your missing fiancée.'

'I've been through all this stuff. She's not missing anymore and you got someone, I heard.'

'Just a few questions. We can make it official if you like; just makes a bit more paperwork.'

'Okay. I'll get my jacket.'

Stafford sets up the recording equipment in Bournemouth CID. Olivia sits close by, hugging files, photographs and hope. She is particularly interested in interpreting Taylor's body language, given that she's observed him under various conditions, more recently employing his deceptive act at the King's Arms pub.

Stafford commences the interview with the mandatory legal cautions before stepping into his droll, official tone: 'Trevor John Taylor. I'm going to ask you some questions about a mobile phone you used to own. Do you recognise this?'

Taylor looks at the photo of a Nokia phone displayed on Olivia's notebook computer. 'I had one like that, but I gave it to Juanita. Don't know if that's the one though. There's probably thousands of them.'

'But your photo wouldn't be on thousands, would it?'

'What photo?'

Stafford clicks to a different file and displays a photo on the screen. 'Who's the girl with you?'

'You know who it is. It's Juanita. Murdered by that Simmons bastard.'

'So where was this taken, Trevor?'

'Don't remember. We had heaps of photos. I just give the phone to someone in the street and ask them to snap. Everyone does it.'

'This photo is of the distinctive Round House in Evesham. When were you there?'

'Never been to Evesham. Maybe Juanita Photoshopped the shot.'

'You'll have to do better than that. We have a lab report certifying no pixel manipulation. What that means to you, is that this photo is original, as are another four in here, and they put you in Evesham on the fourteenth of August. What do you say to that?'

'Well, if I was there… No, I don't remember it. I been to lots of places you know. Work, holidays… '

'I'll refer you to an interview taken on August fifteenth by Inspector Marchant and DS Watts here. You said you'd never been to Evesham and that you didn't know where it is. Do you remember that?'

'Not really. That was ages ago, but if I said it, I said it. So what?'

'Because it suggests to me that you're lying. You're lying because you killed your fiancée and you won't man-up enough to come clean. How about it?'

'Nup. Wasn't me. You already got your man. I read all about it.'

Stafford seethes. His cheeks flush red. With fists clenched beneath the table he calls a break in the interview, hoping to interrupt Taylor's Academy Award winning role of playing the persecuted accused.

Taylor is not exceedingly smart – his stubbornness and slow drawl riles Stafford. In the golden years of Stafford's first joining the constabulary, he had learnt many unofficial 'coercion' techniques. Few officers have survived the days of pushing suspects off chairs; snapping a quick punch to the back of the head; accidentally spilling coffee in their lap; and threatening violence to the suspect, or worse, against their loved ones. Those still in the job struggle with the niceties of audio and video interviews, two-way mirrors and the politically correct complaints procedure that makes police wholly accountable for their actions. In contrast, suspects have at their disposal all manner of Human Rights legislation, civil proceedings, media sympathy and 'no win, no pay' damage litigation.

Stafford resumes the interview. 'Mr Taylor. You ever been to The Rose and Thorn pub in Evesham?'

'Nup. Never heard of it.'

'You ever meet a girl named Amy Anderson?'

'Nup. Don't know her.'

Stafford employs a tactic to throw Taylor completely off-guard; the interviewer's negotiating tool that reinforces supremacy. 'Mr Taylor. We can short-circuit this whole process if you'll give us permission to search your property.'

'Why would you want to do that? I've got nothing to hide.'

'Well you'll not mind showing us through then, will you?'

'And if I refuse?'

'Not a problem. You'll just be delayed fifteen minutes or so while one of my officers arranges a Search Warrant.'

'Look, I don't want any trouble. I done nothin' wrong. You may as well just do it.'

Stafford purposely withholds a still from the Rose and Thorn's CCTV, which shows Taylor with Amy Anderson on the night of her murder. He'll use the photo to gain leverage during the interview as he leads Taylor to the point of no return. The photo will be the proverbial icing on the cake, leaving Taylor no room to weasel out of the tight spot.

DCI Stafford is concerned that this particular photo had been withheld from the trial. It disturbs Olivia too, for she'd insisted to Marchant that the blur in the photo was Trevor John Taylor. She'd had him. Only days after Amy's murder. She could have prevented Hegarty's death if she'd pushed harder. But how could she argue with a supervising officer who always wanted his own way – and got it? Marchant had assured her that Simmons was the prime suspect – there was no one else. 'Move on, Liv,' was Marchant's auto response to her urgings.

Olivia had never before resisted the necessity of having to turn a blind eye to minor events or evidence, but Marchant had stretched the practice beyond accepted boundaries. She had no one to turn to. The situation was too delicate to even mention to Stafford. Despite her disapproval of Marchant's conduct, she continued to abide by the constabulary's unwritten creed: honour and protect your fellow officer. That code, of course, does not extend to overlooking evidence tampering and similar rorts, but to Olivia the line dividing honour and deceit had been blurred. She regretted having not confided in DCI Stafford much sooner.

Stafford suspends the interview, rushes from the room and seeks the officer in charge. Superintendent Deakin is preparing to leave for the day, but begrudgingly welcomes Stafford to his office.

'Sir, we have a situation. Thank you for the use of your room. Can you afford me some bodies to do a residential search? I have the owner, Trevor John Taylor, downstairs. He's given permission. This is the enquiry relating to the deaths of three women in Evesham; you know, the one that's gone balls up. If you could spare a couple of uniforms and someone with computer knowledge, I'd appreciate it.'

'Bit late in the day, chief. See Carolyn on the desk downstairs. Tell her I okayed it.'

'Thank you sir.'

'No chance of any injuries arising, is there?'

'Not a chance, sir. Totally passive.'

'So was Tiananmen Square.'

With the greatest coincidence, John Taylor stands waiting for his brother as police arrive at Trevor's home. He shrinks into the background as Stafford opens the front door to admit his team of four.

'Don't make a mess,' Trevor pleads.

Stafford looks inside and quickly turns back, proffering a look that needs no endorsement: *Make a mess? You've got to be joking.* 'Fine. We'll leave everything just as is,' assures Stafford who accepts license to do as he pleases because restoring the home to a state of disorder will be one easy task. Stafford commences to turn the home completely over, mess or no mess. Trevor, restrained in handcuffs, watches on.

The team sweeps through the house like pest exterminators in protective paper suits. Stafford pores over Taylor's business books and receipts. A fellow officer checks wardrobes in the main and spare bedrooms. There are no torn clothes, no blood, no trinkets stolen as mementos and nothing to tie Taylor to the murders.

Olivia explores wardrobes and drawers in a second bedroom. She finds nothing that might have belonged to Juanita. She calls out to Stafford: 'Sir. Don't you think it strange that he's lost his fiancée, but there's no reminder of her at all. No clothes in wardrobes or drawers, no photos or letters, and no memorabilia of any description. There's something wrong with that.'

'It's four months, Olivia. Don't read anything into it. Some people handle grief in strange ways.'

'But every girl has a jewellery box; you know, full of earrings and trinkets and little mementos. And there's no cosmetics or female stuff in the bathroom either. It looks like he removed all traces of her.'

'You're probably right. But no guy in his right mind would invite a new girl to his home only to have her find perfume and other women's shit in the bathroom cabinet. It would spoil the moment, if you know what I mean. It's all about the element of trust.' Stafford considers his own situation and promptly drops the subject. 'Just be patient. I think we're getting there. I can feel it in my bones.'

'Think you'll find that's the aging process… sir.'

A voice whirls up the stairs like a winter eddy: 'Guv, I think you better come down here.'

Stafford and Olivia rush downstairs, elbowing each other for the lead. Lee Chin grins over Taylor's computer: 'I think you must look this':

August 19, 2015. I've done it again, only this time John saved me. A bloody reporter came round and tried to stitch me up for those two women. I don't know if she knew anything, but it sure was a coincidence that she came here just after that Watts copper left.

I had no intention of doing her in. Just a simple drink and a chat, that's what it started as. But she detailed some things that annoyed me. Stuff she shouldn't have known. How'd she know I'd been in that Evesham pub?

I guess a man is like an animal when he's cornered – he attacks. He'll strike out at whoever and whatever is within range. That reporter was in my line of fire, pushing, pushing: "I can help you; I can make it easy for you; just tell me what happened and we'll share it, just you and me." Of course she wanted to share stuff. She was seeking glory at my expense.

I guess that's why I had to do it. And how easy it was. I did share something with her. I'd had those Hypnos for ages, just waiting for the right occasion. And the occasion presented itself right before me. Just dropped ten into her drink and she was out. Kaput. Nigh-nighs. I suppose it was really over after I Glad Wrapped her. Not a happy time for her, no pun intended, as they say in the magazines. I guess I shouldn't joke about it, but her life just ebbed away like one of those Thai burials where the deceased's soul floats up to heaven from a flaming pyre or whatever the fuck it does.

The look on her face was like nothing I'd seen before. Such dramatic pleading in her eyes. I thought she was out of it because of the Hypnos, but she regained consciousness; eyebrows raised, wide-pupiled – for all of 90 seconds. It may *have been the longest 90 seconds of her life just gasping, reaching, heaving for the smallest wisp of air. Then she was gone.*

Fancy John coming around. Dunno what I would have done without him though. He did the best thing for me he'd ever done and helped me get rid of her. What a brainwave he had taking her back to her home town. Leaving her in the car park of her work. I imagined her boss rolling up the next morning and seeing her there. Front page news.

'Fuck me! Good work Chinny. Got a file date on it?'

Lee Chin looks at DCI Stafford and wonders what gives him the right to call him 'Chinny' after their meeting only thirty minutes earlier. 'August nineteenth, guv. Eleven seventeen p.m.'

'That's enough. Bag it and tag it. And Olivia, you can bag these accounts. What else we got here?'

'Pack of Hypnodorm in a kitchen drawer,' calls out one of the forensics. 'That was in her system.'

'Right. Bag that too. And while you're there, rip those draws apart for a box or roll of that Glad Wrap cling film stuff. Anyone done the garage yet?'

Stafford deploys uniform staff to the single garage which is equally shambolic as the living quarters. A uniformed constable sorts through accumulated bags of rubbish. Amongst food scraps, milk and yoghurt containers, greasy foil takeaway trays and the dusty contents of an emptied vacuum cleaner bag, he looks quizzically at a cellophane, cardboard-backed retail wrap labelled: 'Universal 8-inch Handee Knife'. Thirty minutes later, he retrieves framed photos of Trevor and Juanita, all haphazardly wrapped in newspaper. There is nothing unusual about that; many people of skinflint nature use newspaper for a variety of reasons, from toilet paper to weed retardant.

It is the spots of blood that catches the eagle eye of PC Whitehouse. The spots enlarge to a huge spatter as he leafs open the pages. The masthead reads: *Evesham Record,* August 8, 2015. He calls over DCI Stafford who looks in astonishment at the items. To no one in particular he vents frustration: 'Why the fuck wasn't this place turned over last August?'

Olivia raises her eyes and shrugs her shoulders. She approaches Stafford, and whispers, 'I told him. I bloody told him. He just wouldn't listen. He just didn't want to accept that someone, especially a woman, had figured out something ahead of him. Bloody hell. We were here. In the house. I was here twice.'

'The van. The fuckin' van,' yells Stafford. 'Get the key off Taylor and rip that van apart. And that shit-fighting Orion.'

Uniformed officers pull out rolls of cable, boxes of switches, plugs and fuses, tools and electrical manuals and place them along the footpath like a garage sale in full swing. Fifteen minutes later a constable locates a velvet box in the van's console. He might have known DCI Stafford from an earlier posting, or he is just plain ignorant of police protocol because he opens the box and shouts: 'Hey guv, wanna marry me?'

'I just might, for finding that, son. I just might.' The diamond engagement ring dazzles in the box as it had done on Juanita's finger in front of the Farmers' Market sign.

Trevor Taylor stands bewildered as officers carry out bags of potential evidence from his home. Stafford places a document before him and requests a signature for the seized items. Trevor refuses.

John Taylor cranes his neck trying to see what detectives find so interesting on his brother's computer. Stafford approaches him. 'John, I'll just get you to witness that we're removing five bags of evidence from here.'

'Yeah, sure. I can't believe that Trev's got anything to do with this.'

'With what, John?'

'Err, whatever you're looking for.'

'John, I'm placing you under arrest for being an accessory to murder.' Stafford parrots the legal caution to John Taylor.

'Olivia. Do the honours with his brother will you?'

Olivia grins. A win. A result. *The* result that should have months' earlier climaxed the Simmons debacle. This is the moment she has craved: 'Trevor John Taylor. I'm arresting you for the murder of Juanita Morales, Amy Anderson and Marg Hegarty. You do not have to say anything, but it may harm your defence if you do not mention, when questioned, something you may later rely on in court. Do you wish to say anything in answer to the charges?'

'No comment.'

A uniformed officer takes custody of the bags of evidence as Lee Chin manhandles the computer hard drive and assorted peripherals to his vehicle.

The Taylor brothers accompany officers in separate vehicles back to Bournemouth CID.

32

To a seasoned police officer, interview rooms are likened to toilet cubicles: same equipment – different locations. Stafford commences the official interview, determined to unravel the mystery that Marchant had left behind. Olivia flops into the corroborator's chair without complaint; her knowledge immediately available to Stafford – or to challenge Taylor where necessary.

Before activating the recorder, Stafford offers a sweetener. In his casual 'nice guy' voice – the silky, smooth voice that flows from crooners such as Michael Bublé and the late Frank Sinatra – he announces: 'Trevor. We can do this one of two ways. You can deny everything and make things long and hard and earn yourself a lengthy stretch, or, you can fess up, tell the truth, and maybe pave the way to a few years of freedom. Entirely up to you.'

'I got nothin' to say. You have a guy in jail for this. Do you think anyone's going to believe that someone else did these murders when they already got someone banged up? You got nothing on me.'

'Alright. Let it be recorded that I've offered you an opportunity. Trevor John Taylor, I'm resuming the interview at 6.16 p.m. I am going to ask you further questions in relation to the murder of Juanita Morales, Amy Anderson and Marg

Hegarty. I remind you that you're still under caution. Do you want me to repeat it?'

'Nah. I heard it all before.'

'I'm showing you five bags of evidence removed from your home as a result of a search warrant executed at 3.35 p.m. on this day. Do you agree these are the items seized?'

'I didn't look before so I'm not sure. Whatever it is, I don't know why you want that stuff.'

'We'll discuss that later. For starters, you were engaged to Juanita Morales, right?'

'Yes.'

'Did you have a wedding date set?'

'No. We were working on it. She had six months as a visa condition.'

'When did you first realise Juanita was missing?'

'Somewhere around the middle of August. Got home from work and she wasn't there.'

'I take it then, that it was unusual for her to not be there when you got home. I mean, you were alarmed? You made enquiries of her whereabouts?'

'Yeah. I rang a couple of her friends. There was a couple of numbers on a pad in the kitchen; most she had in her phone.'

'And you made those calls on the night of the fourteenth August? That's what you're telling me Mr Taylor?'

'Yeah, I rang her from home. I was in my lounge room just wondering why the hell she wasn't home because she always had dinner ready for me.'

Stafford shuffles through a manila folder and pulls out a page headed British Telecom. 'Mr Taylor, this is a certified copy of your phone account for the July to September quarter. You will note there is no record of a call to Miss Morales' phone.'

'Must have used my mobile then. I only remember I was in my lounge room.'

Stafford magically produces another page. 'This is your Virgin account for August. You will note that this also records no calls on that date to your fiancée.'

'Well, I don't know then. I told you I couldn't get her. I told you there was no answer, so I wouldn't have been charged would I? That's probably why there's no record of the call.'

'That may be correct,' pipes in Olivia, 'if you did not leave a message. But you may recall that when I spoke to you with Inspector Marchant on the fifteenth of August, you told me that you left Ms Morales a message. So if that is true, there would surely be a billing on your account. Can you explain why there isn't?'

'I don't know how they do their accounting.'

'You also told me that you didn't know where Evesham is and that you'd never been there. Do you recall that?'

Trevor shifts in his seat, clasps his hands together and resumes a confident position with his elbows on the table. 'Yes. I recall that. I don't know where the hell Evesham is and I don't care, except it was the final resting place of my dear fiancée.'

'Also on the fifteenth of August you said: "Evesham. That's ages away. What would she be doing there?" You added: "I can't imagine she'd know anyone that far away." So it seems quite clear that even then you knew where Evesham was.'

'Geographically yeah. I knew it wasn't around these parts, so it had to be far away. Makes sense to me.'

From the folder Stafford removes five photos and lays them on the table in front of Taylor. 'Here you are with Juanita in front of Evesham's Round House, another of you both beside the Abbey and another taken on the bank of the Avon. Do you remember now?'

'You showed me them before. I told you they been doctored.'

'So you're telling me you never even thought to see where your fiancée drowned?'

'Nup. Too traumatic. You probably don't realise how upset I've been over this and the fact that that Simmons guy murdered her. So what's going on here? Are you now trying to say that I killed my own future wife? You've got a nerve.'

Stafford returns to the folder and removes a small receipt. 'Mr Taylor. Do you recognise this?'

Taylor looks at both sides of the receipt and flips it back across the table.

'Am I supposed to? It's just a petrol receipt.'

'Yes, it is. Look at the address. Mobil Fuel Zone, Cheltenham Road, Evesham. Total transaction on your credit card: £32.00. That is your receipt Mr Taylor. Removed from your concertina file. And now look at the date: fourteenth of August 2015.'

'Ah, I must have picked up the wrong one.'

'Maybe you did. But to have done that you had to have been at that particular servo. You were there. It's cross-referenced on your card statement. Not looking too good for you. This puts you in Evesham on the night of the murder.'

'Look, I been to a lot of places. Maybe I'm mixed up with somewhere else.'

'Let me help jog your memory. What about the night of August sixteen? Were you in Evesham then?'

'I still can't remember ever being in Evesham. I'm sorry. So much is just a blur after Juanita going. It just seems as if my life has been on a sort of autopilot, you know; I just do things and go places without really registering what I am doing or where I am going.'

Stafford takes advantage: 'So it is possible that you killed three women without really knowing what you were doing?'

'Of course not. I would never kill anyone. That's just bollocks.'

'But there's more, Mr Taylor. Much, much more.' Again Stafford ruffles through the folder. 'This is a photo of the Rose and Thorn car park in Evesham. If you look in the top right-hand corner of the pic, you will notice a silver Ford Orion. Is that yours?'

'Hard to tell. I don't see a number plate on it.'

'Well, Taylor, I think your number's up. Look at this: photo two, centre left, again in the car park, is a nice snap of you in a cap.'

'Could be anyone.'

'Yes, it could be. But it's you. Trevor Taylor. Look closely at the cap.'

'Sorry, too blurry. Can't focus on anything.'

'All right. I'm showing you a copy of notes taken by Evesham journalist Marg Hegarty. These notes refer to a proposed interview with you on the nineteenth of August, and are supported by an entry of your address and her time of visit. Do you dispute that Ms Hegarty interviewed you at your house?'

'Never heard of her.'

'I'm showing you a packet of Hypnodorm with the name Mr Trevor J. Taylor on the dispensary label. Do you agree they are yours?'

'I don't know if they're mine, but I know that I had some somewhere at home.'

'Traces of Hypnodorm were found in Ms Hegarty's blood. How would you explain that?'

'Ask that Simmons guy.'

'Trevor John Taylor. You are going to be charged with the murders of Juanita Taylor, Amy Anderson and Marg Hegarty. Is there anything at all you want to say in relation to the charges?'

'I don't know if I should be saying anything without a lawyer. I reported my fiancée missing on the night of August 14. Next I know, I get a call from some detective in Worcester and then find they've come to ask me about Juanita. Fair enough – they're doing their best to find her. But later on, Detective Watts comes back and starts hassling me for phone numbers and sort of suggesting that I drowned my own fiancée. Got to the stage where I said I'd call my solicitor, so she finished up and left. Next thing I know, I'm reading in the paper that a guy called Simmons has gone down for her murder plus two others. You guys didn't even have the decency to advise me. I had to read it in the fuckin' paper, so don't now come running to me and suggesting I killed not only my own fiancée, but two other women as well. Don't forget that you guys gave evidence against Simmons. It must have been pretty conclusive – conclusive enough for the court to find him guilty. So no. I got nothin' to say.'

Stafford rubs his forehead in amazement at Taylor rattling off a spiel in the form of a press release and then signing it off with "I got nothin' to say". He completes legal formalities and takes Taylor's fingerprints before placing him in custody to await an official remand application before a local magistrate.

Olivia arranges for John Taylor to be brought to the interview room. Stafford parrots the legal preamble. Olivia defers to the passenger seat, irritated at again being given the minor role.

She believes that she deserves to unfold John's complicity, but accepts that, as with Marchant, she is consigned to a supporting role like a bookend standing rigid on the shelf of knowledge. At that instant, Olivia sees the image of Marchant manifest within herself. So assured had she been of Trevor Taylor's guilt, she had not even considered John Taylor as a possible co-offender. She recounts the phone call when he claimed he hadn't seen Trevor for a fortnight and quietly concedes that she should have acted on the warning flag to probe deeper. *Why would Trevor have nominated his brother as an alibi if he wasn't already panicking?*

Stafford loosens his tie. 'John Taylor. This afternoon you were present when we attended your brother's home. As a result of our enquiries, we have information that implicates you in the commission of a crime. What can you tell us about the name Marg Hegarty?'

'Doesn't ring a bell.'

'We have information stating that you helped your brother dispose of a deceased female from his home. What do you say to that?'

'I'm in a bit of a spot here. My brother's done some strange things in his time, but I don't know what he's been doin' lately. I helped him drive a girl back to her work in Worcestershire somewhere.'

'Did you speak to this girl at all?'

'Nah. Trevor dosed her up with that Hypno stuff. We wanted to get her back to sleep it off so she wouldn't remember where she'd been.'

'She sure won't remember anything, John. She's dead.'

'Bullshit. She was all right when we drove her back.'

'Tell me about the Glad Wrap around her head.'

'Dunno what you're talkin' about.'

'I'm going to read to you an extract from a journal entry written by your brother on August nineteen: "*I had no intention of doing her in. I guess a man is like an animal when he's cornered – he attacks. I guess that's why I had to do it. I suppose it was really over after I Glad Wrapped her. Fancy John coming around. Dunno what I would have done without him though. He did the best thing for me he'd ever done and helped me get rid of her. What a brainwave he had taking her back to her home town. Leaving her in the car park of her work.*" So you see, John, your brother has really dropped you in it.'

John might as well have been confronted by a speed camera photo. Irrefutable evidence. No way out. Sunk by his own brother's stupid diary. *Time for damage control.* 'All right, yeah, look, I'll tell yas everything. I helped him. I had to; he's half useless by himself. As he said in that journal thing, I went 'round. We argued earlier in the week about something else, so we hadn't spoken for a few days. I just went there to cool it, you know, break the ice. He never even knew I was goin' there, but when I got there this woman's croaked it on a chair with plastic round her head like a fuckin' turban.'

He looks to Olivia: 'Sorry about that. I don't usually swear. Anyway, Trev panicked and I panicked and then we just drove her to Evesham after I went through her bag and found a business card.'

'So you agree she was dead when you moved her?'

'Yeah, course she was dead. No doubt.'

'John, I'm going to ask you some questions about Trevor's fiancée. You know anything about her?'

'Sure. I met her a few times. But if you're askin' if I know where she is, I got no idea.'

'But you know something happened to her don't you?'

312

'I know she's missin' if that's what you mean, but only since Detective Watts phoned me.'

'Yes. That's when my colleague here phoned you on the fifteenth of August asking you about Trevor's visit to your home because of a power blackout. You were unable to substantiate Trevor's story.'

'He's a fuckin' bastard. I been coverin' for him all his life. I stood up to him for the first time when he asked me to cover for him about that blackout. There never was a blackout. But I still don't know nothin' about Juanita.'

'Do you know anything about Amy Anderson?'

'Who the... I mean, who's she? I don't know her and Trevor's never spoken 'bout her.'

'Stabbed to death in Evesham on the sixteenth of August.'

'Don't go puttin' that on me. I know nothin' about that. I don't mind tellin' yas what I know, but I sure as shit, sorry, I can't tell yas things what I don't know.'

'All right John. We're going to further our enquiries. In the meantime, you're going to be charged with being an accessory after the fact with the murder of Marg Hegarty. You may face similar charges in relation to Juanita Morales. Do you wish to say anything in answer to the charge?'

'Nah. Guess I'm fucked whatever I do or don't say.'

How right you are smirks Olivia.

33

Interviews finalised, and with the Taylor brothers distanced by separate cells, Stafford and Watts stroll into a local Subway franchise. Olivia selects a six-inch Chicken Breast, while Stafford goes the whole hog with a foot-long Meat Balls with every bit of salad the sandwich artist can ram into the Herb and Cheese roll. The peaceful dine-in allows them to reflect on their day's work and plan the next stage: presenting the result to Chief Constable Nash.

'Should be quick and easy,' says Stafford.

'I've seen enough over-confidence to last a lifetime,' counters Olivia.

A blob of bolognaise sauce slides down Stafford's tie like a baby's first solids rolling down a bib. Olivia laughs: 'You've got a bit of modern art happening on your tie!'

'That's the thing with Italian fashion – it's so realistic.' Stafford slurps his cappuccino and licks his tie. 'Let's get going. The quicker we finish, the quicker I can reward you for your efforts.'

'So that's what you meant when you said Nash approved me to work exclusively *under* you? Well, I got news for you chief. I'm on top of this and I'll be on top of you.'

'I've never been a man to argue.'

They talk non-stop, joy turning to solemnity when they

think of Marchant and his tunnel-visioned zeal. Despite 'The Brotherhood's' deep-rooted bond, it cannot insulate or protect their colleague from the ravages of an impending enquiry. Stafford feels professionally *and* morally obliged to discuss with Marchant the new charges, before reporting his findings to the Chief Constable. A resultant enquiry would likely find Marchant guilty of dereliction of duty, or in the worst case, cite him for perverting the course of justice. Either way, his withholding evidence from an investigation would attract far less attention than if a similar indiscretion had occurred outside the constabulary. Nevertheless, his credibility as a police officer and supervisor will be shattered. As will his career.

'Olivia. You wouldn't know about the file on Marchant. He's been before the board a couple of times, once on a harassment complaint, but to be fair it was withdrawn at the last minute. A WPC had had a torrid time with him; he pulled a few moves on her and then made her life difficult after she confided in the wrong person. Wouldn't surprise me if he put the heat on her to drop the matter. The man can be rather 'influential' and I'm sure you know what I mean.

'The board still interviewed him, unofficially they said, though the bastards still made a file note of it, which is totally out of order. We never had this conversation, but I've seen the file and that bastard Marchant claimed that the WPC, you wouldn't know her, Marilyn someone, had actually made a move on him in the car. He said he thought he was 'on to a good thing' – his words – so he laid his arm across her shoulder and tried to kiss her. Needless to say she freaked, but he saw it as a tease and continued to pull her toward him then planted his fat, ugly face in her breasts.

'The board – his super, a DCI, and the deputy chief

constable for goodness' sake – threatened to move him to a one-man-station in a five-house village on the blustery coast of Devon. Marchant's record, and the fact there'd been no other complaints – officially – saved him from purgatory.

'His other appearance is one that everyone heard about and became the subject of editorials of every daily newspaper in the UK. Even though they'd suppressed his name in the interest of protecting his family, it didn't take long for the word to spread through the various constabularies like that Bovine flu that decimated the country a few years ago. Remember the judge and the brothel case?'

''course I do. That was *Marchant*?'

'The one and only. He'd be a DCI now if it weren't for that stuff-up.'

'But he was only trying to expose rorts. Well, that's what I heard.'

'Expose nothin'. That was just another of Marchant's crooked ploys. Lord Masterton was an eminent judge presiding over the trial of a scroat Marchant had charged with bashing a prostitute in a swanky parlour in the West End. High class pimp the scroat was. Anyway, Marchant thinks the guy's still on the game, so he does his own night surveillance on the parlour. He's just about to leave, it was about 11.30 at night, no sign of his target, but who comes along? The fucking judge! But the best part was the reason the judge gave for being at the bloody brothel. In court, he'd allowed the screening of a video displaying the premises and the proximity of the rooms to the site of the bashing. To ensure the jury would not be misled, His Honour took it upon himself, with no official notification, to inspect the brothel's premises first-hand. That was the official reason. Very commendable. Why a judge would seek to undertake such a study at 11.30 p.m. rather than straight after work in the afternoon must fuel speculation.

'So, get this. Marchant cranks up his camera, snaps the shit out of the bloody thing – the shutter's going up and down faster than a gigolo on steroids – so to cut a long story short, he thinks it'll help his case if he can expose a crooked judge; he goes straight to the papers, accepts an offer of a few grand from his first port-of-call, the ill-fated *The News of the World*, and downloads his snaps straight into their computer. Guess who's on the front page of the paper the next morning? Lord fucking Masterton.

'Masterton, of course, has got the whole legal fraternity at his disposal. He enlists two QC mates; one to go after the paper and the other to go after Marchant. I haven't got the faintest why they let Marchant off the hook by not naming him. He bloody deserved it. That's what happens with Marchant. He just does his own thing; thinks he's always right, and doesn't care about the consequences.

'In the end, *News of the World* paid out a quarter mill to Masterton – solely because they did not verify the circumstances of the photos.'

'So what happened to Marchant?'

'Got off lightly. A written apology to the judge, plus, he had to purchase a two column inch apology in the paper, as well as donate the money he received from the photos – a "token consideration" Marchant called it – to a charity. Bit of a kick up the arse too, I think, but it made no diff; the guy still does as he pleases.'

'Don't I know it.'

They redirect their thoughts to Simmons deteriorating in prison, sleeping on a slab of foam rubber, eating meals contaminated by kitchen inmates who exercise their self-confessed God-given right to impart retribution on behalf of victims; and blanking out the taunts: 'Hey captain. How d'ya like a bit of my good ship *Lollipop*? They'll have ya swabbing the dicks soon, me 'earty.'

Olivia had mentioned nothing to Simmons about continuing the investigation – mainly for fear of planting false hopes, but also because he would draw the conclusion: *if she is checking further into the matter, why had I been charged amid an incomplete investigation?* Whilst she keenly anticipates visiting Simmons to relay the breakthrough, she faces a track of administrative hurdles before Chief Constable Nash will accept the watertight case against Trevor and John Taylor. And then the CPS has to approve it, which, in itself, will prove to be an embarrassing admission of major incompetence.

From there, Rupert Llewellyn-Jones will seek urgent leave to appeal and serve amended appeal papers. A court clerk or supervisor will sling whispers to media contacts – part of on-going 'information bartering' – and in no time the media avalanche will gain momentum, touting special *'Innocent Man Imprisoned'* editions on street corners, interrupting daytime television with 'on-the-spot' bulletins narrated in front of file-footage of the Evesham pier, and streaming internet podcasts to anyone not enraptured by the current reality show winner, whether it be singer, dancer, chef, home renovator or gardener.

But the wheels of justice barely rotate when bringing an action, be it criminal or civil. They turn even slower – barely beyond a standstill – when justice has been found to have been unfairly administered. Historical archives shelve cases of many innocents sharing a situation similar to Simmons. The lucky ones wait many years before the system recognises, let alone unconditionally accepts, their innocence. It is unfortunate that authorities do, behind closed doors, concede that errors of law have denied an accused freedom, but rather than admit those errors and thereby restore public confidence in the judiciary, the key holders of the legal system ensure that every barrier is placed in front of both the innocent victim and his legal advisors, in a concerted effort to parade a system that 'is equitable because it is subject to so many checks and balances'.

'We can't undermine a jury's verdict,' government ministers and officials empathise. Meanwhile, the innocent continue to seek redress through courts and the legal fraternity, both of which will never admit that the system *can and does* make mistakes. The pleas fall on deaf ears because a convicted person has no voice.

The prospect of future difficulties fall heavily on Olivia and dilute the joy of the day's victory. Guilt over Simmons' predicament, as well as the prospective outfall over fingering Marchant, fuels her drive to leave the force. At the very least she would be 'advised' to transfer to another station or area, (in her own interests, naturally) but her compromised reputation as a whistle-blower or one prepared to dig behind colleagues' backs would not aid the transition. That dilemma replays itself during the return to Worcester in Stafford's car.

At 2.00 a.m. they climb the stairs to Olivia's flat. No coffee, no chat and no amorous moments.

Seven hours' later, Stafford and Olivia enter the Chief Constable's office in Worcester.

Janine Nash had rescheduled her morning's duties after receiving Stafford's late evening text advising that their Bournemouth assignment had concluded with the arrest of two brothers, one of whom admits to being an accessory while the prime suspect continues to deny any involvement.

'Morning ma'am,' enthuses Stafford.

Olivia nods her own greeting.

Stafford hands over copies of the Taylor brothers' statements and photos and receipts of evidence already logged in property. The material heavily implies that Marchant had exceeded his authority, contravened provisions of the *Murder Investigation Manual*, and had overlooked matters that warranted thorough investigation.

'Excellent result then.'

'Yes ma'am. Both in custody. We'll work on piecing together the new briefs, but before that I'll go and see Marchant.'

Nash holds up her hand in a gesture recovered from traffic-duty days. 'I've had second thoughts on that. He'll be here in about five. We'll conduct this as a round table discussion; should ease the pain for both of you.'

Olivia flashes a concerned grimace. 'With respect, ma'am. Won't be easing any pain for me. He'll be all smiles and understanding in here, then once we're out of the office he'll turn into a volatile prig, or should I say, change back into one.'

Nash understands her detective's attitude; however, she *is* a stickler for protocol. 'DS Watts. I appreciate the effort you've put in here, and I also appreciate the precarious position in which you find yourself. However, I expect Detective Inspector Marchant to receive the respect of his position, no matter what belief you harbour against him.'

'Yes ma'am. I apologise.'

Olivia flushes with embarrassment, believing she'd said nothing out of turn. She is perplexed how Chief Constable Nash can support Stafford's investigation over Marchant's, but at the same time not allow a slur against Marchant's character. A knock on the office door breaks her thoughts.

Marchant swaggers in, his frown springing at Olivia's and Stafford's presence. Olivia doesn't miss the chance: *I hope he thinks he's here for a promotion.*

Nash throws in a sweetener and commences proceedings. 'Sit down, inspector. You know DCI Stafford don't you?'

'Yeah, seen him around.'

'The reason I've called you here today, is that there's been some developments in the case of the recent murders in Evesham. Information has come to light, and there's no need for me to elaborate, that there might have been another person or persons responsible for at least one of the murders.'

Might have been? Olivia withholds a protest. *It's crystal clear. One has admitted guilt and at the same time tipped in the other.* She holds her tongue, realising that Nash is treading carefully, leading Marchant to his own demise.

Marchant turns and glares at Olivia. Fiercely. Transmitting the unspoken: *what the fuck have you been up to. You haven't got the grace to speak to me about this?*

Anticipating fallout, Chief Constable Nash instinctively deciphers Marchant's reaction. 'Justice must be considered the highest platform governing human cohabitation. We, who enforce its rules, must be proficient in exercising responsibility to ensure that those who cross boundaries of responsible behaviour are prosecuted. Equally, we must also ensure that anyone who might have been subject to an injustice, must, as soon as practicable, be restored to the community without injury or sufferance. That, of course, is virtually impossible, for there will forever remain the stigma of conviction and incarceration.

'We have a situation where DCI Stafford and DS Watts have had cause to pursue an enquiry crossing over an investigation formerly headed by Inspector Marchant.'

'Crossing over!' Marchant rants. 'They've plain, outright shafted me. No one said anything to me about carrying out a covert investigation into a matter where an accused has already been convicted.'

'Be that as it may, Inspector, we now have two males in custody who will face murder and accessory charges, with more than ample evidence, and a confession.

'Our position now is to maintain the fine reputation we enjoy in the county. None of you shall comment to the media, other than to say that all enquiries must be directed to district headquarters. Furthermore, in the interest of personal relations, with the exception of DCI Stafford, I shall hold talks with each of you individually about your work locations.

'Finally, I will ask you, Inspector Marchant, to avail all help as requested by the Crown Prosecution Service to assist their submissions relative to Mr Simmons' anticipated application for bail.'

Nash opens her door signifying the meeting's conclusion. Stafford and Olivia rush out to avoid clashing with Marchant. There is no need. Nash directs him to remain.

Momentarily ignoring Marchant, perhaps offering him a minute to reflect on lost opportunity or forecast what lies ahead, Nash scrutinises the statements and evidence provided by Stafford and Watts. She attaches a file note recommending urgent action and directs a constable to personally deliver the brief to the CPS.

* * *

The CPS has no power to delay Simmons' sentencing. The man has been convicted by a jury. No simple pen stroke can overturn the conviction on the back of the new information. Trevor Taylor denies involvement in the three deaths and is therefore entitled to plea his case before the court. Even should Taylor be found guilty, it will be no simple matter to pardon Barry Simmons. The judicial system travels along a one-way street: no U-turns, no speeding and no regard for warning signs. Self-regulation permits the system to remain parked for an indeterminate period, and no pedestrian or passer-by shall dare query its lack of haste.

Barry Simmons' conviction cannot be overturned through Watts' and Stafford's efforts alone. He must await an appeal hearing even if the CPS agrees to set aside the convictions.

* * *

Marchant contemplates how he will defend a disciplinary hearing. His first thought is to deny any wrong doing. How can anyone prove otherwise? He had simply missed the photos and ignored Olivia's contributions as unfounded and over-enthusiastic presumptions of a promotion-hungry ladder climber. He surmised the meeting with Chief Constable Nash would be a fact-finding mission, a casual rap over the knuckles with the clear message to keep his chin up and above all, stay out of trouble. The carpet would be lifted, and the matter swept beneath.

When finally asked by Nash to account for his actions Marchant lets loose: 'Ma'am. This is indeed an unfortunate turn of events brought about by a junior detective who I took under my wing to groom to the fastidious standards of West Mercia

323

Police. We had a complex investigation, one that, perhaps, on reflection, a more junior member, and I do acknowledge Miss Watts' rank as Sergeant, but this investigation perhaps required a person with a little more expertise in the nature of events we faced. DS Watts' contention that I was brash in pursuing Simmons at all costs is unfounded. DS Watts had every opportunity to present what she considered evidence of Taylor's involvement. Her best offering was 'a hunch'. I am sure DS Watts will verify that I gave her carte-blanche approval to 'go after' I think is the way I put it, this Trevor Taylor. Nothing positive came of my demonstration of confidence in giving her a free reign, other than conjecture and innuendo. It is interesting to learn that the evidence DS Watts *now* submits to implicate Taylor is material located *after* Simmons conviction. I respectfully ask you to question why, if DS Watts *was* so certain of Taylor's guilt, she did not come up with these photos, receipts and the diamond ring during the investigation? She would say she was not given the opportunity, but that is not true. She was involved in the investigation all along.

'I acted upon available evidence; evidence that incriminated, and ultimately contributed to Simmons' conviction.'

Marchant angles to resolve the matter forthwith. He acts true to form and moves to crucify anyone around him, including one of his best detectives, to save his own skin. He sits through the drilling like a meek witness subject to harsh cross-examination: show respect and look professional. He tackles it as experience versus the rookie junior out to make a name for herself. *Well, I'll give her a name. A name she'll be taking to every station she tries for transfer. A loud mouth bitch who'll stop at nothing to get her own way.*

Marchant's record, although blotched by a series of indiscretions early in his career, has painted him as a reliable and congenial officer – police-speak for an average officer who has been treading water for far too long. In contrast, Marchant likens the appraisal to a school report for the dux of class whose only misdemeanour was failing to fulfil his daily duty of emptying bins.

Nash clears Marchant of any wrongdoing, but verbally reprimands him for not controlling the investigation in a thorough and open manner. Chief Constable Nash's personal view is that he's skated on thin ice, but professionally, there is nothing of significance that could be pinpointed as dereliction of duty.

The brotherhood.

34

To ASSIST HIS determining a fair and just sentence, Judge Ainsley had ordered Dr Gerald Matthews to conduct a psychological assessment of Simmons. His Honour was obliged to consider the prospect of rehabilitation, despite Simmons' life expectancy being less than the term of the prospective sentence.

Never had Simmons opened his life to psychologists. He had always controlled his own destiny. Routine assessments throughout his naval career had returned above-average scores pertaining to his mental state and low ratings on the scale of susceptibility to depressive illness.

Dr Matthews probed long-forgotten childhood events like schoolyard fights and participation in 'physically aggressive' sports such as football and rugby. He forced upon Simmons questions about his views on women, about roles played out in Simmons' own marriage and about his opinions on equality. Oddly, there were no questions about relationships with women (or men) outside of marriage.

Rupert Llewellyn-Jones later studied a copy of his client's psychological status. As he delved deeper into the report, he wondered if the document had been mistakenly compiled from another patient's information:

"Mr Barry Simmons exhibits an excitable and irritable temper that flares into contentious arguments and belligerence, at times being mean-spirited and fractious. Although Simmons presents with a cohesive internal structure comprised of routinely modulating controls, defences and expressive channels; surging and explosive energies of an aggressive and violent nature can produce precipitous outbursts that periodically overwhelm/overrun otherwise competent restraints.

"Further, Simmons suffers denial problems and he appears to have given little thought to cognitive, emotional and behavioural states to avoid future aberrant behaviour. He believes that a future appeal will overturn his conviction. That belief seems to be founded from a fantasised view of life that all will work itself out. Mr Simmons' profile reveals a clinically significant character pathology, features of which may interfere with his ability to function productively. On the clinical scales, Simmons demonstrates a degree of elevation on the Sadistic/Aggressive and Anti-social scales, suggesting a degree of endorsement of anti-social patterns.

"Thus Mr Barry Simmons presents with a moderate risk of continued violence if no intervention is provided, though this may be minimised within a correctional facility where there is no exposure to female presence."

* * *

Belinda Pace visits Simmons as part of submission preparations for the sentencing hearing. She hands her client the psychological report, claiming it hinders, rather than assists her plea for lenience. She revises Barry's history, intending to influence Judge Ainsley to deliver a sentence from the compassionate end of the penalty scale. Pace will have to rely on favourable witness testimony of her client's exemplary behaviour within the community. That, of course, will be hotly contested by the prosecutor, although he will face gross difficulty locating contradictory evidence, save for the elements of the convictions.

Pace does not discuss her view of the verdict, expressing only her 'surprise'. She contends the evidence had been too flawed and insufficient to return a 'guilty' verdict – a matter now under intense scrutiny – and a matter that will underscore the pending appeal.

That will not be Belinda Pace's charter, for the process of appeal is the forté of specialist barristers who scan every line of court transcripts searching for elusive legal transgressions that might afford them the chance of standing before an Appeal Court judge to plead their case for a mistrial on the grounds of a miscarriage of justice, an unsafe verdict or a misdirection by the trial judge.

The ominous task of advising Simmons that the appeal process could run to twelve months falls jointly upon Rupert and Belinda. Experience has taught them that conveying such information to a client is akin to a doctor conferring upon a patient that he or she has life-threatening cancer.

Pace faces her client. 'Barry, I must advise you to expect the worst. These crimes – and let's not enter into matters of guilt or innocence – are among the worst this country has seen in the last fifteen years. You cannot expect to receive concessions. In my view a sentence will be pronounced on the light side of thirty years, based on three terms of ten years for each victim.'

* * *

On the twenty-first day of March, a throng of family and relatives assemble in front of the Old Bailey's court number seven. The families of the three victims have pressed the prosecution to pursue the maximum penalty – life imprisonment. Although Juanita's parents' financial position prevented them from attending, the *Evesham Record* had launched a benefit, seeking donations to fund the return of their daughter's body to the Philippines.

Inside the courtroom, Marg Hegarty's parents, both aged pensioners, huddle in the gallery with Samantha, as they had done every day throughout the trial. Amy Anderson's family sit demurely outside the court, supporting Amy's radical friends who wield placards calling for a return of the death penalty.

From the holding cells, Simmons limps to the court. Over seven months his physique has deteriorated into a sinewy shadow of marathon runner – without the commensurate level of fitness. His gaunt face accentuates marked hair loss and his exophthalmic eyes stare straight ahead as if they have frozen in their sockets after endless hours of counting bricks in the cell walls. The hands of a clock adjacent to Barry's cell replicate his predicament – barely moving, constrained to walking circles.

The judge's associate calls the court to order.

Justice Ainsley begins a long oratory: 'Mr Barry Simmons. I am duty bound to exact a penalty and sentence that befits your crimes and the community's expectations. The taking of three young lives is reprehensible. There has been nothing put before me that would offer any explanation for your chain of errant behaviour.

'The community, and women in particular, have an inherent right to walk the streets, pursue their interests and immerse themselves in activities of their choosing. The fact

329

that you indiscriminately took the life of two girls at a time when they were doing nothing other than enjoying the lighter side of life speaks volumes for your level of intent. Worse still, you took the life of Miss Hegarty in circumstances that have not been fully understood by the court. Such is your level of offending that you commit a crime so horrendous that your methods evade the notice of authorities. That reinforces to me, Mr Simmons, that you have shown, and continue to show not one modicum of remorse.

'Perhaps I have painted disparity between the young girls at leisure and Miss Hegarty at work. I do not seek to promote one over the other; I merely point out that you are prepared to prey on women under the most diverse circumstances.

'The community must be protected from the likes of you. I am saddened that a man of your service record should fall into the clutches of criminal activity for no apparent reason. Your psychological report does you no favour, and I am inclined to accept the version of the psychologist over representations made by counsel. You had been a valuable and contributing member of your country and community over many years, but I doubt, given your age, you will ever see that community again.'

Simmons stands motionless. And mute. He cannot address the court, although even if he were permitted, nothing he could say would change the outcome. The judgement is prepared and lying face down on the bench. Barry Simmons has dreamt of this moment in prison and he has dreamt the worst. He foresees the pronouncement of a huge sentence.

'For the murder of Miss Juanita Morales, I sentence you to a term of imprisonment of 15 years. For the murder of Miss Amy Anderson, I sentence you to a further term of imprisonment of 15 years. And for the murder of Miss Margaret Hegarty, I further sentence you to a term of imprisonment of 15 years. Each term shall be served cumulatively, which gives you an effective sentence of 45 years. There shall be a non-parole period of 36 years.'

Handclaps, cheering and shouts of 'rot, ya bastard' roar from the public gallery. The judge does not order silence, believing that Simmons deserves the added humiliation. He callously delays his final words: 'Remove the prisoner.'

Simmons stares at the judge with the same vacant look he displayed upon hearing the guilty verdict. He looks over his shoulder to the victims' families. They have not received justice. For Barry that is worse than the sentence imposed upon him. For many years he fought for the rights of his country and its citizens. Today, those citizens have been denied justice, just as Barry Simmons has been denied his.

One hundred years' earlier he would swing from the gallows with Marchant fronting the crowd of ghoulish onlookers, sipping from a flask of illicit whiskey.

He returns to prison a broken man, like a shattered antique vase repaired with Superglue: appearing intact, but the once valuable specimen now representing only a worthless form. Despite confidence in the prospect of the judicial system at some stage restoring his freedom and his good name, the present moment is lost to despondency and hopelessness.

Families of the deceased accept the sentence, but are disappointed the term of life imprisonment had not been delivered. They feel short-changed and consider their hopes and wishes snubbed. None of them is lucid enough to calculate that from Simmons' present age of sixty-one, he will be ninety-seven years old before being eligible for parole – assuming he survives the years of hell behind prisons' walls.

None of those issues fall on Simmons ears. He is not guilty and will fight to the end.

* * *

Olivia finishes her shift, tired and irritable. The much-vaunted move proposed by Chief Constable Nash has not materialised – she is yet to receive a list of stations identifying a suitable vacancy.

Although her transfer to the Community Policing Squad created distance between herself and Marchant, the work atmosphere remains thick and untenable, prompting Olivia to consider applying for stress leave. The consequence of such recourse would brand her a compensation claimant – not one of the better credentials to be annexed inside the cover of one's Personal History File. That would affix a life-long blight to all future promotional or exterior career ambitions.

Prior to leaving the office, she makes plans to surprise Dave Stafford. She wonders why he hasn't returned her calls, given that she's not seen him since their meeting in Chief Constable Nash's office. She races home, dreaming of a romantic weekend where flowers, fine dining and a raunchy movie would be the appetiser for a relaxing wind-down, emotional contentment, and, well, whatever goes.

She travels by train, crediting its practical purposes for catching up on missed sleep. The stroll through Paddington station returns dark memories of trekking to and from court during Simmons' trial. They fade as she absorbs the bustle of Baker Street – the outer perimeter of city life – where carbon monoxide replaces fresh, oxygenated Midlands' air; where people go about their business with neither a 'hello' nor sign of recognition of anyone within their midst; and where the mix of nationalities is, perhaps, greater than in any other part of Britain. Olivia lets it all flash by. She is on a mission.

She drops her bag on Stafford's doorstep, knocks three times and hides behind a bush. On hearing the door creak, she leaps out. Straight into Shannon's arms. 'What the f— What the hell are you doing here?'

Shannon looks equally startled. 'I could ask you the same thing. I thought that case of yours was over.'

'This is nothing to do with a case. I came to see Dave.'

Shannon stares at the bag. 'You're planning on staying a while?'

'What's going on Shannon? No need to be like that. I haven't seen him for ages and thought I'd surprise him. You know we had a thing going.'

'Well you don't any more. We're getting engaged. How are you anyway?'

'"We're getting engaged? How are you anyway?" Just like that? I don't know, now. Guess I'll just head back home and drink myself stupid.'

'Olivia. If it's any help, I didn't know you were serious. I thought it was just a work thing. Really. He never said anything.'

'Well he wouldn't would he? How long has your 'thing' or whatever you call it been going?'

'Few months now. We bumped into each other when he was working on that triple murder case. 'Bout a month before he went and solved it.'

'Before *he* solved it? He told you *he* solved it?'

'Well, not exactly. He credited you with putting it all together.'

'Whatever. No offence, but I'm not here to see you. Dave around?'

'I think he's still asleep. Been on lates.'

'I bet he's hiding inside 'cause he's not got the bollocks to face me. So maybe you go and wake him, or I'll do it for you.'

'No need to be like that.' Shannon turns and leaps up the stairs.

Olivia enters the hallway. Closes the door behind her.

Stafford appears in a tartan dressing gown; a sort of horror film adaptation of the staircase scene in *Gone with the Wind*.

Olivia doesn't wait for him to step to the floor: 'Why Dave? Why didn't you tell me?'

'We only just started. Don't get hot. You knew we were just working together.'

'We were more than working together, and you know it. And you know what? I'll bet you were screwing her while we were on the Taylor case. You come round to my place, all full of self-righteousness telling me how to fix the case and you're hypocritically deceiving the two of us, not you, but my former friend Shannon here. I bet she didn't know you were whispering sweet nothings in my ear when you told her you would be away on a case.'

'You're right, Olivia. I am sorry. I didn't know it would develop with Shannon and me.'

'But you still chose to have the best of both worlds – maybe in case it didn't work out with her – good old Olivia's in the background. She'll be there for me. Well no more, Dave. You're a great cop and I thank you for your help. I'll have no hesitation in asking for help any time, but as for a personal relationship, just strike me off your agenda.'

'Fair enough. I'm sorry.'

'In fact you probably won't even find me because I'm going to leave the job.'

Stafford stands pensively, holding the front door. *Frankly, my dear, I don't give a damn.*

On arriving home, Olivia follows the time-honoured women's remedy guaranteed to abate emotional breakdowns. Eat. She downs a small tin of peaches, the 425 grams failing to satisfy her cravings. Despite being tired after spending nearly five hours on a swaying train, she walks out to her car, drives to the local McDonald's drive-through and picks up two Big Mac meals and two apple pies. She speeds home, anxious to enjoy the feast before it cools. She stands at the kitchen bench, devours the lot and washes it down with a large strawberry shake. Job done. Five minutes later, she is asleep.

The following morning she phones her office and speaks to the newly appointed Acting Inspector Stanton. She books off sick, but very nearly rescinds after learning that Marchant is on stress leave until further notice.

Coincidentally – or ironically – after hanging up the phone Olivia notices an envelope laying beneath her door. She gives no thought to how a person had gained access through the building's security entrance. The envelope is endorsed with the Chief Constable's return address. Inside is the list. Four stations. She feels deceived. Two London locations she immediately discounts because she cannot afford to live in London. Of equal importance, she does not want to run the risk of running into Stafford.

The third is Gloucester, which isn't too far away, but close enough for members to know the fallout from the Evesham murders catastrophe.

The final option is a small station in Newquay, a coastal town in Cornwall. Very little happens there in winter, but it thrives in summer, courtesy of the international surf centre that attracts an influx of backpacking surfers.

Olivia is not a beach girl.

35

Appeal papers shuffle from office to office. They float in to and out of trays; they are perused and signed, perused and stamped, with the process repeated under scrutiny of high-ranking paralegals before the court will decide whether or not to grant leave to appeal.

In the meantime, appeals lawyers scan testimony and judge's rulings and prepare detailed submissions. The burden facing appeals courts is so great that hearing dates hide in distant calendars. Barry Simmons is fortunate. He will wait only six months.

* * *

On the eleventh day of October 2016, Trevor John Taylor appears before Bournemouth Crown Court charged with the murders of Juanita Morales, Amy Anderson and Marg Hegarty. The solitude of custodial remand combined with his Legal Aid solicitor's impressing upon him that the huge burden of evidence would prove futile any attempt to defend the matter, convinces him to plead guilty, thereby reducing trauma to the victims' family. Taylor cares nothing for the families; it is the incentive of a sentencing discount that encourages him to plead guilty. He's been tipped to expect a sentence similar to that handed down to Simmons.

The hearing is short and sharp. With no need for a jury, the Crown presents its summary. On completion, the defence offers a submission nullifying the acts as a 'temporary mental imbalance' – a token attempt at mitigating sentence. The defence provides no current professional opinion to reinforce its submission, instead relying on dated material from Trevor's childhood. Trevor's parents had provided Legal Aid with a file of material and contacts that might help explain his behaviour. Albert and Irene Taylor's motivation is not so much to assist Trevor, but more to protect the community from the risk of further abhorrent acts. They naïvely believe that he might be released into the community after a short term of incarceration.

Never had Trevor benefitted from the psychological evaluations and treatment. After his ninth birthday, his parents had worried about his attention span, or lack thereof, first brought to their attention by a concerned teacher. Of course they'd had slight inklings that their son was 'different', but like many parents in similar situations, they set aside alarm believing that the stimulation of school would help young Trevor grow out of it.

Two years' later, Trevor settled into a new school. He failed to comprehend the essential subjects of English, Maths and History, but excelled in those demanding practical application, like art and woodwork. There were no marked behavioural infractions. He was a loner who spent time corralling ants into Coke bottles; he would not answer questions in class for fear of giving an incorrect answer; and he shied away from sport after hearing a news report of an international cricketer dying from a heart attack.

His parents had taken him to a place – Trevor remembered his father calling it the 'shrink' – where he feared he would be sent home with his head shrunken like the totems of the South American Indian Jívaro people. He objected to placing different shaped objects into a puzzle in much the same manner as he had done as a two-and three-year-old; he asked why he had to identify numbers embedded within coloured inkblot charts known as Ishihara Plates (which he later learnt were for testing colour blindness, not intellectual capacity) when he believed the answer was so obvious to everyone; and he wondered why he had to count from one to one hundred backwards. *That'll sure crop up in a job interview when I'm older. Why doesn't he make me recite the alphabet backwards too?*

Eminent psychologists and psychiatrists suggested Trevor might be predisposed toward violent acts. Albert and Irene discounted the proposition, believing that over nine years they would have seen signs of aggression displayed at home or been advised of aberrant behaviour having occurred at school.

The nature of psychology in predicting future behavioural patterns of an individual is not an exact science. It is, at best, speculative. It is an educated prediction of the future, often based on psychophysical scales and psychometric assessments, Gossman personality facet scales and a range of clinical tests that supposedly forecast behaviour in the same manner as Myers-Briggs indicators assist recruitment agencies to ensure their prospective employees are socially responsible and have no dysfunctional qualities that might infect the workplace.

The trial judge faces a conundrum in determining sentence. He is accustomed, as are most judges, to extend a discount for a guilty plea, both as a reward for insulating families from horrendous testimony, and also to save the Crown the expense of another protracted trial. On the other hand, he cannot sentence Taylor to a lesser time than Simmons; a bare minimum of parity should be the starting point, although justice had not exactly prevailed in the case to date.

He pronounces the head sentence as three terms of thirteen years, but sets the non-parole period at twelve years for each charge, effectively giving Taylor the same custodial time.

John Taylor acknowledges his fate after his brother changed his plea to guilty. He is clearly implicated. He pleads guilty and receives seven years for his role as an accessory to the 'disposal' of Marg Hegarty. No evidence was found to connect him to the murders of Juanita Morales or Amy Anderson.

John will never learn what drove Trevor to kill Juanita and Amy. He understands the ease with which couples argue, but cannot accept how something could go so terribly wrong during an argument. He tries to understand what had happened to his brother: *What caused his brain to snap, to strangle a loved one to death; to stab the life out of a young woman; and to deprive a woman of life sustaining oxygen, simply because he thought that she might pose a threat?*

Neither John, nor the police, would learn the answer.

* * *

One of the great mysteries of serial killing is the question of their sudden cessation. Granted, some killers are apprehended in the early stages, but people like Peter Sutcliffe, more commonly known as 'The Yorkshire Ripper' who killed at least five women between August and November 1888, [authorities believe there may have been many others]; Rosemary West and Brian Huntley, and Ian Brady and Myra Hindley maintained a 'normal' profile in their communities without neighbours having any indication of their nocturnal activities. They rubbed shoulders with unsuspecting neighbours; they walked down the aisles of Tesco and they attended church and volunteered at local fetes and school working bees.

Trevor John Taylor had followed suit. After killing Marg Hegarty, the murders simply stopped. The police believed the incarceration of Simmons was the reason. Trevor knew otherwise.

He was not suited to co-habitation. He sought the pleasures of companionship, but when the permanence of union became imminent, he panicked and shunned impending change to his highly organised lifestyle. Most would simply sit down as a couple, perhaps with a glass of wine, and discuss the matter, and terminate their relationship with, 'I don't think this is going to work out.' Each goes their own way. Trevor could not do that. Not after two failed marriages. His only means of eradicating the problem *was* eradicating the problem. And then the problem escalated.

After Juanita, his temper remained at boiling point. Amy was a victim of that temper. Nothing less. Had she approached Trevor at any other time she would have been entertained with a drink and a lively night. Possibly many. Instead, she was removed from the equation of Trevor's problems.

Marg Hegarty likewise. Marg knew nothing about Trevor. The fishing expedition changed gear and reversed – she became the hunted, trapped by Trevor's mindset. He was attuned to removing problems – not resolving them.

* * *

Stafford returns to his London office. He sends Olivia a Christmas card and is surprised to receive one in return,

341

addressed to both himself and Shannon. He wonders whether to accept it with sincerity or sarcasm but resolves the conundrum by returning a thank you note, hoping to repair the damage to their once close friendship: *Dear Olivia. Once again, I offer my heartfelt apologies for what happened. I have always valued our friendship and I know that I'm a bastard for seeing Shannon behind your back. I was not motivated by greed or deceit. I thought we enjoyed a level of comfort with each other that was perhaps a work release more than an emotional bond. I apologise for getting that wrong. I have never seen you as a casual fling. Please believe that. I also dearly hope that we can maintain some level of communication, even if only on a professional level. Best wishes, Dave.*

Olivia scrunches up the note and tosses it in the bin. *Your loss, not mine.*

* * *

Marchant's period of stress leave allows him time to follow Simmons' appeal proceedings. By pressing a colleague to return a favour, he obtained a copy of Stafford's brief of evidence. Big mistake. Reading the detailed and comprehensive brief, Marchant reels at the precarious position in which he finds himself. He can only hope that the appeal court will uphold Simmons' guilty verdict.

He sits in the court and glares at Olivia, who in turn, presses emotionless against Stafford's protective shoulder.

Marchant drops his head as the three judges announce their verdict. He calculates the worth of his pension plan, and wonders if it is sufficient to fund early retirement. His current role is now in jeopardy – Chief Constable Nash had forecast that. An alternative position would be offered; certainly not an operational role, and more than likely not as inspector. He sees himself banished to the transport division, monitoring paperwork, service records and new vehicle purchases. He imagines working behind the very desk that he had suggested DS Watts occupy and he imagines being asked to resign to preserve any remaining credibility. If that is offered, he might hastily accept.

He remains in the court – oblivious to the adjournment – as lawyers prepare for the next matter. He ignores a casual wave offered by Olivia and Stafford as they sweep past. His mind floods with images of Trevor Taylor. After John Taylor answered the call from that bloody phone, he'd wondered about its ownership. He curses the day he retrieved it from the back of his drawer and checked the photo and video logs. He did not doubt the phone's ownership. Virgin Mobile confirmed it – Trevor John Taylor.

Olivia had been right all along.

He had prioritised self-preservation and credibility. Marchant comes first. Stuff everyone else. He had smuggled the phone home and smashed it to pieces with a hammer. Dug a small hole, threw in the pieces, doused them with mower fuel and threw in a match. Covered the hole and transplanted a cutting into the freshly dug earth, as one would commemorate the passing of a beloved family pet. Job done.

* * *

Olivia accepts the post to Newquay, but soon finds that she will always be an 'outsider'. After just three months, she tenders her resignation. The job has become mundane. Behind the scenes, innuendo upsets her and colleagues question her attitude and credibility. Gossip whizzes around the office about her enjoying an intimate relationship with Stafford – such is the mentality of some personnel. They believe that Stafford took over the Evesham Murders case not to bring the proceedings to a just conclusion, but because of the power of the skirt – Olivia's skirt. Within the constabulary, many relationships blossom within local precincts and offices. Olivia was penalised for her association because it was, on the face, strictly professional. There had been no association at work other than incident room briefings; no deep, meaningful glares into each other's eyes across canteen tables, and no leaving work together arm in arm. Both Olivia and Stafford are victims of the speculators and rumour-mongers who revel in cultivating gossip, whether true or false and without regard for the reputation of those they seek to discredit.

Olivia has mixed feelings about leaving the police. Her mind is free of recent months' pressure, although it is that lack of pressure that causes her to resign. Procrastination delays many a decision, but once the decision becomes final and non-negotiable, people resume life's role with greater gusto. So it is with Olivia. She takes only a few days to organise her affairs and walk the path to her new career.

She returns to Worcester and sets up with bare essentials of table, three plastic chairs, a small filing cabinet and a phone/fax machine. A pack of business cards and invoice book complete her start-up costs. *Watts Happening? Investigations* is born.

36

SIMMONS WALKS THROUGH Wandsworth's spike-topped prison gates after serving fourteen months behind them. No one greets him. *That'd be right,* he mumbles. *Coming in here there was a press gallery three deep; there was public waving placards, yelling and jeering loud enough to be considered a political rally, yet when the truth comes out and an innocent man is released, no one gives a damn. No one apologises. Sure, I might get an occasional, 'onya Barry', or, 'good to see you out, must have been hard on ya.' Friggin' two-faced idiots. Of course it was hard – if only they knew. If only they were to live one day of the routine: wake up to sirens, get fed by sirens, line up for meals, wait in queues for medication, hope there's a toilet free when you need it – and then hope that no inconsiderate bastard has left mess all over the joint; muster five times daily by command, and every minute of the day be prepared to respond to the beck and call of officers who get their jollies from baiting prisoners and trying to incite trouble, solely to justify flexing their authoritative muscle.*

He uses his free rail pass, courtesy of the government that imprisoned him, to return to Evesham. To nothing. His home had been sacrificed to the legal system – to fund his defence and appeal. Preliminary advice suggests he has little chance of success in a suit against the government. 'There may be confidential ex-gratia compensation,' he is told, but he will receive nothing of substance to reinstate his life to the quality of that enjoyed before the wrongful incarceration.

He walks into the Royal Oak Inn for the first time. Although he'd frequented many Evesham pubs, he'd never patronised the Royal Oak. He chooses to preserve anonymity.

The public reaction to those released from prison, whether on completion of their sentence or after a successful appeal, is one of reservation. If the person was guilty, the public hopes, but does not accept, that they have fully rehabilitated and now present no risk to the public or community. Others subscribe to the theory that a criminal *never* rehabilitates and will always be a risk. Their theory is supported by the prevalence of parole breaches, recidivist rates of drug and sex offences and the unacceptable problem for many who will always *look* like a criminal. Shame on genetics. And tattoos. Strangely, when one is released from prison after a successful appeal, the community expresses reservation. *I wonder if he really did it.* The old cliché hovers: 'Where there's smoke there's fire.'

Barry pads into an upstairs room for £35 per night. He pays for a week and receives a free extra night. Despite having his freedom, there is little relief to be had by walking up the stairs to his new room. A creaky hallway, dimly lit by a sub-standard energy saving fluorescent globe, winds its way to room number four. The size of the room is little more than his cell of fourteen months, but the bed is far superior to the previous hard-based fixtures. Antique furniture of next to no value provides wardrobe space and a dressing table. A funnelled view of Market Square and the Round House that had saved his hide appear through a quaint leadlight window. The toilet and bathroom are far down the hall. *Too bad if I want a piss in the night. Guess I'll use the window.*

The following morning Barry wakes dejected, unmotivated and lacking zest. He ambles downstairs to the breakfast room where the lighting is of similar intensity as the hallway above. He is not particularly hungry, but as breakfast is included in the room rate he scoffs down a bowl of muesli, an English breakfast, orange juice and two cups of coffee. Barry still won't turn down anything complimentary.

He contemplates his future. Sixty-two years and counting down. His love of the sea can hardly be rekindled for it had been transferred to Simmons' Scenic Cruises, in much the same manner as one can be divorced and remarry, but still preserve fond memories of the former relationship – despite it being out-of-bounds.

It is the love of that former relationship that stirs interest in revisiting the Evesham pier. The seven-minute walk restores life's pleasures beyond the razor-wire topped walls that had obliterated his view of the 'outside' world. A gentle breeze whips up the river's silty aroma; swans and ducks replace the prison's scavenging pigeons and starlings, and dewy grass provides a spongy walk after fourteen months of treading crumbled asphalt.

The mounting euphoria quickly subsides when he sees his beloved craft covered by tarpaulins. Admittedly, he was blind to the bank's intent after it advised that his loan would be recalled or the craft seized in absence of payment. Barry had returned correspondence advising his preparedness to resume the repayments at a later stage. He asked for twelve months' grace, but did not receive a reply. He assumed that the bank, of which he had been a loyal customer since his school days, would grant his request. He felt no need to follow up the letter because of his certainty of being freed on appeal. He would easily be able to restore his unblemished credit history. *Bad mistake. Never assume anything with a bank.*

He boards his main craft, lifts the tarp and finds that locals have partied away many nights during his prolonged absence. Vomit, pizza, beer cans and bottles, articles of clothing and papers litter the deck and bridge. Smashed windows and slashed seat covers evidence the rituals of vandals. He throws down the tarp in disgust.

Looking beneath the pier, the hull gleams in emerald lichen, barnacles clamber over each other and river flotsam clings to remaining space. Enough. He looks no further.

He returns to town and cataleptically dawdles through the mall, searching for his past. A previous neighbour approaches, but turns his head as he passes. Barry continues by, not even interested in questioning his ignorance. He props at a sidewalk café, orders coffee and sits at a table strewn with crumbs. The waitress flicks a soiled cloth over the table, not noticing crumbs scurry away from the cloth and dive into Barry's lap. *Story of my life,* he huffs. *The crumbs of life that should be captured always manage to evade apprehension.*

He leans over and grabs a local paper from an adjacent table. The lead story banners:

'*Local Doctor Lost at Sea. Doctor Erich Groenweld, recently retired from the Worcestershire Coroner's Office, is presumed dead after signals from his thirty-eight foot cabin cruiser transponders suddenly disappeared from satellite monitoring. An air and sea search, combined with attempts to contact the craft by radio, failed. Doctor Groenweld had fully expended his retirement funds on a mission to prove that the earth is flat. His sail charts, lodged with Lisbon Coastal Authority and updated to relevant*

European mariners' services, failed to pinpoint a specific route.

*Groenweld claimed, in what might well be his final interview:
'The truth is out there! I depart in the name of science and shall
return in the name of logic and reality.'* The article continued:
*'Doctor Groenweld dwelled as a recluse after becoming the subject
of ridicule upon his "world is flat" theory sweeping all media. His
only interview, given to BBC journalist Michael Johns, topped You
Tube's downloads for three consecutive weeks. This reporter sees the
irony of that number* three.*'*

Page five carries a story of a Bournemouth man jailed for
45 years for crimes coined 'The Evesham Murders.' A single
sentence paragraph, buried within the body of the text, reads:
*'Local man Barry Simmons freed after London's High Court
overturns three murder convictions.'* He reads and re-reads the
sentence. *Bastards they are. They made great mileage pillorying
me when enquiries started. Plastered me all over the front pages:
'Distinguished serviceman arrested for murder. "Captain" Barry
Simmons denies all charges. Inspector Marchant of West Mercia
Police claims: "Our case is more watertight than Simmons'
riverboat".' But now, after all this time the truth is finally revealed,
what do I get? A single fucking sentence hidden in the middle of
some reporter's self-glorifying editorial.* He slumps forward, head
between his knees, coffee untouched.

He returns to his room and wastes the remainder of the
day staring vacantly out of the window. Market Square activity
dwindles after businesses close for the day. Night falls on Vine
Street. Cars' headlights form an umbilical cord of orange, white
and red, joining the Merstow Green roundabout in the south
to Greenhill in the north. Each has a destination; ferrying
home drivers and passengers to family and loved ones, where

they'll exchange banter about work, shopping trips, school problems and next door's cat jumping over the fence into freshly planted nasturtiums; others busting to prepare for the next day's work because that is all that occupies their sheltered and unadventurous lives, and the wealthy few who might plan the annual family holiday to Florida's Disneyland, or, if it has been a bad year for black money, Blackpool.

Barry walks to the doorway, glances across the sparse room, through the partly drawn curtains to the soft, and in a more appropriate setting, the romantic, subtle glimmer of orange-halogen streetlight. He leaves the door unlocked, drops down the stairs to the High Street where he savours the aroma of the evening's culinary preparations: garlic bread, kebabs, pizzas, the vinegary tang of fish and chips and the telltale whiff of supposedly banned monosodium glutamate. He retraces his steps to the pier and tentatively crosses the slippery surface to his boat. He creeps beneath the tarpaulin and crawls into the cabin. Opens a trapdoor in the floor that accesses the motor, fuel and lubricants storage, and reserve safety items. He spots vacant pegs from where life jackets have been stolen, and he notices that diesel fuel has been siphoned from the tank, either as theft or for safety purposes. Two, twenty litre drums of heavy gearbox oil remain, as does the reserve anchor. A coil of frayed rope lies on the floor in a pool of oil and water. He moves the items to the rear of the craft.

For most of the day, Barry has planned to set alight the craft as a final gesture to those, including bank staff, who have persecuted him. The boat, constructed primarily of marine plywood and fibreglass would burn like a scarecrow at the stake. No fire unit could possibly access the pier. Even if it could, the craft would be no more than fragments of charcoal and cinders by the time it arrived. *Not good enough*, he thinks. *Perhaps I should save it for Guy Fawkes Night.*

He uncoils the rope and removes the emergency knife secreted behind the rope-hanging lugs. *Shit! That's the knife that belonged to the receipt. I should have twigged on that had I been thinking straight. Too late now.* He cuts the rope to a length of eight foot six inches and loops one end through the oil drum handle and then lashes it to the anchor. He takes the free end and double-winds it tightly around his waist. He lifts one drum and dangles it over the starboard side rail. The rope bites into his waist like a belt tightened five notches too tight. He sucks in his stomach to ease the pain, bends down, picks up the second drum, repeats the motion, and places it over the rail. The two drums, supported only by his body straining against the handrail, swing from the oily rope like pendulums of a grandfather clock. He stretches for the anchor, straining, grimacing in pain as the weight of the two drums cut into his waist. The grimace morphs to a smile as he realises that this particular anchor has never been used. He flings it over the rail and bellows a chilling yelp as the rope compresses his stomach even further. The drums splash into the river, simultaneously whisking him over the railing like a fish net cast from an ocean trawler.

Descending into the murky depths as had Juanita Morales nearly eighteen months' earlier, Barry faces his feared drill sergeant commanding him to attention; he proudly accepts his first promotion to leading seaman; he enjoys port-side fanfares after returning from mid-pacific commissions – all the while saluting as the weights pull him to the silty floor. He looks into the eyes of his beloved Felicity and squints into the fathoms of endless ocean as above him the half-moon seals its silver sheen over the River Avon.

Felicity does not see her former husband's contorted face.

Nor does she see his thrashing arms and legs.

No one from the community that abandoned him hears his desperate cry for help.

No one sees brown water slosh into his lungs.

And no one hears the final gurgling gasps trapped in bubbles which momentarily rest on the surface as a memorial to Barry Andrew Simmons.

PAIGE OFFERS A PREVIEW OF OLIVIA WATTS' FIRST CASE AS A PRIVATE INVESTIGATOR.

WHISPER OF DEATH. AVAILABLE JUNE 2017.

Meredith Bennington reaches for the shrieking mobile. Knocks it to the floor. Pads her fingers across the bedside rug. Probes for the recently updated iPhone.

She grabs the vibrating sliver. Checks the time. 1.14 a.m.

Answers.

Gasps.

Calls Roslyn and Alexander: 'Get to the hospital. Quick. Mum's deteriorated. Doctors reckon she hasn't got long.'

Alexander's *'How come they called you?'* query sets her on edge. She knows the topic has the potential to widen their cracked relationship into a huge abyss. 'Not now Alex. I think mum might be more important than our squabbling over who's calling who.'

* * *

What the hell. Bloody 2.30 in the middle of the night. I snatch my squawking mobile. I'm not expecting a call. I know that even telemarketers show respect for normal sleeping hours, although that's now subject to change as more and more organisations outsource marketing activities to India and the Philippines. It won't be long before we're inundated with 1.00 a.m. calls, surveying us about banking customs, electricity usage and telecommunications providers. We'll berate them with a mouthful of profanities, and then fume at the pacifying: 'Oh I am sorry. I forgot to account for the time difference.' *Yeah, sure you did.*

I sit up. Pull the duvet to my neck. 'Hello. This better be important.'

'Is this Olivia?'

Duh. Why do people ask the most ridiculous questions? 'Who else would it be at this time?'

'I'm sorry. It's Alex. Something terrible has happened. My mother's just died. I'm at the hospital.'

'Alex. Sorry. I don't know what to say. Is there anything I can do?' I immediately regret my groggy who-the-frig's-this attitude I level to anyone who dares disturb my sleep full of romance and fanciful experiences. 'I'm sorry, Alex. I didn't mean to sound insensitive, I just woke up.' I hoped he'd get the subtlety that he's wrecked my night's sleep. 'I'll come on over.'

I don't mind supporting people in times of need – and this surely is one of those times – but why should I console a guy I hardly know. Truth is, I cannot just ignore him.

I pull on a pair of crumpled jeans, grab my bag, rush into the hallway, and nearly fall downstairs to the front door. Scold myself: *I must get used to this place.*

My Ford Focus sits at the kerb. On expiration of daytime parking restrictions, I move it from the rear car park to the main road. I know that doesn't necessarily guarantee its safety and security because if someone is desperate enough to steal a car, they'll take it from anywhere.

A few months earlier, I wouldn't have given a damn about where I parked my car. A 1973 Reliant Robin painted in sickly blue would hardly raise the testosterone levels of a hardened car rustler. Yes, I ashamedly admit to having owned one of those three-wheeled relics, but that was all my budget would allow in my early years with the constabulary. As I progressed in the job, I considered upgrading. However, living in close proximity to the police station convinced me to save my money and wait. Until when, I had not decided.

Nearly seven years' later, after leaving the police, I preserved most of my final salary to cover living expenses while establishing Watts Happening? Investigations. Knowing that image is everything when promoting a business, I supplemented my remaining £1,000 with a small top-up loan and treated myself to a five-year-old Ford Focus.

For my purposes, it's extremely functional and equipped with a six-speaker sound system, iPod connectivity, air conditioning and comfortable velour seats. Sometimes the most insignificant extras stand out as winners. The cup holder, for instance – within arm's reach – because I'm always buying coffee at take-aways or service centres; the little make up mirror glued to the sunvisor – because a woman can't do without a mirror; and the glove box and door pockets deep enough to store my assorted paraphernalia and notebooks and maps – although I have discarded most fold-out maps after having an integrated GPS system installed. Yep. Suits me down to the ground.

The exterior, however, is disappointing; not from a manufacturer's point of view, but from my own. I have a tendency to switch from introvert to extrovert as the wind changes. My extrovert persona insists that I drive around in a yellow, vibrant orange or iridescent turquoise car. However, my introversion recognises the nature of my work as requiring me to lay low, be unobtrusive and assimilate with society. That limits me to white or silver. Silver is the more appealing, but plain old white is less conspicuous and blends easily with Britain's 34-plus million cars.

Cornwall and District General Hospital is accessed via a half-mile-long road divided by double yellow lines and flanked by bluish-white halogen lights. I could have been driving along Heathrow's Runway 3 East.

I rip a ticket from the automated financial controller of car parks and roll under its rising yellow arm. Anyone who's had the misfortune to drive into a full car park will agree that one spends more time searching for an elusive parking spot than they do attending their loved one. At 3.00 am, there is no such drama. I leave Fiona in the closest bay and rush to Accident and Emergency, signposted only as A & E.

Fiona? Um, yes. I have a penchant for naming my cars. Fiona Focus. It's a juvenilistic trait inherited from my over-alliterative father who animatedly named his vehicles. I clearly recall Victor Volkswagen, Adrian Audi and Verity Vauxhall. There was also an old Renault, late 50s maybe, that he was restoring it. Its name is unforgettable. The model name, designated by the factory was 'Frigate'. Dad prefixed it with a crude name – and it wasn't Freddy. I've merely upheld the tradition.

The glass-fronted entry glows orange from towering floodlights that stand like enormous Chupa-Chups. Hoping to avoid an out-of-hours inquisition, I walk with authority up the wheelchair ramp, showing my distaste – and laziness – for the twenty-odd steps. My resolve fades upon seeing a dishevelled Alexander pacing the foyer.

Alerted by the automatic doors, he greets me with a welcoming hug. Catches me off guard. Holds me with greater intensity than is respectable in the circumstances. It's not one of those European kiss-each-other's-cheek-and-break-off kind of hugs; it is something deeper – I'd describe it as latent desire – reminding me of the 'first date' hug, where the guy holds you, waiting to see if you clench your arms around him as an indication of whether you're going to let him kiss you, but with each breath you feel him drawing you into his body as if he's trying to cast an abstract mould of your breasts into his chest.

4

Before I start to crave more of this little interlude, I return to earth with the realisation that it is probably innocent. *Perhaps I've been left to pasture in fallow fields for too long, agisted to my own paddock and left to wander in expectation of what the mating season – if ever there is to be one – will deliver.* And then my investigative bent weighs in: *Is this an expression of guilt? Is Alexander looking to me as his saviour?* I tilt my neck just enough to see not one tear in his eye. I slowly extricate myself from his tentacle-like grip.

'Sorry Olivia. It shouldn't have happened. She was fine yesterday. No sign of any need for concern. All vitals were within acceptable limits, or so I've been told.'

'These things happen, Alex. Perhaps it was meant to be.'

'Don't give me that sympathetic crap! I've heard enough already from the hospital with their buck-passing and non-acceptance of responsibility. That may wash with some, but it certainly won't with me. I've witnessed far too many bureaucratic cover-ups at work without having them pandered to me in a situation like this. That's why I called you, Olivia. This is a clear case of negligence. Start your timecard or whatever from 2.30 a.m. You're on the job.'

I reel at the aspect of Alexander's nature I had not before witnessed and certainly did not deserve. I'm not here touting for work – I'd much prefer to have stayed in bed – and I don't see this as a time to be discussing business. I soften my approach: 'Alex. I know this is a sensitive time. I've come here as a friend, not as a business proposition. Let's work this through, ask a few questions, *and then*, if there's a reason to explore behind the scenes, I'll take it on. For the moment let's find the charge nurse. And by the way, I'm simply a friend, okay? I'm not here in an official capacity; we don't want anyone to have to think twice about what they're saying. Okay?'

5

We pass the ward where a vacant bed evidences Joyce Beecham's departure. Barely forty minutes after my receiving Alexander's call, the hospital has erased all signs of its recent patient. I shouldn't criticise that, but I do resent the hospital's insensitivity in preparing to admit the next fortunate, or unfortunate, patient. The curtains are pulled open, ready to welcome the morning sun and chirping birds who will sing joy into the freshly bleached, scrubbed and disinfected three metre square of hope. So much for the future. At this minute, only death's darkness fills the ward.

Commanding the Nurses' Station is a diminutive, weary-looking charge nurse, the antithesis of what I expected. 'Nurse Kosinski' shines on an enamelled name badge pinned to the bodice of her uniform. I introduce myself as Alexander's friend, fully intending to soft-pedal around the issue before I hit her with a double-edged leading question. 'Nurse, I wonder if you could tell—'

Alexander rushes in: 'When am I able to find out what caused my mother's death?'

Good one Alex. That's certainly set the scene for refusal. Kosinski offers: 'You'll have to speak to Dr Patel about case details.'

'This is not a "case detail", it is a question about a patient who was vibrantly alive only hours ago but now lays dead somewhere in the bowels of this building.'

I thread my hand through Alexander's arm, not wanting him to eject another blast at the nurse. I also don't want him doing, or saying, something he'll later regret. 'Come on Alex, just a moment.' Then to nurse Kosinski: 'Can we please see Dr Patel, or perhaps a copy of the death certificate?'

'Dr Patel is unavailable, and we can't produce the certificate to anyone other than registered next-of-kin.'

'I am the next-of-kin,' retorts Alexander.

'Just let me check that.' Kosinski clicks through a computer. 'No, we have a Meredith Bennington recorded as NOK.'

Alexander leans over the counter's pedestal and glares at the nurse. 'That can't be – she's my sister. I helped my mother with the form in your own administration office downstairs.'

'You may have completed a medical authorisation form or similar, Mr Beecham, but Mrs Bennington *is* your mother's next-of-kin. All we can say is that Mrs Joyce Beecham was taken by natural causes.'

For the third time I take Alexander's arm, and this time drag him from the verge of passionate confrontation. 'I think we should go now. We can't achieve anything tonight.'

He replies, wilfully enough for Kosinski to hear: 'First thing in the morning I'm going to file a "Contested Decision" report and personally hand it to the hospital registrar.'

At 3.45 a.m. I accede to Alexander's request to leave him alone in the car park. Some people handle grief better on their own. I drive home, detouring via an all-night garage to top up fuel for Fiona and caffeine for me. Two taxi drivers stand alongside their cabs, chatting and slurping coffee as they impatiently inhale huge gulps of nicotine should the next fare be only a radio message away. They're probably recuperating after spending half an hour sanitising the cabin, cleaning out pizza crusts, potato chip bags and all manner of refuse deposited by late-night partygoers. A quick spray and wipe, and they're ready to re-join the excitement and dangers of their occupation – all for little reward.

I complete the ten-minute journey, wondering how best to help Alexander ascertain the cause of his mother's death. Facing me is an investigation that could morph into a malpractice suit or, at worst, a murder enquiry. *That* challenge inspires me to burrow into the Beecham family background from where I might unearth a starting point. Would someone actually murder a seventy-one-year-old grandmother? Logic determines my answer: *Not bloody likely*. Despite Alex's belief that his mother was quite alright yesterday, I've seen nothing to suggest that Joyce Beecham is a victim of foul play.